Hope and Hubris

James McDonald

PublishAmerica
Baltimore

ISBN: 1-4241-4497-3
PUBLISHED BY PUBLISHAMERICA, LLLP
www.publishamerica.com
Baltimore

Printed in the United States of America

To my two grandsons, Michael and Justin

To Ron & June
With best wishes

James

Mind and let me
know how you
liked it or not.
Jim.

E.MAIL
JMCDONALD-98 @
SYMPATICO.CA.

1-800-663-6777

HOPE

In Christian thought, one of the three theological virtues, the others being faith and charity (love). It is distinct from the latter two because it is directed exclusively toward the future.

HUBRIS

In classical Greek ethical and religious thought, overweening presumption suggesting impious disregard of the limits governing human action in an orderly universe.

Encyclopedia Britannica

Chapter 1

Mary Ellen O'Neill was excited. No, excited is too tame a word to describe her feelings on this, the most surprising day of her life! Perhaps ecstatic would better describe the happiness that she felt on being at last given permission to emigrate to America. Her father, Patrick O'Neill, had held off for as long as he could against the pressure of the whole family to let her go. Mary Ellen was a tall girl with long black hair and striking blue eyes. She was certainly the most beautiful girl in the County of Donegal. Lots of the local young men had called to ask her out, but she turned them all down. When her mother asked her why, she simply said she had no time because she was going to America.

Patrick doted on her, not only because she was the only girl in the family, there were four sons, all older than Mary Ellen. She was the apple of his eye because she had been the only one who had been given the chance of an education in Dublin and had succeeded in finishing college as a stenographer, which in 1926 was an occupation reserved strictly for men. Now she was twenty and there were no prospects for female stenographers in Donegal, the northernmost part of the newly formed Irish Free State.

The O'Neill family were not as poor as most of their neighbors in the Glen Finn area of Donegal. They owned fifty acres of land about five miles outside the town of Ballybofey. The river Finn ran right through the middle of their property. Patrick's grandfather, Brian, had been given the land in 1870 as a reward for his service in the Crimea with the British Army. The story was that Brian had saved an officer's life, and in gratitude, the officer's father, who was the absentee landlord of that part of Donegal at the time, found out that Brian actually was one of his tenants and gave him fifty acres as a reward for saving his son's life.

Now the land was owned by Patrick and his brother John, who had emigrated to America in 1916. This was the main reason for Patrick allowing his daughter to go to America; at least there would be family there to look after her. When Patrick wrote to John about Mary Ellen, he was surprised when he got his brother's reply, which came on a Friday morning. John wrote that he would be happy to put Mary Ellen up till she got on her feet, and now that he was settled in New York, he wished to sell his half of the land and start a business in America.

Patrick had never even thought of selling any of the family's land, but John was legally entitled to do so. He talked it over with his wife, Martha, who was shocked at the prospect.

"What about us? We need the land we have now! If we are left with half of it, we'll have next to nothing to sell at the market. You just can't let him get away with this, Patrick." She started to weep quietly.

"Now, Martha," Patrick said gently, "John is within his rights, and remember, he's not charged us a penny rent since he left."

"Charged us rent! He should be paying us for looking after it! You are too soft, just tell him he can't sell it. After all, what's he going to do, come and take it back to New York with him."

"Now, you know I can't do that! It is his half, you know!"

"Oh, to Hell with you, Patrick, you know half this land is no good to us, you might as well sell the lot and give the money to your precious brother! Can't you think of your own family for once?" With that she grabbed her shawl and walked out of the house, slamming the door behind her.

Patrick sat thinking about what she had said. *She was right, half the land was no good to them, but if John wanted to sell it, he did not really have much choice.* He decided to wait till Sunday after Mass and talk it over with the whole family and see if there was a way out.

On the Sunday morning when they got back from church, Patrick told the family about the problem that faced them.

"You don't have to worry, Mary Ellen," he said. "You'll be going to America anyway, and your Uncle John wants you to take the money for the land with you."

Martha broke in. "Oh, he does, does he? Does he think he can use her as a message girl when he's about to ruin us all. Damn him to Hell!"

Patrick held his hand up for silence. "Do any of you have any ideas?" he addressed his four sons, Patrick, John, Robert and Liam.

"Well, Father," Patrick, the oldest stood up. "This decision will not really affect us for long, because the way things are in this country, we'll all be leaving soon anyway. There is no work except on the land and one man can manage that easily enough."

8

"Is he speaking for all of you?" Patrick said. *He knew his son was right, it was just a matter of time before they all left.* It had always been that way in Ireland. It seemed half the young men became priests and the other half emigrated. The others nodded their heads.

Robert spoke up, he was the quietest and the most thoughtful of the boys. "Did you consider buying Uncle John out? I'm sure he would let you pay it in installments."

Patrick laughed ruefully. "I estimate the land to be worth around two thousand pounds. It might as well be two million, and anyway, he wants the money to invest in America."

Robert looked at the others. "How much money do we have between us, minus Mary Ellen's fare?"

"You're not seriously trying to raise two-thousand pounds in here, are you?" Martha laughed shrilly. "And I thought you were the brains of the family!" All of them looked at Robert, who never even acknowledged Martha's outburst. "I asked a question. I have a hundred pounds saved from my four years in the Army!" Everyone became subdued and looked at one another. Patrick Junior broke the silence.

"I have eighty pounds,"Liam said.

"And I have forty-five."

They all looked at John. "Well, I have a hundred and twenty, so there we have it. If we put it all together, we have the grand total of about three-hundred and forty-five pounds."

Martha stood up. "I'm not going to listen to this nonsense. You have to face the facts. We are going to have to sell our half as well and move somewhere else." She started to cry. "Your father's right, it might as well be two-million!" She left the cottage and walked down to the river.

"How much do you have, Father?" Robert asked.

Patrick looked up absently. "Oh, I think we've got about seventy-five all together. I've put aside Mary Ellen's fare. That still is nowhere near two-thousand pounds." Robert walked over to the fire and started poking the turf with the tongs. He thought for a minute and turned around.

"Now, all of you listen carefully. This is what we are going to do. We are going to buy Uncle John's land between us."

Immediately Patrick interrupted him. "Robert, if you can't talk sense don't say anything! It only makes things worse!"

"Father, will you let me finish!" Robert threw the tongs on the hearth. Patrick was dumbstruck. None of his children had ever raised their voice to him. Robert continued. "There are twenty-five acres valued at two-thousand pounds. Divided by five makes five acres each at four-hundred pounds. We have say, eighty pounds each plus our own land, which is valued at two-thousand. Therefore, we are worth more than the value of the twenty-five acres. If we all get a mortgage of three-hundred and fifty each using our own land as collateral, we can buy the land and still have some of our own money left!"

"What the hell is he talking about?" Liam said, shaking his head.

"He's right!" Patrick stood up.

"Only one thing, Robert, who will give us a mortgage?" Robert laughed.

"With the land as collateral and even with a small deposit, any bank in Ireland will do it. Remember, we can't run away with the land, now can we?"

Liam looked bewildered. "What's a mortgage, Father? And what the hell is collateral?"

Patrick jumped up and grabbed him in a bear hug and swung him round. "Never mind, me boy, never mind, just run down and get your mother, tell her all is sorted out and our worries are over!"

John shook his head. "One small question, Robert. How the hell are we going to pay this mortgage if we are all leaving?"

"The same way as the English have done for centuries, John. We rent it out in parcels." John laughed.

"By God you're right. I never thought of that!"

"All right then, I'll go to Dublin tomorrow. I think I can complete this in a couple of days, so I'll be back before the weekend at the latest. Father, I'll need the deeds for the land to take with me. Now gentlemen, if you don't mind, I'll be having the deposits for your investment."

Mary Ellen had sat through the whole conversation with a mounting feeling of dread. Listening to the men arguing about the money convinced her that she would not be allowed to go to America. So when her father rushed over and hugged her she could only gasp. "I'm really going then, Father?"

"As soon as things are settled, lass. Not that I'm happy about it as you know, but if that's what you want, we won't stand in your way."

"Thank you, Father, you know I've always wanted to go!"

Ever since she was old enough to read, Mary Ellen had dreamed about going to America. She drank in everything she could read about it and went out of her way to talk to anyone who had been there. She did not believe the streets were paved with gold, but they had to be at least silver. Everyone who had relatives in America always seemed to be getting money sent to them, so it stood to reason anyone could get rich with a bit of hard work. Not like Ireland where there was no future for a girl except marriage and a load of children. Being the youngest and the only girl, Mary Ellen had been sheltered and spoiled by her father and brothers. Her mother had given up trying to prepare her for the inevitable brood of children which she was bound to have.

She was totally innocent of the ways of the world, trusted everyone and could not conceive of anyone being any different. She was very quiet-spoken and had an aura of grace and kindness about her. Anyone who met Mary Ellen O'Neill knew that they were in the presence of a special person. She had not saved a penny for her fare to America because whatever money that came her way ended up in the poor box at church. She believed with unswerving faith that God would look after her. Her mother had tried unsuccessfully to warn her about all the not so nice things in the world, but it was no good. She trusted everyone and saw no reason not to. When Martha brought the subject up with Patrick he invariably told her to let the girl enjoy her childhood, because there would be plenty of time later on to worry about the rotten world they lived in.

After Robert left for Dublin to arrange for the purchase of the land, and at the same time book Mary Ellen's passage, Martha tried once again to talk to Patrick about her concerns about Mary Ellen.

"Patrick, we are going to have to talk to Mary Ellen. She's walking around singing the whole day and daydreaming about America. You'd better tell her a few home truths. All the Americans are not angels, you know."

"Neither are the Irish, and she's done okay so far!" he replied sullenly.

"What the hell is that supposed to mean? The farthest she's been is that girls' school in Dublin and that's not exactly New York!"

"And you're an authority on New York, I suppose?"

"I'm not only talking about New York, it's just that she's never been away from us and I'm afraid what could happen to her. She's so innocent."

Patrick softened his tone. "Look, Martha, everyone feels the same way when one of their children emigrates. Mary Ellen is not as simple as you think. And anyway, she's going to stay with John, she'll be all right," he said without conviction.

"Well, I tried,"Martha sighed. "I just hope you're right about her."

"That's the spirit,"Patrick said brightly. "Now me stomach is telling me it's dinnertime, so be off with ye."

On the Thursday Robert arrived back from Dublin. Patrick hurried down the road to meet him.

"How did you get on, son, did everything go all right?" he asked anxiously. He had not told anyone he had hardly slept worrying if the deal would go through.

"No bother at all, Father,"Robert replied. "We now own all the fifty acres and the payments are ten pounds a month for twenty years. When some of us move to England, we'll clear it off in no time. It's in all our names and for a few pennies more per month it's insured so if any one of us dies the whole mortgage is paid off."

"Excellent work, Robert, now your mother can stop worrying. By the way, did you book Mary Ellen's trip?"

"Yes, it's all booked. She sails from Londonderry to Liverpool on Friday, the twenty-second and then boards the Mauretania at Southampton bound for New York on Saturday, the twenty-third of October. I took the liberty of upgrading her to second class, and I paid the difference myself."

Patrick drew a deep breath. "That's only two weeks away. Well, I suppose we'll have to arrange a going away party for her leaving."

Robert put his arm around his father's shoulders. "She'll be all right, Father, don't worry. Make the party for two, I booked myself on the ship to Liverpool with her, and seeing it's in England, I might as well stay there and start working."

"By God, you don't waste any time, do you!" Patrick stopped in his tracks.

Robert laughed. "No time to waste, Father! Now let's find Mother and tell her all the good news."

Martha and the other boys were overjoyed that everything had gone so well. But none of them were as happy as Mary Ellen. She ran around showing everyone her ticket.

"Would you believe it," she cried. "Second class no less, I'll be hobnobbing with all the lords and ladies!"

"Not exactly." Patrick laughed. "There is a first class you know, and that's where the lords and ladies will be!"

"Oh, Father, I don't care. As long as I'm going to America." She walked away dreamily clutching her ticket tight to her breast.

Patrick looked at her wistfully. She was so innocent. He decided to have Robert talk to her and try and bring her down to earth.

"I'll try, but don't expect her to change. She's the way she is and I don't think anything will ever change her!" After Robert talked to Mary Ellen, he found his father stacking the turf for the winter.

"I told you it would make no difference, she told me not to worry, God would look after her, so you can't argue with that, now can you?"

Patrick stopped for a moment and looked at his son. "No Robert, you can't argue with that!"

On the following Saturday night they had the going away party for Robert and Mary Ellen. These parties were a tradition in a country that had lost most of its youth each year to emigration. The neighbors came from miles around to sing and dance for hours and tell stories about the successes of the ones who had left.

"Remember Sean O'Casey? He went to Australia with just the clothes on his back and I hear he owns near half of the state of Queensland!"

"And Liam Doherty went to America, they say he made his first million in six months, isn't that right, Mrs. Doherty?"

"Well, he must have spent it in the next six months because I've never had a penny off him!" the old woman snapped.

Everybody roared with laughter, but deep down they all believed that emigration was the best option open to the youth of the country. The party was an all night affair and only ended when the bells of the church started ringing summoning them all to Mass. The women started to gather all the half empty bottles despite the protests of the men who were in no mood to go to church. But, as usual, they were cajoled into going with the promise of a few pints when Mass was over.

"Well," Patrick said jovially, "who knows the next time we'll all be going to church together. Come to think of it, we might never be together again." His mood changed suddenly as he staggered along the road.

"Don't talk rubbish, Father." Mary Ellen took his arm. "When I send for you all to come to America, we'll all be together for good!"

"And just how are you going to do that, my girl"

"Don't you know I'll be a millionaire in no time. Just wait and see!" The whole family roared with laughter "You can't argue with that!" Robert said as they made their way into the church.

Chapter 2

Marcus Browning woke up with a tremendous hangover. He felt as if he had been run over by a lorry. There was a persistent pounding in his head that seemed to stop occasionally then start again. Slowly the realization came to him through the fog in his mind someone was knocking on his door. He lived in a flat in Knightsbridge near the center of London, which came with all the conveniences, including a valet who also doubled as a chauffeur.

Marcus dragged himself out of bed and made his way to the door, holding his hands over his ears to stifle the hammering on the door.

"For God's sake, stop that noise!" he said as he opened the door a couple of inches and peered out to see who was there. It was Harold, his valet.

"Sorry to disturb you, sir, but your father called on the telephone. He wants to see you immediately."

Marcus opened the door. "Come in, Harold. Now, before you say anymore, tell me where the hell I ended up last night?"

"The Turf Club. The one just off Piccadilly, sir."

"How much did I lose? I can tell by the look on your face I sure as hell didn't win." He squinted his burning eyes and looked at Harold. "Well! Tell me for God's sake! Spit it out man, don't stand there like a dummy!"

Harold drew a deep breath. "All I know is you signed a note, sir. You ran out of cash."

Marcus felt the first pangs of uneasiness. His voice dropped to a whisper, "How much?"

"I don't know, sir. All I know is that you gave your note to Mr. James St. John."

Damnation! It had to be that little bastard, I bet he's at father's house already! "And you don't know how much?"

"Not a clue, sir. Now I suggest you get dressed and I'll take you to your father. This is one time I wouldn't keep him waiting, sir."

"No, I'd better go and face the music, give me ten minutes to get cleaned up and I'll be down."

"I'll get the motorcar round to the front and wait for you, sir." Harold left the room and closed the door softly behind him. *What an idiot, his father gives him a life of luxury and he throws money away like water, it proves there's no justice in this world when you see things like this.* Harold had a wife and three children to keep off two pounds a week, which was more than most people got. When he saw Marcus lose hundreds of pounds gambling it made him furious, but it was more than his job was worth to say anything. He smiled grimly. *Things were bound to be different after what happened last night.*

Sir Derek Browning lived in a Georgian mansion just outside Oxford. He was a self-made man who had started a small hardware business in 1912. When the War started in 1914 he saw immediately there was a lot of money to be made in government contracts. Knowing this was a lot easier than getting one of these contracts. After being turned away from every office he went to, rather than getting discouraged, he figured that the only way to have a chance was to talk directly to someone with real power, not some snotty secretary. The problem was how to meet them, because Derek did not move in the same circles as these people. After much thought, Derek devised a plan to enable him to meet some of them. He asked around the pubs off Whitehall at lunchtime and was not long in finding out who he needed to talk to. There were several committees that handed out contracts for the War Office. One in particular that interested him the most was the Quartermasters Procurement Committee. After further visits to the pubs he learned that the members of the committee liked to spend their Saturdays at the racing at Ascot. Now Derek knew what to do.

Dressed in his best, with his life savings of two-hundred and fifty pounds, he made his way to Ascot and put his plan into motion. He waited near the paddock where the racehorse owners gathered and watched for anyone important in the vicinity. Sure enough, there were a couple of Dukes, Peers of the realm, high-ranking Army officers and a few members of Parliament. All six members of the procurement committee were there. Derek mingled with the crowd, making small talk when he could and listened to every word they said. The talk was all about the races, of course, and everyone knew a certainty. Derek asked and got lots of advice on which horses to bet and made notes in his program accordingly. Before the racing started he had the names of most of the men and their tips all listed in his program. These upper classes did not put the bets on themselves, there were bookie's runners who took the bets for them and laid them on at the windows.

Derek gave each of the runners five pounds to give him a list of winners and losers and how much after the last race. The runners were happy to oblige, a fiver was a lot of money to them. There were ten runners, which added up to fifty pounds of an investment. When the racing was finished, Derek gathered the lists, put them in his pocket and went home. After doing the same thing for four Saturdays in a row, he had what he wanted. He was left with only fifty pounds, but he knew it was the best investment he would ever make.

Of the committee members the big loser in the four week period was General Peter Hawkins, who had lost a total of fourteen-thousand pounds. On the fifth Saturday, before the racing started, Derek approached the General with whom he had spoken a few times in the last four weeks. He was standing with his wife talking to a member of Parliament.

"General Hawkins, can I have a word in private please, it won't take a minute." Derek's voice was as sweet as honey.

"Oh, all right, but make it quick will you? I have a bet to put on." The two men walked out of earshot.

"I hope it's better than these!" Derek handed him a slip of paper with all the losers and how much he had lost in the last few weeks. The general's face turned white.

"Where did you get this?" he whispered, stuffing it in his pocket and glancing at the group of people a short distance away.

"That is unimportant, now listen carefully, General. Depending on what you say, both of us can end up very rich or I will be poor and you will have missed the chance to afford as many bets as you want!"

General Hawkins did not panic. For a minute Derek thought he was going to tell him to go to Hell.

"Did you say both of us could get rich?"

"Yes, I did!"

The general wrote something on his racing program and handed it to Derek. "Be at that address at 9:00 a.m. on Monday morning. We can talk there." He turned on his heel and walked away.

That was the start of the Browning fortune. Derek became what was called, derisively, a war profiteer. He never gave that a moment's thought. For 10% of the profits, General Hawkins gave Derek the quotes to beat on everything from boots to toothbrushes. Derek then informed his contacts in the relevant businesses for 20%. There was plenty of government money going around to make them all rich.

By 1918, when the war ended, Derek Browning was a multi-millionaire and General Hawkins could afford his gambling habit quite easily. The two men remained good friends even after the armistice put a stop to their collaboration. Sir Derek was quite happy with what he had achieved in his life. He had married well, and both he and his wife Catherine had good health. The only problem he had was with his son, Marcus. He had named him after a Roman general, Marcus Vicinius. He should have called him Nero. The boy was incorrigible. He had been the bane of Derek's life since he was about sixteen. His academic excellence was only matched by his boorish behavior. He was twenty-two now and seemed to be getting worse instead of better. Thank God for his daughter Matilda, she was eighteen and she'd never given them any trouble.

As Harold drove through the Thames valley on the road to Oxford, Marcus stared blankly out of the window. He was deep in thought. *Why did he have to get so drunk?* He racked his brains trying to remember something about the night before. He could remember drinking in the slums of Whitechapel. He always enjoyed going there and flashing his money around. It gave him great pleasure to watch the hostile glares of the working poor as he flirted with the girls who didn't need to be asked twice to go for a drive in his motorcar. Try as he might Marcus could not remember a thing about gambling in the club. He couldn't even remember being in the club. His mouth was bone dry and his head was pounding. This was part of the hangover and the only way he could get rid of it was to have a few more drinks. Well, he would stop for a few on the way home after he had seen his father. This was another part of the routine, going up to Oxford to be reminded that his father paid for everything, that he would cut him off without a penny; that he should have disowned him for being asked to leave Oxford after Derek had made a sizable donation to get him in. It was always the same lecture. Maybe if his mother wasn't around Derek would punish him, but as it was he got the flat, the chauffeured motorcar and a generous allowance. So what the hell, if the price was a few lectures now and again, it was well worth it.

The sound of the tires crunching along the gravel woke Marcus from his reverie. They were on the mile long driveway leading from the main road up to the house. He looked around at the beautifully landscaped gardens on either side of the road and the horses grazing in the distance. The car drew up to the front of the house and stopped in front of the stairs leading up to the six huge pillars on the colonnade that always reminded Marcus of a Greek temple. *What the Hell am I worried about? It's just a matter of time before this is all mine, so I might as well enjoy myself while I wait for the old man to die.*

The butler met him at the door and whispered, "He's in the morning room, sir."

They entered into the oak-paneled hall with the central staircase arching up to both wings of the second floor. The morning room was on the left. The butler ushered him over to the door, knocked softly, opened door a little and poked his head in the room. "Master Marcus is here, sir."

"It's about time, show him in."

He's got his business voice going. Marcus grimaced as he entered the room. The butler left and closed the door softly behind him. Derek was seated at a small writing desk in front of a massive bay window.

Marcus walked over and stood with his hands behind his back looking over his father's head at the garden beyond. *I should know every flower in that garden considering the amount of time I've spent standing here.* "Where's Mother?" Marcus asked.

"Good morning to you too!" Derek said sarcastically. "It's none of your business where she is! All you need to know is she's given up on you and left me to deal with you as I see fit."

"I don't believe you!"

Derek exploded. "Listen carefully, Marcus! Your mother has had enough. I'd already given up on you, God knows, but this was the last straw for her. Now you are going to learn you've trifled with us too long!"

"What the hell are you talking about? I bet it was that rat St.John. So I lost a few pounds, you can afford it!"

"Yes, I can afford it! Tell me the truth for once. Do you know what you did last night?"

Marcus shook his head. "I only remember the start of the night. I was in some pub in Whitechapel. I remember leaving with a girl, but everything is a blank after that."

"Well, let me fill you in on the rest of your evening out. You took the girl to the Turf Club, no less. You lost so heavily at cards to James St. John that you gave him a note to pay him off."

"Well, how much was it for?"

"It wasn't how much, it was WHO! You tried to pay him off by offering him a young girl of sixteen!"

Marcus was getting a bad feeling about this. *What the hell else happened last night?* "I don't remember that," he muttered in a low voice.

"I suppose you don't remember the police taking her out of the club?"

"No, I don't remember." Marcus' voice was a whisper.

Derek sat back in his chair and smiled grimly. "Well, the girl was so drunk, they called the police to take her home. And if it wasn't for St. John, you'd be in the bloody jail for giving her drink. St. John called me this morning to say that you are no longer welcome at the club. He told the police that the girl must have slipped in herself. I pay fifteen-hundred a year for that club, and you just made it impossible for your mother and me to show our faces there again."

Damn it, Harold should have filled me in on this.

"Anyway, Marcus," Derek said wearily. "I'm cutting you off from all your allowances. No flat, no car, no allowance, nothing. Everything I have is being left to Matilda." He glanced up at Marcus' ashen face.

"Everything is perfectly legal, so don't even think of contesting anything. Because, as you see, I'm very much alive. Now go and get a job and see if you can make something of yourself because I sure as hell can't." He stood up and waved his hand in dismissal.

Marcus could hardly believe what he was hearing. He knew his father and he knew he would never do this without his mother's approval. He became enraged and started screaming "You're lying. Where's my mother, she won't let you get away with this. Where is she? I must talk to her!"

"I'm here, Marcus, and I agree with your father. You should not have shamed us like this."

Marcus whirled around. His mother was standing by the door. She had come in the room while he had been shouting. "But mother…"

Catherine held up her hand. "The decision is final, Marcus. We both love you and feel we are holding you back by continuing to indulge you. With your brains and good looks you can be anything you want."

Marcus laughed bitterly, he was starting to realize that they really meant it. "You make it sound like you're doing me a favor. Throwing me out on the damn street!"

Derek interrupted. "That's exactly what we are doing—we've had enough." He threw some money on the desk. "Here is fifty pounds, take it or leave it. Harold will take you back to the flat to get your clothes. Give me your keys to the flat. I want you out today!"

Shocked, Marcus fumbled in his pockets for the keys. He threw them on the desk.

"All right then, to Hell with you. I'm going and I won't be back!" Catherine started to say something, but Marcus cut her off. "Remember, Mother, it's your choice, not mine. And you'll regret it, not me," he said harshly. She turned away and left the room sobbing quietly.

Derek moved around the desk and grabbed Marcus by the arm. "Do you think we are doing this lightly? Mark my words, it will make you or break you, and if it's the former, you will live to thank us. Now get on your way and I do wish you good luck. Goodbye, Marcus." He turned his back and looked out of the window.

Marcus hesitated, picked up the fifty pounds and strode out of the house without looking back.

Catherine joined Derek at the window. He put his arm around her. "Do you know what's wrong with Marcus, dear?" he asked.

"I suppose he's been spoiled," she replied, sobbing.

"No, that's not it. The boy has no conscience, a very dangerous thing! I shudder to think what he would do in a position of power. Ah well, we've done all we can for him." They turned away from the window and sat on the couch holding one another tightly.

Harold was waiting by the car. Marcus scowled at him and got in without a word. Harold shrugged and drove all the way to London in silence. When they got to the flat, Harold opened the door and said, "I'll wait outside, and when you're finished I'll lock up after you.

No "Sir" today. Marcus gritted his teeth as he went into the flat. *That bastard always hated me.* He hastily gathered everything he could think of and stuffed it into a suitcase and a small valise, looked around him and walked outside.

Without a word Harold locked the door and turned to Marcus. "You are the biggest fool I ever met in my life, Marcus. You had everything and threw it all away."

"Go to Hell!" Marcus replied, and walked down the street carrying the two cases. He walked aimlessly for about fifteen minutes and found himself walking through Green Park, just next to Buckingham palace. He stopped and sat on a bench to gather his thoughts. His hangover had gone and suddenly he was hungry.

It started to rain and with a curse he lifted his cases and quickly walked up to Piccadilly. He turned right and walked into the Ritz. He looked at the tables all set with white linen and silver service and sat down. *This was more like it!*

He'd get something to eat and then he'd feel better and be able to think clearly.

Marcus ordered a steak with all the trimmings and a bottle of Bordeaux to wash it down. When he had finished eating, he bought a cigar and sat thinking while he smoked. His mother was right, he was a very handsome young man and highly intelligent. His expulsion from Oxford had nothing to do with his grades; he easily got firsts in all his subjects. He had been expelled for a series of drunken escapades, none of which he could remember. Now he sat deep in contemplation. After a while he put the cigar out, sighed deeply and looked up at the ceiling. *They are right! I am a disgrace to myself and my family!* A feeling of deep shame swept over him. For the first time in his life he realized his actions affected other people. He slumped in the chair in despair. *Why am I like this? I've got to pull myself together. There must be a reason I behave like this. What the hell is wrong with me? I must snap out of this."* He thought about all the stupid things he had done and there was one common thread in all of them. It was drink that made him turn into a bloody idiot. *So be it!* Marcus straightened up, and at the lowest point in his life he vowed to himself he would never drink again.

His spirits rose when he came to the realization that only he could solve his problems. *He would show them.* He made another vow. When he saw his parents again, he would have more money and power than even his father ever dreamed of. He called the waiter over to bring his bill and for the first time in his life looked at the price. *First lesson! Never eat at the Ritz unless someone else is paying!*

It was dark when Marcus left the Ritz, the rain was falling steadily; all in all it was a miserable night. He pulled his collar up and walked along Piccadilly toward the Circus. *First thing I've got to do is get somewhere to sleep tonight, hotels were out of the question.* Easier said than done, he had no idea where to go. He stopped and took shelter in a shop doorway to decide what to do. *Ah! I'll get a taxi, the driver will know where to go.* After a few minutes, he hailed a taxi and got in with his cases.

"Where to, Guv?" the driver asked

"I'm not sure," Marcus replied. "Do you know where I could stay the night, nothing too expensive?"

"I know lots of places, how much do you want to spend?"

"Could I get something for a pound?" Marcus asked hopefully.

"I thought you said nothing too expensive? For five shillings you can get a top class bed and breakfast. If you want something cheaper there's a working man's home I know for a shilling a night. It's a bit rough, but it'll keep you out of the rain. The driver turned round for a quick look. He saw the tailored coat and fancy shirt.

"I think you'd better go for the bed and breakfast if you're sure you can afford it." *Cheeky bastard!*

"All right, make it the bed and breakfast," Marcus replied.

"Bed and breakfast it is!"

Marcus saw they were headed north up the Tottenham Court Rd. The taxi turned right on Euston road and passed the three massive train stations before turning right again into a narrow street lined on each side with three storey high townhouses.

"Here we are, Guv. Anyone of these will do you. They all charge the same, so take your pick."

Marcus paid the fare and hauled his cases onto the pavement. The taxi drove off into the rain and Marcus turned around and lifted his cases, walked up the five steps leading to the door of the nearest house. He banged on the brass knocker three times and almost immediately the light above the door went on and the door opened. A haggard woman in her fifties stood staring up at him suspiciously. Marcus saw she had no teeth and her breath smelled of cheap wine

"Well, what do you want?" she said, eying the two cases on the ground.

"I'm looking for lodging for the night,"Marcus said.

By this time the crone had sized him up from head to toe. Her manner changed in an instant. In as sweet a voice as she could manage, she croaked, "And you've come to the right place! For seven shillings you can have the best room in the house and a breakfast fit for a king!"

Marcus was just about to agree when impulsively he said, "Oh, I was thinking more about something around five shillings a night. Do you know anywhere around for that price?"

The woman scowled at him and swore under her breath, but she wasn't about to lose five shillings. "For one night only, paid in advance; and you get the second best room. Take it or leave it!"

What a specimen. He pulled a pound note from his pocket and before he gave it over he said, "Can I see the room now?"

"This way now, and mind your cases don't tear the wallpaper," the woman growled as she led him up a narrow staircase.

"Here it is," the woman said as she turned on the light. The room faced the front of the house with a bay window overlooking the street. It was clean enough and had a wardrobe and dressing table along with a double bed.

"I'll take it for four nights," Marcus said, and held out the pound note. Again the woman's manner changed when she took the money.

"You are very welcome to stay, sir. Here is the toilet." She showed him a door on the landing. "There is also a bath on the ground floor. It's only sixpence to use it, and that includes the towel. Breakfast is served from seven o'clock till nine in the morning, after nine there is no service. Anything else you want to know?" She pulled a key from her apron pocket. "Here's the key for the front door. I bar it at ten o'clock."

"No, I think that covers everything," Marcus said and looked at his watch as the woman went downstairs. It was nearly seven o'clock. He closed the room door and took his coat off and threw it on the bed. *What the hell do I do now?* He unpacked his suitcase and put the clothes in the dresser drawers. When he finished unpacking, he walked over to the window and looked up and down the street. The rain was still pouring and the night was as black as pitch. He saw a light in a ground floor window at the corner of the next street. It was a pub!

"Thank God," he said aloud. He grabbed his coat and suddenly realized he couldn't go to the pub because he had sworn to stop drinking. He threw the coat back on the bed and sat in front of the dressing table staring at his face in the mirror. He sat thinking morosely of the fact he would never have another drink. It wasn't so much the drink he would miss, it was the company and the good times he had when he was drinking.

The day had been bad enough without making it any worse. A couple of pints wouldn't do him or anyone else any harm. Why sit here in misery when he could spend a couple of hours with some company? It wasn't as if he was going to get drunk or anything, so why was he sitting here alone? To hell with it, I'll stop drinking when I feel better! Marcus put his coat on, made sure he had the key and went down the stairs.

Marcus hurried through the pouring rain across the street and broke into a run as he neared the pub. He opened the door and entered a typical London pub. There was a middle-aged man playing an old battered piano with the top of it black from cigarette burns. A few men were playing darts in a corner and there were the usual card players. He went over to the bar and asked the bartender for a half of bitter.

"Right you are, sir!" he said jovially as he poured the beer. "A good night to sit by the fire, eh!"

"It sure is," Marcus replied as he looked around the barroom.

A man who was sitting by himself nodded at Marcus and gestured to the empty chair at the table.

Why not? I'll be glad of someone to talk to. He lifted his beer and went over to the table.

"Hello, I'm John Thomas," the man introduced himself. "What a bloody climate, this damned rain looks as if it will never stop," he said as he made room for Marcus to sit.

"Marcus Browning. Yes, it sure is a lousy night."

"I'm glad you came over. I was getting fed up sitting by myself, but I'm not going anywhere in this rain!"

"Funny you should say that, John, but that's the reason I'm here. I was sitting myself over in the bed and breakfast. I saw this place from the window, and as it's just across the road, I hopped over for an hour."

"You're kidding! I'm in a B&B as well. What one are you staying at?" Marcus pulled the key from his pocket and looked at the tag.

"Number twelve. What number are you at?"

"Number fourteen, that's next door to you. How much a night for your place?"

"Five shillings a night."

"Same here. I'm only there till tomorrow. My train for Southampton is at ten o'clock and then I catch the ship to America. No more of this weather for me. What about you?"

"Oh, I don't know yet." Marcus was caught off guard. He hadn't given tomorrow a great deal of thought. In fact, he hadn't given it any thought at all.

"Well, I made my mind up to get out of this damned country over a year ago. It took me all that time to save the fare."

"How much is the fare to America, John?"

"Depends on what ship and what class you go on. I'm going steerage which is the cheapest, and that costs eight pounds. First class can go as high as fifty or even a hundred, but that's out of my league."

Marcus thought about what the man had said. Maybe this was what he should do. Emigrate! There was nothing to hold him in England anyway. "Let me get you another pint, John." He stood up. "And then you can tell me all about America!"

John Thomas didn't have to be asked twice. He only had four shillings left in the world, plus his tickets for the train and the voyage to America. "A pint of bitter, please," he said and settled back in his seat.

Marcus brought two pints back to the table and said, "Now then, John, tell me all about America."

"Where will I start?" John could not contain his enthusiasm. He rambled on and on about the wonderful country where a man could make a million dollars without even trying; about California where the sun shone all the time; about a country so vast you could fit England into a tiny corner of it! Oh yes, America was the promised land all right, and he couldn't wait to get there.

While John Thomas extolled the wonders of the United States, Marcus was making up his mind. He had never even considered leaving England, but now that things had changed there was absolutely nothing to stop him. A feeling of exhilaration swept over him. *This was the answer, a new start in a new world!*

"John, you've talked me into it. Now tell me where do I go to book my ticket?"

John stared at him. "You're serious!"

"Never more so, now how do I go about it?"

"First, you need a passport. And you're in the right place to get one. Just go to the main post office, fill out a form, pay a pound, have your picture taken and wait two days. I had to wait two weeks because I live in Manchester. After that, go to the Cunard Line offices and buy a ticket. Now, emigration is a different thing. You either need a job or a relative to sponsor you. That's all there is to it my friend, but I still think you're having me on!"

Marcus laughed and held out his hand. "Think what you like, John, but I'll tell you something. I don't believe in God, but I do believe providence had a hand in us meeting tonight!" He looked at his watch. "Good God, look at the time! Quarter to ten. I'd better get over there before I get locked out!"

"So will I," said John, gulping the last of his beer. "Look, Marcus, I'm sorry I couldn't buy you a drink, but I've just about enough to get me on the boat."

Marcus was so happy he had made up his mind about going to America, he pulled a pound note from his pocket and gave it to John.

"Here, take this and you'll never know what you did to deserve it. Good luck till we meet again." Before John could respond, Marcus shook his hand and with that he was gone.

Speechless, John Thomas looked at the note in his hand. *Glad to have met you too, Marcus!* he said to himself as he left the pub.

The next morning Marcus was up at eight o'clock, in plenty of time to have the breakfast, which was enough to do him till suppertime. It consisted of eggs, bacon, sausage, beans, and all the bread and butter you could eat. He was not used to having such meals, but he ate till he was full. He was slowly beginning to realize that everything cost money. Before he left his room he had counted what he had spent since he got the fifty pounds. The Ritz had been by far the biggest expense. Including the bottle of wine the four pounds ten shillings could have kept him in the B&B for three weeks. He had just over forty-two pounds, so he made his mind up to be careful from now on.

He left the boarding house at nine o'clock and made his way to the Post Office on the Charing Cross Road. He filled out the form for a passport and went to a small studio to have his picture taken. The passport would be ready in two days. They asked for his birth certificate which he was lucky enough to have in his wallet. He was in the habit of carrying it around because he never knew where to keep it safe. His mother had given him it when he moved to the flat. From there he made his way to the Strand where the big shipping companies had their offices. Cunard was the biggest one, so it was easy to find.

He went into the office and looked around the walls at all the advertisements for travel to just about anywhere in the world. There were models of Cunard's most famous ships in glass cases. Marcus went over to a desk where a bespectacled man about forty was pretending to be busy with papers on his desk.

Marcus knocked sharply on the desk. Using his best Oxford accent, he said, "Good morning, my man. My name is Marcus Browning. I would like to book passage to America as soon as possible, unless of course I'm in the wrong place!"

Flustered at being caught out, the man immediately started to stammer. "Oh no, sir, this is the right place all right. Just let me tidy up here and we'll see what we have available." He looked at Marcus' expensive clothes and said, "I suppose you'll be traveling first class, sir?"

"That depends on two things, if there is first class available on the first ship out, and how much it costs."

The man pored through his schedules and said, "The first ship to America is the Mauretania out of Southampton on the 23rd of October." He looked at the calendar. "That's a week on Saturday." He looked in a large ledger and said, "You're in luck, sir, it looks as if there's one single cabin left in first class, and a premium one at that. Of course I'll have to phone the head office in Liverpool to confirm it."

Marcus looked him in the eye; he wasn't going to let this specimen see he was embarrassed. "How much is this premium first class cabin?" he asked disdainfully.

The man moved his finger across the page. "One-hundred and twenty pounds, sir." He looked up from the ledger.

"How much is second class?"

The man hid a smirk as he turned the pages of the ledger. "In second class the cabins sleep two, so you have to share. There are still a few available. That will cost twenty-six pounds. Now if that sounds a little expensive..."

Marcus interrupted, "That will be fine, now where do I pay?"

"First, I have to call to confirm, then I'll take your particulars and if you want to pay here, I can issue your ticket today. You do have a valid passport, I take it?"

"I'm picking it up on Wednesday."

"We can't issue a ticket till we see the passport."

"I'll bring it in on Wednesday. I'll pay for the ticket now."

"I have to tell you, sir, if you don't get a passport you will lose your money."

"That will be fine. I'll take the risk." Marcus pulled the money out.

"As long as you understand. Now what did you say your name was, sir?" The man pulled a printed form out of the desk drawer.

Chapter 3

On Saturday, the twenty-third of October 1926, the docks at Southampton were alive with people. The great ship Mauretania was being readied for the voyage to New York. The ship was being loaded with thousands of tons of supplies to feed the two-thousand passengers she would transport to the New World.

There were people everywhere milling around, passengers trying to find the right place to have their luggage loaded, children crying and the shouts of the crewmen trying to advise people where to go even though half of them did not speak English.

Mary Ellen O'Neill got out of a taxi in the middle of this immense crowd. She had never seen so many people in her life. Her brother Robert had seen her on the train at Liverpool early that morning. She stood in awe at the gigantic ship at the dockside. It seemed to stretch as far as she could see in either direction, and when she looked up at the people who were on the top deck they looked so far away she couldn't believe that this enormous ship was actually floating on the water.

"I never thought anything could be this big!" she gasped in wonder. She put her hand valise on top of her trunk which her father had fitted with small wheels to make it easy for her to move around. She paid the taxi off and pulled her documents out of her handbag. The instructions read that everything was done alphabetically, so all she had to do was look for a loading gate with the letter O. At first she couldn't see any signs, then she saw that they were on the building which ran the full length of the dock. She dragged her trunk along and joined the line up waiting at the gate marked O.

The line moved surprisingly fast, and when she reached the gate an officer asked for her papers and signaled a porter to take her trunk. He marked the trunk with chalk, stamped her ticket and showed her he had stamped gangway number twelve.

"Go to number twelve, miss, and show the officer your ticket. Here is the receipt for your trunk, you'll get it back at New York under the sign marked O. "Have a pleasant voyage and good luck!"

"Thank you very much, sir." Mary Ellen walked on through the gate toward the line of gangways that stretched along the great liner. At gangway twelve an officer looked at her cabin number on her ticket.

"Straight ahead to the stairs, go up two decks and show the officer your ticket. Next please."

Mary Ellen did as she was told, and after showing her ticket to three different officers, all the while going upstairs, she found her cabin. There were two small bunks made up to look like beds; one with a card and key with her name on it; a small dressing table, a clothes closet and a porthole. There were two enormous life-jackets on top of the closet. There was a card on each bed with information about meal times, where the dining room was situated and lots of information about where to go for advice or help throughout the ship. On the back of the card was a plan of the passenger decks on the ship. Second class was on B deck. Directly across the passage was the toilet, which served four cabins. *Not bad at all,* she thought and went over to open the porthole. She pulled the two heavy brass locking clamps off, pulled the porthole open and stuck her head out. Her cabin faced the dock and she looked down on the scene below in astonishment. *The people looked like ants! Wait till I get up on deck. It'll be even better.*

Mary Ellen closed the porthole and sat on the bed to read the information on the card. She was looking for a place to keep the two-thousand pounds she had in her handbag. Her Uncle John had wanted it in cash rather than a money order. Nobody knew why, and anyway, it was his money and he could have it any way he wanted it. "Ah, here we are." She saw what she was looking for. Any valuables not wanted on the voyage could be given to the ship's purser. The purser's office was on the main deck near the grand staircase. She unpacked her suitcase and stored it under the bed. She lifted her bag and unzipped it. Next to the envelope with the money was a small gold powder box with shamrocks engraved on it. Her brother Robert had given it to her as she got on the train. She remembered his last words to her.

"Mary Ellen, whenever you go through bad times, I want you to read the inscription on this box. It is a quote from Tennyson. I think he must have had you on his mind when he wrote it. It will remind you that no matter how bad things are your family loves you and you will never be alone even though we are far away."

She flipped the lid open and read the inscription. It read. *"My strength is as the strength of ten, because my heart is pure."* Her eyes misted over as she read the words. She sighed and closed the box and put it back in her purse.

Before she opened the door to leave, she noticed a large notice on the door with the lifeboat station number for her cabin. She read the notice and went out into the passage, locking the door behind her and looking at her card to get her bearings.

She made her way up to the main deck and went over to look down at the dockside. There were still hundreds of people milling about. She looked at her watch. It was half past three. *How are they ever going to sail at six o'clock, they'll never make it!* She turned away and went into the middle of the ship to find the purser. It was easier than she had thought it would be, but there were about fifty people lined up waiting at the desk. Mary Ellen joined the line up and made small talk with the people around her to pass the time. As there was only one officer at the desk, it took a long time for her to get served. Eventually she deposited the money and was given a receipt for it. Immediately she felt better. She was not used to having so much money on her and had been worried about losing it ever since her father had given it to her.

Mary Ellen walked out on deck just in time for the ear splitting blast of the ship's horn to go off. Overcoming her fright, she dashed to the railing to look over at the dockside. The great ship was moving! She looked at her watch. It was exactly six o'clock. The noise stopped as suddenly as it started. She said to no one in particular, "I don't know how they managed to get away on time, at three o'clock there were still hundreds of people waiting down there."

"They have to go with the tide, lass," an old man answered. "If they miss the tide they can't go till tomorrow morning." The old man had an accent she had never heard before.

"Oh, I didn't know that,"Mary Ellen replied.

"Is this your first time on a ship then?"

"Yes, it is, I can't get over the size of it! It's enormous."

The old man held out his hand. "Jimmy Switcher of Detroit, Michigan, young lady. Are you traveling alone?"

Mary Ellen shook his hand. She was glad of someone to talk to. " Mary Ellen O'Neill. Yes, I am. I'm going to America to live with my uncle till I get on my feet."

"And where does your uncle live?"

"New York City, in a place called Queens. Do you know where it is? His name is John O'Neill." Switcher laughed, like all newcomers, this girl had no idea of the size of the United States.

"I know of Queens, but I live about five-hundred miles from there!"

"Five-hundred miles! Well, I don't think you'll know my Uncle John then. Where exactly is Detroit, is it north or south of New York."

"You need a lesson in geography, young lady. Why don't you and I meet in the library sometime and I'll show you where Detroit is on the map."

"That's very kind of you, Mr. Switcher. Are you sure it's no bother?"

"It will be my pleasure, my dear, escorting such a beautiful lady. Will tomorrow afternoon suit you?"

Mary Ellen blushed. "Tomorrow afternoon will be fine. I'll meet you right here at one o'clock."

"Excellent, goodbye till tomorrow then." The old man raised his hat and walked along the deck.

"Goodbye, Mr. Switcher." *What a nice man,* Mary Ellen thought and went back to leaning over the rail to watch the people on the dockside getting smaller and smaller as the Mauretania moved out into Southampton Water.

Not twenty feet from where Mary Ellen was standing, Marcus Browning was leaning against the rail wondering if he had just made the biggest mistake of his life. He had spent the last week between the bed and breakfast and various pubs in the vicinity. He had not been drunk and was strangely confident that he was just passing time till he left and would not drink at all once he reached America. Now he had three pounds left in his pocket and not a clue where to go once he reached New York. He had had a good education, but had never worked a day in his life; he had no trade and no experience. *Oh well, I'll have to get some kind of work,* he thought ruefully. *What a bloody idiot I've been. I had everything anyone could want and threw it away because of drink.* The crackling sound of the ship's loudspeakers interrupted his train of thought.

"All passengers go to the lifeboat station indicated on your cabin door for the lifeboat drill. An officer will instruct you on where to go and what to do in case of emergency at sea." This was part of the legacy of the Titanic disaster. Before that, there were no instructions given on safety, whether they had enough lifeboats or not. Marcus had not bothered to read the notice on the cabin door, so he was at a loss as to where to go, and he didn't want to go to his cabin to find out, as it was at the opposite end of the deck. He turned away from the rail and stopped dead. He knew immediately what lifeboat station he would be going to, the same one as the girl who was walking toward him.

Marcus had never taken women seriously, the only women he had anything to do with were the girls in the Whitechapel pubs and his mother's friends, who were the total opposite. *None of them could hold a candle to this one,* he thought as straightened his tie and tried to sound casual as he made his way to her side. With a smile he said, "Number six, I hope?"

The girl looked at him in surprise. "No, sir, number nine."

Marcus laughed. "Incredible! They must have put the notice on upside down in my cabin, so I'm number nine too. I'd be happy to accompany you if you don't mind. I wouldn't want you to fall overboard before we got to know each other. Marcus Browning, esquire, at your service, young lady." Smiling, he held out his arm.

Caught completely off guard, Mary Ellen stammered, "Oh, I don't mind at all, sir. I'm Mary Ellen O'Neill." *What a handsome young man, and well mannered too.*

"So you're Irish!" Marcus took her arm. "And what part of the Emerald Isle do you come from?"

"County Donegal, and where are you from?"

"Oh, I'm from Oxford. It's about fifty miles from London."

"Oh yes, there's the famous university. Now don't tell me you went there!"

Marcus smiled. *Well, I'm not telling any lies.* By now they had reached the lifeboat station and joined the group standing around waiting.

"As a matter of fact I did go to Oxford University. But let's talk about you. Are you emigrating to America?"

"Yes, I am, and I've been waiting for years to go. I can't wait to get there. What about you?"

"Well I am emigrating too, but I don't know if I'll stay there or not."

"Whereabouts in America are you going? I'm going to Queens, New York, to stay with my Uncle John."

What a beautiful quiet voice she has. Marcus was rapidly becoming smitten with Mary Ellen. He thought for a moment. "I hadn't any place picked out, but now that you mention it, Queens sounds good to me!" He looked into her eyes and smiled.

Mary Ellen blushed and looked away. "Oh, here's the officer now. We'd better pay attention!"

Marcus could not take his eyes off her during the drill and never heard a word the officer said. When the drill was finished Marcus said, "Well, Mary Ellen O'Neill, I don't know about you, but I'm getting cold out here. How would you like a hot chocolate or a cup of tea?"

"Yes, I would like that very much. Do you know where we can get one?"

"Not yet, but I'll soon find out!" Marcus could not believe his luck. He asked a nearby steward who directed them to the second class tearoom where all the tables were already set and several stewards were available to serve them. Marcus looked at his watch. It was almost eight o'clock. They ordered tea and cakes and sat talking about what life would be like in America and everything a young couple getting to know each other talks about.

Before they knew it a steward discreetly interrupted them. "Excuse me, sir, madam. I'm sorry, but we have to close now for the night."

Marcus surprised, replied. "Already? But we just sat down!"

Mary Ellen stood up. "My God, look at the time. It's ten o'clock! We'd better be getting to bed."

Marcus didn't want the night to end. As they made their way to their cabins, he said, "Will I see you tomorrow then?"

"Well, the ship's not that big, I'm sure we'll run into one another," Mary Ellen replied, knowing exactly what he meant.

Marcus pretended to look flustered. "I know, but I..."

Mary Ellen put him out of his fake misery. "Are you asking me out on a date, Mr. Browning?" she asked with a smile.

"Yes, I guess I am."

"Well, I'm sorry, but I'm seeing another gentleman tomorrow."

Marcus was completely taken aback. They were standing outside Mary Ellen's cabin. She hadn't mentioned she was with anyone. "Oh I'm sorry, I thought you were traveling alone!"

She opened the cabin door. " Oh, but I am. The fact is I agreed to meet another gentleman in the library at one o'clock. Why don't you come and meet him? Now I'll wish you goodnight." She smiled sweetly and held out her hand.

"The library at one o'clock? I'll be there. Goodnight, Mary Ellen." Marcus shook her hand. *I've got to see this guy,* he thought as he walked along the passage.

Mary Ellen switched the light on as she entered the cabin.

"What the hell! Who's there?" An elderly woman nearly jumped out of the bunk opposite Mary Ellen's.

Startled, Mary Ellen replied. "Oh, I'm sorry. I didn't know there was anyone here. We must be sharing this cabin. I'm Mary Ellen O'Neill, I hope I didn't frighten you."

The woman waved her hand in relief. "I'm Susan Harper. It's all right. I was just falling asleep. I'm exhausted after traveling all day."

"So am I," Mary Ellen said as she undressed. "I'll let you get to sleep and we'll talk tomorrow. Goodnight." She switched the light off and got into the bunk.

"Goodnight," the woman replied.

What a day! Mary Ellen lay looking at the moonlight shining through the porthole. *What a nice young man Marcus is. Well, you never know what can happen,* was her last thought before she fell asleep.

Marcus' cabin was at the opposite side of the ship, as the cabins were always separated by gender. When he opened the door, he was also surprised to find a young man sitting at the dresser reading a book.

"Good evening," Marcus said, and introduced himself.

The young man bolted to his feet and, holding out his hand, started talking excitedly in a language that Marcus had never heard.

Marcus smiled and lifted the book the man had been reading. It was an English Russian dictionary and phrase book. He turned the pages till he found "goodnight" and pointed to it, showing it to the man at the same time.

The man looked disappointed and nodded politely. Marcus shrugged and started getting ready for bed. The man watched for a minute and without another word the two men retired for the night.

The next morning being Sunday, there were church services held on board. They were multi-denominational and were held in the cinema after breakfast. Marcus had tried unsuccessfully to change tables so as he could sit beside Mary Ellen, but the steward told him he would have to exchange seats with someone as they were all pre-assigned. As it was the first sit-down meal and people were finding their seats for the first time, Marcus decided to leave it till dinner to ask for a change. He was seated next to the Russian who managed to tell him his name was Ivan and constantly asked him to read the English words to him out of his dictionary.

If this keeps up, I'll never see America, I'll throw myself overboard to get peace from this fellow. He had only time for a few words with Mary Ellen before she went off to church. Marcus never went to church if he could avoid it. To him, all the talk of God and Saints was all fairytales. He resigned himself to wait until one o'clock and see her in the library.

To kill time he took a walk round the deck, afraid to go back to his cabin in case Ivan the Russian was there. The ship was making twenty-two knots and there was a cold wind blowing off the Atlantic. He pulled his collar up and was just about to go into one of the lounges when a voice shouted down from the first class promenade deck.

"Marcus Browning! I thought I'd seen you earlier! What the hell are you doing down there?"

Marcus squinted his eyes upward to see who was calling. *Oh no!* It had never occurred to him he would meet someone who knew him on the voyage, but did it have to be Samuel Jones, the biggest bloody busybody he had ever met in his life? He and Jones had been classmates at Oxford and had not seen each other much since he'd been expelled. He knew Jones had met his parents at some parties since. *I wonder if he knows I've been thrown out. Well, I'll soon find out,* Marcus thought ruefully.

"Why, Sam Jones. Fancy meeting you here," he replied, thinking desperately of a way to explain why he was on the Mauretania.

"Come on up, Marcus. I've some friends I'd like you to meet. I'll meet you in the lounge." He waved and turned away out of sight.

Goddamn him to Hell, now the bastard will tell my father where I've gone, Marcus thought bitterly, realizing there was no way he could avoid him for the next six days. He made his way despondently up the stairs to the first class where he was surprised to find there was a locked door with a prominent notice. "First class passengers only beyond this point."

What the hell do I do now? Marcus wondered. He was just about to turn away when the door opened and a steward came through carrying a large bag of rubbish.

"Sorry, sir!" he said, and held the door open for Marcus to go through.

Thank God for that! Marcus walked briskly through with a hurried thank you and looked around for the first class lounge. He found the door to the lounge, and when he entered he saw immediately why they called it first class. There was no comparison to the second-class lounge. The walls were covered with mahogany panels with exotic carvings all over the place. There was a huge fireplace with a marble mantelpiece and brass lamps highlighting the numerous paintings that adorned the walls. There were card tables with leather upholstered chairs and reading desks scattered around, and it was at one of these where Samuel Jones was sitting with two older men.

Marcus decided to put a brave face on it, he wasn't about to be embarrassed in front of strangers. He walked over with a smile on his face. "Well, Samuel, how are you doing? It's a small world, isn't it!" he said jovially.

Jones stood up and shook hands. "Marcus, old chap. You're looking well. Let me introduce you. Gentlemen, this is Marcus Browning, Sir Derek is his father. This is Sir William Hawthorne and Jeffrey Walker, both of whom are my colleagues at Hawthorne Financial Group."

Marcus knew of Hawthorne, he was one of the richest men in England, if not the world. The three men were traveling without their families, who were to come to America later. He had never met either of the men before. Both of them stood up to shake hands.

"How are you Marcus?" Hawthorne said. "I've met your father a few times. Nice to meet you."

"Glad to meet you, Sir William. I've only read about you in the papers occasionally."

"All good, I hope!" All the men laughed at his little joke.

Jones called a steward over to the table. He turned to Marcus. "What are you drinking, Marcus?"

"Oh it's a bit early for me, just a soda water please."

The steward scribbled in his notebook. Will that be all sir?" he asked.

Jones looked at the others. They both shook their heads. "Yes thank you, that will be all." He addressed the other men. "Changed days! I've seen Marcus here do a bottle in before dinner, and that was just to get warmed up. Right, Marcus!"

Marcus looked at the men uncomfortably. He noticed Walker watching him carefully. "Changed days indeed! Now tell me what you're up to going to America?" he said cheerfully, all the while thinking, *How can I get away from here without making it obvious.*

"I'll tell you later, but first you have to tell us what the hell were you doing down in second class?"

Marcus had his story already thought out. "Actually, I'm traveling second class."

The three men looked at him in astonishment. Walker spoke first. "You mean you're traveling second class by choice. Whatever for, if I may ask?"

"You may indeed. I did it on impulse when I booked my ticket. Don't ask me why, but I don't regret it. Not yet anyway, I'm quite enjoying myself. I'm stuck in a cabin with a bloody Russian who can't speak a word of English."

"And you're enjoying that!" Hawthorne guffawed. "I hear the Russians bathe once a year whether they need it or not!" They all laughed together.

"And there's the matter of a young Irish lady who I am going to meet at one o'clock."

"Ah, there's method in your madness. You didn't happen to meet this young lady when you booked your ticket did you?" Jones said slyly.

"Maybe and maybe not." Marcus raised his glass. The less they knew the better. "Here's to a pleasant trip."

Jones and Marcus started talking about their days at Oxford. Marcus was relieved that obviously Jones had not heard of his problems. Hawthorne excused himself saying he was going for a walk round the deck. Jones told Marcus he was taking a position in the new office in Chicago and did not know how long he would stay in America. Marcus led him to believe he was going on a sort of working holiday and intended to travel all over the United States.

Jeffrey Walker sipped at his drink, all the time weighing the young man up. Walker was the Director of Hawthorne's firm and the brains behind the operation of the whole empire, which had financial houses in all the capitals of Europe and the Americas. *There was something not quite right about this young man,* he thought. *I think I'll find out more about him.*

"I say, Marcus, pardon me asking, but how did you get in here from second class? I didn't think that was allowed."

Marcus thought fast. The best thing to do was tell the truth. "You're right. When I got to the door to the first class it was locked and by pure luck a sailor opened the door and I just walked through." He smiled broadly. "So maybe I'll not be back up here again!"

"Indeed you will. You come up here anytime you wish." Walker pulled a card from his wallet and wrote something on it then gave it to Marcus.

"Show this to any first class steward and tell them you are my guest and you won't have any trouble again. As a matter of fact, if you want to impress your young lady, I can arrange for you both to come up here for dinner tonight."

Marcus looked at the card. It was embossed with the company logo and Walker's name. He turned it over and looked at the back. It was simply signed Jeffrey Walker.

"That's very kind of you, Mr. Walker. Thank you very much," Marcus said.

"You're welcome. Dinner is at eight tonight. Be here at seven thirty and we'll have a cocktail before going in. Now, aren't you going to invite me to second class? I would like to see the accommodations down there."

Marcus cursed his luck under his breath. *Why did he have to run into Jones.* The last thing he wanted was to become involved with these people. It was a matter of time before they found out he was penniless.

"By all means, anytime you want, Jeffrey." He looked at his watch.

"Oh no, I'm late for my little Irish girl. Sorry, gents, but I have to rush. I'll see you later!" He stood up and gulped down the last of his soda water and hurried out of the lounge.

Walker looked at Jones. "Nice young man that Marcus Browning. Tell me what you know about him."

"Not a lot," Jones replied. "I was at Oxford with him. He was a bit wild and he got the option of leaving or be expelled. He chose to leave. I think it had something to do with a woman."

"Was he any good at his studies?"

"As a matter of fact, he had no trouble getting top grades even though he missed half of the lectures. The word was he has a photographic memory. A shame really, but that's what drink will do."

"So he drinks a lot?" Walker asked.

"Well, he used to drink a lot. I don't know if he still does, I've not seen him in over a year." Jones was wondering why Walker was asking so many questions about Marcus Browning. "May I ask why you're so interested, Jeffrey? You're surely not thinking of taking him on with the firm, are you?"

Walker shrugged his shoulders. "Not yet, Jones, but there's something about that young man I like. I think he could be an asset to someone who knew how to handle him. We're opening the new office in Chicago and I'll be out of New York a lot. I'll need someone to relay information, and maybe Browning might be that man. First though, I'll need to find out why the hell he's traveling second class. There's no way anyone would do that if they could travel first class. There's no comparison!"

"So you think he's lying?"

Walker sipped at his drink. "You said it. Not me."

Typical Walker, never commits himself, but you always know what he means. "Anyway, forget Marcus for the moment. Tell me more about New York." He knew Walker loved talking about America and it was a good way to change the subject.

In the second class reading room Mary Ellen and Mr. Switcher were poring over a large map of the world. Switcher had cut out a piece of paper in the shape and size of Ireland and was moving it around the United States to show Mary Ellen the huge difference in size.

"As you can see my dear, it is as far from New York to Los Angeles as it is to Ireland! That should give you an idea of the size of America."

"It is hard to imagine a country so vast!" Mary Ellen replied. Like a lot of immigrants, all her dreams about America visualized the Statue of Liberty and New York City. She had never given much thought to the rest of it. They sat and talked for a while and she discovered that Mr. Switcher was a retired schoolteacher whose wife had died two years earlier. He was seventy two years old and was returning to America after a three-month tour of Europe.

She felt sorry for him when he told her his only daughter had moved to California and he only saw her and his two grandchildren once a year. He stayed with his ailing sister and a live in housekeeper.

Mary Ellen told him of her ambition to send back to Ireland for her whole family when she became as rich as all the other Americans.

Switcher laughed indulgently. "I don't want you to get the wrong idea, young lady, but everyone is not rich in America. As a matter of fact, there are a lot of poor people and some who can't seem to get ahead no matter how hard they work!"

"You're kidding me." Mary Ellen slapped his arm playfully. "Everyone knows Americans are rich. Look at you, just a teacher and can afford a three-month trip to Europe no less, poor indeed!"

Switcher laughed again. "You don't think I'm rich, do you? I worked all my life and this is the first trip I've had. I admit you can get rich in America, maybe easier than anywhere else, but certainly not as a teacher." He patted her arm. "Don't listen to me Mary Ellen, I'm sure you'll end up a millionaire, and when you do, don't forget to come and see me." He took an envelope out of his pocket and gave it to her. "Here is my home address and telephone number. If you are ever near Detroit, you must promise to come and see me."

Mary Ellen took the envelope and put it in her purse. " Thank you very much, Mr. Switcher. I will certainly look you up if I'm in the Detroit area. And you never know, it may be sooner than you think! Come to think of it, I'll write to you once I get a job and a place of my own."

"That will be wonderful, I'll look forward to hearing from you."

"So this is the gentleman you told me about!" Marcus Browning pulled out a chair and sat down. He held his hand out to Switcher. "Marcus Browning, sir. Mary Ellen told me she was meeting another gentleman, and jealous fool that I am, I just had to meet you."

"Jim Switcher. There's no need to be jealous of me now, young man, but forty years ago, well, that would be a different story."

Mary Ellen smiled at the two of them. "If you don't stop your nonsense, I'll be running away and leaving you."

"No need for that, we won't embarrass you anymore, will we, Marcus?" Switcher said.

"Certainly not," Marcus replied. He looked at the map on the table. "Studying your geography, I see."

"Yes," Mary Ellen replied. "Mr. Switcher was just showing me the size of America. He lives in Detroit." She traced the map with her finger and pointed. "Right here," she said proudly.

Switcher stood up. "Well, time for my stroll round the deck and then my afternoon nap. I'll leave you young people to enjoy yourselves. I'll see you at dinner."

"Not tonight you won't!" Marcus said. "We will be dining in first class tonight!"

Switcher was surprised. "First class! How did you manage that?"

Marcus winked at him. "I have contacts, you know!" Switcher put on his coat and hat.

"There's no need to leave now." Mary Ellen looked disappointed.

"Oh, yes there is! You two have a good time tonight, and let me know all about it tomorrow."

"Oh, all right then, we'll see you later," Mary Ellen replied, and Switcher made his way out to the deck.

"Nice old chap!" Marcus said.

"Yes, he is," Mary Ellen said as she struggled to fold the map.

"Let me help you with that." Marcus took the map and spread it out. "What would you like to do? Do you like playing cards? We could go to the lounge if you like."

"It doesn't matter, let's go somewhere we can just sit and talk."

"That suits me just fine! There's a little bar along the deck we can sit," Marcus said as he finished folding the map. He took her arm and escorted her to the door. "I want to know all about you, Mary Ellen. All about your family and what your plans are for the future."

Mary Ellen looked shyly away and murmured, "Likewise, Marcus."

Marcus smiled inwardly. *She was interested! Well, well!*

"Can I ask you a question?" Mary Ellen asked him.

"Sure, go ahead!" he replied.

"What kind of a name is Marcus?"

"Ah, we may as well get that out of the way right now. My father is a great admirer of the Romans, so in his wisdom, when I came along he named me after a Roman general. My full name is Marcus Vicinius Browning."

"How interesting. Now what's all this about dinner in first class? Nobody gets up there!"

"Well, I suggest you get all dressed up, because we are 'getting up there' as you put it. I met an old school friend, and his boss invited us." He showed Mary Ellen Walker's card.

"Good God! I can't go up there with all the lords and ladies. I'll be like a tramp sitting next to them!"

"No, you won't. You'll be just fine. And, anyway, don't tell me you're just a little bit curious?"

"Well, yes," Mary Ellen said eagerly. "All right I'll go! What time have we to be there?"

Marcus and Mary Ellen had no problem getting up to first class when they showed Walker's card to the first steward they saw. They met Hawthorne, Jones and Walker in the lounge. All of them were very polite to her, but she had a nagging feeling that she was nothing more than a curiosity to them. After they had a drink they left the lounge and went into the first class dining room. Mary Ellen was amazed at the surroundings. She had never seen such luxury, from the linen tablecloths to the sterling silver cutlery. Marcus helped her order from the menu, half of which was in French, and though she felt out of place the whole evening, she was glad to have experienced such opulence, even if it was only for one night. She noticed that Marcus felt completely at home, and joined in the conversation with the three men easily. She did not say much except answer politely when they addressed her, but she knew they had no interest in her, so she kept as quiet as possible.

After dinner, Walker invited them into his stateroom for a nightcap. It was another eye opener for Mary Ellen. The stateroom was more like a luxury hotel suite. The sitting room even had a fireplace and the bedroom was twice the size of Mary Ellen's cabin. Walker's butler brought in fresh coffee and the three of them chatted for a while before Marcus and Mary Ellen said their goodbyes.

When they arrived back in second class, Marcus asked her if she had enjoyed the evening.

"It was an experience I'll never forget! I've never seen such luxury!" she said excitedly.

Marcus laughed. "I'm glad you enjoyed yourself, but I noticed you were very quiet the whole evening."

She took Marcus' arm. "I was too busy looking around. Anyway, I didn't know half of what you men were talking about!"

"Believe me, you didn't miss much! All boring stuff about business,"Marcus replied.

After that night they became inseparable. Every moment they could was spent wandering around the decks arm in arm or sitting in the little bar, which became their favorite place. Marcus even had the steward arrange for them to sit together at mealtimes. It was clear to everyone that here was a young couple in love. Occasionally they would meet Jim Switcher and have a coffee with him and he would listen to all their plans for the future. He started to get to know the both of them quite well.

On the fifth day into the voyage the weather took a turn for the worse. The wind got up to gale force and the great ship was rocking violently, which made a lot of people seasick, including Marcus Browning.

At dinnertime the dining room was almost empty as the storm raged on. Mary Ellen sat alone at her table looking around at the few people who had shown up for dinner.

"Hello, Mary Ellen." She heard a familiar voice.

It was Jim Switcher. "Mind if I join you, there seems to be plenty of room."

"Sit down, I'm glad you came. It's so empty in here tonight."

"Yes, it is. Most people are sick. I guess we're just plain lucky. I don't feel sick at all."

"Neither do I, but I feel sorry for all those people being too sick to eat. If this weather keeps up, they'll have a miserable trip."

The steward came and took their orders. They made some more small talk and then Switcher said, "I can't help but notice that you and Marcus seem to be hitting it off together."

Mary Ellen blushed. "Yes, we are, aren't we?" she replied as the steward served the soup course.

Switcher stirred his soup thoughtfully. "I don't want to pry, Mary Ellen, but I've grown very fond of you these last few days. Promise you won't be offended if I speak my mind." He stopped stirring and looked directly into her eyes.

She looked back at him and said, "Of course I won't be offended, I've grown fond of you too."

"Good. I just hope you're not rushing into anything with Marcus. These shipboard romances are nice at the time, but generally they don't last past the voyage."

Mary Ellen smiled at him and reached over the table to take his hand. "Why, Mr. Switcher, you're worried about me. How nice of you. But don't worry, I've not promised anything to Marcus, although I admit I do like him very much."

In the short time he had known Marcus Browning, Jim Switcher had come to the conclusion that Marcus was hiding something. Switcher prided himself on being able to assess people correctly, and with Marcus he could not shake the feeling that there was something not right about the young man. *Oh, he was very well spoken and good mannered. But underneath the cultured accent and casual elegance, there seemed to be an air of desperation about him. It was his eyes that bothered him most. They were dead eyes. Even when he smiled his eyes never seemed to change. There was ruthlessness there. Maybe even cruelty! Damn it! He can't be that bad!* But deep down he had the feeling he was right. On the other hand, Mary Ellen O'Neill was like an open book. She was the most innocent girl he had ever met in his life, and even if it cost him her friendship, he was determined to warn her. "Well, just be careful. Remember, you hardly know him."

"Mr. Switcher, I'm not a little girl you know. I can look after myself, but if it will keep you happy I will be careful, okay? Now tell me more about yourself."

"Okay. That's all I wanted to hear." *Oh, God! Why do I get the feeling that she's just humoring me?*

They finished their dinner and Switcher entertained her with stories about the places he had been as a young man.

The next morning Marcus woke up feeling a little better. The ship was not rolling nearly as much as the day before. He looked over at Ivan the Russian, who was snoring loudly. He got up and dressed quickly, washed and shaved and went down to the dining room to try and eat some breakfast and to meet Mary Ellen. She told him she had promised her roommate she would accompany her to a ladies card game after breakfast, so that left Marcus with some time on his hands. He decided to go up to first class and pass an hour with Jones and his friends.

He left Mary Ellen after breakfast and made his way up to first class. He showed an officer the card Jeffrey Walker had given him and was shown into the lounge. The three men were sitting at the same table as before.

"Good morning, gentlemen," Marcus said as he pulled another chair over.

"Why, Browning, where have you been hiding?" Walker said.

"I've been waiting to meet your Russian friend. Didn't you bring him along?" Hawthorne asked.

All of them started laughing.

"Not a chance. I snuck out without wakening him. He's probably still snoring away."

Walker smiled over at Marcus. "I thought you were going to show me round second class, Marcus. I've been waiting all week for you."

Marcus had a feeling Walker wouldn't let him off the hook. "Yes, well, better late than never, why don't we go down right now if you want?"

"Why not indeed. Anyone else want to come?" Marcus asked as he stood up.

"No chance!" Jones said. "I've been kind of sick, so I'm just staying around here."

Hawthorne shook his head and waved them away. "I'm not going down there. I'm really not interested in second class," he said disdainfully.

The two men shrugged and left the first class lounge by the staircase door to get down to the second class deck. When they emerged on to the promenade deck the wind had died down and the sun had come out, so it was quite pleasant strolling along the deck.

"Do you want to see my cabin?" Marcus asked.

"I'm not interested in your cabin. I'm interested in you. Is there a place we can talk?"

Marcus, surprised, hesitated and said. "Yes, of course. There's a little café along here." They went into the café and sat at a table for two.

"Do you want anything to drink?" Marcus asked politely. *What the hell does he want with me?* He signaled the steward to come over.

"Coffee, please," Walker replied.

"Make that two," Marcus said. The steward left to get their order. Marcus leaned his elbows on the table and leaned forward. He wasn't going to be intimidated by this man.

"Well, just what do you find so interesting about me?" he asked without smiling.

Walker replied just as seriously, "I don't play games, Browning, and I'm not stupid. Now if you don't want to listen to what I have to say I'll leave right now. On the other hand, tell me the real reason you're down here and maybe, just maybe I can help you."

"What makes you think I need your help?"

Immediately Walker stood up. "Nice meeting you, Browning. Goodbye!" He pushed back his chair.

Marcus instantly regretted opening his big mouth without thinking. He smiled and held his hands up. "Sit down, Walker. Can't you take a joke?"

Walker looked down at him. He put his hands on the table and leaned over Marcus. "When I talk business, I never joke. Now do you want to tell me or not?" Marcus lowered his eyes and gestured to the chair.

"All right, I don't see it can do much harm. You don't even know me anyway."

Walker sat down again and the steward brought their coffees. Marcus told Walker the whole story about being thrown out of the flat and sent on his way with fifty pounds; about making his mind up to go to America on the spur of the moment. "Just one thing, I'd appreciate it if you kept this to yourself. I wouldn't want my father to find out where I am. Now you have it." Marcus finished, and lifted his coffee.

Walker stirred his coffee thoughtfully. "I was right. I knew you were hiding something. To answer your question about why I find you interesting, I pride myself on being able to spot talent. Especially hungry talent, and I believe you are a hungry young man motivated by a desire to show your father that you are as good as him. Am I close?"

"You're dead on. The next time I see my father I want to be able to buy and sell him!" Marcus could not hide the bitterness in his voice.

"Frankly, I don't give a damn what your motivation is. I am looking for a man who will do my bidding without asking any questions. I demand absolute loyalty. Are you interested in a position with Hawthorne Financial Group?"

Marcus could not believe what he was hearing. "Of course I'm interested. What position are you talking about?"

Walker stood up. "Let's go out on deck. First lesson, all walls have ears." He carelessly threw a pound note on the table. They left the café and found a secluded spot on deck. Walker lit a cigarette and turned to Marcus. "Tell me, how badly do you want to become rich?"

"I'm willing to do anything you ask!" Marcus replied.

"Never say anything, Marcus. I might take you at your word." Walker threw his cigarette over the side.

"I meant anything within reason."

"All right, now listen carefully. What I am about to say is between you and me. No one must ever know of this conversation. You can walk away now and forget this ever took place, or you can stay and learn how to become rich. Do you understand!"

Marcus nodded.

Walker stared into his eyes. "What's it to be?"

Marcus had a sinking feeling that if he stayed with this man his life would be changed forever. Yet he knew he could not turn away. Something held him rooted to the spot. He shifted his gaze out to sea. "I'm listening," he said as he looked at the whitecaps rolling all the way to the horizon.

"Good. What I want you to do is become my personal assistant. The company is opening an office in Chicago. I will be traveling back and forth setting the new office up. When I am in Chicago, I will need someone in the New York office to do some work for me that I normally do myself. The pay is fifty dollars a week. After three months, if you are working out okay, I will double your salary. I will place you in a position in the company that will be your cover. The position requires the utmost secrecy. Your real job will be to relay messages and instructions to enable us both to get very rich. Some people might call it illegal, but I call it creative. It is as simple as that. You must do exactly as I say. Do not attempt to think for yourself. And this above all! Never question anything I tell you to do! Are you still interested?"

"Yes, I'm interested."

"What do you know about the stock market?" Walker asked.

"To tell you the truth I don't understand how it works."

"All the better. Now, if I told you I'm about to make ten-thousand pounds today in the New York Stock exchange, what would you say?"

"I'd ask how the hell is that possible when you're out here on the ocean?"

Walker laughed and patted Marcus on the back "Wireless my boy, wireless! The best thing since sliced bread. It enables us to conduct business no matter where we are."

"But how can you know if the stocks you buy will go up and not down?" Marcus was puzzled.

"Let's just say a little bird told me what and when to buy and sell." It started to dawn on Marcus, if you knew such information you could make a fortune in no time. He said as much to Walker.

"Yes, you can make a fortune, but there's one small catch."

"What's that?" Marcus asked.

"A stake, my boy, you need a stake to start with! And from where I'm standing, I don't see yours."

He was right, at fifty dollars a week it would take him forever to get a stake. The bastard thought he was going to use me! But he needed a job anyway. "Look, Walker. If you want me to work for you, I'm your man. I don't want to know the details of your business. I will follow your instructions to the letter and tell no one. In a nutshell, I just want to get rich! But I have one question. I can see how you are rich and getting richer, but you said both of us. Now if I don't have a stake, as you put it, I'm not going to get rich, now am I?"

"No, but if you work out all right, in time I could possibly help to get you started. Let's say, if after three months I'm happy with your performance, we have a review of your position with Hawthorne?"

At that moment Marcus knew he would not last three months. "I don't have much choice, do I?" Marcus replied cynically, knowing Walker was promising nothing.

"I knew you'd understand! We have an agreement." Walker shook his hand. "You have my card. The address in New York is on it. Show it to immigration and tell them you have a job. Be there at nine o'clock Monday morning. Goodbye, Browning." He turned to leave.

"Just a moment, Jeffrey. As you know, I'm a bit strapped for cash. You couldn't give me an advance, could you?"

Walker stopped long enough to sneer. "Do I look like I'm in the Salvation Army or something? And from now on you will address me as Mr. Walker. Is that clear?" He continued on his way without waiting for an answer.

Marcus turned back to staring out to sea. *Walker was right, you had to have a stake to get started.* He grinned to himself. *You shouldn't have done that, Walker. You don't know whom you're dealing with. I'll get my stake soon enough and if it's the last thing I do I'll leave you without the flesh on your bones!* He looked at his watch and went off to find Mary Ellen. He was going to tell her about his new job, but decided against it just to be cautious. He was looking forward to spending the rest of the day with her, as this was their last day on board.

The next morning the decks were crowded with excited passengers waiting to see their first sight of America. Mary Ellen and Marcus leaned over the rail, straining to see through the morning mist. Suddenly a murmur started from the front of the great liner, and as she slowly turned the mist cleared and there it was. The Statue of Liberty with the skyline of New York City in the background. Mary Ellen could not stand still with excitement.

"Isn't it amazing?" she cried. "Just like I've always imagined. And here I am at last."

"Yes, quite the sight," Marcus murmured, unimpressed. *He was racking his brains trying to figure out a way to get some fast money. The faster he got some money, the faster he could put his plan into operation. He had thought of nothing else since his conversation with Walker. If he could get the sort of information Walker was getting, he knew he could not fail, because he felt in his bones he was born for just such an opportunity. The only thing that could stop him was the lack of funds to get started.*

"Look, I've got something for you!" Mary Ellen fumbled in her bag and pulled out a small key ring with "Mauretania" engraved on it. Just a little souvenir of the voyage."

Marcus, surprised, said, "Well, thank you very much, but now I feel bad because I've nothing for you."

Mary Ellen laughed. "It's nothing really, don't be silly."

Marcus put the key ring in his pocket. "Still, it's very kind of you, thanks again." He kissed her on the cheek.

"Marcus, I've got to go to the purser to get something and I don't want to leave it too late. Do you want to come with me?" Mary Ellen took his arm.

"Of course I'll come," Marcus said, glad to have something to occupy him. He couldn't wait to get off the ship. They went into the inner passage and joined the line up for the purser.

"Now what have you got that's so valuable the purser's got to look after it?" He leaned over and whispered. "You've not stolen the crown jewels, now have you?"

"Remember I told you about us having to sell half the land that belonged to my Uncle John? Well, I'm picking up his money for the land. He'll be waiting for it when we meet him today."

"I wonder what he'll say when he sees me?"

"Oh don't worry, he'll be glad I've had company on the ship."

"Oh well, it was the right thing to do. I mean, leaving the money with the purser," he said as they waited in line.

"Yes, I'll be glad to get rid of it. It's always a worry having someone else's money to look after. Ah, here we are." She gave the purser her chit. The purser retrieved her package and she signed a receipt. "Thank you very much, sir," she said

"Aren't you going to change any sterling?" the purser asked. "It's more convenient here than trying to find a bank in New York on a Saturday."

"What a good idea!" Mary Ellen put the package at the bottom of her bag. She pulled her purse from her bag and took out eleven pounds, all that she had. She gave them to the purser and he counted it.

"That will get you forty four dollars, young lady." He took the American currency from a drawer and counted it in front of her."

She thanked the purser and put the money in her purse. She turned to Marcus. "Aren't you going to exchange yours, Marcus? It is convenient!"

Marcus thought fast. He didn't want Mary Ellen to see he only had about twelve pounds. He smiled brightly and said, "Exchange my fortune here? I don't think there's enough money on this ship to cover it! What do you think, my man?" He winked at the purser.

"Quite right, sir. I doubt if we've enough to cover that amount!" The purser had seen everything in his thirty years at sea. *A pound to a penny this one's broke.* He turned to the next in line.

Chapter 4

The Mauretania dropped anchor in the Narrows where the Hudson meets the Atlantic. The third class passengers were transferred to the ferries, which took them to Ellis Island for processing. The first and second class passengers were processed by American Immigration officials on board.

After the processing was finished, the liner lifted anchor and made her way with the assistance of tugs to the pier where the passengers would disembark. The luggage was unloaded and stored in a huge shed with the same alphabetical system as in England. Mary Ellen and Marcus stood waiting impatiently for Mary Ellen's trunk under the O for O'Neill. Jim Switcher came over to say goodbye and wish them all the best in their new country.

When Mary Ellen's trunk arrived they made their way out of the shed and walked to the gates of the pier where a big crowd of friends and relations were waiting. When they got to where the crowds were mingling with the new arrivals, Mary Ellen looked anxiously around for her uncle. A cold rain was falling steadily.

"Marcus, I don't see my Uncle John. He promised he would meet me."

"Don't worry, he'll be here," Marcus replied. "Look at the crowds, give it a little time."

They waited a while longer, then Mary Ellen said, "Look, Marcus, you wait here and watch the luggage and I'll go and find him. I'm too excited to wait another minute!"

Marcus laughed at her impatience. "All right, on you go then, if it will calm you down."

Mary Ellen put her handbag on top of the trunk and disappeared into the crowd.

Marcus watched her go and hesitated for a few seconds before opening the handbag and reaching for the envelope he knew was at the bottom. He had told her to put it at the bottom for safety when she got it from the purser earlier. He pulled the thick envelope out and shoved it quickly into his coat pocket. Without a backwards glance, he lifted his suitcase and quickly walked through the crowd and made his way to the line of waiting cabs.

"Uncle John! Uncle John!" Mary Ellen shouted over the heads of the crowd.

John O'Neill heard her voice and called back, "I'm coming through," and bulled his way through the crowd, which parted easily before his huge frame. John O' Neill was six feet three and built to match. He lifted Mary Ellen off her feet and whirled her around.

"Oh, but you are a bonnie colleen right enough, Mary Ellen. And the image of your mother too! Here's me wife, your Aunt Bridget."

"How are you?" Mary Ellen cried as they hugged each other, "I've got someone for you to meet too, come on, this way."

"A young man, maybe?" they both said at the same time.

"You'll see in a minute." Mary Ellen took John's hand and pulled him along with her.

They made their way to where she had left Marcus with the luggage and saw that he was not there.

"Here's my luggage, but Marcus isn't here!" She looked around for him. "He's probably hiding for a lark," she said, and looked around the rapidly thinning crowd.

"Maybe he's away to the toilet," John said.

"Yes, I suppose that's it," Mary Ellen said.

"Anyway, first things first. I want to give you your money right away. I have it here in my bag." She lifted the bag and started to search through it.

"Your friend wouldn't leave the money unattended, would he?" John asked anxiously.

Mary Ellen, in a panic, emptied the contents of the bag on the ground. "The envelope isn't here! Where can Marcus be?" She looked around for Marcus' suitcase. "His suitcase is gone!" The realization swept over her that both Marcus and the money were missing. She was afraid to think what was beginning to look like the unthinkable. *Had Marcus taken the money?* By this time there were only a few people remaining and still no sign of Marcus.

John O'Neill's face darkened. He grabbed her arm roughly. "How long have you known this man?"

"I just met him on the ship coming over," Mary Ellen stammered. "Uncle John, you're hurting my arm," she cried.

John O'Neill started to shout. "You left my money with a man you've only known for a week. Tell me the truth! How did he know where the money was?" He grabbed her shoulders and shook her like a rag doll.

"He was with me when I picked it up from the purser. He told me to put it at the bottom of my bag to keep it safe." She started to cry. She had never been hit in her life and she was frightened by the violent way he was shaking her.

"He told you to put it at the bottom!" O'Neill laughed hysterically. "My whole inheritance gone! You stupid, stupid girl!"

"I'm sorry. Maybe we can tell the police." She was sobbing uncontrollably.

"Tell the police! They've as much chance as we have of catching him!" He completely lost his temper. He drew back his arm and hit the side of her face with the back of his hand with such force that her feet were lifted clear off the ground. She fell backwards over the luggage and lay sprawled on the ground in front of them.

"Lie there and rot, you stupid bitch!" John O'Neill said bitterly. He grabbed his wife and hurried off, leaving Mary Ellen lying sobbing on the wet cobblestones.

Mary Ellen dragged herself upright. Her face felt like it had been kicked by a horse and her right eye was closing rapidly. She balanced her bag on the trunk and staggered toward the gates. The rain was turning to sleet and darkness was falling. She felt sick and unable to think clearly. Vaguely she noticed people staring at her as she shuffled along the pavement. She turned a corner and looked up a wide street that stretched as far as she could see. The tall buildings on either side seemed to touch the black sky. She walked for what felt like hours, and still there was no end to the street. She noticed at an intersection that the street she was on was called Broadway.

Once she stopped to look in a shop window and what she saw was the right side of her face swollen to twice its normal size. Her right eye was shut and quickly turning black. She shuddered at the sight and kept walking slowly along the endless pavement. She reached a point on the road where it divided into two different streets with a small area in front with a few park benches scattered around. They were all empty as the sleet and rain were lashing the city unmercifully. Wearily she dragged her trunk over and sat on one of the benches.

What has happened to me? What will I do? Where will I go? Oh God help me, I don't know where to turn. She held her head in her hands and wept bitter tears. *Was it only last week she had boarded the ship with all her dreams of America?* After a while she stopped weeping and took her purse out of her bag. She had forty dollars which she had received in exchange for her ten pounds. She put the money back in her purse and stood up to gather her things.

The few passers by glanced at her curiously as they hurried on their way. She decided to take the right-hand fork in the road and look for a hotel. As she started walking, she noticed a policeman coming toward her.

"Officer, please help me!" she called out. "I'm looking for a hotel."

The policeman shined his flashlight on her face. "Good God, girl. What happened to you?" *He was Irish, thank God.*

"I fell and bashed my face, I've just arrived today, and I need to get a bed for the night. I'm exhausted. Is there a hotel or something nearby?"

The policeman looked at her doubtfully. "So you fell, did you? It must have been one hell of a fall. Your face is in a terrible mess. I think it's a doctor you need."

"No, no. I just need a bath and a good sleep. Is there anywhere around here?"

"All the hotels are uptown. You'll have to get a cab. Have you got enough money? By the way, was there no one there to meet you? Have you no relatives here?" *Fall my arse! Someone belted you good.*

"Yes I have money, and no, I have no relations in America."

"I'll tell you what, lass. I know just the place for you. Come on, it's only ten minutes walk." He took the handle of the trunk and turned around. "Follow me. Now I'm taking it you're a Catholic?"

Mary Ellen, relieved, said, "Yes, from County Donegal."

"I'm from Galway, just down the road. What's your name, then?"

"Mary Ellen O'Neill."

"I'm Officer Sean O'Brien."

They turned into a side street and she saw the spires of a church looming out of the darkness.

"Well, here we are, Mary Ellen O'Neill!" He opened an iron gate and went up a short path to knock on the door of the manse. The door opened and a heavyset middle aged woman looked at him with hostility written all over her face.

"You again! What have ye got this time?" with a brogue you could cut with a knife.

Mary Ellen started to wonder if everyone in New York was Irish.

The policeman brushed past her. "Where is he?" he demanded.

The woman looked at Mary Ellen with disgust. "In the lounge." She pushed past Mary Ellen and slammed the door shut, and without a word walked into the kitchen at the end of the hall.

"Wait here a minute, lass." O'Brien opened a door on the left and went into the lounge. Mary Ellen looked hopefully around her as she waited. *I'll be all right now*. Being raised in Ireland where the parish priest was regarded as a direct link to God she was confident everything would be all right. The priest would tell her what to do.

Monsignor James Mooney was sitting on a leather armchair reading a newspaper while sipping a glass of the best Irish Whisky when O'Brien entered the lounge.

"Good evening to you, Father," he said as he lifted the half empty bottle and looked at the label. "Ah, I see prohibition hasn't affected your choice, this is good stuff." He went to the sideboard and lifted a glass. "Do you mind if I have a wee one, it's a lousy night out there."

"Not at all, Sean, help yourself. Now what brings you here at this time of night?"

"I've got a little package that needs looking after for a night. Just off the boat today and already in trouble by the looks of her."

The Monsignor put his glass down and looked up at O'Brien. "What do you mean, by the looks of her?"

"It looks to me that someone belted her one. She's a fine-looking girl except for the black eye she's got."

"And just off the boat? What age is she?" Mooney reached for his dog collar.

"She's about twenty-one I'd say, and she says she has no relations this side of the pond."

Mooney put his cassock on and started buttoning it up. He looked closely at O'Brien. "Are you sure?"

O'Brien returned his look and said quietly. "Yes, she's too scared to lie. After all, I found her wandering the streets, and like I said, someone's belted her one, although she says she fell."

The Monsignor hung a large gold crucifix round his neck and said, "Well, let's have a look at the little lady." He moved toward the door.

O'Brien finished the whisky in one gulp. "Excuse me, Father, but aren't you forgetting something?" He looked at Mooney expectantly.

Mooney laughed. He pulled a wad of bills from his pocket. "Sean, me boy, it's usually the flock that gives the cash in, not take it out!" He peeled a twenty off the wad and held it out.

"Sure enough, Father, sure enough." O'Brien pocketed the twenty as they left the room and went into the hall.

Monsignor James Mooney was six feet three with black hair, which was always combed perfectly. He was the youngest son of a family of eight. Ever since he was a child his mother was determined that he was to enter the priesthood. He was to be her gift to the church. He had never really questioned the fact that he was to be a priest, a lot of Irish families had at least one son in the priesthood. As he grew into a young man and attended the seminary he knew that celibacy would be impossible. He even went to confession and told the priest that he was attracted to women and did not think the priesthood was for him. He was told that prayers would overcome his desires, and after all, he would break his mother's heart if he gave up. So he had entered the priesthood against his better judgement, but he had ultimately bowed to the wishes of his parents who were convinced he was going to be the next Pope.

He didn't regret his decision, because when he was transferred to New York, it was the perfect excuse to get away from his overbearing parents. He knew they would never have let him leave Ireland otherwise. He could have been a film actor if he had wanted to with his dark hair and good looks. When it came to confession time there always seemed to be more women at Monsignor Mooney's box than the curate's on the other side of the church. He was highly thought of in the Diocese because since he had come to Saint Joseph's, attendance had just about doubled and so had the collections. His sermons and his charisma were famous throughout the Lower East Side, even though it was a largely Jewish neighborhood. Insiders in the Church tipped him for Bishop in the near future, even though he was only thirty years old, the youngest Monsignor ever in the Archdiocese of New York. He had a liking for the bottle, but not enough to affect his job as a priest. His main weakness was women.

Deep down he knew he should never have become a priest, but he had learned to justify his sins by believing that he was doing more good for the people than harming himself. He found that being a priest was the ideal job for meeting and seducing vulnerable and gullible women of all ages. Once a week he went to a far off parish and confessed his sins. In his warped perception of his religion, that act of contrition cleansed his soul, even though he knew he would do the same thing the first chance he got.

He came into the hall with O'Brien and said with a kindly smile to Mary Ellen. "Well, young lady, O'Brien here tells me you've nowhere to go? I'm Monsignor Mooney and this is the church of Saint Joseph."

O'Brien lowered his head and squeezed past them. "I'll be on my way now, Father. Goodbye, lass," he said as he closed the door behind him before either of them could reply.

"I didn't have time to thank him for bringing me here," Mary Ellen said in surprise. "Sorry, Father, I'm Mary Ellen O'Neill, and as you can see I fell and bashed my face. I'd be grateful if you could help me get a place to sleep tonight. This is my first night in New York and I'm a bit lost."

Monsignor Mooney looked at her face. *O'Brien was right, this one is a beauty! Even with the black eye you could see it.* "Don't worry, my child, you can sleep here tonight. Now, you must be starving, wandering the streets on a night like this. I'll get Bridie to heat some soup for you and show you to your room. Now, I have to leave you, it's prayer time for me."

"Thank you, Father. I am exhausted and hungry, I don't know if I could have walked another yard!"

Mooney smiled at her. "Bridie, come here!" he shouted. Mary Ellen noticed that it was a totally different tone of voice, no kindness in it. This was the voice of a man who was accustomed to being obeyed.

The heavyset woman came waddling hurriedly back into the hall. Her head was lowered in deference to the priest. Bridget O'Connell had been brought up like all poor Irish Catholics. They had it hammered into them since birth that the priest was the closest they could get to God himself. The parish priests in the countryside had absolute authority over their flock. Nobody questioned the word of a priest. That would be like asking questions of God almighty! Anyone with the temerity to question some of the actions of these men, some of which had no resemblance to the teachings of Jesus, were simply told that these were mysteries that God would answer in his own good time, and through his beloved Holy Father in Rome. Anyone who persevered was told to go to confession and confess their heresy. The alternative was to burn in Hell for all eternity. Bridget was not one to question the authority of one of God's representatives.

"Yes, Father?" she asked quietly.

"Show this young lady to the guest room and run a bath for her. While she is bathing, heat up some soup. The poor girl has had a terrible time today, and this her first day in New York." He turned to Mary Ellen. "Bridie here will look after you. Won't you, Bridie!" He looked at the woman severely.

"Yes, Father," the woman said meekly. She sounded totally defeated. She lifted Mary Ellen's trunk and suitcase effortlessly and nodded to Mary Ellen. "This way, miss," the woman whispered, and led the way upstairs. The priest went back into the lounge, closing the door behind him.

Mary Ellen looked around as she unpacked her case. The room was spotless, with snow white sheets folded neatly on the bed. Bridie had shown her where the bathroom was and started running the bath.

"While you're bathing, I'll light a fire for you to heat your room. When you've finished, come downstairs and your soup will be ready. You'll find some cream and powder for your face in the bathroom cabinet. Is there anything else you would like?" There was something in her voice Mary Ellen could not fully understand. It sounded full of resignation, yet with what seemed like a bitter tone to it. She decided just to go along and not ask any questions.

"Nothing at all, thank you so much for your kindness." The woman turned on her savagely with her eyes flashing malevolently. "Don't thank me. I'm just doing what I'm told. You'll be thanking Father Mooney yourself soon enough. I'll knock when the water's ready." She was almost snarling with contempt.

Mary Ellen, shocked at her attitude, decided not to say another word. She went back into the room to unpack.

After a few minutes the woman knocked and told her the bath was ready. She went into the bathroom and lay luxuriantly in the hot water. She thought about the events of the day and tried to come to grips with what had happened. She could not understand why Marcus would steal the money knowing that it was not hers in the first place. *How could anyone do such a thing?* She remembered some of the warnings her parents had tried to give her with no success. *Are there more people in the world like Marcus?* She wondered long and hard at her situation and started to weep, holding her swollen face in her hands. Suddenly she shivered and noticed the water was turning cold. Hurriedly she got out of the bath and dried herself vigorously with the towel. She got dressed and looked at her face in the mirror.

She recoiled in horror. Her eye was completely closed and one side of her face was almost black. She opened the cabinet and took the cream and powder and applied them to her face. She knew they wouldn't do any good, but it did cover some of the blackness. She took the time to clean the bathtub and tidy up before she went back to the room.

There was a small fire going in the hearth and some coal in a bucket lying next to it. She rubbed her hands together and waited till she felt warm enough to go downstairs. She thought for a minute she would rather stay in the room, but her empty stomach told her otherwise.

Mary Ellen went downstairs to the kitchen and found the woman standing at the stove stirring a pot of soup. She gestured to a chair at a small table. Mary Ellen sat down. Without a word the woman poured a large bowl of soup and put it down in front of Mary Ellen. She went over to a large breadbox and took a half loaf from it.

"There's more in the pot if you want it. Put the light out when you're finished." She turned and left the room.

Mary Ellen tore a small piece of bread from the loaf and dipped it in the soup. The soup was delicious. It tasted nearly the same as the soup she was used to having in Ireland. *I'd better not think of Ireland or I'll start crying again.* She ate three bowls of soup and finished the bread before she felt full. She felt a lot better, but suddenly a great weariness overcame her. Tiredly she got to her feet, struggling to keep her eyes open. She washed the soup bowl and put the light out before going slowly upstairs to her room.

Mary Ellen had just enough energy to get ready for bed and put the light out. She lay in bed watching the room brighten occasionally from the lights of passing cars. Although she was exhausted, she took a long time to fall asleep, with the pain in her jaw and thinking of the terrible things that had happened to her. Eventually she dozed off and fell into a deep sleep.

Mary Ellen woke with a start. *There was someone in the room!* She sat bolt upright

"Who's there?" she asked fearfully. Suddenly a car passed the window and she saw it was Monsignor Mooney.

"Quiet down, girl!" he said hoarsely as he swayed toward the bed. She smelled the whisky from his breath.

"What are you doing here, Father? What do you want?" She held the cover tightly up to her neck.

The priest sat down heavily on the bed and leaned over her. He looked enormous in the glow from the embers in the fireplace. Terrified, Mary Ellen threw the covers off and tried to get out of the bed. He grabbed her arm and twisted her onto her back.

"Time to pay up, girl. You get nothing for nothing in America." His voice was slurred with the drink.

Mary Ellen tried to scream and hit him with her free hand, but it had no effect. Roughly he let her arm go and clamped his hand over her mouth as he tore at her nightdress with the other hand. Mary Ellen grabbed his wrist with both hands and sank her teeth into his hand.

"You bitch!" he yelped in pain. He freed his bleeding hand from her teeth and fastened it round her throat and started to squeeze it tightly.

"I'll teach you to bite me, you little whore!" he said as he increased the pressure on her neck.

Again Mary Ellen tried to scream but all that came out was a choking sound. Desperately she pushed against his chest with both hands, but slowly she felt the strength leaving her as she gasped for breath and then everything went black.

Mary Ellen awoke to the sound of a choir singing a hymn. *Am I dead?* She opened her eyes as the events of the night started to come back to her. She forced herself to move and sit at the edge of the bed. She looked at the bloodstained sheets and felt the pain in her throat. She dragged herself upright and realized she wasn't dead after all. The sound was coming from the adjoining church. She slowly made her way to the bathroom and started to run a bath. She leaned against the washbasin and looked in the mirror. Her face was still swollen and her eye was tightly closed. Her throat was bruised all around her neck and there were marks all over her arms where the priest had grabbed her.

The realization came over her that she had been raped. *Raped by a priest no less! A priest, whom she had been taught from childhood was the repository of trust and kindness, had violated her at the time she was at her most vulnerable.* Slowly she went back to the room and got her clothes together. She went back to the bathroom and lowered herself painfully into the hot water. She took a long time to wash herself and she wept with shame and humiliation as she recalled the ordeal of the night before. She swore to herself he wasn't going to get away with this. When she was dressed and packed she made her way downstairs dragging the trunk with her. The woman was waiting for her in the hall.

"Yes, sneak out, you slut," she shouted. "And don't ever come back here, you bloody whore!"

Mary Ellen was astounded. "I was raped last night!" She could hardly talk because her throat hurt so much. "The priest raped me, and I'm the one who's going to the police!"

The woman rounded on her. "Raped, was it? You come here batting your eyes at the good man trying your best to put temptation in his way. He's kind enough to take you in and this is how you repay him? You're not the first one who's tried this. He's got a hard enough time keeping the married ones away without the likes of you coming here and throwing yourself at him!"

"Get out of my way!" Mary Ellen moved toward the door.

The woman opened the door and shouted in Mary Ellen's face as she left, "Go to the police, you whore. Do you think you're the first one that bastard O'Brien brought here? He knows how to pick them all right. Who do you think they'll believe, a fine man like Monsignor Mooney, or you, that looks

like something out of the trash. Now get on with ye, and don't come back."
She slammed the door violently behind her.

As Mary Ellen left the house, she heard the church choir start another
hymn. The sleet of the night before was reduced to a cold drizzle. She slowly
walked along the street, dragging her trunk after her. It was early Sunday
morning and the streets were deserted. *What if that horrible woman was
right? What if the police didn't believe her?* She turned the corner and walked
along deep in thought. It all started to become clear to her. *The woman was
right, nobody would believe a man in that position was capable of such a
thing. The policeman must go and get girls for the priest. They're in it
together, that's why he left in such a hurry last night.* The reality was, she was
on her own, with nobody to help her.

Eventually she looked around her to get her bearings. She saw that she was
close to the Hudson river and could see the Statue of Liberty in the distance.
She kept walking till she reached the river's edge and looked at the statue.
Was it just yesterday when she first saw it? It seemed like a lifetime ago since
she had gazed in hope and anticipation at the symbol of freedom in America.
She looked down at the black swirling water of the Hudson. She stared at the
currents flowing back and forth for a long time. After a while she started to
feel faint, staring at the water as if hypnotized. Her mind was racing in all
directions. In the last twenty-four hours she had been robbed, raped, betrayed
and assaulted.

Nothing in her life had prepared her for such things. All her dreams of
America had turned into a nightmare overnight. The river seemed to be rising
toward her, and she felt herself swaying forward inexorably. She let go of the
trunk handle and shuffled along the edge of the sea wall.

"Are you all right?"

Mary Ellen felt a hand on her arm. Confused and disoriented, she turned
to see a dark-complexioned man with a long black beard and a small round
cap on the top of his head.

"Let me sit down for a minute." Her voice was a low rasping sound. The
strange man guided her to a nearby park bench. He looked at her swollen face
and turned to call out to someone.

"Rachel! Come here! This girl is ill."

Dully, Mary Ellen heard the man talking in a foreign language. A middle-
aged woman came rushing over and sat beside her. In a heavy accent she
asked Mary Ellen what had happened to her. Mary Ellen tried to talk, but all
she could do was sob uncontrollably.

The woman turned to her husband. "Benjamin, this poor girl has been battered. Look at her face and throat. We have to get her to a doctor right away!"

"Where are we going to get a doctor? We don't even know her! Ask her where she lives and maybe we can take her home."

The woman put her arm round Mary Ellen and asked her where she lived. Mary Ellen stopped sobbing and in a whisper told the woman she had just arrived and had nowhere to live. If they could help her get a boarding house she would be all right.

The woman turned to her husband. "Get her trunk and suitcase. We can't leave her here. We'll take her home to dry out and see if we can help her."

The man lifted the case and grabbed the trunk. "Good idea, I thought she was going to fall into the river."

The woman helped Mary Ellen to her feet. "Jump in more likely, the poor girl. Let's walk over to the road and see if we can get a taxi. This girl's too weak to walk much farther."

The woman took Mary Ellen's arm and they made their way to the roadway and looked for a taxi. Because it was Sunday morning they had to wait for a while. Eventually a taxi came along and they all gratefully got in out of the rain. The man told the taxi driver the address and they were driven to a rundown tenement somewhere in the Lower East Side of Manhattan. The area was populated mainly by Eastern European Jews who had fled to America in order to escape the pogroms in Russia and Poland.

Benjamin and Rachel Swersky were two of these refugees who had come from Poland in 1912. They worked in the garment district, often taking work home with them in order to pay the rent for the dilapidated flat they rented on the third floor. They had two sons, one had just passed through law school and the other was at college, so they needed every penny to pay the bills. The tenement they lived in was typical of the Lower East Side. The building was on Broome Street just south of Delancey. It was in a six- story building with the entrance in the middle. The central staircase led to flats that were laid out like railroad cars. There were three flats on each floor. Inside the flats a narrow hallway went from front to back with three rooms on one side. One of the rooms faced the front of the building, and it was the only one with a window. There was one toilet on each floor, which served three families.

They helped Mary Ellen up the stairs and Rachel lit the gas fire. She put a kettle of water on the stove to heat and then turned to help Mary Ellen. "Now let's get you out of these wet clothes, you must be freezing." She took Mary Ellen's coat and hung it on a hook on the back of the door.

The three of them sat round a small table and waited for the kettle to boil. Mary Ellen looked around the room. There was a gas fireplace and stove against one wall, a window that overlooked the street at the front of the building, a small sofa, the table with four chairs and a treadle sewing machine in the corner. There were bundles of books piled haphazardly on a ramshackle bookshelf.

"I'm Rachel Swersky and this is my husband Benjamin. Now you say you have just arrived in America? For God's sake, girl, what happened to you? You're in a terrible state, were you attacked?"

Mary Ellen covered her face with her hands. "It's worse than being attacked. I wish I'd never came to this cursed place, I've not been here a day and look at me." She stopped herself from starting to weep again and said, "A thousand thanks for helping me at the river. I was starting to feel weak and dizzy—I might have fallen in if you hadn't come over."

Rachel said, "Just a minute, there's the kettle boiling. I'll get some tea and you can tell us all about it." She busied herself making the tea and put a small plate of bread slices on the table. "Here you are. Now tell us all about it and we'll see if we can help you. Won't we, Benjamin?"

Benjamin muttered something under his breath and nodded his head. Rachel patted Mary Ellen's hand.

"All right, I'll tell you what happened, but you probably won't believe me. I can hardly believe it myself!" Starting from when she met Marcus Browning on the ship, she started to recount everything that had happened to her up till they saw her at the river.

At about the same time, resplendent in his vestments, Monsignor James Mooney was giving his weekly sermon to a packed Saint Josephs. His bandaged hand was hidden under the lace cuffs of his white smock. This week's sermon was about the three virtues of Faith Hope and Charity.

"Yes!" he thundered in conclusion. "Yes, you can have Faith! Yes, you can have Hope! But the greatest of all is Charity! For without Charity we are as cymbals of clanging brass!" He turned away from the congregation basking in their approval to the strains of the choir singing "Faith of Our Fathers."

When Mary Ellen finished telling the Swerskys her story, Rachel said immediately that she must go to the police no matter what the housekeeper had said.

"You can't let him get away with it, think of the next girl they get!"

Benjamin held up his hand. Speaking slowly and deliberately he advised against going to the police. In his thick accent he tried to explain. "If you go to the police to complain about this priest, first it's your word against his. Who will they believe? Second, and this is the main problem. Most of the police force in New York City are Irish Catholics. They will stick together to protect one of their own. Third," he paused for a moment and took Mary Ellen's hand, "if you go there to complain, they could arrest you for lying about the policeman, and God knows what they might do to you. Regarding the man who stole the money, well, he could be just about anywhere by now."

"Benjamin, what are you talking about? This is not Poland! This is America. They don't just arrest you for nothing! I say she goes to the police!"

Mary Ellen listened to the two of them arguing about what to do, then she made up her mind. She signaled to them she wanted to say something and they reluctantly quieted down. "I agree with Benjamin. I would have no chance of convincing anyone that this man raped me. I hope someone catches them, but it won't be me. I've no proof I was even in the house last night! You're right about Marcus, he could be anywhere!"

"When you look at it that way, I suppose you're right," Rachel said. "But it makes me so angry that they get away with such things."

Benjamin sighed. "Not so much different from Poland after all! So, what are you going to do?" he asked Mary Ellen.

"The first thing I have to do is get somewhere to stay. I need time to let my face heal up. I've got about forty dollars. What will that get me? Do you know a place I could go?"

"We'll find a place for you tomorrow. Today you stay here with us. We have to go to work at twelve o'clock, it's ten thirty now, so we have a little time."

Surprised, Mary Ellen said, "You work on a Sunday?" She had never heard of such a thing.

"Of course. We work six days out of seven, twelve noon to midnight and sometimes more. We don't work on the Sabbath," Rachel replied.

"But this is the Sabbath!" Mary Ellen replied. "It is Sunday, isn't it?"

Benjamin and Rachel looked at each other and both of them started laughing.

Mary Ellen's face reddened. "Well, what's so funny?" she asked.

They stopped laughing and Rachel said, "Don't tell me you can't see we are Jewish?"

Mary Ellen had never seen a Jew before. All she knew about Jews came from reading the Bible. She looked at them and said in surprise, "What am I supposed to see? The only thing I see different is your little cap, Benjamin. Is that what you mean?"

Both of them started roaring with laughter again.

Benjamin paused for breath and panted, "You're serious, aren't you? You don't know what a Jew is, do you?"

"Only what I read in the Bible. Jesus was a Jew, wasn't he? I never met a Jew before, so how am I supposed to know you are Jewish. You don't look much different to me!"

They looked at her and Benjamin said seriously, "You know, Mary Ellen, that is the nicest thing anyone has said to us for a long time!"

Impatiently, Mary Ellen replied, "Really! I'm sure I don't know what you are talking about. It would be nice if you let me in on the joke!"

They sat silently for a moment and Benjamin sighed. "Sadly, my dear, it's anything but funny." He went on to tell her how the Jews had been persecuted all over the world for hundreds of years and how in Poland they were hunted down and killed during the pogroms. Even here in America they stayed in their own neighborhoods in fear of attacks by gangs in other parts of the city.

"We usually stay around this area," he said. "Sometimes people have been attacked uptown. We look different, you see. So we get noticed and some of these idiots call us names or worse."

Mary Ellen was unimpressed. "Well, that sounds the same as what happened to the Irish Catholics. We've been persecuted for hundreds of years by the English. At one time they even banned people from wearing green, and our religion had to be practiced in secret under pain of death. And I read that even here in New York they used to have signs saying no Irish need apply!"

"Not anymore, they don't. The city hall is run by the Irish!"

Rachel interrupted. "Let's not argue about who was persecuted the most! What Benjamin means is it's harder for us to blend in because we had to learn the language, and we do look different from the Americans." They went on to tell her how they had fled Poland and struggled to make ends meet, working seventy hours a week in the sweat shops of the garment district. They told her how they had lost their daughter to influenza. One of their sons was a lawyer and the other one was at college. Now they were just about ready for Benjamin to start his own tailor's shop. Occasionally they rented out the back room to save money faster. In a few more months they would have enough money.

Mary Ellen listened in horror to their story. "And I thought everyone here was rich! You must regret leaving Poland to come here and work so hard for so long!"

Benjamin and Rachel both started to talk at once, then Benjamin signaled Rachel to go ahead. "You tell her. You're the one who took English classes."

Rachel clasped her hands together and talked passionately about leaving Poland. "Regret leaving! It was the best thing we ever did in our lives. Yes, we work hard. But we can see how we can have our own business, then our own house uptown. In Poland there was no future, only fear and uncertainty. In America anything is possible with hard work. So, for all its faults, and there are many, it is the best place on earth for working people. It doesn't matter where you come from. Anything is possible here. You must have heard about people who came here with nothing and ended up millionaires. Look at Carnegie, he became the richest man in the world. Where did he come from? He came here from Scotland with nothing! The whole point is that the children will be better off. Here they can get a good education, even though it's expensive. In the old country they could never have become doctors or lawyers, or even teachers." She paused for breath.

"Yes, I suppose you're right," Mary Ellen said morosely. "But I'm afraid at the moment I can't see any future here for me, and I looked forward to coming all my life!" She started to weep again.

Rachel tried to comfort her. "And no wonder you feel that way, after what you've been through. Now, Benjamin and I are going to work. Just you lie on the sofa and try and sleep. If you need anything just help yourself. We'll be back after midnight." She showed her the pantry and told her where the key was for the toilet. Benjamin took her case into the back room, which had a fold down bed in it. The two of them went into the other bedroom to change into their working clothes.

"Well," Rachel said when they returned, "we're off to work now. Just go to bed when you feel like it. Don't wait up for us, we'll be late." She went over and held Mary Ellen by the shoulders and looked into her eyes. "Believe me, things will get better for you. I know it looks hopeless right now, but time heals everything. Isn't that right, Benjamin?"

Benjamin came over and patted her back. He looked at her sympathetically. "Yes, time heals everything."

They both said goodbye and were gone, leaving her alone in the flat looking around in despair. *Oh, sweet Jesus. Why did I leave Ireland? Why did I leave my family?* Great waves of homesickness overwhelmed her as she cried herself to sleep.

Mary Ellen awoke to what sounded like someone shouting in a foreign language. She rubbed the sleep from her eyes and looked at the clock. It was three-thirty. She wearily roused herself and went to the window to see what all the noise was all about. She looked down on a sea of people, horses and carts, trucks and pushcarts, everyone jostling for space, with the people all seemingly shouting at once. It was a street market selling everything from fruit to pots and pans, live chickens and goats, and from what Mary Ellen could hear, not a word of English being spoken. She opened the window and leaned out to get a better view. The market stretched for about four blocks on either side of the building where the Swerskys lived. Hurriedly, Mary Ellen shut the window to keep out the cold. She had never seen so many people together in her life. Not even in Dublin on a Saturday morning.

She lifted her bag and went over to sit by the gas fire to keep warm. She opened her purse and counted her money. She still had the forty four dollars the purser had given her. She replaced the money and rummaged through her purse and found the little box her brother had given her. She opened it and read the inscription. *I wish I understood what this means,* she thought ruefully. She sighed and put the box on the table and busied herself heating some water on the stove to make some tea.

She spent the rest of the day soaking a cloth and holding it to her swollen face and dozing off and on between times. She was awakened with the sound of the door opening. It was the Swerskys and it was nearly one o'clock in the morning.

"Still here? I thought you would have gone to bed by now," Rachel said as she held the door open for Benjamin who was carrying a large sack.

Benjamin laid the sack down next to the sewing machine. He gestured at the sack. "Extra work, means extra money."

"I was too lonely to go lie in the room with no windows. The noise from the street made me feel I wasn't so alone," Mary Ellen replied.

Rachel hung her coat on a hook on the back of the door. "Homesick, I suppose. Don't worry, it'll pass after a while, won't it, Benjamin?"

Benjamin sat at the table. "Yes, it'll pass. The secret is to keep busy, then you don't have time to think." He picked up the little box with the shamrocks engraved on it. "Nice box! Did someone give it to you?"

"Yes, my brother gave it to me before I left. Look inside the lid, it's engraved."

Benjamin flipped the lid up and read the inscription. "Listen, Rachel." He read the inscription. "Isn't that beautiful? Your brother was very thoughtful, Mary Ellen."

"Yes, but I don't really understand it. Robert told me to read it when I was having bad times and it would make me feel better, but it's not doing me any good at the moment! Do you know what he meant?"

Benjamin closed the box. "Yes. It's from Tennyson. It means that if you keep true to yourself, you will be too strong for your enemies to hurt you. What has happened to you is through no fault of your own. So you must not blame yourself. Your brother gave it to you for inspiration."

Mary Ellen listened carefully. "So that's what it means!" She opened the box and recited the words slowly. *"My strength is as the strength of ten, because my heart is pure!"* Yes! Yes! Now I understand. These terrible things were not my fault! I was blaming myself. Oh, thank you, Benjamin, I feel better already!"

"Well, we're glad of that! But it's bedtime now, we should all be getting to sleep," Rachel said as she turned the fire off.

Mary Ellen said "Yes, goodnight, and thank you both again, I don't know how I'll ever repay you for your kindness this day."

"Nonsense, just try and get a good night's sleep and tomorrow morning we'll get you fixed up. Okay?" Rachel ushered her into the back room.

"Goodnight, Benjamin! Thank you."

Goodnight!" Benjamin replied as Rachel came back into the front room. They looked at each other. "Before you say anything about what we should do, Rachel, I think we should wait till the morning before we decide anything, I'm exhausted."

"You're right!" she replied. "Let's go to bed." They doused the lights and went into the bedroom.

When Mary Ellen got up the next morning, Benjamin was already hard at work at the sewing machine. Rachel was just pouring the coffee.

"Good morning, how are you feeling? What would you like in your coffee?"

"Milk and sugar, please," Mary Ellen replied. She looked at the clock on the wall. It was eight o'clock. "How long have you been working, Benjamin?" she asked.

Benjamin rose up and stretched. "Since six. We take turns each. Tomorrow it's Rachel's turn, and I get to lie in bed. Every morning we do two hours only, then we go out for a walk for an hour."

Mary Ellen went over to the sewing machine. There were piles of shirt collars all finished. "How many of these did you do this morning?"

"I can do forty an hour. Rachel can do fifty or more. We get two cents each."

Mary Ellen thought for a moment. "So you made a dollar sixty this morning."

"Yes, it all adds up. Another three months and we will be able to start on our own."

"That's good news. Now do you know where I could get somewhere to live and how much it will cost? I have forty-four dollars. I can't go looking for a job looking like this, so I'll have to wait till my face gets better."

Rachel sat beside her. "Well, in this area you can get a room with food for five dollars a week. I don't know how much they charge uptown, or even over in Queens. Maybe you should try Queens, there's lots of Irish people over there."

Mary Ellen looked at her in disbelief. "Rachel, after what's happened to me since I came here, I don't care if I never see an Irishman again! This area will be fine for me till I get a job."

"Well, in that case we'll look for a place this morning. We'll try and get somewhere near so as you can come and visit us."

"That's fine with me,"Mary Ellen said.

"Just a minute!" Benjamin stood up and leaned on the table.

"Listen to the both of you! Why look for a place when we have room here. You're welcome to stay here for a while, at least till you get a job and get to know the place. I won't let you go out on your own after what you've been through! Can you use a sewing machine?" He was getting flustered and upset.

"Yes, my mother had one something like that one,"Mary Ellen said, wondering why he was getting so worked up.

"Good. The matter is settled. We can bring you home some work and you can make some money till you get well enough to get a better job. Now I'm going out for a little while!" He grabbed his coat and left them sitting looking at one another. Rachel had a little smile on her lips.

Mary Ellen sat open mouthed in surprise. "What are you smiling at, Rachel, and what was that all about?"

" I knew what Benjamin would do, but I had to wait till he said it. After all, he's the man of the house!" She burst out laughing.

"What's so funny?" Mary Ellen was smiling too.

Rachel stopped laughing and said seriously. "We couldn't let you go out on your own after what you've been through. Our own daughter would be about your age now and Benjamin and I would never forgive ourselves if something happened to you before you find your feet and get better. It's not a very safe place for a young woman on her own. So we would like you to stay as long as you want."

"Oh, thank you so much. I'll be glad to stay with you. I was dreading going to a strange place again. But why did Benjamin go out?"

"He was a little embarrassed, that's all." Rachel went on to tell her how Benjamin was very clever and was just about to start university in Poland when the pogrom started. The soldiers burned the Swersky house down and threw the family out. They wandered around southern Poland doing odd jobs and sleeping in barns before finding a village with more Jews. After that he had to go to work to help them make ends meet.

"That's when I met him and we got married. The whole thing made him determined that his family would not be denied an education, so we scraped enough money to come to America. You see all these books? They are in different languages and he can read them all. Our two boys, David and Isaac, are both as bright as their father and they are working their way through university. David is going to be a lawyer and Isaac is taking business courses. You'll see them soon enough. They visit us at least once a week."

Mary Ellen could hear the pride in Rachel's voice as she talked about her sons. "I'll look forward to meeting them. I knew Benjamin was well read when he answered my question. Now, will you show me how to sew these shirt collars."

Just then Benjamin came back into the flat rubbing his hands. "It's a nice morning, a bit chilly, but not cold enough to stop us going for a walk. Come on the both of you, let's go!"

"Just a minute, I was going to show Mary Ellen how to do the shirt collars," Rachel replied.

Benjamin waved his hand in dismissal. "We can show her later. Now let's go and we'll show you the neighborhood, young lady!"

"Oh, all right then, come on!" Rachel grabbed her coat.

Mary Ellen said, "Look at my face, everybody will stare at me. You two go and I'll stay here."

Rachel put her arm round her. "Wear a head scarf and nobody will notice. You'll have to go out sometime you know."

"Yes," Benjamin said. "You're so beautiful on one side, nobody will look at the other! Isn't that right, Rachel?" They all laughed and Mary Ellen agreed to go with them.

"Oh, all right, I'll wear a scarf and keep my head down."

Chapter 5

Marcus walked over to the first cab in line and said to the driver, "Take me to a reasonable bed and breakfast place in a good neighborhood near public transport. Not too far away from the business district."

The driver took his suitcase and put it in the trunk. "No problem, sir. Queens or Brooklyn is your best bet, no coloreds around there!"

"Make it Brooklyn. Just a minute, I only have pounds, where can I change them into dollars?"

"On a Saturday I don't know. Don't worry, I'll take you to Brooklyn for a pound." The driver waited for an answer before he closed the trunk. Marcus smiled cynically, *He's probably overcharging, but so will the rest of them.*

"That'll be fine," Marcus said, and hurriedly went into the back seat, sitting as far back as he could. The driver closed the trunk and got into the driver's seat.

"First time in New York, sir?" the driver said as he turned the cab around slowly.

"Yes," Marcus replied irritably. "Look I'm tired out, could you speed it up?"

"Sure thing, pal. *"Damned Limey, I should have charged the son of a bitch two pounds! I'll take the bastard to the expensive area, he won't know the difference."* He blended the taxi into the traffic and headed for the Brooklyn bridge.

Marcus waited till they had cleared the dock area and pulled the envelope from his pocket. He opened it and riffled through the bundle of notes. *There must be a thousand at least here! I'll wait till I'm alone before I count it,* he thought and shoved it back in his pocket. He felt something else and pulled it out. It was the key ring Mary Ellen had given him. He looked at it for a moment and wound down the window and threw the key ring out of the moving cab. He closed the window and sat back in the seat. If he thought about what he had done to Mary Ellen it was only in regard to her seeing him again. That was very unlikely in a city as big as this, and anyway, she couldn't prove anything. There were no pangs of conscience with Marcus. He had his stake now and that was all that counted. Sure, she was a beautiful girl, and he had enjoyed her company. He was honest enough with himself to know that he could never really love anyone. That sort of thing could get in the way of his primary purpose. The making of money! Thus he put her out of his mind and never really thought of her again.

In about half an hour the taxi stopped in front of a row of houses in a nice looking neighborhood. There were trees on either side of the street and the houses were all detached two-stories. Some of them had notices on the widows advertising either full board, rooms, or bed and breakfast.

"Here we are, take your pick!" The driver got out and retrieved the case from the trunk, dumping it unceremoniously on the sidewalk.

"Here you are. Thank you." Marcus gave him a pound note. Without a word the driver jumped in his taxi and drove away. Marcus shrugged and looked for the nearest bed and breakfast.

He knocked on the door and a woman answered. Yes, there was a room available; it cost six dollars a week; two weeks in advance; yes, pounds were acceptable. The subway was a two minute walk along the street. One change of train took you straight into Manhattan. Marcus agreed and she showed him where the amenities were and took him upstairs to his room.

He curbed his impatience and unpacked his suitcase and looked around. It was a very well furnished room with a nice view of the street from the bay window. He went to the washroom in the hall and washed his face and hands. Back in the room he took a deep breath and emptied the envelope on the bed and started counting.

When he finished counting the money, he lay back on the bed with his hands clasped behind his head. *Two-thousand pounds! Eight-thousand dollars!* He grinned in anticipation. *If what Walker said was true, and he was privy to that information, he could not go wrong! All he needed was a stockbroker.* Dreamily he started counting in his head how fast he could compound money. *If he could double his stake once a month he would be rich in a very short time! To hell with a month! What about doubling it every week. There was no reason why he couldn't if he knew the right stocks in advance.* By the time Marcus fell asleep he was doubling his money every day and calculating how much he would have after a year.

He spent the Sunday walking around the neighborhood and finding his bearings. He bought a map of New York and took the subway into Manhattan and found the address Walker had given him. Hawthorne Insurance was located at the corner of Broad street and South street. It was a brown colored ten story building with the name emblazoned in huge brass letters across the front between the first and second floors. The whole journey took him forty minutes door to door. He did not want to be late on his first day. The building was closed. He was amazed at the length of the avenues and the size of the place. The streets were nearly deserted in the business district. He noted there were lots of banks near where he was going to work. He'd have to get to one tomorrow. *Much different from London, easy to find your way around.* He bought a newspaper and went back to his boarding house and read the paper cover to cover.

The next morning Marcus was standing in front of the Hawthorne building at eight thirty. *What a difference a day makes*, he thought as he watched crowds of people hurrying in all directions, cars honking horns and police whistles drowning out the hum of the crowds. He looked up at the surrounding buildings and tried to imagine how many people worked in all these offices. He turned around and went through a revolving door that led to the foyer. To the right there was a receptionist sitting at a desk with a phone and appointment book lying open in front of her. She was an elderly woman with her hair tied in a bun and thick glasses. *You'd think they would have a younger woman at the front desk!*

"Good morning, I have an appointment with Mr. Walker." He smiled at the woman who answered crisply without looking up from her book.

"Name please?"

Sour faced bitch! Probably been here so long she thinks she owns the company. He had decided to abbreviate his name because he had always hated his name and what better time to change than starting anew in America. While he was at it he might as well abbreviate Browning as well. It also wouldn't hurt if the police were looking for a Marcus Browning.

"Mark Brown," he answered casually as he looked around the huge foyer with the oak paneled walls and a gigantic portrait of Sir William hanging directly opposite the front door. There were four elevators on the left side opposite from the receptionist.

She looked at her book and then ran her finger down the page to check.

"Sorry, there's no Mark Brown here."

Marcus turned to face her. "But there must be, madam. May I?" he said in his best Oxford accent. He took the book and turned it toward him. He pointed to his name and said, "Here we are, it's just that you have my Sunday name down!" He said it in a manner that made her feel foolish as he intended.

Flustered, she replied. "Oh, I see. Use the right-hand elevator and go to the top floor, Mr. Walker's secretary will be expecting you," she said in dismissal as she lifted the phone. *Snobby Limey bastard*!

"Thank you very much." Marcus grinned as he turned away. When he got to the top floor he noticed immediately there was lots of space. The area just outside the elevator was about thirty feet square, with a big class aquarium with tropical fish right in the middle. There were couches and armchairs scattered around and coffee tables with magazines in front of them. A floor to ceiling window took up almost an entire wall that looked over the East river. Two engraved frosted glass doors bracketed the window. The one on the right read Sir William Hawthorne and the other one read Mr. Jeffrey Walker. Immediately in front of the window sat a middle aged woman at a roll top desk. There was a nameplate on top of the desk that informed the reader that Miss Steinhoff was behind the desk. She looked at him over her horn rimmed glasses.

"Can I help you?' she called over to him.

Marcus looked at her. *They must have got all the secretaries from the same stable!* A smile would surely kill this one.

"I have an appointment with Mr. Walker, Mark Brown's the name." He didn't wait to be asked this time.

"Mr. Walker will be here shortly. Have a seat," she answered as she lifted a folder and opened it. Marcus walked over to the picture window and looked over the East river to Brooklyn and Queens.

"Nice view you have here," he said pleasantly. The woman never even acknowledged his presence and kept her head down at the desk. Marcus gave up and sat on one of the armchairs. He took his newspaper from his pocket and started reading while he waited. He looked at his watch. It was eight fifty five. He read the newspaper for a while, glancing at his watch and trying to stifle his impatience. *Walker was playing games, making him wait like this!*

At last the elevator door opened and Walker came striding out with a beautiful blonde girl about twenty years old. The girl went to his office and opened the door. Walker came over to Marcus and said, "Good morning, Browning. Have you been waiting long?" It was ten o'clock.

"Since about ten to nine," Marcus replied.

"Well, not to worry, come in to my office and we'll get you going in no time." He turned to the woman at the desk. "Good morning, Greta. Bring in a blank employment form and we'll get Mr. Browning here organized." *Greta! Well named! She sure as hell looked like a 'Greta,' the hatchet-faced bitch.* Marcus laughed inwardly.

The woman looked up and said, "Good morning, Mr. Walker. I have one ready for your attention."

"Excellent, follow me." He led the way into the office.

As soon as Marcus walked into Walker's office he knew that this was what he wanted. Everything was the last word in luxury. There was a fire going in the antique English fireplace, the mahogany walls gave the impression of warmth, which offset the light coming in from the huge window that also looked over the East river. The paintings on the walls set off to perfection the light-colored maple furniture. There were two doors at the far end of the office between bookcases that went right to the top of the twelve foot walls. The hand made Persian rug was almost wall to wall. The blonde girl was nowhere in sight.

Walker sat behind his desk and Marcus stood with the secretary waiting to be asked to sit down. Greta put the folder in front of Walker and stood ready with her pencil and notepad.

"That will be all, thank you, Greta. Have a seat, Browning." He gestured to the chair in front of the desk. Greta left and closed the door quietly behind her. Walker opened the folder and passed a sheet of paper over to Marcus.

"This is a standard employment form. Fill it in when you go home. Your hours are from nine a.m. to four p.m. with an hour for lunch between twelve thirty and one thirty. The hours are most important. Do not deviate from them or you will be fired immediately. Now, your duties will consist of doing confidential work for me. You will have an office with a private phone number. I will give you two phone numbers. You will receive a call at ten o'clock every morning, and also at two thirty. Occasionally you may receive more. You don't need to know where from. The caller will instruct you on what to buy and what to sell and how much. You will then call one of the two numbers I will give you. The first one you will call every day, this is for amounts up to two-thousand dollars. The second one is only for larger amounts. You will note all the transactions and meet with me once a week to go over them. When I am out of town, I will phone you for the information. The meeting place is on this card. The two phone numbers are there too. Don't lose it." He passed a business card over.

"I will stress for the last time that what you are doing is strictly confidential. You are sworn to secrecy and you will be well rewarded. Well, that's about it. Our weekly meeting will be every Friday at five o'clock. Any questions?"

Marcus decided against asking anything about the person who would be calling him. He had a feeling that if he did Walker would fire him on the spot.

"Yes, why are the hours of work so important?"

"Because the person who will be calling expects an answer! If you are not there, it could cost a lot of money. Now do you understand?"

"Yes, perfectly. One other thing, I will be calling myself Mark Brown from now on. You don't mind, do you?"

Walker looked blankly at him. "I don't give a damn what you call yourself, as long as you do your job." He pressed two buttons on the console on his desk. A moment later one of the doors opened and the blonde appeared with a tray with two cups of steaming coffee on it. The main door opened and Greta appeared with her pad and pencil.

"Greta, Mr. Brown is my new personal assistant. Please show him to his office and make sure he has everything he needs. Thank you." He stood up and walked round to Marcus. He shook his hand and said, "Welcome aboard, Mark. Here's to a successful partnership!"

Marcus shook his hand "Thank you, sir, goodbye for now."

Walker hesitated for a moment, and said, "Look, I'm looking after things today, so after Greta fills you in why don't you take the rest of the day off. I'm sure you can put the time to good use. You can start in earnest tomorrow."

Excellent. I can open an account and familiarize myself with the neighborhood. "I sure will, sir. Thank you very much."

Greta led Marcus back to her desk. She opened a drawer and lifted out a key. "Do you have a bank account where we can deposit your salary, Mr. Brown? Or would you like it in a check?" she asked.

"A check will be fine," Marcus replied. He didn't want anyone knowing where he did his banking.

"Very well, your check will be at the front desk for pick up every Friday morning. Now, if you will follow me, I will show you to your office."

They went over to an elevator in the corner with the doors open.

"I couldn't help noticing the young lady. What's her position in the company?" Marcus asked.

Greta looked at him severely. "I don't know, and neither do I care!" she snapped.

"I see. You'd think someone would have used the lift by now,"Marcus said conversationally, trying to change the subject. He could see Greta did not approve of the young woman, whoever she was.

"This is a private elevator for Mr. Hawthorne and Mr. Walker; and myself, of course," Greta said smugly. They went in and she pressed the button for the basement.

"That's a nice office Mr. Walker has!" Marcus said.

Greta became animated. "It's nothing compared to Mr. Hawthorne's. You can look right over to New Jersey past the Statue of Liberty from it. There's no finer sight than seeing the big liners coming in with all the tugs and smaller ships accompanying them. Mr. Hawthorne always lets me watch with him."

As the elevator descended, Marcus was thinking surely his office was not in the basement. It wasn't in the basement, it was two floors down from the basement. *The elevator didn't even go that deep,* he thought bitterly. Greta seemed to take great pleasure in showing him to a dingy cubicle in a dark corner of the cavernous room half filled with dust-covered filing cabinets and old office furniture. She used the key to open the door and when she switched on the light, a single bare light bulb cast a feeble light on a dilapidated old desk, on top of which lay a black telephone. A wall clock ticked loudly in the silence.

"Is this where I'm supposed to work?" Marcus asked incredulously.

"Yes, sir. There is a toilet through that door at the back and you have a desk and telephone. You'll find stationery and pen and ink in the desk drawer. I believe you have everything you need. You will please leave the form at the front desk tomorrow morning. I'll pick it up there. So, if you don't have any questions, here is your office key. Please lock it when you leave at night. The janitor will clean it at the weekends."

"One thing, if you don't mind, how long did the last person last in this job?" he asked, knowing she would think he meant because of the lousy office.

"Nine weeks, if I remember correctly." She handed him the key and walked briskly back to the stairs.

Marcus was too dumbstruck to even answer her. He walked slowly over and slumped into the swivel chair in front of the desk. *That didn't give him much time.* He looked around him in disgust. *You can't see any bloody Statue of Liberty from here,* he thought ruefully. This was not what he had expected at all. He sat for a long time debating whether to go back up and tell Walker where to stick his job. *The bastard did this deliberately to humiliate me!* At last he got up and put the light out. He had made his mind up to give this a try. If Walker was telling the truth about the information he was getting, and he was going to be out of town frequently, then Marcus knew exactly what he was going to do. On the other hand, if he was lying, Marcus would find out soon enough. *To hell with the lousy office, he wouldn't be there very long no matter what happened.*

Greta knocked on Walker's door and went in with a smile on her face. "Mr. Brown's all settled in, sir!"

Walker was sitting behind his desk with the blonde standing beside him looking out at the view.

"So did he like his office, Greta?" He laughed sarcastically.

"I'm sure he'll be all right, plenty of privacy, sir."

"Very well, that will be all, Greta."

Marcus locked the office and left the building. He had noticed a branch of the Bank of America a short distance away that morning, so he went in to open an account. He went over to a counter with an 'inquiries' sign above it.

A young man came over and asked, "May I help you, sir?"

"Yes," Marcus replied. "I want to open an account, change some sterling into dollars and find a stockbroker."

"The first two are no problem, sir. But I'm afraid you'll have to go across the street to find a stockbroker."

"Oh, and where would that be?"

"Straight across, if you look up when you walk out the front door you'll see a sign that reads. "Norwood Stockbrokers." You can't miss it.

"Good, now I have two-thousand pounds I wish to deposit. Make it an account that the stockbroker can access with my permission."

The teller looked at him quizzically. "Are you intending to buy and sell stocks with this money?"

"Yes, I am. Why do you ask?"

"Because your best bet is open your account and give your stockbroker a check for the amount you wish to invest. They will all deposit any profits here for you. If that is what you want to do."

"Excellent, set it up and give me a hundred dollars in cash please."

"Good, I need your name, place of employment and your address."

The teller opened a checking account in the name of Mark Brown. When he was finished with the paperwork, he said, "Here's your bankbook and checkbook. One-hundred dollars to you and that leaves you eight-thousand two-hundred and forty. You know, after a month you can apply for a line of credit equal to half of your balance. It might come in handy if you want to invest in a sure thing."

Marcus took the money and put the books in his inside pocket. "That's good to know. Do you have a card? I am most impressed with your service. And thank you for the advice."

The young man replied. "Not me, I'm only a clerk. My name is John Reynolds."

"How long have you worked here? I think you should be more than a clerk."

"I've only been here three months. I'm going to night school to get a degree in accounting, so this is how I pay for it."

"Well, I still think you're more than a clerk. Thank you, John, I'll be seeing you, goodbye."

"Goodbye, Mr. Brown," the teller said as they shook hands.

Marcus walked out of the bank and crossed the street to Norwood Stockbrokers. A receptionist directed him to a lounge and told him someone would be there shortly. He had hardly made himself comfortable when a bespectacled man about fifty came in.

"Jack Norwood at your service, sir. Normally one of our associates would look after you, but I'm available right now. So this is your lucky day," he said with a smile.

"Mark Brown's the name. I need advice on how to buy and sell stocks. The young man in the bank sent me over here." The two men shook hands.

"Come this way Mr. Brown. My office is much more comfortable." He led the way to an elevator that whisked them to the top floor. Norwood's office was nice, but not in the same class as Walker's. *Still a hell of a lot better than mine*, Marcus noted as he sat down.

"Now what exactly do you want to do, Mr. Brown," Norwood said briskly.

"I want to know if it is possible to buy and sell stocks over the telephone with your company and if so, how to go about it."

"Well, that's easy. You just leave us a check to open your account, and for five percent of each transaction we'll be happy to oblige. Now, if you want advice on what to buy and sell the fee is seven percent per transaction and three percent of any profit. Said profits to be deposited in your bank or added to your account with us." He spread his hands wide on the desk and smiled expansively. "Easy, isn't it? Now, how much were you thinking of starting with?"

This guy doesn't mess around. Nice money if you can get it. "I won't be needing advice on buying and selling, I was thinking of starting with five-thousand. For three percent of each transaction, I think we could do business, Mr. Norwood."

Norwood kept smiling as he spoke. "For a new customer, a special deal. Would you be happy with four percent, Mr. Brown."

"Perhaps if I started with eight-thousand instead of five?"

Norwood laughed. This guy was no fool, very sharp for one so young. Something told him he was going to make money with him.

"All right, Mr. Brown, Eight-thousand will get you three percent."

"Three percent will do for now. No fee for profits. Will everything be ready to start for tomorrow morning about ten?"

"If you leave the check with us today, I'll set up your account and give you my private phone number for any problems you might have. Use the other number for your transactions. You'll be dealing with a young man called Joseph Cassidy. He'll be available each day from seven in the morning to eight at night. Is that suitable for you?" He handed him two business cards.

"Just what I wanted, Mr. Norwood. I'm looking forward to a long and profitable partnership!" He pulled out his checkbook. As he wrote the check out, Marcus asked, "Is there a good library around here?"

"You know, I've worked here for years and I honestly don't know! I only leave this building either to eat or go home. There is The New York Public Library at 42nd St. and Fifth Avenue. It's the best library in the country, but it's a good bit away. What exactly are you looking for?"

Marcus gave him the check. "If I'm going to be in the stock market, I'd better start learning more about it. So I'm going to start reading up on how it operates."

"Good idea, Mr. Brown, but in my experience there's no sure way to pick winners. A lot of people have lost a lot on sure things. It's a lot like horse racing."

"I see," Marcus replied. "If that's the case, then you must be the bookie!"

Norwood burst out laughing. "By God, you are a quick learner, Mr. Brown. One thing. Make sure you read the *Wall Street Journal* every day, it's a must." He stood up and held out his hand.

Marcus shook hands, and said in parting, "I think I'd like to be a bookie too, Mr. Norwood. The bookies always win!"

When Marcus left the building, he pulled out his map to orient himself, then rode the subway to 42nd St. The New York Public Library was actually at Sixth Avenue, but he found it easily. Anyone who moved from London to New York found it very easy to find their way around. The city was like a grid. Nothing like London where you could get lost in a few minutes. After giving his address and showing his immigration papers, Marcus obtained his library card and for the next month read everything he could get his hands on relative to buying and selling stocks. He did most of his reading in his little office while waiting for the phone calls from the mystery man, as Marcus came to call him.

After Marcus had left the Library with his first batch of books, he bought two small ledgers that he could fit in his inside pocket. The next morning when he went to the office, he realized that this day would set the course for his future. He was beginning to think that the phone would never ring, even though he was reading to pass the time. At last, around eleven fifteen the phone rang. Marcus let it ring twice then picked up the receiver. He had his report notepad ready and the two cards Walker had given him.

"Good morning, Mark Brown here," he answered in his best Oxford accent. A thick southern accent replied immediately.

"Good mawnin, Mr. Brown, Mr. Black here." The voice was full of sarcasm. Are you ready?" Marcus smiled to himself. *Black is it? Well, I'll find you, my friend, one way or another.*

"Go ahead, Mr. Black." The man proceeded to give Marcus instructions to buy and sell specific stocks at specific amounts at specific times. He realized, as he wrote them down that any mistakes could be fatal. There were a total of seven stocks to buy and three to sell, which Marcus assumed Walker already owned. Painstakingly he entered them in the pad. He noticed that all of the purchases were less than two-thousand, so he called the appropriate number and relayed the instructions. He then looked over the stocks that were bought and noted two of them had to be sold at three thirty the same day.

He took his own ledger and entered under purchased. Four-thousand dollars worth of each stock and the values of them. He then called his new stockbroker, Joseph Cassidy. When Cassidy took the instructions down, he whistled softly into the phone, "Mr. Norwood told me to expect your call, Mr. Brown. I see on your file that you prefer not to accept advice from us? Is this correct?"

"Yes, Mr. Cassidy, that is correct. Why do you ask?"

"It's just that I see you're putting everything you have in your first transaction. That is unusual for a new client."

"Just do it, Mr. Cassidy, and please call me back when you sell them and let me know the value!" He hung up the receiver and was surprised to notice that his hands were wet with sweat. He wiped his hands and copied all Walker's transactions into the second ledger. At lunchtime he went out for a walk and found out where the local speakeasies were. He decided against going for a drink. Now was his chance to stop, he was glad that there were no pubs handy. The afternoon seemed to crawl no matter how hard he concentrated on his reading, the thought kept surfacing that he could lose his money. Maybe not all at once, but still...at three forty the phone rang, startling him even though he was expecting it. Closing his eyes, he slowly lifted the receiver.

"Hello, Mark Brown here, can I help you?" he said softly.

It was Cassidy. "By God, Mr. Brown, you sure know how to pick them. I have good news and bad news, what do you want first?"

Marcus' spirits lifted. One out of two wasn't bad. "Give me the bad news first," he whispered.

Cassidy's voice boomed over the phone. "All right. The first one made you twenty percent clear, and wait for it, Mr. Brown. The second one made forty-two percent clear. That makes a clear profit for one day of two-thousand four-hundred and eighty dollars. And that is with the fees deducted. Congratulations, Mr. Brown."

"Thank you very much, Mr. Cassidy, I'll call you tomorrow morning. Goodbye." Marcus put the receiver down, clasped his hands behind his head, leaned back in his chair and stared at the ceiling, thinking things out for a long time. *By God, if this business is as easy as this, it's better than I could have hoped. Walker must be worth millions!* The next step would be to find out who "Mr. Black" was. That would be hard to do, considering he was convinced that Walker would unload him before long. He slowly unclasped his hands and carefully noted the numbers in his ledger. In the second ledger he copied the day's profit on Walker's money. He would update it daily as the investments were sold using the *Wall Street Journal.*

For six weeks Marcus steadily increased his stake, some days making more than others, but never losing. His weekly reports to Walker were more of a social nature. They were held in an upscale speakeasy off Times Square. Marcus noticed the clientele were well heeled and included a lot of big name city politicians. He simply gave Walker a sealed envelope containing the reports. Walker would put it in his briefcase and then have dinner and a couple of drinks. Marcus always turned down the offers of drink. Walker would tell him when the next meeting was if he was going away. Marcus' stake had more than doubled. He now had more than twenty-thousand dollars.

All this time he had read everything he could about how the stock market worked. He knew that what "Mr. Black" was doing would land all of them in jail. It was called insider trading and was a criminal offence. Marcus studied every transaction he made very carefully. He was looking for some kind of pattern. He noticed that now and again various tool company stocks were bought and kept for around seven days before being sold. It was never the same company, but the returns were staggering. Why then was Walker only buying a thousand dollars worth at a time? Maybe it was so it was not so noticeable. Some of the transactions had tripled in value in six or seven days. Marcus was impatient to make even faster money than he was doing. He knew time was going to run out on him. If he couldn't find out who Black really was, then the opportunity would slip away. He decided that he would go and see John Reynolds at the bank one day after work. He now had ten thousand on deposit and the other ten with Norwood.

On Wednesday the eighth of December, just six weeks after landing in America, Marcus decided to gamble everything he had.

John Reynolds sat and listened to Marcus' proposal and nodded his head in agreement. "Mr. Brown, what you say makes sense and I'm all in favor. But I'm afraid I don't have the authority to do it. You'll have to talk to the manager, Mr. Tweed."

Marcus had asked for a line of credit equaling his deposits and would repay the full amount in ten days plus interest. That would give him twenty-thousand, not counting what he could get out of Norwood with his other ten.

"Do you think he'll go for it?"

Reynolds leaned over to Marcus and said slowly, "Impress the hell out of him and ask for more than you really want. Give him the impression that you have other options and I think you'll be okay."

Marcus smiled. "Lead the way, John, and thanks for the advice."

The two men walked over to a secretary sitting at a desk outside a frosted glass door marked in gothic letters. Gordon Tweed, Manager.

"Hi, Lucy," Reynolds said. "Is the boss available?"

The girl pressed the intercom button. "Mr. Reynolds with a customer to see you, sir. Can they come in?"

"Yes, of course. Send them right in!" the voice answered immediately.

The girl shrugged and pointed to the door. "In you go, gentlemen."

The two men went into the office and Reynolds introduced Marcus to Tweed.

"Well, how can I help you, Mr. Brown?" he asked pleasantly, as he signaled them to be seated in two chairs at the front of his desk.

"Actually, I'm here to help all of us here make a nice profit, Mr. Tweed. I need some capital to invest for around ten days. I have ten thousand on deposit here, and I would like a line of credit for thirty thousand, to be repaid in full in ten days with seven-percent interest. Of course I know I'm asking a lot, so I'm prepared to offer you personally, and Mr. Reynolds here the chance to make a little money for yourselves. This is a once in a lifetime opportunity. I am absolutely certain of the investment paying around twenty-percent. I am giving you the first chance at this because of the courtesy shown me by Mr. Reynolds when I opened my account. Now, Mr. Tweed, what do you say?" He sat back in his seat and glanced at his watch.

Brilliant! Reynolds thought. *This guy is away ahead of me.* He saw Tweed's eyes light up when Marcus mentioned the investment return.

"An interesting proposal, Mr. Brown. Unfortunately, I simply cannot do it. The best I could do is give you a line of credit for five-thousand dollars. If your offer for us to invest is genuine, I suppose I could risk around a thousand, What about you, Reynolds?" He looked at Reynolds, who was wondering what Marcus next move would be. Before Reynolds could answer, Marcus was already on his feet. He held out his hand.

"Sorry we can't do business, Mr. Tweed, but I did give you the first chance! I will be terminating my account today. Goodbye." He turned to leave. His heart was pounding under his calm exterior. He was gambling everything on this moment.

"Mr. Brown, please sit down. I am prepared to negotiate a little." Tweed stood up and pointed to the chair.

Got you! Greed always wins. He looked at Tweed and deliberately sat on the edge of the chair, giving the impression that the next time he stood up he would walk. "Mr. Tweed, with all respect, I am not here to negotiate. If you can't or won't give me what I asked for I will go elsewhere. This is an opportunity for you to make a tidy profit, depending on how much you wish to invest. I urge you to put as much in as you can comfortably afford. You too, Mr. Reynolds. You won't be sorry! Now what's it to be?"

Tweed stared dumbfounded at him and Reynolds looked on in amazement. *Good God, he's turned the tables on him. It's like he's doing us the favor!*

The three men sat in silence for what seemed like minutes.

At last Tweed said hoarsely, "I don't know how you talked me into this,

Mr. Brown. Thirty-thousand dollars at seven-percent for ten days. And put me in for ten-thousand. What about you Reynolds?"

Reynolds face reddened. "I'm sorry, I'll have to pass on this one," he muttered.

"Oh, I see. Well, Mr. Brown, Mr. Reynolds will prepare the paperwork for you. Will tomorrow be all right."

Marcus stood up. "Excellent, Mr. Tweed. I'll call Mr. Reynolds when I want it deposited. It will be in the next few days. Just put your ten in my account and I'll handle it from there. You will not regret this day, Mr. Tweed. I think this is the start of a long and fruitful friendship!"

The three men stood up and Marcus shook hands with Tweed. When Reynolds got Marcus alone, he exclaimed, "Boy, Mr. Brown, you handled it beautifully. I never saw anybody handle Tweed like that. Congratulations!"

Marcus shook his hand. "It would never have happened if it wasn't for you, John. I won't forget that! Thank you, now I must rush. Goodbye."

He left the bank and went straight across the road to Norwood Stockbrokers. He looked up Cassidy on the directory and took the elevator up and went into Cassidy's office without knocking. A young man was hunched over a desk full of files and papers. There were three telephones and he was talking into one of them. He swivelled round in his seat and waved to Marcus to sit down on a wooden chair that was also piled high with papers. Marcus just stood and looked around till Cassidy hung up the phone.

"Yes, sir, can I help you?" He stood up and offered his hand.

Marcus took his hand and said, "Mr. Cassidy, I'm Mark Brown. I think it's about time we met, don't you?"

"Mr. Brown! What a surprise, I was wondering when we would meet." He swept the papers off the chair and said, "Have a seat, it's the least I can offer you after the last six weeks." Cassidy had never had a client like this. Everything he touched turned to gold. He knew Brown had to be getting information, but that was none of his business. He himself had secretly invested in some of the one day deals and netted himself a tidy profit on the side apart from his commission. He returned to his seat and spread his hands wide.

"Well now, to what do I owe the honor? Something tells me you're not here for the good of your health?"

"You're right about that. Now, let's get down to business. You may have noticed that every transaction I give you makes a profit."

Before he could say another word, Cassidy interrupted, "Mr. Brown, I do not care what your system is for picking these stocks, I just put it down to a run of good luck!"

Marcus knew Cassidy did not want to hear he was getting information. He laughed and said, "Yes, and I hope it lasts a while longer. As a matter of fact, I know it's going to last till next week at least." He looked at Cassidy to make sure he got the message.

"That's good to know, I hope you're right," Cassidy answered carefully.

"All right. Down to business." Marcus drew his chair over next to Cassidy and leaned toward him. Without giving anything away, he explained that he had a sure thing coming up which would reap a huge profit and needed extra capital to maximize his profit. Could Cassidy help him?

Cassidy thought for a while. *I bet it's one of those tool stocks coming up again.* He too had noticed the cycle. This guy was a gold mine, and he wanted some.

"How much were you thinking of Mr. Brown?"

Marcus leaned back, and without taking his eyes off Cassidy, said quietly, "Fifty-thousand dollars."

Cassidy didn't blink an eye. "And how much do you think this will make?" He was frantically trying to remember how much the tool stocks had made. Marcus knew this guy was smart enough to know what he was getting at.

"Let me put it this way, Mr. Cassidy. I have great faith in tool companies. They are the future of this country!" He sat back to see Cassidy's reaction.

"Mr. Brown, correct me if I'm wrong. What you are asking me is can I help you acquire fifty-thousand dollars to invest in a short term stock option?"

Marcus nodded. "Correct, Mr. Cassidy. Can you do it?"

Cassidy shrugged and said, "Depends what you want to pay for it. I know where it can be gotten, but you may not like the price."

"Okay. Let's have it. How much?"

"Up to a hundred thousand, payable at twenty percent a week." He sat back to see Marcus' reaction. Marcus had already calculated the percentages. *If the stock performed the same as the others, he would make a bundle of money. Twenty percent was a hundred percent safe.*

"A hundred it is. After two weeks I will repay a hundred and forty-two-thousand. When can you have it?"

Impressed by Marcus' mental arithmetic, Cassidy replied, "It's a phone call away, but you should be aware that if payment is not made on time the lender will increase the interest at his discretion. In plain English, you will owe them for the rest of your life, and believe me, you cannot hide from them. Not here, not in England, not anywhere!"

Marcus knew he was talking about loan sharks, but the risk was worth it. He took a deep breath. "One other thing, I'm sure you will be making an investment in this too. So I think it would be a nice gesture if you forfeited your commission on this one. After all, I'm the one who's getting you the information, not to mention taking all the risk!"

Cassidy smiled. *What a greedy bastard!* He nodded in agreement. "You're sure about this?"

"Yes. Let's get on with it!"

Cassidy stood up. He looked at his watch. "Be here at the same time tomorrow. You have to meet someone. Bring your passport and all your personal information, bank accounts, place of employment, everything including your family background. Clear enough?"

Marcus understood perfectly but he was determined. "I'll be here. Thank you and goodnight, Mr. Cassidy." He rose from the chair.

Cassidy lifted the phone, and turned to face Marcus. "Just curious, Mr. Brown. Why come to me and not to Norwood?"

Marcus smiled and replied, "I don't think Mr. Norwood has as many friends as you, Mr. Cassidy."

He left Cassidy shaking his head and went out into the December night. In a few short hours he had put in place the first part of his plan. He now had a total of a hundred and fifty-thousand of his own to invest, plus the ten for Tweed. It had not been easy. He knew the second part would be doubly difficult, but the rewards would be immense if he could pull it off. He shook off the urge to go for a drink and went for something to eat.

The next night Marcus showed up at Cassidy's office at the same time. In his briefcase he had all the information he could gather. If the people did not want to lend him the money, then so be it, he would have to try something else in the short time he felt the had left at Hawthorne's. He had spent hours thinking how he could find out who Mr. Black really was. He had come to the conclusion that it was not Walker's money he was investing. It had to be a cover for Black, who had something on Walker. Either that or Walker was doing Black a favor, and that was highly unlikely, because all of them were out for themselves. All he really knew for certain was that his time was running out and if he couldn't find out who Black was, then the golden goose would die a sudden death.

He knocked on the door and went into Cassidy's office. Cassidy was sitting at his desk and there were two other men standing smoking cigarettes. The place was blue with smoke. Cassidy introduced Marcus and told him the men's names were unimportant. Marcus nodded in understanding.

"Have you got identification?" One of the men asked abruptly. He was a small man with thick spectacles and a hat that looked three sizes too big for him. The other was the heavy.

If he was there to scare me, then he was doing a good job of it, Marcus thought. He was not very tall or well built, but one look at his eyes told you this was a stone-faced killer. Marcus suppressed a shiver and opened his briefcase. "I think everything is here." He put all the papers on the desk. The small man lifted his landed immigrant papers and his passport, glanced at them and put them in his own briefcase.

"Mr. Cassidy has explained the terms of the loan, Mr. Brown. You will get your papers back when our business is complete." He handed him a legal document to sign and a check for a hundred thousand dollars made out to Mr. Mark Brown.

"You understand that this money must be deposited with Norwoods. After fourteen days, either the full amount plus interest or the remainder will be returned to us. If your investment does not cover the total then you will owe us the balance at twenty percent per week. Your documents will be returned to you when our business is complete. Do you understand?"

Marcus signed the paper and the check and handed the check to Cassidy. "Thank you, sir. Put that in my account, Mr. Cassidy. I'll call you tomorrow morning." He offered his hand to the small man who studiously ignored him as he stuffed the document in his case. The other man had not stopped staring at him since he had come into the office. Marcus stepped over to the door and left without looking back. He couldn't shake the feeling that he'd gone in over his head. The more he thought about what he had done the more afraid he became. He knew he would not feel better till he had finished the business with the loan sharks.

On Friday morning Marcus carefully wrote down the latest round of investments. "Mr. Black" did not mention any tool companies, so Marcus invested a thousand in a one day deal. He wanted to make sure he could put the maximum in when he needed to. He sat for a while with all kinds of thoughts going through his head. *What if Black never gave him any more tool companies? What if Walker fired him?* He felt a dread overcome him that he had just ruined his life. *How could he have been so sure yesterday?* All his confidence left him and he sank into a deep despair. For the rest of the day and the whole weekend Marcus worried constantly. At night he could barely sleep and took to going for walks in the middle of the night.

When he went to work on Monday morning, he was almost throwing up with worry and dread. It did not help matters that Black still never mentioned any tool companies in his instructions. On Monday night Marcus never slept at all. By now he was convinced that he had made the biggest blunder of his life. He lay on his bed weeping with remorse and dread. He tried to think clearly but the fear overwhelmed him at every turn.

On Tuesday morning he sat staring at the phone drumming his fingers incessantly on the desk. After what seemed an age the phone rang. The familiar southern accent started to read the instructions. Then it happened.

"Weir Tool Company. Buy one-thousand shares at nine fifty and sell on Wednesday the twenty-second of December." Marcus made his notes as the relief swept over him. He was not out of the woods yet, but if this performed like the others, he would have been worrying for nothing. He made his phone calls and then called Cassidy. He instructed him to put everything he had, a hundred and sixty-thousand dollars in Weir shares.

"Thank God for this, Mr. Brown, I was beginning to get a little worried."

"Whatever for, Mr. Cassidy? Do me a favor on this one, call me every day at closing with the value, will you?" Marcus said innocently.

"You bet I will. I'm putting a bundle on it myself."

Marcus put the receiver down and then called the bank to let Tweed know everything was going as planned. He had settled down now and started to read his books to pass the rest of the day. Just after four o'clock the phone rang. It was Cassidy.

"Twelve fifty-five!" His voice was hoarse with excitement "How the hell do you pick them?"

Marcus grinned. He was starting to relax now. "Thank you very much, Mr. Cassidy," he said quietly. He stood up and rubbed his hands together in glee.

"YES! YES! YES!" he cried as he held his hands in the air. Suddenly he felt foolish and sat down, dreaming once again how much he could make on Weir Tool.

Even his most optimistic estimates fell short. Every day the value of the shares went up. To fifteen dollars, then twenty and never stopped rising till at last on the Wednesday morning they peaked at thirty-two dollars. Marcus sat and calculated the total. It came to just over a half million dollars. In a week and a half! He checked and double checked. Even after he paid the loans he still had three-hundred and fifty-thousand. He would only give Tweed the twenty percent and use the rest of Tweeds profit which came to twenty three-thousand to buy a house. He called Cassidy and told him to get the loan sharks to his office. He told him to have the check ready for the loan sharks and one for himself for a hundred and fourteen-thousand. That would leave him around two-hundred and thirty-thousand on deposit at Norwoods.

He could not wait to see Cassidy after work. All day he pondered his future. His priority now was to find Mr. Black. *There had to be a way.* He decided to ask John Reynolds if he had any ideas. During his conversations with Reynolds he had discovered he was taking law at night school. He was a very shrewd young man and Marcus valued his opinions.

Marcus swept into Cassidy's office smiling from ear to ear. The two loan sharks were there stinking the place up with cigars this time. There was a magnum of champagne half empty on the desk. The celebration was in full swing.

"Have a drink, Mr. Brown!" Cassidy poured a large glass of champagne."

Marcus held up his hand. "Not until we finish our business. Have you the check for these gentlemen?" Cassidy beamed.

"Here it is, all signed and sealed, you just have to sign here."

Marcus addressed the little man with the big hat. "Do you have my papers?"

"Yes, everything is right here." He spread the papers on the desk. Everything was there. Marcus signed the check and Cassidy cosigned it for Norwoods.

Marcus read the figure. "One-hundred and forty-two-thousand dollars. Thank you very much, gentlemen. Our business is now at an end." He handed the check to the little man who put it in his briefcase. He took a card from his inside pocket and handed it to Marcus.

"A pleasure doing business with you, Mr. Brown. Don't hesitate to call if you need our services again."

That'll be the day! Marcus shook hands. "I most certainly will, Mr…" He looked at the card and smiled. "Quick Cash?" Every body laughed heartily and drank their champagne.

"Listen, Mr. Brown, what are you doing over Christmas?" Cassidy asked.

"Nothing at all," Marcus replied. He had almost forgotten that Christmas was just a few days away. All he had been thinking about was his investment. Now he could afford to relax for a few days.

"Look, how would you like to come to Norwoods Christmas party. It's at the Waldorf Astoria on Christmas Eve. I can assure you it's a great night. I can get you an invitation. There's lots of important people go to it. So what do you say?"

Marcus was delighted to accept. He had not made any friends and now he had something to really celebrate. This would be his best Christmas ever. He had the Christmas holiday off, which meant he did not have to work till Tuesday.

"I'll be glad to come. Thank you very much, Mr. Cassidy," he said as he sipped his champagne.

"Excellent. I'll meet you at the front door of the Waldorf at six o'clock on Friday."

Jeffrey Walker strode into his office at ten o'clock on Thursday morning. Greta was waiting with a message for him. She handed him a note.

"You have to call this number right away. The caller said you would know who it was." Walker took the note and went into his office and locked the door behind him. He hung up his coat and hat and sat behind his desk staring at the number on the piece of paper. *There must be something wrong.* It was from his contact in the stock exchange. The number he had been given was only for emergencies. With a slightly trembling hand he dialed the number. The phone had not completed one ring when a familiar voice snarled.

"Walker, what the hell are you doing! How many Weir Tool shares did you buy?"

"The usual. About ten grand worth. What's the problem?"

The voice on the other end turned menacing. "The problem is that someone bought a bundle! There was close to three quarters of a million dollars worth sold yesterday. The shares are down fifty percent already this morning. Now there are only two of us who knew what was going down, and it sure as hell wasn't me! So that leaves you, you greedy bastard! I told you to keep it low and steady, but no, you had to get greedy. Now there is bound to be an inquiry! If this gets to me, I'll crucify you. How could you be so stupid?" The voice paused for breath.

Walker was stunned. This was serious stuff, an inquiry could cost him everything he had. "I swear! I only bought ten-thousand dollars worth. In fact, I don't even know how much it went up. I've not been watching it."

"Well, if it wasn't you and it wasn't me, then that only leaves one other. It must have been your Mr. Brown, he's the only other person in the loop! I told you only to hire new immigrants for the job."

Walker thought fast. *No, it was impossible.* "Look, that is impossible. The man had nothing when he landed. He even tried to get an advance from me on the ship. No, it's not him. It must be just a coincidence, someone taking a gamble, maybe?"

The voice at the other end hissed, "I don't believe in coincidence. Till you find out who bought those shares there will be no more business between us. Now, for starters you should get rid of Brown today."

Walker was really scared now. He had made a fortune from this arrangement. "I'll do my best. But it's not going to be easy. Christmas is coming up and people are on holidays. I'll fire Brown next week. It won't make any difference if you're not doing business today."

" I want names, Walker! If I don't hear from you by next week I'm going to see Mr. Hawthorne. I'm sure he'll be interested in some information I have." The caller hung up the phone.

Walker stared at the receiver in disbelief. He pressed the cradle impatiently till he got the dial tone and frantically started dialing his stockbroker.

Marcus spent the Thursday at work looking at some properties in the newspapers, but did not see anything he wanted. He decided he would get an apartment near Central Park so as he would not have far to travel to the business district. He thought it strange that he never got his usual call from "Mr. Black," but put it down to the holiday season. He tried to call John Reynolds, but he was off for the holidays. He went for dinner at a fancy restaurant that doubled as a speakeasy, and as he drank in the atmosphere he took stock of his position.

Within a few months he had accumulated a small fortune. *What a country! Yes, a man could indeed become a millionaire. All he needed was a bit of luck.* Not for a moment did he think how he had gotten the money to start with. It never entered his head. He was concentrating on finding a way to find out who the elusive Mr. Black was before he lost his job.

On Friday, as promised, Cassidy was waiting outside the Waldorf at six o'clock. "Merry Christmas, Mr. Brown," he said ebulliently.

"Merry Christmas to you too, Mr. Cassidy," Marcus replied.

Cassidy walked him into the foyer and showed the doorman his tickets. They went over to the cloakroom to check in their coats.

"Well, what do you think of this place? Amazing, isn't it." Cassidy waved at the grand entrance to the famous hotel.

"Yes, quite spectacular," Marcus replied, not wanting to tell him in his opinion it wasn't a patch on the Ritz, or even the Savoy.

They made their way to the ballroom, which had tables set all round the dance floor. The band was playing Christmas music in the background. All the men wore tuxedos and the ladies were all dressed to the nines with their long gowns and diamonds glittering everywhere. Cassidy led him over to their table that was set for eight. There were a few bottles wrapped in brown paper sitting on the table, a futile attempt to disguise the fact that all the cups in the room were filled with liquor. There were two men and four women at the table. Marcus recognized Norwood. Cassidy introduced him to everyone. Cassidy's wife and Norwood and his wife were there. The other man was introduced as one of Norwood's clients. He too had his wife with him.

Marcus knew then that he was a valued client. He realized as he looked around that only those and such as those were invited to this party. *Well, he shouldn't be surprised. The speed that he had accumulated his money had been truly astounding, and Norwood and Cassidy were making money off him too. They did not want to lose a client like him.*

"And this is Miss Emily Norwood."

He bent and kissed the young lady's hand. *Norwood's daughter! And unaccompanied too.* Without being uncharitable, Emily Norwood was no oil painting. As a matter of fact she was very plain, and her personality did not help. She was very shy and self conscious, and tended to sit quietly and speak only when spoken to. Even with the Norwood fortune behind her, at the age of twenty-eight she had never had a steady boyfriend.

Marcus turned on his full repertoire of charm. He knew he was in with big money here and the more contacts he made the better it would be for him. Concentrating on shamelessly flattering Mrs. Norwood, he was the perfect gentleman, drinking water only, regaling them with stories of his father's castle, (an exaggeration) quickly realizing they were easily impressed with stories of titles and royalty. Funny, considering they had fought a revolution to get rid of it. But if that's what they liked, then that's what they would get.

When dinner was served, they asked him stupid questions like, "Do they have turkeys in England?" to which he replied to roars of laughter "Yes, we keep them in a place called the House of Commons!"

After dinner the ladies excused themselves to powder their noses. Cassidy asked Marcus if he'd like to accompany him round the room to see some acquaintances. He explained that he always had to tell Cardinal O'Leary of New York that his mother was asking for him. She had known him since he was a parish priest.

Marcus readily agreed. He was curious to see some of the celebrities.

Cassidy pointed out the Mayor of New York, Jimmy Walker, reputed to run the most corrupt City Hall in the city's history. He was also the most popular mayor the city ever had. He pointed out a few more politicians and a couple of famous show business people. Cassidy stopped at the table where Cardinal O'Leary was sitting with the Attorney General, his wife and two daughters and three other priests. He introduced Marcus and started chatting with the Cardinal.

Marcus noticed one of the priests, a big handsome man, whom Cassidy had introduced as Monsignor Mooney, was whispering in the ear of the giggling wife of the Attorney General. He was stroking her leg under the overhanging tablecloth. Marcus stifled the urge to laugh out loud. A blind man could see what was going on.

Cassidy was chatting with the Cardinal when Marcus suddenly froze. *There was no mistaking that voice!* A Southern accent you could cut with a knife! He turned around slowly and saw that it was a man leaning against a pillar surrounded by a group of men who were hanging on his every word. The man was at least three-hundred pounds with a face that had cost a fortune in whisky. He nudged Cassidy's arm. "Who is that man leaning against the pillar?"

Cassidy glanced over. "See you later, Your Eminence," he said as he straightened up.

"That is Mr. Louis Robideau, The Chairman of the New York Stock Exchange. Why do you ask?"

Marcus shrugged. "I just noticed he's got a big crowd of admirers and was curious as to who he was."

"Yes, they are all his flunkeys. He's got a lot of power. That's why they all suck up to him. Look at him, you'd think he was the damn President!"

They continued on their walk till Cassidy stopped to talk to someone he knew.

Marcus politely left him with his friend and made his way back to where Robideau was holding court. He thought for a minute how to approach Robideau without making it obvious. There were too many people around.

He took his notebook out of his pocket and hurriedly scribbled on it. He tore the page out and waited for a waiter to come round with the fake drinks. When the next waiter came round, Marcus gave him the note and a five dollar bill. He nodded in Robideau's direction.

"Would you please give that gentleman this note." The waiter smiled and went directly over to Robideau and handed him the note. Robideau glanced at the note which read:

Good evening, Mr. Black. Where can we talk? Mr. Brown.

He looked around with a mixture of surprise and anxiety. Marcus waited till he caught his eye and nodded in recognition. Robideau stuffed the note in his pocket and excused himself from the crowd. He brushed past Marcus and whispered. "Room 102 in five minutes."

By the time Marcus had made his exit from the ballroom and found the room ten minutes had elapsed. He knocked on the door and Robideau opened it immediately. He pulled Marcus in and glanced along the hall before shutting the door and locking it.

"Did anyone see you coming in here?" he asked brusquely.

Marcus shook his head. "No, I'm not stupid. Nobody knows I'm here."

Robideau sat on an armchair. He did not ask Marcus to sit down.

"What do you want, Mr. Brown, and just who the hell are you?"

If that's your attitude pal, then so be it. Marcus leaned over him. There was only one way to deal with bullies and that was to bully them. Something useful he had learned from his father. "Listen carefully, Mr. Robideau, or Mr. Black, or whatever your name is. We can do this the easy way or the hard way. You know very well who I am and why I'm here, or we would not be in this room together. Don't interrupt! I have written down every transaction you have given me since I started, along with the profits you made. Dates; amounts; everything is on paper. Your two stockbrokers can be traced through the phone numbers I have. It will be an easy matter for the authorities to check them and put two and two together. Now what's it to be?"

Robideau knew he was beaten. *That stupid bastard Walker. If this got out he would not only be ruined, he'd likely go to jail. Now the question was what did this guy want?* He gestured to a chair. In a voice quivering with emotion he said, "How much do you want for the records you made?"

Marcus sat down. "Calm down, Mr. Robideau. We can leave this room with an agreement between gentlemen. I am just as greedy as you are, and I don't give a damn about the past. If you agree, I will take the heat for Weir Tool if there is an inquiry. I'll put it down to dumb luck. After all, I'm just off the boat, and it was me who made the bundle. Now what I want is simply to carry on the way we were. Only Walker is out of the picture. Also, I'm interested to know just how you get the information. If you agree, then nothing will change for you, and I will take Walker's place. Only I won't have a middleman. Is that clear? Now you know the alternative, so I want an answer now or I'm going straight to the authorities and then the newspapers!"

Robideau's florid face had turned chalk white at the thought of the consequences of his actions. He regained his composure and said, "That's not much of a choice, is it?"

Marcus smiled. "Indeed it is not, Mr. Robideau."

Robideau loosened his tie. He had no choice at all, and Brown knew it. He was back in control now. After all, he needed a middleman, and it might as well be this guy.

"All right, Mr. Brown, we have an agreement. I'll deal with Walker myself. To answer your question, in my position, I can sway the value of stocks simply by starting rumors. It's as simple as that. In the case of Weir tool, I let it be known that General Motors was interested in buying it. When the stocks went up, I simply let it be known that the deal fell through. The secret is keep it small and steady. No big amounts, it attracts attention. Now I have a question for you. Where the hell did you get the money?"

Marcus held his finger to his lips. "None of your business, Mr. Robideau. Now give me your phone number and I'll be in touch after the holidays. I don't think I'll be with Hawthorne's much longer."

Robideau was relaxed now. "Neither will Walker!" he said grimly. He gave Marcus his private phone number.

Marcus patted his back. "Don't do anything about Walker till we talk more. We'd better get back to the party. One other thing, why do you need a middleman? Why not make the calls direct?"

Robideau laughed out loud. "How did you find me, Mr. Brown?"

"It was your accent that gave you away!"

Robideau was still laughing. "You just answered your own question!"

Marcus looked at him and joined in the laughter. *Now I don't need to ask Reynolds after all.* "Glad to do business with you, Mr. Robideau. Let's get back to the party and have a good time!"

Robideau stood up. "Yeah, why the hell not!" The two men shook hands and made their way back to the ballroom.

"Where have you been, Mr. Brown? We were beginning to think you got lost!" Cassidy asked when Marcus returned to the table.

"You were right, I did get lost looking around this place. It is enormous, isn't it?" Just then the band started playing a new song. Marcus held his hand out to Emily Norwood. "May I have the pleasure, Miss Norwood?" he asked in his Oxford accent.

Emily stood up. "Certainly, Mr. Brown," she answered breathlessly. They made their way to the dance floor.

"I wish you would call me Mark. Mr. Brown sounds so formal, don't you think?" he murmured smoothly as they glided across the floor.

She smiled up at him. Summoning up her courage, she said, "Only if you call me Emily."

"By all means, Emily. Do you know how beautiful you are tonight? I haven't been able to take my eyes off you." He turned the full charm treatment on her, and by the time the dance was over, Emily wanted to find out more about this handsome young Englishman.

When they returned to their seats, she turned to speak to her father. "Father, Mr. Brown is all alone here in New York. Could we not ask him for Christmas dinner tomorrow? It must be terribly lonely for him at this time of year."

Marcus pretended to be embarrassed. This was even better than he'd hoped.

Mrs. Norwood immediately said. "But of course, you must come!"

"Not at all, Mrs. Norwood. I wouldn't dream of imposing myself!"

"Nonsense, my boy!" Norwood boomed. "Great idea, Emily. I wish I'd thought to ask myself. No argument, Mr. Brown. You're coming for Christmas dinner and that's that!"

Marcus tried hard to look uncomfortable. "Well, it looks like I've no choice. Thank you very much, I'll be happy to come."

"Excellent. We're having it in the Hamptons this year. You don't have a car now, do you, Mr. Brown?"

"No I don't," Marcus replied.

"It doesn't matter. Give me your address and I'll have you picked up. Will ten be all right with you?"

"Yes, ten will be just fine, thank you."

"Wait a minute, Mr. Brown," Mrs. Norwood said. "We are all going to ten o'clock Mass in the Cathedral. Why don't you get picked up at nine thirty and that way you can join us and we'll all go to the Hamptons together?"

"Mother!" Emily said. "We don't even know if Mr. Brown is Catholic!"

Marcus mind raced. He knew that Mrs. Norwood knew exactly what she was doing. He smiled at her and said, "What a great idea! I was planning to go to six o'clock Mass to miss the crowds. You know, they all come out of the woodwork at Christmas!"

"Excellent! Now don't forget to bring an overnight bag with you." Mrs. Norwood smiled. Only a Catholic would have answered like that.

Marcus returned her smile as he stood up. "Now, Emily, how about another dance?" As they waltzed their way round the floor Marcus was formulating the next part of his plan. Everything was falling into place. Never in his wildest dreams could things have gone better. It was just a matter of time till everything fell into place.

"You know, Emily," he whispered. "I've a feeling that this is going to be my best Christmas ever!"

She looked up at him with shining eyes and said, "Yes, Mark, the best ever!"

Chapter 6

Mary Ellen was getting faster at sewing the shirt collars. She was up to thirty an hour, nearly as much as Benjamin. A month had passed since the Swerskys had taken her in. Her face had healed up and she was feeling better physically but she still had the homesickness. She wrote to her family and told them about having the money stolen, but did not mention that Uncle John had hit her or that she had been raped by a priest. She knew nobody could imagine such a thing happening. She told them not to worry, she had a place to stay and was saving up to pay Uncle John his money. She started looking for a real job, but found herself afraid to stay out when it got dark. Every day she would walk around the crowded neighborhood, which was ninety percent Jewish. She was fascinated by the babble of a dozen different languages and often stood and listened to the haggling between the buyers and sellers, some of whom were arguing in different languages. The daily experience of street life in the Lower East Side helped her to stop brooding about her misfortunes. The Swerskys encouraged her and occasionally they would accompany her in the mornings. After looking for a week she found a job in an office starting as a filing clerk. It would do till she could get a job as a stenographer. The pay was not bad, twenty dollars a week.

She was getting used to New York, but still had no peace of mind. She could not shake the feeling that something else was going to happen to her. The trauma of the rape was causing her to have nightmares and the homesickness kept dragging her down. Her natural optimism had deserted her and she was afraid she would never be happy again. She decided not to say anything to the Swerskys, but decided it would be better if she just saved up her money and went back to Ireland. Then she would be safe again living with her family.

One weekend, the elder son, David, came home to visit. On the Saturday morning they were talking and Rachel told him all about what happened to Mary Ellen. He listened to the story carefully and asked her a few questions without upsetting her because she was trying to forget what happened.

"The reason we didn't go to the police was nobody would believe her and they're all Irish anyway!" Benjamin finished telling David the story.

David Swersky sat thinking about what they had told him. He had the rare gift of being able to think things out logically in a very short time. He never answered a question or said anything without thinking out the consequences. Most of the time he never said anything at all. He considered small talk the waste of time, which would be better spent reading and broadening his mind. He had graduated first in his class and was the youngest lawyer to be called to the bar in the history of the State. He had been hired by the most prestigious firm in New York, and was the first Jew they had ever hired.

"Both the theft and the rape should have been reported at the time, Father. You made a mistake."

Benjamin stood up angrily. "They would have arrested her or worse. I was afraid of what they would do!"

David held up his hand. "Calm down, Father. It's not too late. These people should be accountable for their actions." He looked at Mary Ellen. "I am willing to help you, Mary Ellen. I think you should report this matter to the police. We have the names of the three men involved. That is all we need."

"What good will it do? They will never admit it and I'll look like a fool for waiting so long."

"I agree they will not be punished. It will not even go to court. You have no witnesses or any evidence." They all looked at him as if he was crazy.

At last Rachel asked the question they were all thinking. "Then what is the point! It will not do any good and might make things worse! They might even charge her for God's sake!"

David shook his head. "Nothing will happen to you, Mary Ellen. I am a lawyer and you are my client. The whole point is I want them to deny it and I want it in writing. If this O"Brien is doing this on a regular basis, eventually someone else will make a complaint, and when they do I will have your case to throw in the mix. Maybe there has already been a complaint against them. The priest will be harder to get at. The Church is the most secretive organization on earth. If someone in power knows what Mooney is doing they will likely transfer him to another country. Remember, most of the judges and politicians in this state are Catholic. Now, are you willing to do this, Mary Ellen? Remember, if your testimony can help catch them, even if it's years from now, you may save another young girl from what happened to you."

Mary Ellen thought for a while. The last thing David had said had made her mind up. "What do you want me to do? I'm afraid to face these people and get made out a liar. You know they won't admit anything."

"All I want you to do is sign a legal document naming me as your attorney. You won't have to meet any of them. I will send them all letters to arrange a meeting with them individually. They will deny all involvement in any wrongdoing, but all I want is for them to deny it in writing. I'm gambling that they don't know they don't have to sign anything, but I'll put it in such a way that they probably will go along with it. The housekeeper will be first. The way you describe her, she won't have the cunning to deny ever seeing you."

You mean I don't have to confront them?"

David smiled. "Exactly!"

Benjamin stood up and said. "I still don't see what good this will do. All you will get is three written statements, all denying any knowledge! What use is that?"

"Right now, no good at all. But I've learned that you never know what is around the corner, and maybe, just maybe I'll run into one of them someday. When that day comes I will be ready."

Benjamin shrugged his shoulders. "That's an awful lot of maybes, David. I think you're wasting your time!"

"Whatever you say, Father. Anyway, Mary Ellen, I want you to tell me every detail about what happened starting from you got off the boat. Try not to miss anything out. I'll prepare a document for you to sign, and don't worry, it's pro bono. That means free in lawyer's language."

Rachel waved her arms above her head and shouted, "For this you go to university? For this you go to law school? You take clients for free? You'll be getting Jewish lawyers a bad name, David!"

They all roared with laughter and soon the talk changed to the exciting prospect of the Swerskys opening their own shop.

David Swersky's plan worked out as he predicted. He timed his visit to St. Joseph's when Monsignor Mooney was saying Mass. He first went to the housekeeper and asked her if she remembered Mary Ellen. At first she denied ever meeting her until he told her they were thinking of charging Monsignor Mooney. The housekeeper exploded.

"Ungrateful little wench!" Bridie spluttered. "The good man takes her in off the streets and this is the thanks he gets! Sure, I'll write a statement. Give me a pen and paper!" She took David into the kitchen and David coached her to write a statement testifying that Mary Ellen had indeed spent a night in the house, but no rape or assault had taken place to her knowledge. She signed the paper with a flourish.

"That should fix her. If you need me again, I'll swear on a stack of Bibles the good man never touched her!" As David was putting the paper into his briefcase, Monsignor Mooney came in, still with his vestments on after saying Mass. David handed him his card and introduced himself as Mary Ellen's lawyer and the reason for the visit.

"Your housekeeper has just made a deposition that refutes my client's claim of assault. If you and Officer O'Brien would do the same I think we can put this matter to rest. It's quite clear to me it's my client's word against three, so I think I can safely say this matter will be closed."

Mooney looked at him suspiciously. "How do I know you are the girl's lawyer? What was her name again? I've taken a few girls and boys in off the streets for their own safety, I really can't remember them all." David pulled out Mary Ellen's deposition and her signature appointing him as her attorney.

"I'm sure Bridie here will remind you which one it was, Father,"David said smoothly. "Now, would you like to give me a short statement and I'll be on my way!"

Mooney knew he was trapped. "Of course, now what poor misguided girl was this, Bridie? Tell me about her and maybe I'll remember."

"O'Brien brought her here. Remember, she had a terrible black eye?"

Mooney furrowed his brow as if in deep thought and then said, "Now I remember her. And this girl is claiming that she was assaulted here at Saint Joseph's?" he said in feigned astonishment.

"I'm afraid so, Father. Worse, she claims that she was raped."

Mooney sat down as if in shock. "The poor girl, she must be ill. What would you like me to write?"

What a performance! David gave him the pen and paper. He made sure he got a good look at Mooney's right hand. He saw the scar of the bite mark where Mary Ellen said it would be. "Just the truth, Father, and that should take care of it."

Mooney wrote his statement and signed it. David took it and put it in beside Bridie's statement. "Just one thing, could you tell me what precinct Officer O'Brien is in?"

Abruptly Mooney stood up. "I've no idea. Now if there's nothing else?"

"I'm sorry to have bothered you. Good day, I'll let myself out,"David said as he walked quickly to the front door.

As soon as the door closed, Mooney turned on Bridie in a fury. He grabbed her by the throat and hissed. "You stupid cow! Why did you write a statement? You should have denied everything and told that little Jew to get lost."

"But I lied to protect you! If you'd learn to keep your trousers on none of this would have happened. Anyway, you wrote a statement too!"

Raging, Mooney threw her to the ground. "After you admitted she was here I had no choice, you stupid bitch! And never talk to me like that again, do you understand!" His face was contorted with fury.

Terrified, Bridie nodded her head. "I'm sorry, Father, I didn't mean it!" she said weakly.

He looked at her with contempt. "Get up and get the breakfast on, and when you finish get over to confession and confess the sins you committed this morning!" He stormed into the lounge to get a drink. He poured a large glass of whiskey and downed it in one gulp, then immediately poured another. He sat in his armchair and started thinking about what had happened. *He had been told he was being promoted to bishop in the near future. It had been arranged for him to meet Cardinal O'Leary on Christmas Eve to get his approval. If anything like this got out he would be doomed to a life in some remote parish, or worse, put in a monastery.* He looked at the card David had given him. Wills and Watson. *How the hell could that girl afford a lawyer, especially a lawyer from such a prestigious firm?*

He sipped at his drink. *Well, the lawyer had told him the matter would be closed after taking the statements. The girl had no proof of any assault, and if not for the stupid housekeeper nobody would ever have known she was even in the house! O'Brien would say the same on his statement. Still, there was something not quite right about this. Why would the lawyer come knowing he would never get an admission of guilt? Could it be he just wanted to show the girl he was trying? Yes! That must be it. He looked at the card again. Yes, for the fee this guy was charging no wonder he wanted to show her something for her money. He flipped the card into the fireplace and watched it burn. The little Jew was right. The matter was closed.*

It did not take David long to find O'Brien. A few phone calls to the local precincts did the trick. He arranged to go down to the station the next morning to meet O'Brien. O'Brien listened to what David had to say and was openly hostile in his answer.

"Are you accusing me? You lawyers are all the same, coming after hard-working cops. All I did was try to help a girl in distress and you come here accusing me. Get the hell out of here!"

Calmly, David replied, "I'll go if you want, but I don't think Monsignor Mooney will be happy at the fact you never corroborated his statement." He pulled the statement out of his briefcase and showed it to O'Brien.

He read it over and said sullenly, "All right, I'll write a statement, but I don't know what good it will do. What do you want me to write?"

"Just the truth will do."

O'Brien sat down at a desk and started writing. "What did you say the girl's name was again?" he asked.

"Mary Ellen O'Neill," David replied. At that moment he knew that Mary Ellen was one of many. This low-life bastard was procuring young girls for the priest!

O'Brien finished his statement and signed it. He handed it to David and said slyly, "You know, I should charge you for this! I bet you lawyers charge plenty for your statements!"

David looked at him with disgust and turned on his heel and walked out of the station. '*This one likes money! Something to remember!*'

"Well, how did you get on?" Rachel asked when David returned home.

"Just as I thought. They all admitted that Mary Ellen spent the night in the church house but they swear there was no assault. I have their statements. I checked at the courthouse for any other complaints but came up empty."

"So you wasted your time!" Rachel shook her head. David never answered her.

"Answer your mother!" Benjamin said angrily.

David shrugged. "If you think I wasted my time. I'm not going to argue with you. Maybe I have. But as far as I'm concerned, I wanted them to deny it in writing. You see, I believe Mary Ellen and I know they are lying."

"In writing! What's the difference if you can't prove it anyway?"

David held his hand up and said quietly, "No, I can't prove anything now. But I will be watching and waiting. They will slip up sometime, because I know they have done this to others. Now let's leave it at that! Mary Ellen wants to forget it and we'll just make it harder for her if we continue to argue!"

"Yes!" Mary Ellen said. "Now when are you going to open your own shop? Have you found a place yet?"

They all took their seats at the table. Rachel spoke first, "We've been waiting for a good time to tell you." She appeared flustered and embarrassed. "David, will you explain things to Mary Ellen please?"

"Of course, mother," David said. "Mary Ellen, my parents were afraid to tell you, but we have found an ideal location for a tailor's shop on West 25th street. The only problem is that the apartment that comes with it has only one room. So they can't put you up in it! You know they won't see you out on the street. They worry about you. So you can see their dilemma!"

"There's no dilemma at all!" Mary Ellen replied. "You must take the place. I can't be living with you the rest of my life. I was going to start looking for a place of my own anyway, now that I have a job. The only thing stopping me was I didn't know where to look, but now I do."

"And where might that be?" Rachel asked anxiously.

"Actually I'm thinking of looking for a place near a little tailor's shop on West 25th Street!"

Benjamin clapped his hands. "Excellent! That way we can keep an eye on you!" They all embraced and started planning to move before Christmas and Hannukah.

Mary Ellen did find a flat half a block away from the Swersky's shop. She went to the opening the week before Christmas and watched how happy they both were to have realized their ambition. They knew they were about to start working even longer hours, but that paled in comparison to the fact that at last they were their own bosses.

On Christmas Eve, Mary Ellen went along to the Swersky's flat to visit. The whole family was there celebrating Hannukah. They all had a good dinner and a few glasses of wine before the inevitable argument started between Benjamin and his younger son Isaac. Isaac had given up his religion and Benjamin could not understand it. They argued constantly, but Isaac was determined and nothing Benjamin said would change his mind. David and Rachel were used to it and chatted away as if they were in a different room.

After a lot of shouting and screaming, Benjamin said, "Wait a minute, Isaac, let's hear what Mary Ellen thinks." He asked Mary Ellen, "What do you think of a man who gives up his religion because he thinks it's old-fashioned!"

"I never said that!" Isaac shouted. "You're twisting my words, Father. I simply think that we should change a bit to suit the modern world. After all it's the twentieth century!"

"Gentlemen, if you are asking me about religion, I cannot answer because I have given mine up too!" Mary Ellen replied.

David, who had been listening to the argument, spoke up. "Now why did you give up your religion, Mary Ellen?"

"You know why, David. After what happened to me I swore I'd never go to church again."

Rachel moved over behind her and put her hands on her shoulders. "And no wonder, you poor girl." Benjamin and Isaac nodded in agreement.

"Yes, we are asking the wrong person about religion. I'm sorry child, I didn't think," Benjamin said, patting her hand.

"I think you're wrong to give your religion up because of one man!" David said abruptly. They all looked at him in astonishment.

"David! Apologize to Mary Ellen at once," Rachel said.

Shocked, Mary Ellen stared at him. "David, you of all people know what happened. Why would you say such a thing?"

David answered sympathetically. "Now listen to me, Mary Ellen. You told me that back in Ireland you loved going to church every Sunday with all your friends and neighbors. You said you felt nearer to God when you were praying. Isn't that right?"

Mary Ellen bowed her head. The memories of home washed over her like a wave. "Yes David, I did," she said quietly.

"All I'm saying is, if you want to give up your religion you should have a better reason than that. One rotten priest is not the Catholic Church. Why stop going to church because of him! You're only depriving yourself of some solace. Have you not been hurt enough without making it worse for yourself? No, Mary Ellen, don't give him that victory. I say you go back and pray to God for guidance. There again, if you have other reasons for not going back that will make a difference."

"That's quite enough, David. Can't you see you're upsetting her!" Rachel hugged Mary Ellen. "Don't listen to him, my dear."

Mary Ellen smiled at Rachel. "I'm not upset at David, I was just thinking of home." She wiped her tears away. "David is right. I do miss going to Mass, and I'm not going to stop going because of that monster."

David sat back in his chair. "Just what I wanted to hear, Mary Ellen. I'm sure it will help your recovery."

"Yes, I'll go to Mass tomorrow morning for Christmas. I feel better already,"

David looked at his mother and said with a smile, "Well, I got Mary Ellen back to church, I think you should try the same with Isaac!"

"Good idea!" Benjamin said. "What about it, Rachel!"

"I think that's a father's job, Benjamin, but we've had enough religion for one night. Let's change the subject and talk about something else. Now who wants more wine?"

Mary Ellen did go back to attending church and she did feel better for it. She started to feel that she would recover from her ordeal. By the end of January she was beginning to put some money away in a bank account. She had decided to get back to Ireland as soon as she could and try to repay Uncle John from there. She had made up her mind that she had just about enough of America.

One morning at work, Mary Ellen fainted in the office. When they revived her, the manager insisted she see a doctor before she came back to work. That was the day Mary Ellen found out she was expecting a baby. After the doctor told her, she was dumbstruck. Never for a moment had she given a thought to the possibility. She made her way back to the Swersky's shop in a daze. When she went in she asked to see Rachel alone.

Rachel took her into the back shop and sat her down. "What's the matter? You look as if you've seen a ghost!"

Mary Ellen started weeping. In between sobs she managed to tell Rachel the news. "What will I do?" she cried. "A baby! What will I do with a baby! I'm not even married! Now no one will want me. Oh, Rachel, what will I do?" She started sobbing uncontrollably.

While Rachel was comforting her, Benjamin came back to see what was wrong. Rachel told him and he just shook his head and sat down.

"What more can happen to her? Goddamn that priest! Now he'll have to pay! He can't get away with this. I'm going to call David."

He left before Rachel could reply. She took Mary Ellen upstairs and made a pot of tea. There was nothing Rachel could say that made any difference. The damage was done. As Rachel tried to comfort Mary Ellen, she knew within herself there was nothing anyone could do. She just hoped David would know what to do.

Benjamin came back and said that David was on his way. By this time Mary Ellen was lying in the Swersky's bed weeping. Benjamin went back down to the shop knowing he was just in the way. Rachel was sitting next to her holding her hand. She was still holding her hand when David arrived. He came into the room and nodded at his mother.

He sat on the bed and said. "Stop weeping, Mary Ellen. You'll just make yourself ill. Come to the table and drink some tea and we'll talk. Weeping will just make you feel worse." He raised her to a sitting position. "Go and wash your face and Mother will heat the tea."

They helped her to her feet and she went to wash up while they went into the living room.

"I don't know how much more that girl can take, David. I'm afraid she'll do something stupid. What will we do?"

Just then Mary Ellen came in and sat down. Her eyes were swollen with the crying and she was as white as a sheet. She looked at them both with a strange look on her face. "I want to kill myself! I don't know what else to do. I can't have a baby. I've no husband and will not be able to care for a baby."

David took her hand in his. "Listen to me, Mary Ellen. You will not kill yourself. You will have this baby. And yes, you will care for it, do you understand?"

"But how? I'll lose my job! Nobody will want anyone with a baby."

"Plenty of women look after children without husbands. What about all the widows? Some of them have more than one child and they manage to survive."

"I'm not a widow and don't know the first thing about babies. And now I'll never even have a husband."

"Mark my words, Mary Ellen. You will have a husband and family. Now, I want you to do me a favor."

Mary Ellen looked at him dolefully. "What favor can I do for you?"

"Take one day at a time. Don't think of doing anything foolish like having an abortion. Come here every day for the next week and we'll work something out, that's the favor I want. Now, I think that's enough for today."

"Oh, my God. An abortion! How could you think of such a thing!" Shocked, Mary Ellen stared at him.

David sipped his tea. "I'm sorry, I shouldn't have said that. I know you wouldn't murder your own child. But you see if you kill yourself, you are also killing your child. So like I said, Mary Ellen, that's enough for today." He knew the mention of an abortion would shock her out of her despair.

She sat up straight in her chair. "I should think you'd be sorry! And you're right, David. That is enough for one day," she said angrily.

"One more thing, Mary Ellen," David said kindly. "I wouldn't tell the boss you're expecting just yet."

Rachel felt a great sense of relief. David had known exactly how to handle this. She knew then that Mary Ellen would be all right.

Mary Ellen went back to work and took David's advice not to tell anyone she was expecting a baby. She went through the motions of working and living day to day. She worried constantly about what would happen to her. She knew she could not stay where she was. It was a matter of time before she was fired. They did not look kindly on unmarried girls who got pregnant. The

Swersky family could not do enough for her. She went along most nights after work for the company. They offered to keep her till the baby was born. But she knew they could not keep her in their little flat. She did not have enough to go back to Ireland, and, anyway, her family must never know she was having a baby. It would shame them all over the county. So what was she to do?

One night she was going through her belongings, sorting things out when she came across an envelope with the name J. Switcher written on it. She opened it and started reading. It was a note from the old man wishing her a good life in America and an invitation to visit him anytime she wanted. She sat deep in thought for a long time. *She had nothing but bad luck in New York. Maybe if she went to see Mr. Switcher things would be different. After all, there was nothing holding her back.* As she didn't have a phone in the flat, she resolved to call him from work and see how he was before deciding on anything. Anyway, she didn't have to decide anything till she lost her job.

The next day Mary Ellen called Jimmy Switcher from work. He was both surprised and delighted to hear from her. He told her that when he got back home he discovered that his sick sister had died when he was on the Mauretania and the housekeeper couldn't get in touch with him. As there were no relatives in Detroit at the time, the local church had taken care of the burial. Shortly after that the housekeeper left, saying he didn't need her anymore, so he was on his own. Now he wanted to know when she was coming to visit him.

Mary Ellen had made her mind up not to tell him just yet what had happened. She wanted to consult with David Swersky first and follow his advice. Suddenly an impulse came over her and she told him everything that had happened in a torrent of words. By the end of the story she felt herself breaking down again. Before he could reply, she hung the phone up, saying she would call at the same time the following day. She hurried to the washroom to wipe her tears and pull herself together.

'Why did I tell him like that? What came over me?' She wondered why had she blurted out everything like that, it would just upset the old man.

The next day she called him back to apologize.

He wouldn't hear of it. "Mary Ellen, whether you wanted to tell me or not, I think deep down you had to tell someone. Why don't you come out to

Detroit and stay here till you have the baby. As a matter of fact, I've been thinking about hiring another housekeeper. Why don't you consider it? It won't pay much, but I've got a big house and there's plenty of room for you. You say your friends have no room and you don't want to impose, so there's nothing to keep you in New York. You don't have to make a decision right now, but promise me you'll think about it."

Mary Ellen promised him she would think about it. The next time she was at the Swerskys and David came over she broached the subject with them.

Rachel was all against it. "You hardly know this old man, haven't you learnt anything? Your problem is you trust everyone. He could be a murderer for all you know!" Rachel scolded her.

"He's nothing of the sort!" Mary Ellen said indignantly. "Granted, I trusted Marcus Browning to treat me better than he did, but you can't blame me for trusting a priest for God's sake, it's the way I was brought up!"

"Oh, I'm not blaming you for anything, dear. I just don't want anything else to happen to you. I'd feel better if you stayed here so I can take care of you,"

David, who had been sitting in silence, said, "From what you've told us, I don't think Mr. Switcher is a murderer. But before you decide, why don't you give me a few days to check up on him and see if he is what he says he is."

Rachel interrupted impatiently. "How can you check up on someone in Detroit? It can't be that easy."

"Our firm has contacts all over the country. We do background checks on people every day, so it's no big thing."

"I don't know," Mary Ellen replied. "I feel like I'm sneaking behind his back, and him being so kind to me."

"I understand how you are feeling," David said. 'But you must understand how we feel. It would ease all our minds, and you must admit, you are a bit too trusting of people. Now what do you say?"

"Well, when you put it like that, I suppose it's the best thing to do, but I still feel bad about it," Mary Ellen said reluctantly.

The next week Mary Ellen's mind was made up for her by two different occurrences. The first one was when David told her that Switcher was just as he said he was and there was nothing against him. The second one was that she was let go from her job. She was politely and firmly told that the firm did not employ pregnant women, especially single pregnant women. Mary Ellen was too naïve to understand how they knew she was expecting because she hadn't noticed the knowing looks and giggles directed at her when she wasn't looking. She decided to take Switcher's offer and go to Detroit, at least until the baby was born.

The Swersky family were not too happy about her going, but they told her that if she wanted to come back she was welcome. Benjamin was livid with anger about the fact that the priest responsible was getting away scot free. He smashed his fist on the table.

"David, you're the lawyer. There must be something that you can do to make this man accountable!" he said in a fury.

"Believe me, Father. If there was something then I would do it. I've made inquiries and the consensus is it's his word against hers. I'm sorry, but at the moment there's nothing can be done."

"Couldn't you at least tell him there's a child coming? Maybe then he'll take responsibility!"

"Yes!" Rachel said. "He doesn't know about the baby, maybe it will change his mind. You must tell him, David."

David held his hands up in surrender. "All right, I'll inform him, but I doubt if it'll do any good."

"We'll never know till you tell him!" Benjamin said angrily.

"Just a minute," Mary Ellen said. "If anyone should be telling him it should be me, not David!"

They all stared at her.

"Do you think you could confront him, Mary Ellen?" David asked her gently.

She thought for a minute, and suddenly the memory of that night came back to her. She remembered the room door opening and the smell of whisky and… "No! I don't ever want to go near that man again!" She held her hands over her face and started sobbing quietly.

Rachel moved quickly to comfort her. "Well, David, it's up to you. It certainly can't do any harm."

A few days later David went to Saint Josephs to see Monsignor Mooney. A woman he didn't recognize answered the door of the church house. She told him that the Monsignor was now in another state, and no, she didn't know the name of the parish. From there David went back to the office and called the Archdiocese. After a few more calls he found out that Monsignor Mooney was now a bishop and was attending Boston College. He called Boston

College and after getting the run-around for a while, eventually he found a secretary who told him that Bishop Mooney was taking business accounting and teaching theology at the same time. Quite a brilliant man, the Bishop. And very handsome too, if you want to know. Diplomatically, David managed to get the Bishop's phone number without hearing any more about him from the woman.

"Hello, your Grace, this is David Swersky from New York. We spoke before about a young woman, Mary Ellen O'Neill."

To David's surprise, Mooney answered immediately, "Yes, I remember, the poor girl with the black eye. How can I help you?" he asked unctuously.

"The young lady is expecting a baby, and she claims that you are the father." David waited to hear his reaction.

Without the slightest change in tone, Mooney replied, "Are you looking for help for the poor girl, Mr. Swersky. Perhaps I could help to get her into a convent for the duration of her confinement." His voice took on a slightly menacing tone. "Or perhaps she needs another kind of help. By that I mean there are some fine psychiatric institutions? Obviously this girl is deeply disturbed. You have the depositions from myself and the others. If this offer of help is not acceptable, I suggest you never call here again with such accusations or I will take legal action against both you and this girl. Is that understood?"

"Perfectly! Goodbye, your Grace." David replaced the receiver and sat looking at it, thinking, *What a scumbag, and a bishop no less.*

The last thing Bishop Mooney wanted was any sort of scandal. He was approaching what could be the defining point of his career in the church.

He was first in his accounting class and was being touted as a potential financial adviser to Cardinal O'Leary. That was the job Mooney wanted. He would have an office in New York City and the power to control tens of millions of dollars. All he needed to do was keep his marks up to scratch, which came easy for him. The hard thing was to avoid being caught with any of the three women he was having affairs with. Boston College was not that big, and he had to be very wary both of the women he was seeing and the other students. So far he had been both careful and lucky. But if he got the job in New York, he would have the whole city as his playground and less chance of being caught. The fact that Mary Ellen O'Neill was carrying his child must not be allowed to interfere with his plans, so therefore neither she nor her child meant anything to him.

David duly told the family that Bishop Mooney did not want to know anything about Mary Ellen, so they had to resign themselves to the fact that there was nothing they could do. Mary Ellen called Switcher and made arrangements to go to Detroit at the end of March. She had paid her rent up to the end of the month and it would give her a couple of weeks to spend with the Swerskys before she left.

When the day came for her to leave, the whole Swersky family saw her to the train station. David gave her his card and told her to call him whenever she wanted. Just before she boarded the train, Benjamin gave her an envelope and they all hugged her and said their goodbyes.

"This reminds me of when I left Ireland. I might never see you again,"Mary Ellen said tearfully.

"Not at all, girl," Rachel said. "You're only a phone call away and a day on the train, so dry your eyes. Remember, you promised to come back to show us your baby."

She boarded the train and made her way to her compartment and leaned out of the window. The deafening noise of the steam whistle drowned out all the shouted goodbyes as the train slowly started moving out of the station. Mary Ellen waved till she could no longer see them, then closed the window and sat down.

The train rapidly gained speed and the steady clicking of the wheels on the tracks made her think of the last time she had been on a train in England with her brother Robert. It seemed like years ago, so much had changed. *Was it only a few months ago that she had boarded the Mauretania with such high hopes for the future. Now everything was uncertain. Here she was going to live with a stranger with a baby on the way. How could things have gone so wrong for her?* She closed her eyes and prayed to God that she was doing the right thing going to live with Mr. Switcher.

The train journey took most of the day. She had to change trains in Buffalo, and it was after seven when the train steamed into Detroit. Jim Switcer was waiting for her as promised. When she saw him, all her fears left her. She knew instinctively that she could trust him.

"Well, Mary Ellen O'Neill," he said jovially. "You look just as beautiful as I remembered." He hurried over to hug her.

"Mr. Switcher, how can I thank you? I don't know what I would have done without you taking me in," she replied, relieved that he had shown up to meet her.

"Glad to have you, my dear. Now let's get you home, you must be tired out from the trip." He called a porter to get Mary Ellen's luggage and led the way to his car. He lived in Royal Oak, a leafy suburb of Detroit, in a tree-lined street with dark brown stone houses with front and back gardens. There was even a driveway and garage for the car.

He drove into the driveway, and said with pride, "This is it, Mary Ellen. It took a long time, but it's all mine now. Come in and I'll show you around."

To Mary Ellen the house was like a mansion. The main floor had a living room and dining room with a huge kitchen at the back that looked onto a big back yard surrounded by a tall cedar hedge. There was a washroom directly off the hall. He took her down to the basement where he had shelves full of jars of preserves and pickles. Upstairs there was a bathroom and three large bedrooms. He opened the door to one of them and said, "This was my daughter's room before she got married. I had it decorated for you, so I hope you like it."

"Like it! It's wonderful!" Mary Ellen had never had a room to speak of. In Ireland she had a little box room with a cot where she slept, but there wasn't even enough room for a chair in it. This room was big and had bay windows that overlooked the street. It was freshly painted and furnished with old, but solid furniture. "This is a marvelous house, better than I ever thought it would be. Thank you so much for putting me up."

"Come on and we'll get your luggage up here, and then we'll have a coffee and talk for a while. It's awhile since I've had someone to talk to."

After they put the luggage in the room, they went into the kitchen and Switcher made the coffee. They sat down at the table and Switcher said, "Now, Mary Ellen, start from the beginning and tell me everything that happened since I last saw you. Take your time, I got the most of it on the phone, but it's not the same as talking face to face."

Mary Ellen told him the whole story again, leaving nothing out, and when she finished, he said, "By God girl, what more can happen to you? How have you survived so many calamities and still keep your sanity?"

Mary Ellen took a long time to answer. "I suppose what kept me going is hoping things will get better. Hoping that someday all this will be a distant memory. Hoping that God will look after me in the future. Yes, Mr. Switcher, it's hope that keeps me going."

Switcher looked at her sympathetically. "You must be exhausted, so let's get you to bed and we'll talk more in the morning."

He escorted her upstairs and showed her where everything was and said goodnight. He went back downstairs and sat in his rocking chair smoking his pipe. Sorry as he was for Mary Ellen, he was glad she had come to him. He had been terribly lonely since the housekeeper left and was glad he had some company, even if it was temporary.

The next morning at breakfast Switcher explained the duties of a housekeeper to Mary Ellen. She could tell he was making it up as he went along.

She let him talk for a while before she interrupted, "I think I know how to keep house, Mr. Switcher. All you have to do is show me where things are around the house and I'll take over from there. You'll also have to show me where the shops are and tell me what foods you like."

"You haven't asked how much it pays?" he said, trying to change the subject.

"Well, full board is quite sufficient for me, thank you."

"Don't talk foolish, girl. Everyone needs a little money, it gives you independence. The job pays twenty dollars a week plus full board. I insist on it! It comes from the insurance money I got when my wife died. If we hadn't insured each other I would have had to sell the house, so don't argue. One other thing, would you please call me Jimmy, Mr. Switcher sounds too formal."

"Of course, Jimmy, and thank you for being so generous."

"Not at all, now this morning we'll go along to my doctor and get you registered. I imagine you'll be seeing him regularly from now on. Oh, I nearly forgot. That's a benefit that comes with the job."

Mary Ellen gasped. "But doctors cost a lot of money?"

"Don't you worry about that. Now there's one other thing I have for you. Now don't misunderstand me, it's for your own good." He took a small box from his pocket and gave it to her.

"Open it. It was my wife's wedding ring. I think you should wear it, and if anyone asks, I suggest you tell them you're a widow. Believe me, it will make your life a lot easier. People act funny around single girls who are expecting."

Mary Ellen looked at the worn gold band. "How long were you married?"

"Forty-five years,"Switcher answered.

"I understand what you are saying, and I'll do as you say. I will wear your wife's ring with pride, Mr. Switcher, and thank you for everything you are doing for me."

He stood up and said gruffly, "You're welcome, but remember you have a job to do, so it's not all free. Now I think we'll take a drive around this morning and show you the neighborhood."

"Well, maybe later. I'll have to make the beds and start cleaning the house. Then we'll have to decide what's for dinner. And then…"

Switcher interrupted, "Nonsense, everything can wait till tomorrow. Come on, get dressed and let's go!"

"But I'd better start my work," Mary Ellen protested.

Switcher thought for a moment and said, "I'm not hiring you officially till tomorrow, so you have nothing to do today, now will you get ready?"

Mary Ellen laughed out loud. "But I will start work tomorrow, agreed?" She held out her hand.

"Agreed." Switcher smiled back at her. "Now let's go!"

From the day Mary Ellen arrived in Detroit she started to feel better. The more she got to know Jimmy Switcher, the better she felt. He showed her around Detroit, which was different than any place she had ever been. It was a totally different city than New York. There were no high buildings in Royal Oak. The streets were wide and every house had a garden. With spring just starting, she amazed Switcher by creating a vegetable garden in the backyard and transforming his front yard into a dazzling display of shrubs and flowers. He would sit on his porch for hours and watch her working in the garden. Gradually Mary Ellen became more like her old self. She regularly looked at her little box and read the inscription, and like Benjamin Swersky had explained, the more she read it the more she felt her strength and confidence returning. She attended church regularly and joined a women's social club. They organized dances and bake sales for charity and Mary Ellen became friendly with a few of the other women.

It was a new beginning for both her and Switcher and they spent many nights together talking into the small hours. He had been a history teacher, and he never tired of answering her innumerable questions. She discovered that he went to play poker every Friday night, and once a month his three old friends would come to his house to play. After a few weeks she cajoled him into teaching her the science of playing five card stud. After a while, he found that instead of just keeping score had they been playing for real he would have been bankrupt.

After another losing night with her, he sighed and said, "Mary Ellen, you are a natural at this game, but I think you use your beauty to distract me. If we were playing for real money, you wouldn't win a hand because I simply wouldn't look at you!"

She shuffled the cards expertly and said innocently, "I'm sure I don't know what you're talking about. Anyway, we're not playing for real now, are we? But if you're so confident, why don't you let me play with your friends one night?"

"You'd be out of your depth!" he said indignantly. 'Anyway, you couldn't afford it. We play for big money!"

Mary Ellen knew they only played for nickels, but she just sighed and said, "Oh well, I'll just have to save up my money to get a game."

"I don't care how much you save up, you'll never get into our game. Not that I would mind, but the others wouldn't want a lady playing with us."

"I think they're just afraid a lady might beat them," Mary Ellen said with disdain.

Switcher glanced at her suspiciously, then he said, "Yes, maybe you're right, but you still won't get to play."

The months passed slowly during her pregnancy and spring changed to summer. Occasionally her friends from the church club came to visit her when she could no longer go to the functions. Switcher was glad to see her make friends with women who could tell her things about her condition that he knew nothing about. Mary Ellen had never experienced such temperatures. It regularly passed ninety degrees and she would sit on the porch with the old man drinking lemonade and fanning herself in a vain attempt to keep cool. On the fourth of July Switcher asked her if she would like to go and see a parade celebrating Independence Day. Sick of having to stay around the house, and fed up with her pregnancy, Mary Ellen was glad to get out. The day started out hot and only got hotter. By early afternoon the thermometer was approaching a hundred degrees. Switcher and Mary Ellen were sitting on the fold-down chairs they had brought with them, waiting for the bands to appear when she suddenly doubled over.

Gasping for breath she said, "Jimmy, it's time!"

Like a man forty years younger, Switcher took off to get the car. In what seemed like seconds he was back and speeding to the hospital. They made it with not a moment to spare and within an hour of arriving she had given birth to a healthy boy. The nurse came out and called Switcher in to see the baby. Mary Ellen was sitting up in bed holding him.

"Congratulations! He is a beautiful baby," Switcher said happily. "Have you thought of a name for him?"

" Oh yes, I've known his name for a long time now. His name is Patrick James O'Neill. Patrick after my father and James after his American grandfather."

Switcher went over and lifted the baby from her arms. "I'm honored, Mary Ellen. Thank you very much. Now, how soon can we all go home?"

Mary Ellen laughed weakly. 'I don't know, you'll have to ask the doctor. But there is one thing I want you to do."

Switcher was still doting over the baby. "Anything you want, my dear," he said absently.

'Will you call the Swerskys in New York and tell them the news for me?"

Switcher gave her the baby. "Of course, I'll call them as soon as I get home. Now I'm off to see the doctor to see when I can get you both out of here."

Chapter 7

After the Christmas Eve party at the Waldorf, Marcus took a taxi home and lay in bed thinking about what had transpired. He now realized what it was he wanted from life. *Money! The more money the better. He knew that with a lot of money came a lot of power. Everything he would do from now on would be for the purpose of making money.* Neither sentiment nor conscience would stand in his way. When he thought of the money he had made it gave him a feeling that he had never had before. Now he knew what he wanted from life! Everything else paled in comparison to the accumulation of wealth. The night at the Waldorf had been very profitable. Not only had he found Robideau and made a deal, which was perfect for him, but maybe not as important for him as meeting Emily Norwood. He had as much feeling for Emily as he did for the table in the corner. Only the table could not come close to the profit he saw in Emily Norwood. She was an only child, and heiress to a fortune. Marcus knew it wasn't just her looks that had kept her single for so long, it was her mother. Right from the start of the evening, Marcus knew that the way to Emily was through Mrs. Norwood. She was the type who watched every move he and Emily made. That was why he had to concentrate on getting her on his side. He had to find out more about being a Catholic, the mother would not entertain anyone who wasn't. If he could do that, Emily would be a pushover. He fell asleep wondering just how much the Norwoods were worth.

As promised, the limousine picked him up at nine thirty on Christmas morning.

"Good morning, sir, and a merry Christmas," the driver said as he held the door for Marcus.

"Merry Christmas to you too," Marcus replied. "What time will we get to the Cathedral?"

"Oh, about ten to ten, the roads are quiet this morning."

Marcus leaned over the seat and dropped a twenty on the front seat. "Could you make that ten past, I wonder?" Marcus asked. He wanted to be alone so he could observe the procedure of the Mass. He did not want Mrs. Norwood suspecting he was a non-Catholic, that would put paid to his plans before he even got started.

The driver picked the twenty up and slipped it into his pocket. "Ten past it is, sir!"

When Marcus went into the packed church fifteen minutes late, he had to stand at the back, so he could not see or hear what was happening. All he could tell was that the congregation took turns at standing, sitting and kneeling at different times. He looked around in desperation. If Mrs. Norwood asked him anything about this, he was sunk. He noticed a rack full of different pamphlets and took one of each and started hurriedly reading them. They were no help at all, not explaining anything about the Mass. He stuffed them in his pocket and resigned himself to hoping he could bluff his way through the day. Anyway, today was all about the birth of Christ and he knew the basics about that.

When the Mass finished, Marcus waited outside till he saw the Norwoods coming out. He met them at the bottom of the steps and apologized for being late, blaming it on the traffic. The Norwood limousines came to pick them up and Emily asked if she could ride with Marcus to keep him company on the two hour drive. Emily never mentioned the church, all she wanted to talk about was how happy she was that he was coming to dinner. Putting his misgivings about her mother aside, Marcus put all his considerable energy into charming Emily, asking her all about herself and her family, hanging on her every word and whispering how lucky he was to have such a beautiful young lady invite him along for dinner. Emily happily chattered all the way, flattered that such a handsome young man was taking such a keen interest in her.

As they approached Southampton, Marcus noticed that they were passing some enormous mansions, some of which were partly hidden by trees. Emily started telling him who the owners of these palaces were.

"See that one, that's the Vanderbilt cottage. They say it's bigger than the White House. There's the DuPont place, and coming up is the Rockefellers. It was a who's who of American millionaires.

Marcus was impressed, he couldn't wait to see if the Norwood cottage was anything like these fabulous houses he had just seen.

The Norwood cottage was not on the same scale as the ones they had passed, but it was impressive in its own right. There were fifteen rooms in the main house and there were two smaller guest houses. It had a fine view of the Atlantic and a private beach. *This property must be worth a fortune!*

Marcus did his best to listen as Emily showed him around, but his mind was racing. After he had been given the tour, they went into the enormous lounge where the guests were mingling before dinner. There was music playing in the background, someone was playing records on a gramophone. Emily never left his side, introducing him to everyone and making sure they all knew that he was her guest.

There were a lot of important people at the dinner party, and Marcus made sure he spent time cultivating as many as he could. Before long he had half a dozen invitations to dinner parties. After a while Emily excused herself to talk to some friends, and even though the drink was already being served, Marcus continued to drink only soft drinks. He had started to realize that it was no coincidence that when he stayed sober good things tended to happen.

Mrs. Norwood was very gracious to him, but he had the feeling that she would be a hard nut to crack. He was under no illusions that she was aware her daughter's main attribute was the Norwood fortune and that she would protect her like the proverbial lioness. Mr. Norwood introduced him to some very important people and dropped hints both ways that Marcus was a good man to know, even though he was a newcomer.

"That was very good of you flattering me like that to your friends. I know they are all business acquaintances, and I might be looking for a job after the New Year, and every introduction helps,"Marcus said.

Norwood looked at him in surprise. "What kind of a job, Mark? I thought you were happy at Hawthorne's."

"Remember I told you I wanted to be a bookie? That's what I want, and I'd like your advice on how to go about it."

Norwood narrowed his eyes and said quietly, "You're serious, aren't you?"

Marcus returned his gaze. "Never more so, Mr. Norwood. In three months I've made over three-hundred thousand dollars. How much would it take to get my foot in the door of a brokerage house?"

Norwood didn't answer right away. He took his time taking a cigar from his pocket and unwrapping it before going through an elaborate procedure of cutting it and lighting it. Marcus stood patiently watching him, knowing exactly what he was going to say. Greed always won in the end.

"I know you've done very well, Mark, but your luck can change very quickly. Before I answer your question, let me ask you one. It has all been luck, hasn't it?" He puffed at his cigar and looked out at the ocean view.

"I don't believe in luck, I have a system," Marcus replied. *Here it comes.* Norwood was checking if he had a source of information.

"And you still have a system?"

"A better one than before." Marcus had a slight smile on his lips.

Norwood took another puff of his cigar. "Come and see me on Wednesday morning in my office. I think I may have what you're looking for. Now I'd better see to my other guests, and I see Emily coming over for you. I'll see you later, enjoy yourself, Mark." The two men shook hands and Norwood left just as Emily came rushing over.

"I've been looking for you all over. I want to show you around the house," she said, taking his arm. Marcus tried to look enthusiastic as he let her guide him.

"I thought you'd never come back. Yes, let's have a look around, shall we?"

The tour around the house became a constant stream of introductions to everyone that Emily knew, no matter how vaguely. Marcus was the first young man who had shown an interest in her for a long time and she was determined that everyone should know about him. After they had stopped for a chat with Mrs. Norwood and a couple of her rich friends, Mrs. Wheeler and Mrs. Parsons, the two women immediately turned on Mrs. Norwood, salivating at the prospect of some gossip.

"Now, Mary Norwood, who is that young man and where did Emily meet him? I must say he's very charming! And they seem quite taken with one another!" Mrs. Parsons gushed.

"And very handsome too! Come on, don't leave us hanging!" Mrs. Wheeler added breathlessly.

"Slow down, girls, he's a business acquaintance of my husband's. We just met him last night at the Waldorf. I don't know much about him at all except he's only been in the States a few months." She sipped at her drink, watching Emily and Marcus mingling with the other guests. She turned to the two women and said without a hint of a smile, "But rest assured, girls, if he starts calling on Emily, I'll find out all about him quicker than you can say Jack Robinson!"

After what seemed like hours, Marcus managed to get Emily to show him the upstairs part of the house so he could get her alone for a while. She started to show him round the bedrooms, but he stopped her in the upstairs hall and sat her down onto a captain's bench. He sat beside her and took her hand in his. Emily Norwood never stood a chance. Within twenty minutes, he had her convinced that he had been looking for her all his life. He told her that he had fallen in love with her the first time he set eyes on her and couldn't keep his feelings hidden any longer. Nobody had ever spoken to her like that and he said it with such sincerity that she didn't doubt him for a moment. She was quite literally swept off her feet. He finished his virtuoso performance by asking her if she had any feelings for him.

"I have to ask you, Emily, I must know if you feel anything for me? Please be honest with me. I know it's too much to hope for that you, with all your beauty would be interested in me, but I have to ask because I simply can't go on without knowing how you feel." He dropped his head as if waiting for an axe to fall on his neck.

Emily replied in a voice choked with emotion, "I'm so glad you told me these things, Mark." She raised his head and looked into his eyes. "I do believe in love at first sight, and yes, I think I'm in love with you!"

Marcus struggled to keep his composure, it was going perfectly so far, and he did not want to jeopardize what he had accomplished so far. Without answering, he pulled her close to him and kissed her passionately on the lips.

As they sat close to each other, she whispered in his ear, "Let's go downstairs and tell my parents you will be calling on me, Mark."

Marcus did not answer right away, he pretended to think for a moment. "My dear, I'd love to, but we only met last night and people might get the wrong idea!"

"You mean they'll think you're taking advantage of me! Mark, I know I'm not the best looking girl in the world, and I know they all laugh behind my back because I've never had a beau, but it would mean everything to me if you did this for me."

For a moment, Marcus hesitated. Then he sighed and said, "Emily, I meant what I said, and if it will make you happy I'll do it, although I don't know what your parents will say. They may bar me from seeing you again, and I couldn't bear that."

She jumped to her feet, beaming with joy. "Don't worry about my parents, I'll take care of them." She kissed him again. "I know it's sudden, but I really can't wait to tell everyone. Thank you, Mark. I'll never forget this."

Marcus held her tightly, and said quietly, "Emily, if you want to tell your parents now, I think it would be better if we told them in private, just to show them the respect they deserve."

"How thoughtful of you, Mark. You wait here and I'll go and bring them up here." Without waiting for an answer she whirled down the stairs as fast as she could go.

Marcus strolled over and looked out of the huge bay window at the gardens and paths through the woods. The Norwoods were bound to give Emily a substantial wedding gift, even if only to impress the neighbors. *If I play my cards right I'll be halfway to getting some of it if I can get her mother on my side.* He knew it would not be easy. He heard the footsteps coming up the staircase and braced himself for the performance of his life.

He turned around to see Emily rushing up the stairs with her parents behind her. She rushed over and grabbed his arm and waited till the Norwoods reached the hallway.

Mrs. Norwood was the first to speak. "Well, what's the big surprise, dragging us away from our guests! Out with it, Emily,"

Emily looked at them and said, "Mark has something to tell you." She looked up at him adoringly.

Marcus smiled and said, "I wanted to wait a while to tell you this, but Emily insisted I tell you today, so without further ado, I'm in love with your daughter and would like your permission to call on her!"

They stared at him in stunned silence. Mrs. Norwood sat down heavily on the bench. Mr. Norwood regained his composure first. "You've only met each other! If this is a joke, Brown, I sure as hell don't see the funny side of it!" Marcus knew Norwood would be easy, it was the mother he was worried about.

"No joke, Mr. Norwood, and I wasn't aware there was a timetable for falling in love!"

Emily held his arm tighter. She couldn't believe how brave Mark was standing up to her father like this.

Norwood turned white. "Don't be insolent, young man!" he spluttered.

"Mr. Norwood, the last thing I want to be is insolent. It is with the greatest respect for both you and Mrs. Norwood that I'm asking your permission to call on Emily!"

Mollified, Norwood nodded his head.

Mrs Norwood addressed them in a tone that Marcus couldn't quite figure out. "What if we refuse you permission to call on Emily on the grounds that you don't even know her, and more importantly, none of us know the first thing about you?"

Marcus put on his most sincere voice. "The whole purpose of asking your permission is two-fold. It is so we all can get to know each other better, Mrs. Norwood."

This guy is smooth! Mary Norwood thought fast. *The worst thing I could do is refuse him permission. I can see Emily is besotted with him already. I need a plan to deal with this man. I can see he's no fool and I'll have to find out his agenda, because there's no chance he's in love with poor Emily.* She forced a smile. "Well, if Mr. Norwood has no objections, since you put it that way Mr. Brown, you have my permission to call on Emily at our home on the condition that you wait a while before you take her out unaccompanied."

Mr. Norwood answered in surprise. "If you have no objections, dear, then it's okay with me."

Emily rushed over and embraced her parents. "Thank you both so much, I'm so happy I could cry!"

Marcus shook Norwood's hand and kissed Mrs. Norwood's cheek. " Thank you both very much, I know this is not easy for you, but you won't regret it! Now, would you please call me Mark from now on. Mr. Brown sounds so formal, don't you think?" He bowed respectfully and treated them to his most dazzling smile. "Come on, Emily," he said. "Let's go downstairs. Your guests will be thinking you've disappeared."

"Yes, on you go!" Mrs. Norwood said. "We'll be down in a minute."

When Marcus and Emily left, she turned to her husband. "There's something about that young man I don't like! I can't put my finger on it, but I'm going to find out what the hell he's up to before it's too late! Just where did he come from and how did he get invited to the Waldorf? Sit here and tell me everything you know about him!"

Jack Norwood sat down next to his wife. Unlike most husbands of the day, Jack knew his wife was smarter than him and wasn't ashamed to admit it. She was the one who made the important decisions at the shareholders meetings. He was merely the mouthpiece. He sought her advice in everything he did and had prospered greatly from it. "All I know is that he came into my office asking how to buy and sell stocks. I'm convinced he is getting information from somewhere because he's made a small fortune in the short time he's been dealing with us. Cassidy has been jumping on the gravy train and says I should do the same. Everything he touches turns to gold. Just today he asked me in so many words how he could invest in our company—he's very ambitious. Right now he's got a job of some sort at Hawthorne's. I told him to come to the office on Wednesday morning. That's all I can tell you for now. If you like, we'll put a Pinkerton man on him and find out everything about him, but that will take some time."

Pinkerton's, the famous private detective agency, supplied investigators to all the big firms with absolute discretion assured.

Mary Norwood listened carefully, when Jack had finished talking she sat back and closed her eyes. "What better way to get into the company than marrying the owner's daughter? Have you looked into his eyes, Jack! They are like fish eyes, no expression at all. He gives me the creeps. Emily has no chance with this man. My instincts tell me he's an adventurer, and a very dangerous one! The worst thing we could do right now is tell Emily how I feel. It will only make her more determined. No, we'll play along with Mr. Brown for the time being!" She opened her eyes and leaned toward her husband, speaking with such intensity that made him listen to every word she said. "We've no time to lose! Get the Pinkertons on him first thing Monday morning. Have your meeting with him on Wednesday, offer him a position with the company. Leave the possibility of him buying in to the company open. That way we can keep an eye on him and it will stop him suspecting anything is going on. It will also keep Emily in the dark. We'll see what Mr.Brown is really up to. Remember, we've no time to lose. Look how fast he's got himself into this family already! Now let's get downstairs, it's nearly dinnertime."

"Just a minute, Mary. If you dislike Mark so much, why do you want me to give him a job?"

Mary patted his hand. "Remember, Jack, keep your friends close, and your enemies closer!"

They both got up and walked down to the ballroom.

"You know, Mary, I must admit I quite like him, maybe your instincts are just a mother's reaction to seeing her child growing up."

Mary laughed out loud. "Jack my dear, when will you ever learn?" He laughed along with her, knowing she was always right.

For the rest of the day and evening, Marcus and Emily were inseparable. They sat together at dinner, and when the dancing started to the music being played on a gramophone, they danced as if they were the only couple on the floor. They made the rounds of all the guests, Emily telling everyone that she and Mark were seeing each other and accepting all the good wishes with a sense of victory over all the hypocrites who laughed behind her back and now were falling over themselves to be introduced to her beau.

"Look how happy she is!" Jack Norwood said to his wife as they danced to the music.

"Yes, I can see her, Jack. That's what worries me. Already she's madly in love with him. The longer it goes on, the harder it will be for her when he breaks her heart, and I know it's only a matter of time!"

"Are you sure about this, Mary? After all, we hardly know him. Why not give him a chance before you condemn him. He seems just as taken with Emily."

Mary looked at her husband with pity in her eyes. "It's all an act, Jack. He's good at it too! Why, he's even got you believing it! Please don't let him pull the wool over your eyes. He's not after Emily, he's after what Emily can give him! And that is access to this family's money! That is what he's really after."

"I think you're wrong, Mary. How can Emily give him access to our money?"

"Emily can't, but you can! And you've never refused Emily anything. Just promise me one thing. No matter what happens, you will consult with me before either giving or selling any part of the company to Emily or Mark Brown!"

Norwood looked at her in amazement. "I've no intentions of giving or selling part of the company to anyone!"

Mary squeezed his hand tight. "Just promise me Jack, just promise me!"

He realized she was deadly serious. Quietly he said, "All right, Mary. I promise."

"Thank you, Jack, now let's enjoy the rest of the evening."

They left the dance floor and went on socializing with the rest of the company.

Marcus stayed the night at the Norwoods and the next day Emily and her father took him a tour of the estate. Mrs. Norwood claimed she had a headache and stayed behind. The place was about the size of his father's estate in England, only much more wooded. There were two guest houses apart from the big house that had a beautiful view looking over the Atlantic Ocean.

Around four o'clock, Marcus said his goodbyes and was driven home in the limousine. He had arranged to call on Emily at the New York townhouse on Friday evening.

The next morning he stayed away from work and called Robideau and arranged to have lunch with him. Robideau hated being held to ransom, but he had no choice but to go. Walker had called for him three times but he told his secretary to say he wasn't in. The two men took a private booth in an upscale eatery and Marcus wasted no time in getting down to business.

"Don't look so miserable, Robideau, it's not the end of the world. You and I are going to make a lot of money, so relax. Now, first things first, tell me what you've got on Walker, I don't care how you know!. The quicker you tell me the quicker we'll be finished, so leave nothing out!"

Robideau sighed. *Damn this smart ass Limey son of a bitch. He had him over a barrel.* "He's been using company money to invest for himself."

Marcus grasped the implication immediately. "Hawthorne's money? How long for and how much? You have proof, haven't you?"

"Slow down! About a year and a half. I don't know how much, maybe half a million! And of course I have proof!"

Marcus sat back and smiled broadly. "Tell me exactly how he did it!"

"He has the authority to write company checks, so it was an easy matter to transfer money to his personal account. He would then invest the money in the stock market, wait till it went up in value then sell. He would then transfer the money back and keep the profits. It was a good system."

"Okay. How did you find out about it?"

Robideau laughed. "You're not going to believe this, but it was me who suggested it to him! That way I could get him to invest for me because it's illegal for me to do it. Everything was going well till he hired you. That's the whole sorry mess."

"So he'll do just about anything you want to keep it quiet."

"Yes, but I'm going to crucify him for being so careless. He should have had you checked out before he gave you the job!"

Marcus held his hand up. "You'll do no such thing, Louis. You don't mind if I call you Louis, do you? All you have to do is introduce me to Walker as your friend, and that I also have the proof of his embezzling. No rush, but I'll expect everything you have on him in writing by the end if the week." Marcus' voice changed and his face darkened. "Believe me, Louis, by the time I'm finished with Jeffrey Walker, he'll be wishing it was you he was dealing with!"

Robideau stared at him. *What a cunning bastard. I'd better go along with this. I don't want this guy as an enemy. He's totally ruthless! He'd have no hesitation in bringing me down.* "I'll get it to you tomorrow if you like, Mr. Brown."

Marcus' demeanor changed and he said pleasantly. "Thank you, and please call me Mark, Louis. We might as well be friends seeing we are partners in crime, pardon the pun. Now let's enjoy a nice lunch before we go and see our mutual friend!"

Robireau had met a few cool customers in his career, but none as cool as this one, the bastard knew he had all the aces. He shrugged his shoulders and laughed in resignation. "Might as well, Mark, after all, we won't be seeing each other for a while."

"That's the spirit, Louis. We may not be able to meet as much as we'd like, but we'll talk regularly, just as good friends should, right?"

Louis Robideau grinned cynically. "Right, we'll talk regularly! You call me as soon as you get your new number. Now where the hell's the waiter?"

After lunch, Marcus and Robideau took a taxi to Hawthorne's. As they strode through the foyer to the private elevator, Marcus noticed the looks of both respect and curiosity on the receptionist's faces when they recognized the Chairman of the Stock Exchange. Robideau called over to the receptionist with a smile.

"Don't call upstairs! This is a surprise visit!"

"Of course, Mr. Robideau."

No questions asked! Not like the way he was treated. Marcus grinned inwardly. *Things were about to change in a big way.*

When they exited the elevator, the secretary Greta looked up in annoyance at not being notified then quickly recovered her composure when she saw who it was. She hurried out from behind her desk and said obsequiously, "Good afternoon, Mr. Robideau. What a nice surprise! I'll tell Mr. Walker you're here." She ignored Marcus completely.

"No need, I'll let myself in! Just carry on with your work." Robideau brushed her aside and opened the door of Walker's office without knocking. Marcus followed him inside and closed the door behind him.

Jeffrey Walker nearly jumped out of his chair when the two men barged in to his office. "Louis!" he stuttered, "what's he doing here?"

"Shut up and listen!" Robideau roared. "Your prodigy here is the one that made the big profit on Weir tool. He managed to figure out who I was and now he knows everything! Is that clear enough!" He put his hands on the desk and leaned over Walker menacingly. "I'm finished with you, Walker. Brown here has something to say to you. Never try to contact me again, or else you know what will happen!" He turned on his heel and walked toward the door. Marcus stopped him in his tracks.

"Just a minute, Louis. You should hear this. Now listen carefully, both of you. I will be leaving a letter with my lawyer tomorrow once I get certain items from Louis. It will be opened in the event of my untimely death so neither of you will get any foolish ideas. You can go now, Louis." Robideau left the office, closing the door behind him.

Walker sat white-faced, staring at Marcus. The realization that he was ruined hit him like a ton of bricks. Unable to think straight, he was stunned into silence. Marcus pulled a chair over and sat in front of the desk, savoring every minute.

"I'd get you a drink if I knew where it was. Believe me, you're going to need one!" Walker waved vaguely at the door at the back of the office. Marcus went over and opened it to see a well stocked bar and refrigerator.

He poured Walker a large Scotch and a soda water for himself. He gave Walker his drink and sat opposite him waiting for him to speak.

Walker drank half the Scotch and said hoarsely, "What do you want, Brown?" He sounded totally defeated. He knew that Marcus could ruin him, even send him to prison. *Robideau had been right, it was all his fault for not checking more thoroughly. Yet he still couldn't understand how Marcus had got started.*

As if reading his mind, Marcus said, "Don't torture yourself, Walker. You'll never find out where I got the money to start with. Now I'm here to do business with you. You know I'll destroy you if you don't do as I say, but it doesn't have to be that way if you agree to my conditions."

Walker looked up in surprise. Perhaps there was some hope yet. "I'll do anything in my power to do what you want. Just don't make this public. It will ruin my family. I've got plenty of money, please don't do anything till we at least talk about it." He drank the rest of his drink and looked at Marcus pleadingly.

"Stop whining and listen carefully. I'm already employed here as your personal assistant, so a promotion to a senior position would not look too out of place. Now, you are in charge of Hawthorne's world headquarters, correct?"

"Yes," Walker replied. He was beginning to recover from the original shock.

"You travel frequently between London, New York and Chicago, correct?"

Walker nodded his head. *What was this bastard getting at?*

"You will put me in charge of the New York office with all the authority that goes with it, except for writing company checks. You will continue to do that with one slight difference. When you transfer company money temporarily, as you have been doing for your own use, it will now go to a numbered account which I will be opening tomorrow. I will let you know when to deposit and withdraw the funds. This will be my office. Due to your heavy work schedule you no longer can cope with all three. I will be starting my new job next week in the New Year. You can have an office available for your visits to New York somewhere else in the building, but not in the basement where I was. It wouldn't look right, would it?" Marcus was enjoying this.

"My salary will be fifty-thousand a year. You will give me a nice starting bonus of let's say a hundred thousand of your own money. I will require a company car and chauffeur. That's all for now. I suggest you let me know your whereabouts at all times. Now is everything clear?"

"How am I going to get Hawthorne to agree to this? It's not possible."

Marcus looked in contempt at Walker's ashen face. He stood up and leaned over the stricken man. "The same way you got him to agree to let you use his company money! Now what's it to be?"

Walker gulped and tried to answer, but he couldn't speak. He looked up at Marcus and nodded his head and in a whisper said, "I'll try."

Marcus walked to the door and turned round. "You are lucky, you know. If I was a vindictive man I'd show you up for the thief you are. But you'll still have your job only under different conditions. Now I suggest you get busy, I'll be back tomorrow afternoon to finalize everything." He left the office and walked over to the elevator, glancing over at Greta who was pretending to look busy. Marcus knew she had heard the raised voices and was afraid to get involved. *She's smart enough, maybe I'll keep her on.* He smiled at the thought as he pressed the down button.

He walked briskly the short distance to the Bank of America. John Reynolds was behind the desk serving a customer. Marcus caught his eye and signaled to meet him in Tweed's office. He went over and knocked once before entering.

Tweed looked up at him with a worried look. "Glad to see you, Mr. Brown. How did our investment go?" he asked anxiously.

Marcus sat at the desk and pulled out his checkbook. "To Mr. Gordon Tweed, the sum of fourteen-thousand dollars," he said, and signed the check with a flourish. "Don't cash that one until you deposit this one!" He slid the Norwood check for the hundred and fourteen-thousand over the desk. Tweed grinned from ear to ear.

"Well done, Mr. Brown. Any time you need another advance, make sure you let me know."

"Of course, Mr. Tweed. It was a pleasure doing business with you."

They heard a knock at the door and John Reynolds came in. He shook hands with Marcus. He looked at Tweed's face and said, "I gather your investment went well!"

"Exactly as Mr. Brown here promised!" Tweed held up the two checks. "Please deposit this one in Mr. Brown's account, John."

Reynolds took the check and whistled. "Congratulations, Mr. Brown!" he said enthusiastically.

Marcus was writing another check as he spoke. "And a little bonus for you, Mr. Reynolds. After all, I couldn't have done it without you."

Reynolds took the check and looked at it in surprise. "A thousand dollars! Good God, Mr. Brown, I don't know what to say. Thank you very much."

"You're welcome," Marcus replied. "Now, Mr. Tweed. From now on I'll be depositing larger amounts of money in this bank. I want Mr. Reynolds to handle my account. I'm sure you'll consider a bonus for him for bringing in such an account to your bank. A promotion might be in order as well. Also, I'm sure we can discuss preferred status for overdrafts and advances at a later date."

Tweed narrowed his eyes. "We are not in the habit of handing out bonuses to our employees, Mr. Brown. Just how much money are we talking about?"

Marcus stood up to leave. "Speaking conservatively, in the region of a half million dollars in the first six months, and rapidly increasing after that."

Tweed sat open mouthed. "Speaking conservatively! I'm sure we can accommodate your requests, Mr. Brown."

"Excellent, Mr. Tweed, I'll be in touch." He turned to Reynolds as he opened the door. "Can I have a word in private, John?"

Reynolds looked at Tweed who nodded his head. "Of course, Mr. Brown."

The two men left the office and stopped in the main foyer.

"I want you to do me a favor, John. And please call me Mark from now on."

"Of course, Mark. You just paid my full tuition for me. Anything I can do to help, just ask."

"There may be certain people making enquiries about me. Will you tell me if anyone comes around here asking questions?"

"I'll do better than that. Just tell me what you want me to tell them."

Marcus smiled and shook Reynolds's hand. He knew then he had this man's undying loyalty "Just tell them the truth. I'll be back tomorrow and hopefully I'll have a phone number for you to reach me. Goodbye for now."

"See you tomorrow, Mark." Reynolds returned to his desk and sat deep in contemplation. Mr. Brown had definitely taken a liking to him. He looked at the check in his hand and thought, *Sure, it was overly generous for what he had done, but what the hell, why question Brown's motives. Just take the money and be thankful for it and stop analyzing the reasons. There may even be a promotion coming thanks to Brown. Yes, John. Keep your mouth shut and hang on to this guy's coattails. You never know how far he could take you.*

Outside the bank, Marcus looked at his watch. It was too late to go and look at an apartment. It was unseasonably mild for January. He decided to walk for a few blocks to gather his thoughts. A lot was happening all at once and he did not want to make any mistakes. He had known immediately that the Norwoods would try and find out about his background. That's what he would do in their position. He just didn't know how they would go about it. They were bound to go to Hawthorne's. First, he'd make sure Walker gave them a glowing report about him. Second, make up a plausible story about why he came to America. They must not find out his parents had cut him off, so he had to make sure that there were no links to England. That would be easy enough. Then it would be a matter of time before he married Emily, and the sky would be the limit. He now knew the way to beat Mrs. Norwood's opposition was through Norwood himself. The man doted on his daughter and would give her anything she wanted.

He walked for a long time, perfecting his plans and double checking everything in his mind. At last he found himself in Times Square, and suddenly he felt very tired. It had been a busy day and tomorrow would be just as busy. He bought a sandwich to eat on the subway and went home for an early night. He would need all his wits for his meeting with Walker.

The first thing Marcus did in the morning was call Robideau. They arranged to meet at Grand Central station for Robideau to give him the records of Walker's transactions.

When they met, Robideau handed him a large manila envelope. "You'll find everything in there. Dates, account numbers, amounts, everything. Now if you'll excuse me I'm in a hurry!"

"Of course, I'll be in touch!" Marcus watched him walk away without a goodbye. *Well, I suppose I would feel the same if the shoe was on the other foot,* he thought as he sat down on a bench and opened the envelope. Robideau was right. Walker had trusted him with information that could ruin him. The evidence was clear that it was company money that was being invested. Marcus stuffed the papers into the envelope and put it in his briefcase. He walked out of the station and took a taxi to the Bank of America.

John Reynolds had just sat down at his desk when Marcus came in. "Good morning, John. I'm in a hurry, what I want you to do is open a safety deposit box in my name. Have you a paper and pen I could use?" Reynolds pulled his drawer open and handed Marcus a pad of paper embossed with the bank's name. As Marcus hurriedly scribbled a note, Gordon Tweed came in and noticed him sitting at the desk.

He came straight over and said, "Good morning Mr. Brown, you're in early!"

Marcus finished writing and looked up. "Just in time, Mr. Tweed. Would you be good enough to read this and witness it for me? It'll have to do till I get myself a lawyer."

Tweed put his briefcase down and read the note aloud. "In the event of my death, I authorize John Reynolds to open my safety deposit box and make public the information that it contains. Signed Mark Brown." Tweed hesitated for a moment and then shrugged his shoulders and signed his name as a witness.

"Would you do me the favor of keeping it for me till I get a lawyer?"

Tweed nodded and put the note in his briefcase.

"You will do what I ask, won't you, John?" Marcus looked at him without smiling.

"Of course, but I don't think you're about to die just yet!"

"Neither do I, John. Neither do I! Now I am in a hurry so could we get this done right away?"

Reynolds sprang to his feet and Tweed said goodbye and went into his office. It was done in five minutes. The boxes were inside a vault. Reynolds gave him a numbered key and left him alone. Marcus put the envelope Robideau had given him and the other with every transaction he and Robideau had done since he started at Hawthorne's inside the box and locked it. He left the vault to find Reynolds waiting outside.

"Thank you, John. One other thing, I want you to open a numbered account for me. Now I'm late for an appointment. I may be back later today."

"Goodbye, Mark," Reynolds called after him as he hurried out of the bank.

It was eleven thirty when Marcus got to Walker's office. Greta was a different person. When Marcus came out of the elevator she was all over him. She practically bounded out from behind her desk.

"Good morning, Mr. Brown. I'll take your coat and hat! Mr. Walker said you're to go right in!" She smiled grotesquely as she held the door open for him.

"Thank you, Greta!" He handed her his coat and hat and entered the office. Greta closed the door behind him.

Walker was on the phone and writing at the same time. He glanced up at Marcus and signaled him to be seated. When he finished talking on the phone, he made a note and threw down his pen. Marcus noticed that he looked full of energy and was not at all the broken man he had left the day before. Walker had spent the previous night evaluating his position. He knew Brown wanted him to continue to write the company checks so nothing could be traced back to him. The thing he did not want was his conduct being made public. On the other hand he would only be blackmailed so far. If Brown thought he would blackmail him for the rest of his life with ever increasing demands, then so be it. He refused to live in fear, so he would tell Brown to do his worst and take the consequences. Being ruined was not as bad as being owned by a man like Brown.

"Before you say anything, Brown, I want you to listen carefully. I have come to a decision about your ultimatum. I agree to all your requests regarding your promotion. I was just informing London. As from January first you will be vice president of the New York office with all the authority that comes with it. I retain the authority to write company checks. I will be spending most of my time in London from now on. The Chicago operation is up and running. You will have to learn to do some of my duties here. This will have to look legitimate. The salary is no problem. Hawthorne doesn't usually question my decisions, but I think he'll want to know about this one. Especially about giving up my office. He's in Florida at the moment, he'll be back in two weeks. I'll handle him when he gets back. I will write you a personal check for a hundred thousand dollars as you requested.

"As far as a company car is concerned, the answer is no. Nobody in this company has one. Now, listen to me. I have agreed to your demands because of my family. I do not want this to be made public. I have also decided that if you make any further demands, I will go to the police and confess. I will not live the rest of my life being blackmailed. So this must be an end to it. If you do not agree, I will go directly to the police this morning!"

He stood up behind the desk and looked at the stupendous view. "Yes or no?"

Marcus had paid attention to Walker. Apart from listening to what he had to say, he had been watching his demeanor. He realized Walker had been taken as far as he would go, and was deadly serious.

"Yes, I agree. As regards the company checks, feel free to use them if you want. I'm not out to stop you making money just because I want to!"

Walker turned around and faced him. "Greed got me into this mess, so no thanks. I would rather we communicated only by phone from now on. It will make my life more bearable if I don't have to be in your company."

"Fine with me! But I'll need some idea of what my duties will be in this position. Come to think of it, what exactly are your duties?"

Walker sat down and sighed. "My duties are to make decisions on where the company can make the most profit on investments. The money for these investments comes from all the small investors who are dabbling in the stock market. All the people who work here advise the small investors for a percentage. They are called financial advisors. That is how we make our money to invest. Your duties will be to oversee our financial advisors. That is the part of my job you will be doing. If you interfere too much and cost the company money, I cannot protect you. Does that answer your question?"

"Yes, but there is one other thing that's most important. I will need help to take over your duties and I can think of no better way to legitimize the whole thing than keeping Greta on as my secretary. I hope you didn't want to take her with you."

Walker looked at him as if he were mad. "Who the hell would want to take her with them? You're welcome to keep her if you want to," he lifted his notes and said, "Is there anything else? I'll give Greta these notes. She will notify everyone of the changes. You can take the rest of the week off and start on Monday. That will give me time to clear my office out. I will leave ten signed company checks in the desk drawer. My phone numbers for the various offices and my home number in England are in there. Here is the key. When you use them up, notify me and I'll send you more. I suggest you limit their use to no more than twice per month. These funds must be returned to the account in the Chase Manhattan bank within four business days. If you keep them out longer than that then it will show up and your little scheme will be finished. Are you clear on everything?"

"Just a couple of details. I'm expecting some questions to be asked about me. You'll have to give me a glowing reference now that you've promoted me."

Walker grimaced and nodded.

Marcus stood up and held out his hand. "Let's shake on our arrangement, Walker. Remember, you still have your job!"

Walker looked at him with hate in his eyes. "Never in a million years, you insolent bastard!"

Marcus shrugged as the two of them left the office. *That was the second time you've insulted me.* "Have it your own way," he said evenly, holding the door open for Walker to pass through.

Walker walked over to Greta and laid the papers on her desk.

"Greta, you are the first to know that as I'll be spending most of my time in London, Mr. Brown is now vice president of this office. You'll find everything is here in writing. He will be starting on Monday morning. I have to go now, so good morning to both of you." He walked straight to the elevator and disappeared from view.

Greta looked at Marcus in astonishment. "Congratulations, Mr. Brown. I must say this comes as a surprise!"

"Yes, I suppose it is, Greta. Now I know we didn't get off to a good start, but I would like you to stay on as my secretary. I'm sure you know everything that goes on around here, and you will make my job a lot easier. Now what do you say?"

Greta nearly sat down with relief. She was afraid to lose her job and was already thinking Marcus would want a younger and better looking woman for his secretary. Her face reddened. "I'm sorry about that, Mr. Brown. I'd be delighted to stay on, thank you very much."

"How much is your salary, Greta?" Marcus looked behind her through the picture windows out at the East river.

"Four-thousand a year, sir."

"Your first duty as my secretary is to give yourself a raise to five-thousand. Have the documents ready for me to sign on Monday morning."

This time Greta did sit down. She stammered her thanks. "I don't know what to say, sir. Thank you very much."

Marcus sat on the edge of the desk. He leaned over and looked right into her eyes. He knew he was taking a chance, but if his hunch was right, it would make it easy for him to put his plan into operation.

"Greta, this is very important. I'm your boss now. Not Walker. You will tell me the truth, won't you."

Greta looked at him fearfully. She knew it would be a mistake to cross this man. "Of course I will, sir. How can I help you?"

"Are you aware that Mr. Walker has some special investments that need large amounts of funds moved back and forth on a regular basis?"

Greta never changed her expression. She knew exactly what he was talking about. "I'm not aware of any such investments, sir. If there were, he must have handled them himself."

Immediately Marcus knew she was lying. "I admire loyalty, Greta. Make sure that is the last time you lie to me, because I demand your loyalty now. I know we can work well together. See you on Monday." He strolled over and looked at Walker's name on the frosted glass door. He called over his shoulder as he went to the elevator. "One other thing, Greta. Please have my name on my office door when I return."

Greta, her face crimson, bent over and scribbled on her notepad. "Of course, sir." She watched the elevator doors close. *Yes, I think I'll get on all right with Mr. Brown. He's just as greedy as Walker, but a lot smarter.* She smiled to herself as she sat down. *A raise of a thousand to start with! Not bad at all.*

The next morning Marcus went for his meeting with Norwood. After some small talk, Norwood asked him what exactly he wanted to know.

Marcus did not beat about the bush. "I want your advice on how to go about becoming an owner of an investment company?"

Norwood thought for a minute. He realized that Marcus was serious. "Look, Mark, investment companies are complicated. To answer your question, you would need a sizable investment of your own and one or more partners with the same commitment. Apart from having a thorough knowledge of the business, of course."

"I have enough knowledge as to how this business works. How much would I need and would you know of anyone interested in such a venture?"

"If you insist on an answer, I would say to start you would need around a million dollars, and that is just for buying into the stock exchange and renting an office for the first year. It may even be more by now. I don't know of anyone offhand who would be interested, but I'll keep my nose to the ground for you if you like."

Marcus pretended to look disappointed. "Never mind, I guess I'm aiming a bit too high."

Norwood saw his chance. "Look, Mark, how would you like a job here at Norwoods? That way you could learn the business and save some money at the same time."

Marcus stood up abruptly. "Is that what you think I came here for? A job! For your information I'm now the vice president of Hawthorne Financials New York office. I don't need charity, Mr. Norwood, I came here only for your advice!"

Norwood thought fast. *Hawthorne's was a big player. How did one so young get a position like that?*

"Sit down and relax, Mark. I was just trying to help. And call me Jack from now on. Congratulations on your new job. Let me talk to some people and we'll see what comes of it. Now, when are you coming round to see Emily. She told me to ask you?"

When Mark left the office, Norwood called his wife and told her what had happened.

"What do you think of that? And you thought he was after something! He's the vice president of Hawthorne's for God sake!"

"All that's fine and dandy, but I still don't trust him!"

"Oh, Mary, you'll come round to my point of view. He'd make a fine match for our daughter."

Mary Norwood slammed the receiver down. She knew she'd better back off and wait for Mr. Brown to make a mistake. Whatever happened she did not want to lose her only daughter.

Mary Norwood was wrong. Marcus never made any mistakes. He bid his time and played the perfect suitor for the next six months. He had one more thing to do as part of his plan and decided to do it as soon as he had the chance. The chance came sooner than he expected. Sir William Hawthorne came back from Florida on the seventeenth of January and found Marcus waiting for him.

On Wednesday, January nineteenth Mary Norwood opened her copy of the *New York Times* and looked at the lead story in disbelief.

Jeffrey Walker, Vice president and Chief Financial Officer of Hawthorne Financial, has resigned amid allegations he had been embezzling company funds for his own use. There is to be a full inquiry both in England and America. All his assets in both countries have been frozen and charges are expected to be forthcoming. Mr. Walker's attorney says his client has already left for England. He will probably have to face charges there as well as here in America.

Sources tell us that Walker's criminal practices were brought to light by the new vice president of Hawthorne's, Mr. Mark Brown. Mr. Brown is well known in financial circles for his honesty and integrity...

Mary Norwood sighed and put the paper down. It seemed this paragon of virtue could do no wrong. The Pinkertons had found nothing on him. She resigned herself to listening to her husband telling her that he told her so.

After Marcus had his revenge on Walker, he took a vindictive pleasure in firing Greta personally for the way she treated him on his first day. He immersed himself in learning everything he could about the stock market. He decided to move his portfolio out of Norwoods to another house. In March he opened his own investment trust company and named it Roman Investment Trust. He rented a small office and hired Joseph Cassidy as manager. Norwood had no objections. Marcus continued to work for Hawthorne. With the constant flow of information from Robideau he could not go wrong. Word went around that Roman was the place to put your money. Marcus was working sixteen hour days and still found time to see Emily Norwood every Friday night and Sunday afternoons. Despite Mary Norwood's misgivings, they were married in St. Patrick's on June twenty-fifth, 1927. Before the banns had been published, two-hundred dollars to the priest served as well as a Roman Catholic baptismal certificate with no questions asked.

The Norwoods gave them a town house as a wedding gift, but they only had a weekend honeymoon. Marcus had to get back to work. His company accumulated money at an incredible rate. The stock market boom of the twenties was reaching its climax. Everyone was investing on margin and with the cheap money available from the banks, even ordinary working people were getting in on the action.

In June, 1928 Marcus resigned from Hawthorne's. By this time Emily had her first baby, a boy whom they named Jack after his grandfather. Marcus had about as much interest in the baby as he did in Emily. But he knew the baby would keep both her and the mother from bothering him. He had used his time at Hawthorne's to learn everything about how the financial world worked. He took to dying his hair gray at the sides to make him look older because all of the men he dealt with were old enough to be his father, some of them his grandfather. He made a name for himself as a man to listen to. He put his newfound knowledge to good use, borrowing more and more from both the Bank of America and the Chase Manhattan.

Everyone wanted a piece of the action. Norwood would ask Marcus for advice on good investments and Marcus would oblige. Even without Marcus' advantage vast fortunes were being made on the inflated value of the stocks.

After another year of making more and more money from these investments, Marcus took stock of his financial situation. In less than three years in America he had accumulated a fortune of around fifty-million dollars, all of it in the stock market. *What a country!* But there was a doubt creeping into his mind. This rate of profit could not go on forever. The trick was when to get out of the market, but the way things were going, there was no sign of the easy money stopping, or even slowing down. He studied the newspapers endlessly, reading reports on everything he could get his hands on, looking for a sign.

The sign came when he least expected it. As was his custom, every morning Marcus would buy the *Wall Street Journal* at Grand Central Station and have his shoes shined while he looked it over. One morning in early May, 1929, his shoe shine boy, a black man in his thirties, asked him had he any tips for the day's trading. Marcus gave him a good tip and told him to put it in the bank. He left the station deep in thought and decided to walk downtown. It took him two hours to get to his office, but by that time his mind was made up.

First he called John Reynolds at the bank and asked him if he could buy gold bullion. Reynolds told him it was legal only if bought in large amounts. The government did not want the whole population having a few ounces of gold each. He called Cassidy into his office and told him to slowly start selling his stocks and buy gold bullion from the Bank of America. When Cassidy asked him why, Marcus had his answer ready. He swore Cassidy to secrecy and told him a pack of lies about moving the money temporarily till he had set up a huge deal, which would make even more profit. He would let Cassidy know when to move his money in time to join in the venture. Cassidy left the office rubbing his hands in anticipation.

Marcus then called Jack Norwood and asked if he would know of anyone interested in buying Roman Investment Trust, but to keep quiet about it. Then he simply waited. When the shoe shine boy had asked Marcus for a tip, an alarm bell went off in his head. *If a man who made his living shining shoes was into the market, there was something drastically wrong with it.*

It took four weeks for Cassidy to transfer Marcus' money into gold. Meanwhile, Marcus kept giving Cassidy the information from Robideau. After one particularly profitable session, Cassidy came into his office and said jovially, "You know, Mark, I hope this deal of yours is a good one, you're losing money every day you keep that money tied up in gold!"

"Yes, I know I am. But I've had it with this business. I'm burnt out and I need to spend more time with my family." Then Marcus dropped the bombshell. "That was John Reynolds on the phone. I've sold the company. You now work for Norwood and Hawthorne Investment Trust."

He had played it perfectly. He knew Norwood's greed would prevent him from letting anybody else get Roman. Hawthorne had bought thirty percent because Norwood could not come up with the hundred and fifty-million needed to buy it. Marcus had just instructed Reynolds to transfer the lot to his account in the Bank of England. It was small potatoes to Hawthorne, but Norwood had mortgaged everything he had to come up with the money.

Cassidy stood open mouthed. "But you never mentioned anything about selling!"

Marcus stood up and looked around the office. "Don't worry, Joe. You'll be working for your old boss. It'll be just like old times for you. See you around."

Cassidy sat down in shock. *What a lousy bastard, he never dropped a hint about this. Why would someone sell a money maker like this?* He did not believe for a minute that Mark Brown was doing this for his family. There had to be another reason, but what? As hard as he had tried, Cassidy had not found out where Marcus was getting the inside information, so now the golden goose had died! *Oh well, no use crying over spilt milk. He did all right before Brown came on the scene and he'd do all right without him.*

Marcus had one more thing to do before he went home and told Emily his plans. He went to the bank and took everything out of the safety deposit box. Then he called Robideau and arranged to meet him for lunch. Robideau was not keen, but Marcus insisted and he had to agree much as he disliked it. When the two men met and were seated, without a word Marcus pulled a large manila envelope from his briefcase and laid it on the table.

Robideau stared at it. "Is that what I think it is?" His voice was hoarse.

"Yes, that is everything I had on you. You may as well have it now, because I don't need it anymore," Marcus said blandly.

"Just like that! You blackmail me for two years and now you simply don't want to? I find that hard to believe after what you did to Walker."

Marcus leaned forward and his voice changed. "Walker was different. He got what was coming to him. You have never harmed me. I have nothing against you. I just wanted to use the information to make money. So there you have it, it's all yours to do what you want with."

Robideau took the envelope and stuffed it in his briefcase. He looked at Marcus and said, "Well, I must say I'm glad this business is over. I'm not going to thank you, but I will buy you lunch."

"That's fine with me!" Marcus replied and beckoned to the waiter.

After his lunch with Robideau, Marcus went home and told Emily that he had sold the business and how would she like to go on a grand tour of Europe?

Emily was ecstatic that she would have her husband and baby all to herself for a while. Now she could tell the doubters that Mark truly cared for her, otherwise they wouldn't be going on an extended trip. She couldn't wait to tell her mother and start planning.

"When can we go, dear? I hope it's soon," she asked him, already doubting that he meant it. After all, he had never taken a day off since they were married.

Marcus turned on his most dazzling smile. "As soon as you want, Emily. You take charge of the whole trip. Only one thing! Make sure you include England in the itinerary."

She hugged him excitedly and exclaimed, "Now why would I miss England out. That's the first on the list!" She ran into the front room and grabbed the telephone.

Before he went to bed that night, Marcus burned everything that he had kept in the safety deposit box. All the records of his dealings with Robideau were gone. He was not about to take the chance that they could come back to haunt him.

Chapter 8

On July 4th 1929 Mary Ellen was celebrating her son's second birthday. The last two years had passed so quickly it seemed like a blur. She had settled in to a busy schedule of looking after Switcher and the baby. She was involved in the local Catholic charities and spent a lot of time helping families in need. Switcher doted on little Patrick and never tired of bragging about him. Mary Ellen had written a few letters home, but couldn't bring herself to tell them about her child. She still felt ashamed of her situation, although nobody in Detroit except Switcher knew the truth.

There were about a dozen other children at the party, along with their parents and some of the neighbors. The house was crowded with people and children running in and out to the backyard. Mary Ellen had just finished playing a game with the children when she noticed a young man standing in the doorway looking at her. She had seen him before at some of the functions in the church hall, but had never spoken to him. She caught his eye and turned hurriedly away in embarrassment. She asked one of the women who the young man was and found out that he was the brother of one of the women. She did not have time to find out more before he made his way to her side.

"Hello, I'm Adam Corbett," he said, holding out his hand.

"Mary Ellen O'Neill," she replied shyly, wondering what kind of accent he had.

"And what part of Ireland are you from, Mary Ellen?"

"Donegal, and where might you be from? I can't make out your accent."

"I'm a neighbor of yours from across the Irish sea. I'm from Lanarkshire, in Scotland."

"And how long have you been in America?" Just then one of the women called on Mary Ellen to bring out the birthday cake and she excused herself.

"I'll talk to you later!" Adam called as she hurried off.

Adam Corbett was twenty-five years old and had emigrated to America by way of Canada in 1921. He had been born into a family of coal miners and started work in the mines when he was twelve. The conditions the miners had to work in were horrendous. They had no rights whatsoever, and if they did not toe the company line then the company simply fired them. They had to put up with breathing in the black dust all day or night, twelve hours at a time. The dampness and the dust took the lives of thousands of miners all over Britain, but the government was indifferent to their plight. Adam's father and his two brothers had helped him save enough to get out of Scotland, but he never forgot the brutality of the coal mines. The experience had made him into a fighter for workers rights. In America that meant he was a union organizer.

Such men were anathema to the auto companies and their subsidiaries. They would go to any lengths to keep them off their premises, including violence and even murder. With the courts on their side, they were free to hire gangs of thugs to break up union meetings and intimidate the workers. The plants were full of informers, and the organizers had to be very careful in their work. If they were found out, they were fired and immediately blacklisted and could not get a job in the industry. Adam worked in an assembly plant and secretly tried to recruit workers to join the union. He had very limited success given the mood of fear that permeated every plant in the area. Everyone was afraid of losing their job.

After the stock market crashed in October, 1929, the fear turned to terror. Gradually the layoffs became a weekly occurrence. The next two years became a nightmare as the great depression took hold of the United States.

This was the period when Adam Corbett was trying to court Mary Ellen O'Neill. He would go round to Switcher's house and sit on the porch talking with the two of them, but try as he might, she would not agree to go out with him. Over the months he wondered what was wrong. She always seemed glad to see him and old Switcher always made sure he gave them plenty of time alone. Everyone said that she was a widow, but she never once mentioned her husband. Adam was afraid to come right out and ask in case she was still in mourning.

After six months of getting nowhere with her, Adam decided to take the bull by the horns and ask her outright if he was wasting his time. He waited late one night till Switcher went to bed and the two of them were left alone. After the usual talk about who was losing their job or their house that week, Adam asked her the question.

"Mary Ellen, I have something to ask you. But before I ask I want you to promise me you won't take offence."

"Not at all, ask whatever you want, Adam."

143

Mary Ellen had grown very fond of Adam over the months. She instinctively knew that he was a good and kind man. She still felt that she could never be married because of what had happened to her, so she was careful to keep men at a distance, even the ones she liked.

"Why won't you come out with me some night? God knows I've asked you often enough."

Mary Ellen had known this was bound to come sometime. She bowed her head and said in a low voice, "I cannot tell you, Adam, I'm sorry."

"So there is a reason?"

"Yes, but I cannot tell you what it is." She looked at him desperately. She knew that he had forced himself to ask her.

Adam Corbett stood up. "If you cannot tell me, then I must accept that. You must know by now that I love you and little Patrick, and you still cannot tell me what it is. I thought that you had the same feelings for me, Mary Ellen. But it appears that I am mistaken. I wish you goodnight." He lifted his jacket and was gone.

Mary Ellen sat rooted to the chair. She folded her arms on the table and dropped her head on them and started to weep. She knew she loved Adam Corbett but she also knew that if he found out the truth about her he would not want her. She wept for what seemed like hours and fell asleep with her head still on her folded arms. She was still in that position when Switcher came downstairs for a drink of water. He shook her awake.

"What are you doing, Mary Ellen? What's the matter? You'll freeze to death down here!" She lifted her tear-stained face to him and cried, "Adam's left and he won't be back."

Switcher sat opposite her, and said, "Come on now, calm down and tell me all about it."

Between sobs, Mary Ellen told him what had happened then reverted into weeping again.

Switcher thought for a long time about what he was going to say. "Listen to me, my child. Someday you will have to tell someone what happened to you. If a man loves you enough, it won't matter to him, and if you love that man enough you will tell him. That's about all I can say."

Mary Ellen looked up at him and suddenly stopped weeping. "But I'm afraid to tell him in case he walks away!"

Switcher looked at her kindly. "He's already done that, and that's because you didn't tell him."

Stunned, Mary Ellen realized he was right. Adam had left not because she told him her secret, but because she hadn't. Wearily she got up from the chair.

She bent over and kissed old Switcher's head. "Goodnight, Jimmy. Where would I be without you?"

By the fall of 1931 the Depression had affected everyone in America. Its effects were to cause the whole world to sink into what became known as the Great Depression along with the United States. One Thursday morning Mary Ellen was cleaning up the leaves in the garden when she noticed old Switcher driving erratically toward the house. The car swerved into the driveway and came to a sudden stop. Mary Ellen rushed over to see what was wrong. When she saw Switcher's stricken face she thought that someone he knew had died.
"What's the matter, Jimmy?" she cried as she pulled the car door open.
"The bank's closed." Switcher stared at her blankly.
"What do you mean, closed? It's only eleven o'clock!" She knew he went to the bank every Thursday to draw the money out for the week
"I mean it's closed for good and I've lost everything in it!" Switcher was in shock. He struggled out of the car and slowly walked up the porch steps to the front door.
Mary Ellen grabbed little Patrick and hurried into the house after the old man.
Switcher collapsed into a chair and held his head in his hands. "Look at me, worked all my life and saved enough to live on, only for it all to disappear. How can they get away with this?' the distraught man cried out in anguish.
Mary Ellen held his head in her arms. "Surely it can't be that bad, maybe they'll open tomorrow."
Switcher shook her off. He had calmed down enough to talk sense. "Sit down, Mary Ellen. I know you never bother reading the papers, but there have been banks closing all over the country. Our little world here is finished. Everything I had was in that bank. The insurance money, my savings, everything. Listen carefully, Mary Ellen. We have no money! Do you know what that means? I'm seventy-seven years old. I'm too old to work, even if there was a job opening! We have no income, nothing. Do you understand?"
Mary Ellen could not believe what he was saying. "But how can this happen? Is it legal for them to shut the door and not give you your money?"
"It doesn't matter if it's legal or not. The government can't do anything about it."
"I can get a job! You can take care of Patrick and I can work. Don't worry, everything will be all right."
Switcher shook his head impatiently. "No, everything will not be all right. In fact, I don't think that things will ever be the same again. It goes deeper

than the stock market crashing. Even deeper than half the banks in the country going bust. No, there's something wrong with a system of government that allows this to happen. No jobs means no money. No money means no food. No food means revolution! This government is rotten and should be turfed out!"

Mary Ellen listened to Switcher's outburst without understanding half of it. She had finally understood that he had lost all his money. The ramifications were beginning to sink in. She knew that hardly anyone worked anymore, not by reading the papers, but by talking to people she knew. It would not be easy to find a job, but she would find one. She had to find one, because the alternative did not bear thinking about.

Suddenly Switcher stood up. "Where's that bottle of whisky kept?" he demanded.

Mary Ellen was surprised. Switcher only had a glass of wine on special occasions. There was something in his voice that told her not to argue with him.

"It's in the cabinet, I'll get it." She went into the living room and returned with the bottle.

Switcher poured himself a large glass and slammed the bottle down on the table. "Here, have one yourself, you're going to need it!"

Mary Ellen took little Patrick's hand and said, "No thanks. I think I'll go for a walk and think things out. I'll be back in a little while." She did not like the mood that Switcher was in. She had never seen him so upset. She knew he had good reason, but did not want to be around him till he came out of it.

"Suit yourself!" He drank the whisky in one gulp and immediately poured himself another.

Mary Ellen took Patrick and went out into the damp, drizzly day and started walking down the street. She walked around the neighborhood for about an hour to give Switcher time to calm down and then made her way back to the house. The first thing she noticed was the car was gone. *Where can he have gone?* She went over and asked the neighbors, but nobody had seen him driving off.

After waiting for around two hours, Mary Ellen was frantic with worry. She called the police and told them what had happened. They said they would send an officer round to talk to her. After a while the police car drew up in the driveway. The two officers came into the living room. Mary Ellen told them to sit down and she would describe the car and Mr. Switcher to them. The officers remained standing, looking uncomfortable till at last one of them broke the silence.

"We don't need a description, miss. Mr. Switcher had his bankbook on him."

Before he uttered another word Mary Ellen knew that Switcher was dead. She covered her face with her hands and started to weep uncontrollably. One of the policemen put his arm around her awkwardly, and said, "I'm sorry to have to tell you, but Mr. Switcher died of a heart attack. Are you his daughter, miss?"

Mary Ellen lowered her hands and pulled little Patrick to her. "No, I'm not his daughter, I'm just a friend who lives with him," she replied through her sobs.

"Do you know of any relatives? We have to inform the next of kin."

"He has a daughter in California, I can get you the address." She went into the writing bureau and gave them a notebook. "You'll find it in there." She sat down and started weeping again.

The policeman opened the notebook and copied the information. "Is there anything we can do? Would you like us to take you to a friend's house or something?"

"Can I see him? I'll have to arrange the funeral. Oh God, what will I do?"

"Calm down, miss. He has been taken to the City Morgue. You'll have to talk to the coroner. I don't know what the rules are, you not being a relative."

"When can I talk to the coroner or whoever he is? I'm the closest thing to family he has!"

The two policemen looked at one another, then one of them said, "Look, I'll tell you what we'll do. We'll go down and ask the coroner to send someone round to see you. He'll know what to do all right."

Mary Ellen nodded. "Thank you, now I'd like to be alone for a while."

The two men were relieved to have finished their duty and told her to call if she needed anything.

When they left, Mary Ellen put Patrick to bed and lay on her own bed thinking of what had happened. She had never given a moment's thought to the ramifications of Jimmy Switcher dying. It was clear that she would outlive him, but the thought had never entered her head that he would die so suddenly. She began to wonder what would happen to her now that he was gone. She had no money, her habit of giving to the poor box at church had never stopped and she had never given any thought to saving. She did not even have the right to live in his house. Maybe his daughter would come back from California. Switcher hardly ever mentioned his daughter, and Mary Ellen never asked about her because she instinctively felt he did not want to talk about her. She did not know what had happened between them. The rest of the day became a blur of neighbors coming to pay their respects and asking questions that she could not answer. At last Mary Ellen got rid of the last one and went to bed exhausted.

The next morning a young man from the coroner's office came to see her, and in typical bureaucratic fashion told her she could go and see Switcher's body if she wanted, but the funeral arrangements would be made by his daughter. Mary Ellen had no say in the matter. When she told him that the daughter was in California, he just shrugged and told her that he didn't make the rules and if she wanted to know any more then she should get a lawyer. Mary Ellen was glad to see the back of him.

She sat for a while weeping occasionally and worrying what would happen to her. She had kept in contact with the Swerskys and decided to call Rachel and tell her what had happened. When she gave the operator the number to call, she was shocked to learn that the number was no longer in service. It had been only a month since she had spoken to Rachel, but the operator was adamant. There was no such number available.

She decided to go to the police station and see if they had contacted Switcher's daughter. The officer told her that the police in California had indeed contacted Switcher's daughter and she had instructed the police to talk to Switcher's lawyer about arrangements for the funeral and the sale of the house.

"You mean to tell me she's not coming to her father's funeral!" Mary Ellen was shocked at the news. The part about selling the house did not register with her in her anger.

"Look, miss, here's the lawyer's name and address, I suggest you go and talk to him." The officer gave her a slip of paper.

"That's just what I'll do!" Mary Ellen walked out of the station with tears running down her cheeks. How could anyone be so heartless? When she thought of how kind Switcher had been to herm she could not conceive of his own daughter not coming home to pay her respects. *To put a lawyer in charge of the arrangements for her father's funeral! What kind of a person was she?* Mary Ellen counted what was left in her purse. She had eight dollars and fifty cents. She looked at the address on the paper and decided to go by bus. It took her almost an hour to get to the lawyer's office. It was just off Five Mile Road in a red brick building. She went in and asked the receptionist for Mr. Holmes, the lawyer.

"Have you an appointment, ma'am?" the receptionist asked brightly.

Mary Ellen thought fast. If she said no, she would have a hard time seeing this man, so impulsively she answered, "No, but if you tell him Jim Switcher's daughter is here I'm sure he'll see me."

The receptionist gestured to a couch and pressed a button on her desk console. Mary Ellen sat on the couch with Patrick and waited nervously.

After a minute the elevator door opened and Mr. Holmes walked out briskly and came straight over to her.

"Miss Switcher? I thought Jim had only one daughter, and she's in California. My deepest condolences. Come this way and we can talk." He led her to the elevator and they went up to his office on the third floor. He seated her on a chair in front of his desk and sat behind the desk and lifted a folder.

"I'm just going through your father's will, now what is your first name?"

Mary Ellen interrupted him. "I'm not Jim's daughter, I just said that so as I could see you. I'm a friend who's been living in his house for the last four years. The police gave me your name. I don't know what to do, and I thought you could give me advice or something? I just don't know where to turn!" She burst into tears and hugged Patrick to her.

The lawyer pulled a handkerchief from his pocket and handed it over to her. "Calm yourself, miss. Now what did you say your name was?"

"Mary Ellen O'Neill. I met Mr. Switcher on the boat coming over and he's been like a father to me. What will I do?" she sobbed.

"And you are no relation to the deceased?" The lawyer was unimpressed by Mary Ellen's tears. He had seen it many times. An older man had taken a housekeeper in to look after him and they ended up thinking they were somehow entitled to his money when he died. His time was too valuable to be taken up explaining the law to anyone who asked him. He stood up and said coldly, "I'm sorry, miss, but to put it bluntly, I've been instructed to bury Mr. Switcher and sell all his assets, including the house as soon as possible. Not that we'll get much for anything these days." He turned his back and looked out of the window.

Mary Ellen regained her composure. "Are you telling me his daughter is not coming to the funeral?"

Mr. Holmes turned around and looked at her. "Miss O'Neill, I'm sorry to have to be so blunt, but this is simply none of your concern. Do you still have the key to Mr. Switcher's house?"

"Of course I have the key. What has that to do with anything?" She had not understood his meaning.

"Well, as Mr. Switcher's attorney I'm afraid you'll have to give the key up and vacate the premises as soon as possible."

She looked at him in shock. "Give you the key? Get out of the house? Where will I go?"

Holmes decided to let her down gently in case she became hysterical. "Look, miss, why don't you go home and pack your belongings and find another place to live. I'll give you two days to vacate the property. If you do not, I'll have to inform the sheriff's office. You must realize you have no right to live in that house now that Mr. Switcher is dead!"

The reality of the situation hit Mary Ellen like a blow. Here she was with a child and no money or a roof over her head. She looked at the lawyer pleadingly. "Will you at least tell me when the funeral is?"

Holmes closed the folder and filed it in his drawer. Without looking up he answered, "There will be no funeral service as such. There will be a viewing at seven o'clock tonight at Ward's funeral home. Tomorrow morning Mr. Switcher will be buried in the family vault at...let me see." He paused and pulled the folder out and opened it. "Ah, it is located at Gratiot and Twelve Mile road. He will be buried at ten o'clock. The funeral home is just down the road on Gratiot. When you vacate the house, leave the keys inside. Now, if there's nothing else?" Gently but firmly, he took her arm and escorted her to elevator.

Mary Ellen walked away from the lawyer's office in a state of numbness. She could not think clearly and the realization that she was going to be homeless in a couple of days terrified her. She did not know anyone that she could ask to take her in for free. She could not get a job without having a babysitter, and she could not get a babysitter without money. She walked all the way home trying to think of what to do. When she got home she fed Patrick and put him to bed. She could not eat or sleep all night, and sat in the darkness alone in despair over her situation. She came to the conclusion that her only recourse was to go to the priest and ask for help. She shuddered when she thought of the last time she had gone to a priest, but she knew Father Daly well enough by now.

In the morning she dressed Patrick and had a bath and put on her best clothes for the funeral. It was a cold and damp November morning and only five people showed up at the funeral. The funeral director said a few words and signaled to the grave diggers to lower the coffin into the gaping hole in the ground. Mary Ellen lifted a handful of earth and slipped Switcher's wedding ring off her finger. As the men shoveled the dirt on top of the coffin, she said a prayer aloud and threw the dirt and the ring into the open grave.

What a sad way for such a good man to go, she thought sadly. *No family and only five mourners.* She took her little boy's hand and walked slowly away as the drizzle turned to sleet and the wind lashed the people on their way out of the cemetery.

She walked from the cemetery to the church, a distance of five miles, and both her and Patrick were soaked and shivering by the time she knocked on the chapel house door. Father Daly answered the door himself and ushered them inside.

"What are you doing walking in this weather, Mary Ellen? You'll both catch your death of cold!" He took her coat and led the way into the kitchen. "Sit down and I'll make you some coffee, and what will I give little Patrick? The poor child is frozen."

"Some hot milk will do." Mary Ellen braced herself to tell the priest what had happened.

He boiled the kettle and served the coffee and hot milk. He sat across the table from her and asked her, "Now, my dear, what can I do for you?"

Mary Ellen could not have picked a worst time to look for help. The country was at its lowest point since the Revolution. Banks were closing all over the country, and there were millions of people out of work. With no Social Security to fall back on, people who had saved some money for a rainy day now were left with nothing. Because they could not pay their mortgages or rent, they ended up on the streets selling apples or lining up daily at the soup kitchens that had opened up in all the cities across America.

At first Father Daly had let some poor families sleep on cots in the church hall, but the numbers were so great that it was impossible to help them all. He had appealed for help from the Bishop, but the Bishop was getting the same thing from every parish in the city. It was like a hurricane of poverty that seemed to grow in strength as the depression dragged on. He listened to Mary Ellen sorrowfully because he knew that she was the first to give to charities and anyone in need. Now that she needed help he was unable to help her.

"Have you no one who can put you up? Even for a little while?" the priest asked morosely.

"I don't know who to ask. All my friends from the church are just as bad off as I am."

The priest suddenly brightened up. "That's the answer! Your friends will need every dime they can get their hands on right now. You say you have eight dollars. Well, believe it or not, eight dollars is a lot more than a lot of people have! You can stay here tomorrow night after you leave the house, and I'll ask around and see if we can get you a room to rent." Mary Ellen was doubtful.

"How much would it cost to rent a room?"

"I'm not sure, but the way things are now, people will take anything they can get just to stay in their houses. Now, you go home, and if I were you I'd take every morsel of food in the house with you when you leave. Believe me, you will need it."

Mary Ellen got up to leave. "Thank you, Father, I'll see you tomorrow night."

"Goodbye, Mary Ellen. I'll send someone round about six to help you with your belongings."

Father Daly was as good as his word. He arranged for one of the parishioners who was in dire straits to meet Mary Ellen when she arrived at the church house with her belongings. He introduced the woman as Mrs. Gorman. Her husband was away looking for work and she had three children all under the age of six. She happened to live one block over from Switcher's house, but Mary Ellen had not met her before.

"Well, Mrs. Gorman, I'm afraid I can't pay much. How much do you want for renting a room to my son and I?"

"God knows I'm not looking for much. My husband left two months ago and has not sent a penny since. He's riding the trains hoping to get something, but he's had no luck at all." The woman looked close to tears. "The truth is if I don't come up with thirty dollars at the end of the month, we could be thrown out on the street!"

"All I have is eight dollars," Mary Ellen said. "You can have it all if it will help you keep your house."

"It'll help all right, but how long do you want to stay for the eight dollars?" Mary Ellen took the money out of her purse. She put it on the table. "If you need it all right now, take it. I'll leave it up to you how long we can stay for it."

Father Daly looked on in amazement.

Mrs. Gorman took the money and leaned over to Mary Ellen. "Mary Ellen, get your things. You're coming to stay with us for as long as you want! That's the kindest thing anyone has ever done for me, so it's only right that I can put you up."

Mary Ellen smiled up at the priest. "You see, Father, everything will be all right."

Father Daly looked at the two women and smiled happily. "Yes, everything will be all right."

Mary Ellen and Mrs. Gorman got on well together right from the start. Mrs. Gorman had a friend who owned a small bakery and needed occasional help during the night. Now that the two women could babysit for each other, they took turns helping out at the bakery. The pay was very little, twenty-five cents an hour, but they could take home any extra or damaged cakes and pies and a couple of loaves a day. This was more important than the wages, because they all had plenty to eat.

The winter of 1931-32 was the worst of the Depression. Millions of people were close to starvation. The soup kitchens were the only source of food for hundreds of thousands of city dwellers. In the countryside, at least there seemed to be always something to eat, but in the inner cities it was not uncommon to see women and children raking through the rotten garbage dumps looking for anything that might be edible. Most of the people could not afford to heat their houses adequately and between the cold and the poor diet the infant mortality rate soared.

In the middle of January, Mrs. Gorman and Mary Ellen were sitting discussing what to do about the mortgage payment. Mr. Gorman had sent forty dollars at Christmas. He had found some work with the railroad clearing snow in the mountains out west. That had paid December, but January was another matter. The bakery was on its last legs. Very few people could afford bread now, let alone cakes. They still got enough food between them to survive on, but they both knew it was coming to an end. The two women had tried everything they knew to get some kind of work, but they were just two of millions. Mary Ellen took to walking the railroad tracks to pick up lumps of coal that had fallen off the trains. They learned all kinds of ways to make the little food they had go further. They got the bones that the butcher used to give to dogs for making soup out of the damaged vegetables they picked up at the fruit market.

All of this helped them survive, but the mortgage was another matter. A lot of the neighbors had simply walked away from their homes because they had no way of paying. The impossibility of finding work meant that there was simply no cash. Mrs. Gorman wrote to her husband telling him that the collection agency was giving people an extra month to come up with the payment or they would be evicted. That meant going to live in one of the city shelters that did nothing more than put a roof over their heads. They used derelict buildings and put army cots in them. There was no privacy and whole families had to share rooms with others in the same predicament.

"I'll die before I'll go into one of those places!" Mrs. Gorman said bitterly. "What has happened to this country? A few years ago everyone was working!"

Mary Ellen shook her head. "I sometimes wonder myself what I'm doing here. You know, all my life I wanted to come here, and now look at me. No house, no job, no husband and a baby I can hardly feed." She took Mrs. Gorman by the hand. "Don't despair, God will take care of us. We haven't died of hunger or cold yet, have we? You must have hope in the future. It's the only thing that keeps me going. If I didn't have hope, I think I would be dead by now, after all that's happened since I came here."

"I suppose you're right, but hope isn't going to pay the mortgage, is it?"

Mary Ellen stood up briskly. "No, it won't, but neither will sitting around moaning. I'll go down to the market now and see if I can pick up anything. Now cheer up, something will come up and we'll be all right, wait and see!" she said without conviction.

Mrs. Gorman sighed. "I hope you're right, Mary Ellen, because I'm reaching the end of my tether."

Mary Ellen was half right. Something did come up to help Mrs. Gorman. It came in the form of a letter from her husband telling her that he had got a full time job with the railroad out in Colorado. He was going to send her the money for the family's fares to join him out west. He told her to put the house up for sale, but if it didn't sell to just walk away and leave it. He would send her the money in two weeks, so she could start packing right away. When Mrs. Gorman told Mary Ellen the news, she was embarrassed, knowing that it meant that Mary Ellen would have to find somewhere to live.

"Never you mind about me! Just think of your own family and how lucky your husband was to get a full time job. Patrick and I will find a place, and, anyway, we have two weeks before you go, haven't we?" Mary Ellen tried to put on a brave front, but inside she knew that this was her worst fear coming true. She had no money to pay rent anywhere and the bakery was only open three days a week, and was about ready to close down.

Mrs. Gorman put the house up for sale, but with the place already mortgaged at pre-depression prices, there were no offers. The two weeks flew and the money duly arrived for the Gorman family's fares. Mrs. Gorman gave Mary Ellen twenty dollars of the money.

"It's the least I can do!" Mrs. Gorman said, brushing aside Mary Ellen's protests. "It still leaves us enough to get our tickets. Look, here's the keys to the house, just stay here until they throw you out. It will take them awhile to figure out that we're gone and won't be coming back. Here's a note giving you permission to stay here till we come back. When they come, just tell them you're still waiting for us."

Mary Ellen was shocked. "But isn't that illegal? Will we get into trouble?"

Mrs. Gorman laughed out loud. "Trouble! You'll be in worse trouble without a roof over your head. This will give you some time to try and find a place, and if you're still here when they come looking, all they can do is put you out!"

"I suppose you're right. How long do you think it'll take for them to come?"

"Probably a couple of missed payments. I'd say about six weeks for them to get here after all their paperwork."

Mary Ellen brightened up. "Well, it will give us some time to find a place, or maybe even a job!

"That's better, now come and help me get packed."

After the Gormans had gone, Mary Ellen had the house to herself. Every minute of every day was spent waiting and worrying about being put out on the street. She realized she could not live like this and started to look for a room to rent. She went back to Father Daly, but he couldn't help her with a place to stay. He told her that the church was having a big sale of anything that people wanted rid of that Saturday and offered her the chance to help sell the stuff. She would get a ten percent commission off anything she sold. Mary Ellen was glad of the chance to make a little money and maybe find someone with a room to rent.

On the Saturday morning the church hall was crowded with people bringing in their goods to sell and lots of people looking for a bargain. Mary Ellen was stationed at a stall full of used pots and pans. She looked at the stuff in disgust. Half of the cookware had no handles and every second pot seemed to be burnt beyond repair. *How will I make anything off this rubbish? Nobody in their right mind would buy any of this.* She made a half-hearted attempt at sorting them in some kind of order.

Strangely enough, Mary Ellen's stall turned out to be one of the most popular. To her surprise, people were actually buying the old pots and pans, and the more she sold there always seemed to be more coming in. She was kept busy most of the morning, and at lunch time, when Father Daly filled in for her she had fifteen dollars. That meant she had made a dollar fifty and got a free lunch into the bargain. She was feeling quite pleased with herself when she went back to the stall after lunch.

She chatted for a little while with the priest about finding somewhere to live, and he promised to keep a lookout for her. When he left, Mary Ellen sat down to wait for customers. Suddenly she heard her name being called and looked up in surprise. It was Adam Corbett coming through the crowd to greet her. Dumbstruck, her face reddened remembering their last meeting.

"Hello, Mary Ellen, how are you doing? It's a long time since we met, but you're still as beautiful as ever!" Corbett smiled at her and hugged her in order to disguise his shock at her appearance. In the few months since he had last seen her, she had lost about twenty pounds and her face was drawn with worry and tiredness.

"Fine, Adam, and how are you?" she stammered, trying to sound calm, when inside she was bursting to tell him how glad she was to see him.

"I'm doing okay. I'm still working, which is more than most people can say. Now tell me how you ended up selling old pots in a church sale?" He was laughing, but she sensed that he knew she wasn't there by choice. She remembered Switcher's advice to her the night Adam Corbett walked away. She would tell him the truth this time and see what happened. She started off telling him about Switcher dying and told him everything that had happened since, including the fact that she was homeless and was trying to find a place for her and Patrick to live. When she finished telling him, the tears welled up in her eyes and she turned away in embarrassment. "So there you have it, Adam. That's why I'm standing here selling old pots."

He looked at her with pity in his eyes and said harshly, "Why didn't you get in touch with my sister, you know how I feel about you!"

"I was too ashamed after the way I treated you the last time we were together."

Corbett stood for a while in silence, looking at her. He held out his hand and took her hand in his. He looked into her eyes and said seriously, "Mary Ellen, you have nothing to be ashamed of. The fault was mine for prying into your business. When you're ready you can tell me whatever you like, but for now your worries are over. You and Patrick are coming to live with me. I have a three-bedroom house all to myself, so there is plenty of room!"

Mary Ellen started to protest halfheartedly, but Corbett brushed her aside. "Come on, Mary Ellen. Let's get Patrick and get out of here. I have a car with me so we'll go and get your belongings and get you home as quick as possible. You look as if you need a good rest."

Mary Ellen started feeling better immediately. Corbett's no nonsense way of taking charge made her feel the way she used to in Ireland so long ago, when she had her father and brothers to protect her.

Adam Corbett rented a house from the United Auto Workers, a new union he worked for as an organizer. He got the house cheap because of his position in the union, who also let him use their car when it was available. As he explained to Mary Ellen, it was the worst of times to try and get men to join a union when they would do just about anything to keep a job, let alone jeopardize it by joining a union. That being said, it did not stop him from trying. He worked steady night shift in an auto parts plant and spent half of his day going around trying to get people to sign up for the union. His job was on the outskirts of town, so he confined his activities with the union to the downtown area where no one from his work would see him. He knew if his employer found out what he was doing he would be fired immediately. At work he never mentioned unions because, like everyone else, he needed the job.

Mary Ellen soon settled in and was both happy and relieved to have a place to stay. Corbett gave her and little Patrick two of the rooms, which were sparsely furnished, but Mary Ellen soon had them quite comfortable.

The next Saturday morning when Corbett came in from work, Mary Ellen had a fried breakfast ready for him when he came in.

"Well, what a nice surprise, Mary Ellen!" He sat down and started eating with obvious enjoyment. "Boy, I could get used to this! I'm fed up having porridge every morning, this is great."

Mary Ellen smiled. "Well, enjoy it while you can, but you know you can't have this every morning."

"I'm not thinking of any other morning, thank you very much. Once a week will be fine, if you don't mind!" He pushed his plate away and lit a cigarette. "Thanks again, Mary Ellen, that was just great!"

"Don't thank me, it's you that's paying for it, I just made it!"

Corbett looked at her with a serious look on his face. She knew when he looked like that he had something important to say. "Sit down, Mary Ellen. Pour yourself a coffee. We have to have a talk, and the sooner the better, I'm thinking."

Mary Ellen poured her coffee, and suddenly started to feel nervous. She instinctively knew what he was going to say, but had not expected him to bring it up so soon. He was going to ask her about her dead husband and she knew she was still not ready to tell him the truth. She sat down facing him and braced herself. "Well, Adam, I'm glad you enjoyed your breakfast, now what is it you want to say?"

Adam leaned over the table and looked into her eyes. "I need to know a couple of things, Mary Ellen. Don't be offended or afraid I'll throw you out or anything, just answer me two things truthfully and that's all I want. Can you do that?"

Mary Ellen nodded her head. "I'll try," she said quietly.

"Are you really a widow, Mary Ellen?" he asked softly.

Immediately Jimmy Switcher's face appeared in front of her. *She heard his voice telling her that if someone loved her enough, the truth would not matter to him, and if she loved someone enough, she would tell him the truth. Did she love Adam Corbett enough, or was she just grateful for his help? And did Adam Corbett love her enough to overlook what happened to her?* Her face became drawn as the memory of that terrible night returned to her.

Corbett looked at her anxiously. "Are you all right? Look, just forget I said anything! I'm sorry I upset you, it's the last thing I want to do!"

Mary Ellen shook her head and took a deep breath. "It's all right, Adam, I'll answer your question. No, I am not a widow. I have never been married." She lowered her head and felt the tears slowly trickling down her cheeks. She waited for the second question, and prepared herself to tell him about her ordeal. He reached over and took both her hands in his. She looked up slowly and was amazed to see that he was smiling.

"Good! Now that's out of the way, I can ask you the second question. Will you marry me, Mary Ellen O'Neill? I've loved you since the first time I laid eyes on you!"

Mary Ellen was dumbstruck. She had expected him to ask about where Patrick came from if she was never married.

"Don't you want to know about Patrick?" she asked hoarsely.

"It's not Patrick I'm asking to marry. I'm sure you'll tell me all about it when you're ready. Right now I'm waiting for an answer to my question."

Mary Ellen started to relax and think clearly. "Adam, I'll answer your question after you hear what I've got to say. First, you have to hear me out, then you can ask me again if you want to. Fair enough?"

Adam leaned back in his chair. "If you're sure that's what you want to do. But it won't make any difference."

"All right then, we'll see." Mary Ellen gathered her thoughts. *Where would she start her story?*

She started from the time she met Marcus Browning on the ship and told Corbett everything that had happened since. The theft of her money; the rape by the priest; the kindness of the Swerskys and Jimmy Switcher, right up to the Gormans leaving her in the house alone.

Corbett sat in silence listening to her. When she finished he shook his head in disbelief. "How did you survive all of that? What kept you going? Why didn't you ask your family to send you the fare to get back to Ireland?"

Mary Ellen looked at him sadly. "I couldn't disgrace the family going back with a baby and me not married. Who would believe that a priest could do such a thing? I doubt even my own mother would believe it. I still haven't told them about Patrick."

Corbett"s voice was quiet. "The disgrace is not yours, Mary Ellen. It's that thief whom you trusted and the priest who violated you who are the disgrace. You have done nothing wrong."

"I still don't think my family would understand that. Things are different in Ireland, you know."

"And you still go to church after what happened to you! For God's sake why would you go back?"

She smiled at him. "Faith in God, Adam. And the hope that things will get better."

Again, Corbett sat in silence. Eventually he shook his head and looked up at her. "Well, I've been told before never to try and understand a woman, because they are totally irrational. Now I know what they were talking about, so I give up. Now will you answer my question? Will you marry me, Mary Ellen?"

She stood up and looked out of the window. "You're sure you still want to marry me, Adam? Even after hearing that?"

He stood up and turned her around to face him. "All the more so, Mary Ellen. All the more so!"

Suddenly she flung her arms around his neck. "Yes, Adam Corbett, I will marry you. I was just afraid to tell you what happened before in case you didn't want me."

"Well, let's try and forget all that for a while, we've got the future to think of now." He put his hand into his pocket and pulled out a little box.

"Open it, it's your wedding ring, girl!" He lifted her up exuberantly and whirled her around.

She fumbled the box open and said seriously, "I can't put it on till we're married, you know!"

Corbett put her down and shook his head. "All right! We'd better get you married soon. Now where would you like to be married?"

"In the church, of course. I'm sure Father Daly will marry us."

"You reckon he'll marry us even though I'm not a churchgoer?"

"Yes, I'm sure, because I'll turn you into a churchgoer!"

Corbett laughed out loud. "We'll see about that later on! First let's go and see the priest."

Mary Ellen took Adam's hand in hers. "I'll need to tell my family in Ireland and I don't know how to explain little Patrick. I could never tell them the truth about what happened."

Adam thought for a moment. "A white lie never hurt anybody, Mary Ellen. Just tell them I'm a widower and Patrick is my son. That should solve your problem."

"I've never lied to them before, but I'm sure God will forgive me this one time."

Adam patted her hand. "I'm sure he will, Mary Ellen. I'm sure he will."

Mary Ellen was right. Father Daly was happy to marry them and didn't even ask Adam if he went to church. They had a small wedding with only Adam's sister and her husband and a few of his friends.

They soon settled into the routine of married life. Adam did not want her working, even if she could get a job. His job paid poorly as did all jobs at the time, but it was enough to pay the rent and feed them quite comfortably. Occasionally he would get the use of the car from the union and they would go for drives in the country. Adam's sister and her family became good friends and they would go to each other's houses for dinner on Sundays. For the first time since she landed in America Mary Ellen felt happy and safe. Corbett was a good and kind husband and she soon found out that he was passionate about his union activities. He told her about his experiences in the mines and described the way they were treated at his work. More and more the conditions were worsening. The breaks were cut in half and the workers were expected to produce more for the same wages. Some places even cut the wages and the workers were told to take it or leave it. This was like telling them to choose between starvation and working, so they had to accept steadily worsening conditions.

When President Roosevelt was elected in 1933 and "The New Deal" started to take effect in the huge government-backed projects, more people were getting jobs, but it was just a drop in the ocean of unemployment and it was a very slow process for the country to get back on its feet. Things would not get back to the 20s level of employment till the United States started rearming in 1940. In 1934 more and more companies were resorting to hiring thugs to break up union meetings and it was becoming dangerous to hold such meetings, because the police were often called in to help the company men, and there were many cases of split heads and broken limbs at the end of these confrontations.

After John L. Lewis, the great union leader of the A.F.L. took out more than 70,000 miners in Pennsylvania, the labor wars of the 30s really started. Munitions sales soared as both the companies and police forces readied themselves for what they regarded as a war against them. The depression had brought out the worst in many employers. In Pennsylvania employers deducted thirty-three cents off children's pay to pay the fines levied for working them ninety hours a week. The union organizing was more a measure of desperation than a war against unfair labor laws.

It was in this atmosphere of almost war fever that Adam Corbett went about the business of organizing unions in the worst of conditions. The targeted companies were the worst abusers of their workers and they soon had gangs of thugs waiting for the opportunity to break up the meetings. Mary Ellen worried about the danger Adam was in and tried to talk him out of going to the meetings.

"Someone has to stand up for these people, Mary Ellen. The working conditions will only get worse unless we organize. Strikes seem to be the only language the bosses understand."

"Well, let someone else organize them! You've done enough and I don't think they appreciate what you're trying to do for them!"

Adam quieted her down and said, "If you saw the conditions some of these people are working under you would be the first to help, Mary Ellen. Do you know that in some mines out west the miners are led to the pits at gunpoint? No, it's just a matter of time till the government gives us our rights, and that is all we want, the right to negotiate our working conditions!"

"I suppose you're right, but please be careful, Adam. There's too much violence going on at these meetings," she said resignedly.

"Ach, you worry too much woman, I'll see you when I get back." And off he went to another meeting.

One night Adam came back with twelve stitches in a cut on his head. He hid it from Mary Ellen and went to work as if nothing had happened. When he got to work, the foreman, Robertson, was waiting at the door with a policeman.

"You're fired, Corbett. We know what you've been up to. Now get the hell off this property or I'll have you arrested!"

Adam knew there was no use arguing. "All right, just give me my tools and my wages and I'll be on my way!"

The foreman, a creature who would literally have licked the bosses' boots if they told him, knew he had the upper hand, and was enjoying his chance to bring Corbett down. He had never gotten over the feeling that Corbett always seemed to treat him with contempt without saying so directly.

"What tools? You never had any tools when you started here. We'll mail your wages on to you, now get the hell out of here!"

For an instant Adam thought about beating the hell out of him, but the policeman already had his hand on his nightstick. He held his hands up and smiled at Robertson. "All right I'm going, but I'll probably see you around sometime soon!" He turned on his heel and walked away.

Robertson felt a shiver of fear go up his back. He turned to the policeman. "You heard that! He just threatened me! Go on, do what you're here for, arrest him!"

The policeman looked at him in disgust. "I never heard any threat! Let him go home, the poor bastard just lost his job and you want to arrest him into the bargain, come on get inside!"

Mary Ellen was not surprised to hear that Adam had lost his job. "It was a matter of time before they found out what you were up to. So what will you do now?"

"Don't worry, I'll get another job. The union does have some power, you know. We have sympathizers in places that hire union men as long as the other employers don't find out."

Suddenly Mary Ellen noticed a trickle of blood on his forehead. She jumped out of her chair and rushed round the table. "My God almighty, Adam! What happened to your head?" She pulled his hair back to see the stitches."

"Ach, that's nothing, just a scratch. There was a bit of a tussle at the meeting and I got whacked, that's all."

She wiped the blood off his face and said, "Adam, the next time it could be worse than this. Promise me you'll stop going to the meetings. I'm afraid you'll get killed one of these days."

Adam put on his serious face and replied, "You know I can't do that, Mary Ellen. I want a promise from you. You know I'll do anything for you, but I want you to promise never to ask me to give up on the union. It means too much to me."

She sighed and washed the cloth in the sink. "I promise, but please be careful in future, will you?"

"Of course, now you stop worrying. Tomorrow I'll go and see about a job. We can't live on nothing, you know."

Adam was right, he got another job without too much trouble. He also got his tools back. One night when the foreman Robertson was going into work, he was approached by two strangers who told him in no uncertain terms to bring Adam's tools out of the plant in the morning. They did not threaten him directly, but he knew he'd better give them the tools.

Mary Ellen had a gut feeling that it was only a matter of time before Adam got hurt or worse. The papers were full of the violence between the unions and the strikebreakers and police. The abuses by the employers continued even though the government passed laws giving the unions the right to negotiate. General Motors subsidized an expanded police force to jail suspected organizers. At the smaller companies they were not so particular. They simply hired gangs of thugs to beat and terrorize anyone who tried to organize their workers. There were cases throughout the country where workers had been shot and killed for simply having meetings. At one of these meetings Adam was mingling with the crowd of workers trying to get them to sign up when suddenly they heard the police sirens as about twenty cars came from different directions and screamed to a stop, with armed men jumping out all over the place. The police didn't bother to warn anyone, they simply waded in to the crowd with their nightsticks, battering anyone in their way. The crowd scattered in all directions and a couple of shots were heard over the noise of the shouting men.

As Adam tried to calm the men nearest to him a plain-clothes man ran at him with a piece of pipe intent on smashing his head in. Adam was no stranger to violence, being raised in a mining town in the west of Scotland. He sidestepped the onrushing thug and tripped him up, then kicked him brutally in the face. In a rage he grabbed the man by his lapels and repeatedly smashed his head into the concrete till he stopped moving. The whole place was a mass of shouting men, the screams of the injured mixed with the occasional gunshot being heard above the din. Adam Corbett lifted the pipe and waded into the masses of blue uniforms, swinging in both directions, battering everyone that came near him. He was blindly swinging the pipe when suddenly he felt a sharp pain in his neck and everything went black.

He woke up in a cell in the police station along with a dozen of his friends. One of them was holding a wet cloth to his head, which felt like it was being drilled by a jackhammer.

"Are you all right, Adam?"

Adam raised himself to a sitting position and groaned as he felt the huge bump on his head. "I'll be all right," he said ruefully as the events of the night started to come back to him. He looked around the holding cell and saw a lot of bandaged heads and cut and bruised faces.

A policeman appeared and barked at the group of prisoners. "On your feet and face the front so as we can get a look at you."

The men dragged themselves upright and shuffled toward the barred doors. Through the haze of pain in his head, Adam saw a man in plain clothes with a bandage round his head peering into the cell. It was obvious his nose was broken and his eyes were already turning black.

"That's the bastard there!" he shouted, pointing at Adam.

Adam looked foggily at the man and realized it was the man who attacked him with the pipe.

The policeman opened the cell door. He pointed at Adam. "You there, come here!" Adam walked slowly to the door. The policeman turned to the man with the bandage. "Are you sure it's this one?"

The man walked right in front of Adam and looked him in the eye. "I'm sure, all right! I hope you've got a good lawyer, pal, because you just tried to murder a Federal agent!"

Mary Ellen knew immediately something was wrong when one of Adams' friends came to the house. She was not surprised to hear what had happened, she just felt a kind of relief that he had not been killed. The next morning she went to the courthouse where the men were being arraigned.

The prosecutor shouted a name and the charge which was always the same. "Incitement to riot and trespassing on private property." The union lawyer put up the fifty dollars bail to get the men out till a trial date was arranged. When it came to Adam, he was brought in to the courtroom in handcuffs. The prosecutor read out the charge. "Adam Corbett, you are charged with the attempted murder of a Federal officer in the fulfillment of his duty. How do you plead?"

The courtroom went silent as Adam stared at the man in disbelief. "I never tried to murder anybody! I was just defending myself!"

The judge hammered his gavel furiously. "Just plead guilty or not guilty! You'll get a fair trial when we arrange a date."

"Not guilty, your honor!" Adam caught sight of Mary Ellen who was white-faced with shock.

"The people request that this man be held without bail, your honor. We believe he would flee to escape punishment for his crime."

The union lawyer interrupted, "What crime? He just pleaded not guilty, didn't he?"

The judge hammered his gavel furiously. "This is a Federal crime he's charged with! I have no authority here. Prisoner to be remanded till a hearing is arranged with a Federal judge. Take him away." The bailiff led Adam back to the cells.

Mary Ellen pushed her way to the union lawyer. "What's happening? What are they doing to him? Can I see him? Please help me!"

The lawyer took her by the arm. "Don't worry, we'll sort this out. There's been a mistake in the charges. Now come with me and we'll go and see Adam."

The union lawyer led Mary Ellen to a waiting room and told her to wait till he got back to her. He was gone for an hour and Mary Ellen started imagining all sorts of things. *What if the man died? What if Adam got life? God forbid, but what if he got executed?* Her mind was flying in all different directions when the lawyer came back. "What's going on, I'm about round the bend with worry?" Mary Ellen stood up and gripped his arm.

The lawyer eased her back into the chair. "The man Adam hit is indeed a Federal agent. We have three witnesses that will swear that Adam acted in self-defense, so the attempted murder charge will be dropped. We still have to wait till a Federal judge is available to try the case, so they will hold him in jail till then."

"How long will that be?"

"A few days, a week at the outside."

"When can I see him?"

The lawyer stood up. "They're transferring him to the State courthouse. I'll drive you there and you can talk to him before they lock him up."

They left the courthouse and drove to the state facility, which was a half hour's drive. The lawyer signed some papers to allow them entry and led Mary Ellen into a sort of hallway with glass partitions separating it down the middle. The room was empty. The partition was divided into cubicles with a small hole in the glass for speaking to the prisoners. There was a chair in front of each cubicle and the lawyer guided Mary Ellen to the first one.

"I have a couple of questions, then I'll leave you alone with him. Ah, here they are now."

A door opened and Adam came in with a guard. He sat opposite Mary Ellen, and before he could say anything the lawyer signaled to the guard to leave.

The guard shrugged, looked at his watch and growled, "Ten minutes!" He left and slammed the door behind him.

The lawyer leaned close to the glass. "Just two questions, Adam. First, did the agent show you a badge identifying himself?" Second, did he attack you first?"

"The answer to the first is he identified himself with a lead pipe! And the second question is answered in the first!"

The lawyer leaned back, satisfied. "That's all you need to say to anyone. I'll be in touch." He turned around and left the room.

Adam looked at Mary Ellen through the glass. "I'm sorry to put you through this, Mary Ellen, but that man was trying to kill me. I had to defend myself."

"I believe you, Adam. Are you all right? You don't look well."

"Apart from my head, I'm all right, now. Don't worry about me. The union will look after me in here. I'll be acquitted at the trial, we have three eyewitnesses."

"I hope you're right, I just hope it's soon so as we can get it over with."

"The lawyer says it will be a week at the outside. No jury, just a judge."

"Why no jury, Adam, I thought that was the law?"

"The lawyer said if we chose just the judge it would be over faster. It's an open and shut case anyway."

"If you say so, but I think a jury would be better. You never know with a judge!"

Adam laughed. "That's the Irish coming out in you. It'll be all right, don't worry."

"All right, time's up, pal. Back to your cell!"

The guard came in and roughly grabbed Adam's arm and pulled him upright.

"Don't worry." Was all Mary Ellen heard before the door slammed shut and left her alone.

The lawyer was right about the timing of Adam's hearing. Federal Judge George Russell was holding court on Thursday, the sixteenth of August, 1934, at the courthouse in Detroit. Mary Ellen left Patrick with a neighbor and went to the courthouse filled with trepidation. She could not shake the feeling that something terrible was going to happen, regardless of what the lawyer told them. When she arrived at the courthouse, she saw the lawyer standing outside talking to some men. She went up to him and asked where she should go.

He took her arm, and saying goodbye to the men, led her up the stairs into the building. "Now, I don't want you worrying, Mary Ellen. I've spoken to the prosecutor and he's dropped the attempted murder charge. Adam will plead guilty to simple assault and he'll get a fine. The union will pay it and he'll be going home with you for dinner."

"Did Adam agree to plead guilty? It doesn't sound like him."

"Well, it took awhile to talk him into it, but if he didn't, there was the risk of jail time, so he came around to seeing it my way."

They entered the courtroom and Mary Ellen sat on a bench and looked around. The two prosecutors were sitting at a desk in front of the public benches and the man whom Adam assaulted sat beside them. The clerk of the court came in and sat at her machine, and the bailiff came in and looked at his watch. It was five minutes to ten.

A door opened on the side and Adam came in accompanied by a guard. He nodded to her as he walked over and took his seat beside the lawyer.

"All rise!" the bailiff called as the judge came in from a door behind the bench and took his seat. The bailiff read out the charges and the clerk handed a folder up to the judge. Judge Russell glanced at the papers and looked through bloodshot eyes at Adam. The judge was nursing a terrible hangover and wanted another drink badly. The sooner this thing was over the sooner he could have a nice glass of whisky to steady his shaking hands.

"Adam Corbett, you are charged with assaulting a Federal officer in the line of duty. How do you plead?"

"Guilty your honor," Adam said clearly.

The judge looked again at the papers in front of him and said, "You have waived the right to a jury trial for this most serious charge. Is that correct?" He looked at Adam's lawyer.

"Yes your honor, we will accept the court's decision without benefit of a jury."

The judge turned to address the prosecutor. "I see you dropped the charge of attempted murder. It's a big difference from assault. Why did you do that?"

The prosecutor was used to dealing with cantankerous judges. He knew if he mentioned witnesses the judge would order a jury trial, and that was the last thing he wanted.

"We decided to go with the lesser charge because of lack of evidence, your honor."

Russell looked at him cynically. "Lack of evidence? I see. Stand up Corbett!"

Adam and his lawyer stood up.

Russell cleared his throat. "I'm sick and tired of these union thugs causing honest hard working Americans to lose business. I'm going to make an example of you, Corbett! We can't have Federal agents going in fear of their lives because of hoodlums like you. I sentence you to two years in Federal prison, and furthermore, the sentence will be served in Sing Sing prison in New York State. That will keep you from inciting your friends to riot here in Michigan! Take him away!"

He hammered his gavel on the desk and was out of the courtroom in an instant.

Adam turned to his lawyer open-mouthed. Before he could say anything, the guards were putting handcuffs on him.

The lawyer looked over at the prosecution. "What the hell happened? This usually gets a fine!"

The prosecutor shrugged. "I guess old Russell was in a bad mood." He lifted his briefcase and left. The Federal agent looked over at Adam on his way out and smirked at him.

Mary Ellen, white-faced, grabbed the lawyer by the lapels. "You said he'd be fined! Two years in prison for defending himself. What kind of justice is that?"

The lawyer hung his head. "I'm sorry, this has never happened before."

"Can't we appeal it or something?'

"There is an appeals process, but it would take months and a lot of money. You'd have to get a lawyer who knows Federal law better than me. I'm sorry I can't help you. What will you do, Mary Ellen?"

"You heard what he said. Adam is going to Sing Sing in New York." Mary Ellen sighed bitterly. "I've lived in New York before, so I suppose I'll have to go back. I have to be near him. He'll need me to visit him and, anyway, there's nothing to keep me here."

The lawyer looked at her sympathetically. "I'll see if the union can at least pay your fare to New York. I'll come by tomorrow and let you know."

"Can I see Adam now?"

The lawyer dropped his eyes and shook his head. "I'm sorry, Mary Ellen, but the next time you see your husband he will be in Sing Sing prison."

Chapter 9

Marcus and Emily arrived in England in August 1929. They took a suite in Selfridge's hotel and spent a few days sightseeing. Emily kept asking Marcus to take her to meet his family. Marcus explained to her that he had left on bad terms with his parents and did not feel right about showing up unannounced. It was all an act to make Emily doubly determined to meet them. He wanted to make sure she thought it was her cajoling that made him go. After a few days, Marcus pretended to reluctantly agree to take her to meet his parents.

"If you insist, we'll go. But don't be surprised if they don't let us in the door!"

"Nonsense! Wait till they see little Jack. They'll welcome you with open arms!"

"One thing, Emily, do not under any circumstances mention my sale of the company or anything at all about money. Leave that to me. Do you understand?"

Emily, like most people born into great wealth, had no interest where it came from, as long as it was there. She looked at him with a puzzled look on her face. "Of course, dear, whatever you say."

Emily was right. They hired a car with a chauffeur for the day and drove to Oxford in the morning. When the car drove up the driveway, Marcus saw his father talking to one of the servants on the front steps. The car slowed and stopped, and Marcus put his hand on Emily's arm.

"Stay here till I see what kind of reception I get." He opened the door and walked over to his father who looked at him, dumbstruck.

"Marcus! Good God!" Derek pushed the servant toward the door of the house. "Tell her ladyship Marcus has come home!" He rushed over and hugged Marcus, then held him at arm's length.

"By God, Marcus, look at you! You look wonderful. Where were you all these years?"

Emily opened the car door and came out holding the baby in her arms. Sir Derek looked at her in amazement. "Don't tell me you're married! And with a baby, too!" Marcus' mother came rushing out of the house and hugged him with tears running down her face.

"Thank God you've come back, son." She turned and looked at Emily and the baby. "And what have we got here?" She clasped her hands together and turned to Emily and the baby.

Marcus laughed. "If you give me a chance, I'll introduce them. This is my wife, Emily, and your grandson Jack. Emily, these are my parents, Sir Derek and Lady Catherine."

Sir Derek called on the butler to unload the luggage from the car.

"Father, we left our luggage in the hotel."

"Why did you do that? You are not staying in any hotel, what hotel is it? I'll send a man to go get your luggage."

Marcus pretended embarrassment. "Well, after the way we parted..."

Emily interrupted. "That's all in the past now, isn't it, Mr. Browning?"

"Of course it is, now tell the driver to go and get your things and you can stay with us."

Marcus nodded to the driver and told him to tell the hotel manager to give him the luggage. He pulled a wad of notes from his pocket and carelessly handed the driver some of them.

"Pay the hotel what we owe and I'll see you when you get back."

Catherine Browning took the baby from Emily and said happily, "Let's all get inside and you can tell us everything. My God, Marcus, I'm so happy you came back.

Emily looked at Marcus with a knowing smile on her face as if to say. *I told you so.*

After they had settled in and Marcus had told his parents about his time in America, they were more impressed by the fact that he didn't drink alcohol than anything else. Marcus was deliberately vague about his wealth and simply told them that he worked for a financial institution in New York.

"You must be doing very well for yourself," his father said when they were alone that night. "Tell me, why did you go to America?"

"It could have been anywhere or nowhere, I just went on the spur of the moment. At the time it seemed like a good idea."

"Well, you seem to have done all right for yourself!"

Marcus stifled a grin. *You don't know the half of it, old man.* "Yes, I'm doing all right. Of course, Emily's father owns an investment firm. I'm sure he would help us out if we got into any trouble financially."

"Yes, I'm sure he would. Still, I'm glad things are going so well for you. You went to the right place," Sir Derek said thoughtfully.

The next morning Marcus told his parents their plans to tour Europe for a couple of months, and then come back to England to book their passage back to the United States before winter set in. Before they set off for Europe, Marcus' parents arranged a dinner party for all their friends to come and see Marcus and his American wife. Marcus knew that appearances meant everything to his parents. That was why they had thrown him out. The good name of the family meant more to them than just about anything else. That was why they could not handle being unwelcome at the club where Marcus disgraced them.

This was a golden opportunity to show all those who shook their heads over Marcus that they were wrong and to show them what a success he had turned out to be. At the party Marcus' parents took the chance with both hands, bragging about their new grandson and reveling in the success of the prodigal son. All their friends and acquaintances were all over Emily and the baby. After dinner the men moved into Sir Derek's smoking room for brandy and cigars.

"Marcus, you remember General Hawkins, don't you?" his father said.

Marcus looked at the old general, whom he vaguely remembered visiting his father on occasion during the war. "Yes, it's been a long time. How are you, sir?' Marcus asked respectfully.

"I'm not dead yet, if that's what you mean!" the old man replied gruffly. It was obvious that he had a few brandies already.

Marcus laughed rudely. "I only asked to be civil, you old bastard. To be honest I don't give a damn if you live or die!" He turned to walk away, but the general grabbed his arm.

"Well said, Marcus! That's the first honest thing I've heard all day. Now sit down and tell me all about America. Your father says you're doing well there."

Marcus looked at his father, shrugged, and followed the general to a sofa and sat beside him. Sir Derek hurried after them and sat in an armchair next to them. Before Marcus could say a word, Hawkins started telling him about the time he was in America, South Africa, Australia and just about everywhere Marcus had heard of and some he had not. Every time he tried to escape, Hawkins would grab his arm and start again.

Sir Derek tried to rescue him. "Come on, General. Tell Marcus our news."

Hawkins stopped his ramblings and looked at Derek in surprise. "You mean you haven't told him yet?"

"Not yet, why don't you? I was going to tell him tonight anyway."

Hawkins grabbed Marcus' hand. "Your father is running for Parliament as the Conservative member for Oxford!"

Marcus had been letting everything the general said go in one ear and out the other, but this was news indeed. "Running for Parliament! I never knew you had any political ambitions."

Hawkins laughed rudely. "Politics doesn't come into it, my boy. Money is what it's all about. Isn't that right, Derek?"

Sir Derek looked around him in embarrassment. "Keep your voice down for God's sake. Some of the opposition are here tonight."

Hawkins made an exaggerated show of looking over his shoulder, and whispering. "Yes, Derek, we must be careful. We wouldn't want anyone to hear our little secrets, would we?"

Marcus ears pricked up at this exchange. He sensed there was something between the two men. He leaned over and whispered to the general, playing the same game. "And what little secrets might you have? Come on, I won't tell anyone, especially the opposition." He winked at his father. He thought his father looked a little uncomfortable at the way the conversation was going.

"You're talking nonsense, General. You'd better leave off the bottle. I think you've had enough for tonight." Sir Derek stood up. "Come on, Marcus, I want you to meet someone."

Hawkins grabbed Marcus' arm, looking at Sir Derek slyly. "On you go, Derek. Marcus can stay with me. After all, I don't even know the boy!"

Derek shrugged and sat down again.

Marcus said, "Now what were you saying about secrets, General Hawkins?"

Sir Derek broke in impatiently. "What he's saying is that he has a very valuable parcel of land that is slated to be expropriated for a power station. If the plan for the power station goes through, he will only get the value of the land taken for the power station, which will leave all his surrounding land virtually worthless. Now if I get elected, with the general's help, my first order of duty will be to crush these plans for the power station before they take root."

The old general laughed and patted Sir Derek's knee. "Well put, Derek. You scratch my back and I'll scratch yours, just like we did in the war."

Marcus interrupted. He instinctively knew that his father had tried to change the subject. What had gone on between these two men that his father didn't want him to know? "I didn't know you were in the war together!"

Old Hawkins roared with laughter. "Oh yes, my boy! We went right through the whole war together, didn't we, Derek?"

"What the hell is he talking about? You were never in the Army, father."

Sir Derek sighed in resignation. "He's telling you we had a business partnership during the war, that's all."

Marcus started to sense he was getting somewhere. He leaned over conspiratorially to Hawkins, and baited the trap. "And a right profitable one I bet!"

Hawkins jumped in with both feet. "Profitable isn't the word for it. It was a license to print money. I was privy to all the bids coming in for war supplies, so I just let your father know the prices to beat. The war could have gone on forever as far as we were concerned."

Sir Derek felt a pang of panic. None of them had told anyone else about what happened.

Marcus slapped old Hawkins knee. "Brilliant! I wish I could get into something as easy as that. Anyway, Father, I hope you get elected and help the General keep his land. Now if you'll excuse me I'd better go and see how Emily's getting along." He walked out of the room nodding politely to people on his way out.

Sir Derek rounded on the General. "What the hell did you tell him that for, Hawkins? Those things are better kept quiet! What if someone got wind of it? What were you thinking of?"

"What's the matter with you? He's your son for God's sake. Anyway, it's ancient history and nobody can prove a thing."

Sir Derek sipped at his drink thoughtfully. "Yes, I suppose you're right, but do me a favor and never mention those times again."

Hawkins answered huffily. "All right, if it means that much to you."

Marcus' mind was racing as he mixed politely with the guests. *So that was how his father had made his fortune! Yes, business was the same the world over!* He looked around at all the ladies glittering with jewels and the men standing around talking and he grinned cynically. Yes, everybody has something to hide, it's just a matter of finding out what it is!

Emily telegraphed her parents and told them they were living with Marcus' parents for a couple of months before they headed for Europe. She was delighted to mix with the so-called upper classes. She loved the way of life in the country with its fox hunts and the outings to London to the shopping centers. So much so that she broached the subject with Marcus about maybe moving permanently to England.

"I think it's time we resumed our trip, Emily. After we come back, we'll talk about it!" Marcus had no intention of moving back to England, but he let her think what she wanted, it made no difference to him. She would do as he said and that would be the end of it.

They left for Europe on the day the stock market crashed on Wall Street. The next morning in the Ritz hotel in Paris, Marcus read the newspaper accounts of the stock markets collapsing. He let the newspaper fall on his lap and thanked God for that shoe shine boy in New York. His premonition had been right. As they traveled, he read with a strange sense of satisfaction of the collapse of the stock market, the suicides, and the billions of dollars lost by investors. They traveled through France and Italy buying antiques and by Christmas they were in Vienna. They went skiing in Salzburg and then went to Switzerland and Germany. By February they were back in England after having what they both thought the trip of a lifetime. For the first time in his life, Marcus had been truly happy and swore to himself to have more such trips as often as he could. Emily thought she was married to another man the way he laughed and played with the baby.

"This holiday did you good, Marcus. You're a different person now, a lot happier than you were in New York," Emily said on the train to Oxford.

"Yes, Emily, but you know we wouldn't enjoy it so much if we lived here. It would be just the same old thing once you got used to it. But don't worry, we'll come back, and often." Unsaid was the fact that they would not be staying in England. Emily got the message, but was not too disappointed, she was getting a little homesick after so long away from home.

When they got to Marcus' parent's house there was a telegram waiting for Marcus from New York. Sir Derek gave it to Marcus. "This came last month for you, but we didn't know where you were."

Marcus opened the telegram. It was from Jack Norwood. *COME HOME IMMEDIATELY. STOP. LOST EVERYTHING. STOP. JACK.* Marcus handed the telegram to Emily and lifted the baby.

"Have cook rustle up something to eat, will you, Father, I'm starving."

Emily looked at the telegram in shock. She handed it to Sir Derek. "What does it mean? Lost everything?"

Marcus answered over his shoulder. "Exactly what it says, Emily. Don't you know what's been happening in the world?"

"Yes, but I never thought that it would affect Father."

Sir Derek answered. "It has affected just about everyone, my dear."

Marcus grinned cynically as he handed the baby to his mother. "Everyone except the poor, they had nothing to lose!"

Emily started crying. "We'll have to go home right away, Marcus. They need us over there!"

"We'll not be going anywhere for awhile, Emily. I believe it's March before the first boat." They sent a telegram telling Norwood they would be home at the end of March.

Despite the miserable winter weather, Marcus and Emily left the baby with his parents and traveled around England and Scotland seeing the sights. They ended up back in London where they booked their tickets for the Ile De France on Sunday, the twenty-fourth of March, leaving from Southampton. They went back to Oxford and stayed for a week before packing their trunks for the voyage home. On Thursday, the twenty-first of March, Sir Derek and his wife had a dinner party to say farewell. After the guests had all gone, Sir Derek called Marcus into his study.

Marcus looked around the study. It was smaller than he remembered, and the fire in the grate made the room stifling hot. He went over and opened the window to let some air in.

"Look, son, the last time we were in this room we had harsh words. I'm sorry about that, but now you've turned your life around, I'd like to offer you this." He took an envelope from his desk and handed it to Marcus.

"I don't know your financial situation, but the way things have gone with the stock markets, and the telegram you got from Emily's father. I thought perhaps this may come in handy."

Marcus opened the envelope. Inside there was a check for ten-thousand pounds. He looked at it and put it back in the envelope. He shook his head and laid the envelope on the desk.

"Yes, the last time we were in this room I asked you for help and you threw me out." He looked directly into his father's eyes.

Derek suppressed a shudder. He had forgotten that look. He should have known Marcus would never forgive him.

"I don't need anything from you, Father. Now let's join the ladies, shall we?" he said coldly.

Sir Derek was in shock. He dropped his head and muttered in a low voice. "You go ahead, I'll be there in a minute."

Marcus left him alone staring into the blazing fire. Sir Derek crushed the envelope and threw it in to the flames and watched it burn to ashes along with his hopes for a reconciliation. He had had misgivings about offering Marcus the money, but Lady Catherine had insisted.

The next morning Marcus and Emily left for London. No one mentioned the incident with the envelope, and they all said their farewells as if nothing was amiss.

As Sir Derek and his wife watched the car leave the estate she looked at him and said sadly, "Do you think they'll ever come back?"

Sir Derek watched the car disappear among the trees and answered, "Catherine, I simply don't know."

Marcus and Emily arrived at their hotel at one o'clock. Marcus left Emily with the baby and arranged for transportation to Southampton on Sunday morning. That would give them the full Saturday in London for their last day. He left the hotel and walked to Fleet Street to the *Times* office. He went into the foyer and asked to see the editor.

The desk clerk looked at him with disdain and replied, "Anyone can't just walk in here and see the editor! You need an appointment and a good reason, sir."

Marcus didn't bothering answering him and walked straight into the first office he saw with the clerk in hot pursuit. The room he walked into was a hive of activity. The clatter of typewriters was deafening. He looked around and at the far end he saw the frosted glass door with "Editor" engraved on it. With the clerk still running after him Marcus opened the door and walked in. The editor looked up in surprise as the clerk stammered apologies and tried to pull Marcus by the arm.

"What the hell's going on?" the editor roared.

Marcus pulled a large thick brown envelope from his pocket and held it toward the editor.

"News! My man. And damn big news. Now do you want it or do I go across the street?"

The editor waved the clerk outside and motioned for Marcus to sit down.

"This had better be good, young man. Now start talking or I'll have you out on your arse in two minutes."

"First, you must promise to wait till Sunday to print it, or I walk out right now!"

The editor was a hard-bitten old newshound and he sensed that this guy had something big. He grinned cynically. "Sorry, if it's as big as you say, I'll publish it tomorrow."

Marcus stood up. "Have it your way."

The editor lit a cigarette and waved him back to his seat. "All right, I'll wait till Sunday. Now what have you got?"

Marcus opened the envelope and pulled the first sheet of paper out and handed it over.

The editor read it over and threw it back on the desk. "This is nothing but an old receipt for some army goods during the war."

"Look again, it's a list of bids from different companies."

The editor looked again. He looked up at Marcus. "Is this what I think it is?"

Marcus nodded. "It's exactly what you think it is!"

"How many in the envelope."

Marcus shrugged. "Enough to do the damage."

The editor stubbed his cigarette out and glanced through some of the papers. He shook his head. "Who would have thought it! That old idiot Hawkins and Sir Derek Browning! Strange bedfellows indeed, but money talks, doesn't it? How much do you want for this?" *It's worth at least a thousand,* the editor thought.

Marcus stood up. "Nothing, just make sure it's in Sunday's paper!" He turned to go.

"Just a minute, who are you and where did you get these papers?"

"Remember, Sunday's paper. On the front page!" Marcus shut the glass door behind him and walked through the office. He heard the editor's voice roaring above the clatter of the typewriters.

"Jones! Stewart! Drop everything and get in here!"

Marcus grinned grimly and, pulling his collar up, went out into the drizzle on Fleet Street and hailed a taxi.

On Sunday morning as the taxi sped through the countryside toward Southampton Marcus, folded his copy of the *Times* and lifted the baby.

"Anything interesting in the paper?" Emily asked.

"Nothing at all, just the usual stuff about the stock markets crashing."

In Oxford, Sir Derek's butler left his copy of the newspaper on the breakfast table as was his custom. Sir Derek sat down and opened the paper as the maid poured his tea. Lady Catherine sat at the other end of the table facing Sir Derek. As she stirred her tea she noticed a change come over her husband.

"Anything wrong, Derek?" she asked.

Sir Derek's face was gray. Without answering he threw the paper on the table and knocked over his chair in his haste to get out of the room. Catherine pushed her chair back and hurried after him shouting

"What's wrong? Where are you going?" She followed him into the study. He was leaning on his desk with his head bowed. He was weeping. Catherine rushed to his side shouting hysterically. "Tell me what's happened for God's sake, Derek!" He gestured at the file drawer on the desk. She could see by the splintered wood that the drawer had been broken open. "If you don't tell me what's happened I'll scream!"

Sir Derek composed himself and took a deep breath. He held his wife in his arms. "We're ruined, Catherine! Ruined! The *Times* has got all the records of my dealings with Hawkins. They were stolen from this desk!"

"It's years since you did business with Hawkins! What damage can old records do?" Catherine had never taken any interest in the business and had no idea what Derek was talking about.

Derek held her at arms length. "Go and read the front page of the *Times* and you'll see. I have to make a phone call." She looked at him strangely and went back into the dining room. Sir Derek lifted the phone and called his lawyer.

Lady Catherine spread the front page open on the table and looked at the headlines.

SIR DEREK BROWNING, GENERAL HAWKINS IN WAR PROFITEER-ING SCANDAL! Stunned, she continued reading:

The Times has obtained irrefutable proof in the form of records kept since the War that General Peter Hawkins gave lists of bids for war contracts to Sir Derek Browning...

Lady Catherine crushed the newspaper and staggered backwards, stumbling over the fallen chair and into a dead faint.

In the study, Sir Derek paced back and forth impatiently, waiting for his lawyer to answer the phone.

"Derek! What can I do for you this fine morning?" the lawyer answered brightly.

"Shut up and listen!" Derek replied harshly. He told him about the *Times* article and made arrangements to meet that afternoon.

The lawyer listened intently and signaled to his wife to get the paper. He grimaced at the headlines and read a few lines of the story. "One question, Derek?" the lawyer asked.

"Go ahead."

"If there was no burglary, do you have any idea who broke into your desk?"

Derek stood as if in a stupor staring out at the rain lashing against the windows.

"Derek, are you still there?"

Derek regained his composure enough to whisper into the phone. "My son, Marcus! It was he who betrayed me! " He put the phone down and sat down heavily in his chair and sat in silence listening to the rain.

The taxi drove right onto the dockside at Southampton, and Marcus told the driver to stop at the first class gangway for the Ile De France. This was a lot different than the last time he was here. Two porters immediately started unloading their luggage from the taxi.

"Your newspaper, sir!" the driver called out.

"Keep it!" Marcus said as he paid him and gave him a generous tip. Their trunks had already been sent ahead and were already on board. An officer came over for their tickets and a steward led them on board to their stateroom.

Marcus left Emily to unpack and walked along the promenade deck deep in thought. *Less than five years ago I left here with nothing. Now I'm going to start all over again, only this time I've got my stake and with it a chance to make some big money.* The fact that he was already a rich man meant nothing to him. He was looking beyond the money to the next level. *Power!* He had no interest in politics, but he knew you could buy politicians. The more money you spread around, the more you owned them. His first priority was finding a moneymaking venture. He couldn't leave his fortune doing nothing. It would take years for the markets to rebound, so it would have to be something else. Maybe real estate. Or munitions. There was always a market for weapons. He would have a good look around when he got to New York, meantime, he would enjoy his last week of vacation.

When the great liner docked at New York, being in First Class meant the customs officials came on the ship and cleared them so they could walk off without being bothered. Their luggage was already on the dock when they disembarked. It was pouring rain. Emily was looking frantically for her parents, expecting them to be waiting with the car. Marcus engaged a cab driver and paid him to get a truck to deliver their luggage to the townhouse. At last Emily saw her parents and hurried over to meet them. Marcus followed close behind carrying the baby.

Mrs. Norwood rushed over and took the baby in her arms. She gave Marcus a quick kiss on the cheek. "Welcome home, Mark. It seems like you two have been away for years! Isn't that so, Jack?"

Marcus shook hands with Norwood. He was shocked at the older man's appearance. He had aged twenty years in eight months.

"Good to see you, Jack!" Marcus said. "Where's the car? Let's get out of this bloody rain."

Norwood's haggard face fell. "There is no car. It got repossessed along with everything else. We're living in your house, you know. I hope it's all right, but we had nowhere else to go," he stammered nervously.

This man's heading for a nervous breakdown! Marcus pulled his hand free. "I'm so glad you came back!" He was close to tears.

"Never mind that now." Marcus hailed a taxi. "Let's get home and you can tell us all about it."

Back at the house, Marcus greeted the servants and they all went into the sitting room for coffee. "All right!" Marcus said." Let's have the bad news. From Mrs. Norwood if you don't mind?" He knew Norwood was in no shape to talk coherently.

Mary Norwood was a proud woman. It went against her grain to tell this young man, whom she still did not trust, all about the misfortune that had befallen them. But she was also pragmatic. She would not let her pride be the cause of both herself and her husband being thrown out on the street.

She told Marcus the whole story of how, not only did they lose everything they had in the stock market, but also their houses, including the mansion in the Hamptons. Everything had been mortgaged to buy Roman Investments. Now they had nothing and were officially bankrupt. If they had not had a key for Marcus' townhouse, they would literally be on the street. She went on to explain that all their friends were even worse off than them, three of them had committed suicide and others had simply disappeared.

Marcus listened carefully to her story. He had known it was a disaster, but it was worse than even he had thought.

Emily sat next to her father clasping his hand. "Marcus! You've got to help them! We can't let them lose everything!"

Marcus' glance was enough to silence her. "In round figures, how much do you owe, and to what banks? What are they offering for the houses?"

Mary Norwood looked at her husband, but he just waved his hand and signaled her to continue. "Forty-five million dollars to the Bank of America and ten million to Hawthorne's. The bottom has fallen out of the real estate, we'll be lucky to get a hundred thousand for the brownstone, and maybe a million for the property in the Hamptons."

"So nothing has been sold yet?"

"No, I imagine the bank is trying to sell them, but it makes no difference to us, we signed everything over to the bank two weeks ago."

Marcus sat in silence for a few minutes. The ticking of the wall clock seemed to get louder by the minute. The tension in the room was becoming unbearable.

The bastard is making us suffer! Mary had to stop herself from telling him to go to Hell, and Emily sat in terror of either losing her parents, or husband, or both!

Finally Marcus broke the silence. "You did the right thing signing everything over to the bank. Legally you have nothing left to give. Now listen carefully, all of you. This is what is going to happen. You can have this house to live in for the rest of your lives. After all, you bought it! I will buy the brownstone for Emily and I to live in, and I will buy the house in the Hamptons. You will be welcome to use it any time you want. I will buy a car for you to use and will pay all the bills till Jack starts work with me. Everything will remain in my name, because the banks have long memories. Now, if there is nothing else, I'm tired and I want to get an early start in the morning." He stood up and Emily jumped over and hugged him tightly.

"Thank you, Mark!" She turned to her parents in triumph. "Everything will be all right. Mark will look after us all, won't you, Mark?"

Marcus felt embarrassed by Emily's outpouring of affection.

Jack Norwood looked as if a great weight had been lifted from his shoulders. "Mark, I don't know how to thank you!" He was having difficulty controlling his emotions. "You mentioned something about work?" he said hopefully.

Marcus gently pushed Emily aside. "Yes, Jack. I have big plans and I'm going to need a good man at the top, so why look elsewhere when you are available. You don't mind working for me, do you?"

Norwood could not contain his excitement. "Of course not! Can you fill me in on your plans? Or is it too soon?"

Marcus burst out laughing. "I should say it's too soon! But relax, it won't be long before I decide which way to go."

"Isn't that wonderful, Father! Come on, I'll make you a coffee." Emily grabbed her father's arm and led him toward the kitchen.

Marcus turned toward Mary Norwood who looked more shocked than embarrassed. She walked over and took both of his hands in his. "Mark, I have a confession to make. I never fully trusted you. I always felt you had an ulterior motive for everything you did, including marrying Emily. But what you did for us this night makes me ashamed to admit how I felt. I hope you accept my sincere apologies. And my thanks."

Marcus looked at her seriously. "Are you telling me that you felt I couldn't be trusted?"

Mary dropped her eyes in embarrassment. "Yes, I'm sorry to say I did feel that way, Mark. Please forgive me."

Marcus lifted her chin up and said with a roguish smile, "You have nothing to be sorry about, Mrs. Norwood. You were right all along about me! I can't be trusted! Not for one minute!" He started roaring with laughter.

Mary looked at him in amazement. Despite his laughing, she could not shake the horrible feeling that he was being deadly serious. She had the feeling she would never really know Mark Brown. Puzzled, she started laughing along with him and the two of them left the room arm in arm.

The next morning at breakfast Jack Norwood was back to his old self, talking non-stop about all the people who had lost everything in the crash.

"What happened to Joe Cassidy?" Marcus asked.

Norwood put his fork down. "Funny thing about Joe. Nobody has seen or heard from him. It's like he disappeared altogether."

Marcus looked at his watch. "Well, I've got to get things started. I shouldn't be too late. I'll see how I get on today before we finalize what we talked about last night."

"Can I come along, Mark?" Norwood asked anxiously.

"Not today, Jack. Don't worry, in a month you'll be so busy you'll be asking for time off!" Marcus lifted his coat and hat and went outside to look for a cab.

The cab dropped him off at the Bank of America and he went in to a scene he could not believe. Lines of people were waiting to withdraw whatever money they had. There were handwritten notices around saying today the most the bank would give was twenty dollars each. The amount varied each day as the bank juggled its enormous resources to avoid using all of its cash. The panic caused by the crash was being compounded by the closure of a few smaller banks out west. The people were just starting to try and withdraw their savings before any more banks closed their doors.

Marcus walked past the lines of people and headed straight for Tweed's office. He saw a flustered John Reynolds trying to explain to the irate customers that the limit on withdrawals was only a temporary measure.

He knocked once and opened the door. Tweed was on the phone and looked up angrily when he heard the door open. When he saw it was Marcus he hurriedly got off the phone and stood up to shake hands.

"Where the hell have you been, Mark? Boy, you sure got out of the market at the right time. I lost everything I had in it, but I was lucky I had nothing on margin. I still have my job though, and believe me, things are going to get worse. Much worse! Now, what can I do for you?"

"I've been in Europe on business," he lied. "My father-in-law, Jack Norwood, was telling me he's in hock to you for millions. He says that you have power of sale of his two houses, a brownstone and an estate in the Hamptons."

Tweed looked at him slyly. "And you want to make an offer?"

"Yes, I do. Pull the file and let's have a look at how much we're talking here."

Tweed went over and pulled the file for Norwood's estate. He thumbed through it and pulled a sheet of paper. "Let's see. Last spring the brownstone was valued at four-hundred thousand. The estate in the Hamptons was five and a half million." He looked up at Marcus.

"I'll give you thirty-five cents on the dollar in cash for both properties. That is my final offer."

Tweed did some math in his head. The offer was a good one. *Why did he always underestimate Brown?* The offer was just high enough to make him agree because real estate was only worth twenty percent of last year's prices.

"That comes to over two-million dollars, Mark. All your money is in bullion, and the government has limits on selling large amounts of gold. Now for fifty cents on the dollar maybe we could arrange something."

"I'm not touching the gold yet. The longer this downturn lasts, the higher it will go. Last chance, Mr. Tweed. I could give you a check today, and judging from what's happening out there," he nodded toward the door. "I'm sure you could use some extra cash."

Tweed frowned and went back to the filing cabinet. He pulled a file out and glanced at it for a moment. "Mark, you are aware that you only have around forty-thousand on deposit?"

Mark pulled a checkbook and bankbook from his pocket and threw them on the desk.

Tweed looked at them in surprise. "You have money in The Bank of England?"

"All my eggs are not in one basket Mr. Tweed. Go ahead, I don't mind if you look."

Tweed narrowed his eyes and pulled the bankbook over. He opened it at the first page and nearly fainted with shock. "A hundred and fifty-million! Is that what you got for Roman?" He gathered his wits quickly. "Whatever they're giving you I'll give you a quarter point more if you move it here. What do you say?"

"I say thirty-five cents on the dollar for the two houses, Mr. Tweed. You could not give me what the Bank of England gives me." He pulled the two books toward him.

"And what exactly are they giving you?"

"Peace of mind, Mr. Tweed. Peace of mind. Now is it a deal or not?"

"Come on, Mark! You don't think for a minute that Bank of America could go under! Be realistic, if we go under, the whole banking system would collapse!"

Marcus pointed toward the door. "Take a look at the people out there. They don't look too sure, do they?"

Tweed knew then that Marcus would not change his mind. He got back to the subject at hand. At the rate real estate was dropping, Tweed knew he had to take the offer. If he refused and then couldn't sell he would lose his job. Thirty-five percent was better than nothing and he needed the cash badly.

"You say you'll give me a check today?"

"Look, I'll do better than that. I'll go over myself and get a bank draft for you and you'll have the cash in your bank tomorrow! That will look good to your bosses, even though it's just thirty-five percent of last year's price. Is it a deal?"

"I'll start the necessary paperwork, who's your lawyer?"

"I don't have one. You must know someone who needs the commission."

Tweed thought for a moment. "Yes, I think I do. I'll call him and set up a meeting. Would tomorrow morning at ten suit you?"

Marcus stood up and shook hands. "That will be just fine, I'll see you then."

On his way out of the bank he waved to John Reynolds who was trying to pacify an old couple who were demanding that he give them all of their savings in cash, but he didn't see him. *People were getting scared with the bank closures,* Marcus thought. And he suspected that there would be many more to follow. If the ordinary working Americans withdrew all their savings, the country would come to a standstill. No government would allow that to happen. He figured the big banks would be all right, but there were hundreds of smaller banks who had invested in the market and lost the people's savings. They were the ones that would close. He went out into the rain and started walking.

After Marcus had left the house, Emily went upstairs to attend to the baby and Mary and Jack sat down at the table.

"Well, Mary, you must admit you were wrong about young Mark! He's saving our lives by letting us stay here!"

"Jack, I admit this. I still don't trust that man! The way things are, he could put us out at any time. Everything will be in his name."

"What else do you expect? We are bankrupt, Mary. We're damned lucky he's letting us live here or we would be homeless. I know you've never liked him, but you must admit you were wrong about him! For God's sake, he's giving us a roof over our heads, and he's promised me a job!"

"I can't help how I feel."

"Well, for God's sake, don't let Emily know. She'll go crazy if you tell her, and maybe we will be thrown out!"

Mary Norwood sighed. "Don't worry, Jack. I'm not that stupid." But she couldn't shake the memory of Marcus' answer the night before.

Marcus walked to the Bank of England offices and arranged to pick up the bank draft in the morning. He thought that he could probably get the houses for less, but he did not want to spend time on the wheeling and dealing. His immediate concern was to find a venture to make more money. He had the feeling that this Depression was going to be a long one, and who knows what would happen. He had to be 100% sure of any investments he might make. He made his way to the library and started poring over the histories of past depressions to see if he could find a way of increasing his wealth. He came to the conclusion that real estate was the safest way to guarantee good returns. The problem with that was it could take years to generate profit. No, it would have to be something else. There had to be something out there just waiting for someone to see the potential. He left the library and hailed a taxi.

At exactly ten o'clock the next morning Marcus walked into Tweed's office. The scene in the bank was even worse than the day before. There were three men sitting around Tweed's desk when he entered the office. Tweed lost no time in introducing them. The first man was the bank's lawyer, a white haired man in his sixties. "This is Jonas Hall, our attorney."

Marcus shook hands and turned to the other two men. One of them was in his seventies and looked like he should be retired. The other one was a short dark-skinned man with jet black eyes and a business-like look about him.

"This is William Wills of Wills and Watson, the most prestigious law firm in New York, if I may say so. And this is Benjamin Swersky, who will be handling your end of the transaction."

The older man shook hands with Marcus first. "I won't be staying, Mr. Brown. I just wanted to meet you. I've read a bit about your success, and to tell you we'd be honored to have you as a client."

"The honor is all mine, Mr. Wills!" Marcus had read a lot about Wills and Watson. They had a stellar record of winning difficult and complicated corporate cases, especially against all levels of government. They would not come cheap, but they were the ones you wanted on your side when it came to court cases. "But surely a simple real estate deal is not what you are here for?"

Wills nodded in agreement. "Mr. Swersky will handle your transaction satisfactorily. I am here to ask you to consider having our firm as your attorneys. Mr. Tweed tells us you have not yet retained anyone."

"Not yet, but you're right, I will be needing legal counsel."

"So you'll join our list of distinguished clients?"

Marcus shook David Swersky's hand and David gave him his card.

"Not so fast, Mr. Wills. Let's see how Mr. Swersky handles the Bank of America before I decide."

Tweed was right, Wills thought. *This one was as sharp as a whip.*

"A wise decision, Mr. Brown. I'm sure we'll be hearing from you! Won't we, David?" He looked over his glasses sternly.

Swersky returned his gaze unflinchingly. "I'm sure we will, sir," he said with a tone that implied the conversation was finished. Wills shook hands all round and left the office.

"Well, gentlemen, down to business!" Tweed said briskly. "Do you have the bank draft, Mr. Brown?"

Immediately Swersky took control of the meeting. Marcus took the draft from his pocket and Swersky held out his hand. "I'll have that if you don't mind, Mr. Tweed. I know this is a straightforward transaction, but I would like a chance to read it over with my client!"

Tweed was not pleased. "I was under the impression that this was to be done today?"

"Don't worry, it will. Look, give me the copy to read over lunch and I'm sure it will be completed this afternoon."

Tweed looked at Jonas Hall helplessly. "No problem, Mr. Swersky, here you are." He handed over the papers. "We'll see you back here around two o'clock?"

Swersky took the papers and stood up. He looked at his watch. "Fine, let's go, Mr. Brown. I know a nice restaurant where we can talk."

Marcus shrugged and stood up. "All right, if you say so, Mr. Swersky." The two men left Tweed's office.

Worriedly Tweed turned to the lawyer. "Everything's in order, isn't it? If this doesn't go through, I'm finished here." He had been on the phone since the day before convincing his bosses it was a good deal for the bank.

"Don't worry, there's nothing wrong. Everything will go smoothly."

"I hope you're right!" Tweed said. Something about Swersky bothered him and he could not put his finger on it. "I just don't like that little man, and I don't know why. I wish Wills had brought someone else."

Jonas Hall zipped up his briefcase. He stopped on his way out. "It wouldn't have anything to do with the fact he's a Jew, now would it, Gordon?"

Tweed's face reddened. "Certainly not!" he replied angrily, but Hall had already closed the door behind him.

Marcus and David Swersky ordered lunch, and while they waited they talked about the deal they were about to make. They were also weighing each other up. Both men recognized that the other was not to be taken lightly. Immediately David saw through Marcus' veneer of being a simple client looking for advice. He knew Marcus had a keen intelligence and was totally ruthless in matters of business. Anyone who had made such a fortune in so short a time was no fool. Things at the office were not too good. Most of the well-heeled clients had cancelled their retainers, and David was the last of the junior members of the firm to still have a job. He was expecting to get his walking papers at any time. He was hoping to impress Marcus and maybe get a bonus along with his commission. While he was chatting to Marcus, he was reading the contents of the agreement.

On the other hand, Marcus watched him closely, asking him if everything was in order. He noticed the speed that Swersky read the agreement and thought, *If this guy can read that fast and understand all the fine print, he certainly was a man worth having on your side.* He liked the way that

Swersky had taken control in Tweed's office. He had noticed how annoyed Tweed was, and was willing to bet that the bank's lawyer was even more annoyed.

Swersky finished reading the agreement and laid it on the table.

Marcus picked it up and flipped through the pages. There were fifteen pages, all neatly typewritten. "Everything in order?" Marcus asked.

"Well, there is something…"

Marcus slapped the papers down on the table before Swersky could finish. "Who do you think you're kidding, pal?" Marcus said. "Do you expect me to believe that you read all this in the time we've been sitting here?"

Swersky looked at him evenly. "Try me!"

Marcus grabbed the papers and picked a page. "All right! Page ten, paragraph three item one." He held the page open to read it and looked at Swersky expectantly.

Without a moment's hesitation Swersky read the passage word for word. "Now would you like me to explain what that means?"

Marcus was not easily impressed, but this was different. He had met a lot of clever men in his life, and he admired intelligence. He knew he was in the presence of a special mind.

"I think you've proved your point." He swore never to test this man again. "Now, before I so rudely interrupted you, what were you going to say?"

"The furnishings in the properties are not mentioned in the agreement. I presume you understood it would be included?" David spoke slowly, looking into Marcus' eyes. Marcus had not given a thought to the furnishings in the houses, but he got the message immediately. *The furniture and works of art had to be worth plenty.*

"Of course I did! I'm glad you noticed. By God, they were trying to keep it all!" he lied easily.

Swersky took the agreement and scribbled an addendum at the end. He folded it and put it in his briefcase. "Everything else looks in order."

"What if they turn it down now you've added the furnishings?"

"When we go back to the bank, leave everything to me. Do not say a word. This is what you hired me for, so there's no need for you to be involved."

Marcus was not used to being talked to like that. But he realized what Swersky was telling him. Why hire a lawyer and then stop him doing his job! If he had confidence in his lawyer, then he should let him get on with it. An idea was forming in his mind. He would need a sharp lawyer, one he could trust to do what he wanted, and he sensed David Swersky was that man. First, he would see how he handled this deal.

Back in Tweed's office, Jonas Hall had all the papers ready for Marcus' signature. Without saying anything, Marcus nodded to David.

"If you will read this, Mr. Hall, you will agree that we will have to alter the agreement a little!" He handed him the papers. Hall read what David had written and without changing expression, handed them to Tweed. Tweed read the addendum and turned red with rage. The pressure of this deal had been building up in him. He knew if it did not go through it could cost him his job. That did not bear thinking about, but this change was totally uncalled for. All his years of experiencing setbacks and successes with the same outward calm were forgotten in a moment of madness.

"You little bastard!" Trust a Jew to think of this! Trying to make a name for yourself, are you? Well, it won't work here! The furnishings were never in the deal to start with! For God's sake, we can get at least a hundred thousand at auction for them!" He turned to Marcus. "We've done a lot of business together, Mr. Brown. Do me a favor and fire this guy before he spoils our relationship." He looked expectantly at Marcus who simply shrugged his shoulders and walked to the window.

Gazing out of the window, he replied without looking at Tweed. "From now on, Mr. Swersky will be my counsel. When you deal with me you will go through him." He turned around and faced the three men. "Do we understand each other?"

The two lawyers nodded. Tweed was white-faced with shock. He knew by Marcus' tone he meant every word he said. Now he regretted his outburst and tried to find a way out of his predicament. He smiled uncomfortably and tried to laugh his way out of it. "You didn't take my little joke seriously, Mr. Swersky?"

David looked at him coldly. "Forget it. Now, Mr. Hall, you've read the addendum. Do we have a deal or not?"

Hall looked at Tweed inquiringly. Tweed was not going down without a fight. "You can't just change a deal like that! You're practically getting the houses for free, and now you want everything in them too? It's preposterous. The answer is no. The furnishings and works of art will be auctioned off, you can bid on them at auction if you want!"

David stood up and lifted his briefcase. "This is our final offer! If you sign the deal today, including the furnishings, I will give you this bank draft for the agreed amount. If not, the offer drops five percent per day for five days, after which time it will be withdrawn. Do you understand, Mr. Tweed?"

Tweed looked open mouthed at Hall. "This is blackmail! Can he do this?" Hall looked nonplused. "I'm afraid he can, Gordon. Nothing has been signed yet."

Tweed totally lost control. He hated this little Jew who was destroying everything. "Well, to hell with it! Someone else will buy these houses. So my answer is this. No deal! Now get the hell out of this office!"

Marcus, who was still standing by the window, turned around and said quietly, "I told you when you spoke to Mr. Swersky, you were speaking to me! I will be transferring my gold deposits to the Bank of England! Frankly, I expected more from you, Mr. Tweed. Let's go, Mr. Swersky."

Tweed was on his feet in a flash. He practically raced to the door to block their exit. His face was twitching with anxiety. He hated to do it, but he could talk his bosses into letting the furniture go, but if he lost Brown as a depositor of fifty-million dollars, he would be crucified. He held his arms out, his face contorted in an unnatural smile.

"Come on, gentlemen, can't anyone take a little joke these days? Jonas, give me the papers. What's a little furniture between friends? Come on now, sit down and we'll finish our business, and then I'll take you for a drink."

Swersky looked at Marcus, who hesitated for a few moments, then said, "I suggest you be careful with your little jokes, Mr. Tweed. Some people may not have my sense of humor!"

They returned to their places at the desk. Tweed was thinking furiously. *What if Brown double-crossed him and withdrew his gold anyway. No matter what, he could not let that happen.* He put down his pen and cleared his throat. By now he had regained his composure. "With all due respect, Mr. Swersky, I must have written assurance that your client will not move his assets in Bank of America to another institution. To put it bluntly, that would cost me my job, and I simply cannot let that happen. Even at the cost of this deal. I hope you understand my position," he added respectfully.

Eyebrows raised, David looked at Marcus expectantly. Marcus thought fast. He knew Tweed was not bluffing. *On the one hand he was tempted to move the gold anyway, and cost the little creep his job, but that would cost him the houses. He knew if he moved the gold, Tweed would never sell him the houses.* Pragmatism took over. "With the volatility of the financial sector at the moment, I can only guarantee that I will leave my assets here for one year. That's the best I can do!"

Tweed looked visibly relieved. "I can't ask for any more than that, given the state of the markets. Jonas, have the secretary type up a paper to that effect, and we can conclude our business today! Everyone in agreement?" He sat back in his chair and spread his arms wide.

Marcus and David both nodded and Hall excused himself to have the agreement put in writing. While they waited, Tweed engaged Marcus in some small talk, but David never said a word.

Tweed found him sitting there disconcerting. *I wish I'd never met you, you little bastard. I'll be glad to see the back of you! The little Jew had cheated him out of a good commission,* he thought bitterly. He was sure Brown had never given the contents of the houses a thought. *Trust a Jew to get something for nothing.*

Hall came back into the office with two copies of a statement which Marcus signed. Hall witnessed them and then the four men passed the bill of sale around for all the signatures. Each of the lawyers stuffed their copies in their briefcases.

"All that remains is this! And then we'll be on our way," David said, handing the bank draft to Jonas Hall. Hall took the two bundles of keys from his briefcase and gave them to David.

"A pleasure doing business with you!" Hall shook hands with David and Marcus.

Tweed stood up and shook Marcus' hand but David was already opening the door. "Just a minute, Mr. Swersky," Tweed said. "Would you two gentlemen like to come for a drink to celebrate?"

Marcus answered quickly. "Some other time, Mr. Tweed. I've things to discuss with my attorney!"

Swersky and Marcus both left and Hall looked at Tweed curiously. "You didn't expect them to go for a drink after that performance, did you! The little lawyer hates your guts, and I can't say I blame him after what you said."

Expressionless, Tweed looked at the lawyer and replied, "I don't give a damn one way or another!"

Outside the bank, Marcus and David pushed their way through the crowds.

"What other business do we have, Mr. Brown? I was under the impression that this was only one transaction."

"We can't talk here, Mr. Swersky. Let's find a quiet place we can talk."

"I know just the place, Mr. Brown. Come on, it's not far, we can walk it." He led Marcus to a small hotel with a deserted lounge.

"It never gets busy till around six!" David said, calling the barman over. "What would you like to drink?"

"Coffee will do for me, thank you!"

"Two coffees, please."

The two men sat in a booth facing each other.

"I won't waste your time, Mr. Swersky. I was most impressed with your handling of the transaction. I would like you to be my attorney, are you interested?"

David tried to keep his voice level. "You'll have to go through Mr. Wills if you want the firm as your attorneys, Mr. Brown."

"I did not hear any mention of Wills and Watson. I'm asking you to be my attorney, not the firm."

David thought fast. He decided to find out a little more about Mr. Brown. "I'm always interested in other opportunities," he answered carefully.

Marcus leaned toward him. "I understand your concern, Mr. Swersky." As if reading his mind, Marcus asked bluntly, "If you have any questions, ask me now. This is the only chance you'll ever have!"

David knew there was more to this man than met the eye. He decided discretion was the best way to go for the time being. "Just that I would like to know exactly what you want me to do? Is it real estate deals, like today? Or corporate law, or even criminal cases?"

"Right now, I have nothing for you to do. But as soon as I decide the way I'm going, you will be a very busy man. How much of a retainer do you want? And remember, as my attorney, I don't want you to be distracted from your job by being unhappy with the compensation."

"If you have nothing for me to do, why would you pay me anything?"

"I want you to be prepared to come and work for me at a moment's notice! When I call you, I expect you to be there. That is what you'll be paid for."

David tapped his spoon on the table. He thought carefully how to respond. He did not want to fully commit to leaving Wills and Watson for a few cases then be left without a job.

"I'd need some security if I left my job now. Things are bad everywhere!" He allowed himself a little smile. "Even for lawyers."

"That's understandable," Marcus replied. "Look, why don't you think about it for a couple of weeks, if I need you I'll be in touch. I will be busy with my new house in the Hamptons. You know where to find me, write your own ticket! Now, can I have the keys to my new houses?"

David laughed and lifted the briefcase on to the table. Marcus put the keys in his pocket and shook hands. David held his hand for a moment and said, "You don't have to answer this, but I noticed Tweed's reaction when you said you'd move your assets to the Bank of England." Before Marcus could answer, David pulled his hand back and muttered in embarrassment. "I'm sorry. Forget I said that! It's none of my business."

Marcus looked at him in amusement. Theatrically he cupped his mouth with his hand and whispered, "I've no secrets from my lawyer, David. Around fifty-million dollars in gold." He turned around and left David Swersky standing with his mouth open.

David sat down and sipped at his coffee with a smile on his face. His mind was made up. This was the opportunity he had been praying for. Brown was young, and very rich. Just how rich, David would soon find out, and then he would write his own ticket, as Marcus had so lightly put it. He decided to talk to his parents before making his decision final. He owed them a visit anyway. He left the hotel and hailed a taxi.

Marcus walked a few blocks thinking about what his next venture would be. He knew Swersky would take his offer. He would be a fool to turn it down, and Marcus knew he was no fool. The first thing Marcus had to do was move into the brownstone. He looked forward to going to the house in the Hamptons and have it decorated to his own specifications. He had coveted the property since the first time he saw it and could not help congratulating himself for getting it for a bargain price. He decided to take a few months to refurbish it before he started seriously looking for new enterprises. If anything good came up in the meantime, fine. It had started to rain, so he hailed a taxi and went home to tell the family his news.

"Is everyone home?" Marcus asked the butler as soon as he got in the door.
"Yes, sir."
"Have everyone come to the lounge, I have some news for them."

When the whole family was seated, Marcus stood behind a chair and dramatically threw the keys on the table.
"Recognize these?"

Emily sprang to her feet. "You did it! Mother, Father! We've got our homes back. How did you do it so fast, Mark. You're wonderful! Isn't he, Mother?"

Mrs. Norwood smiled uncomfortably. "You really bought our houses?" Jack Norwood sat shaking his head.

Marcus continued. "Yes, I did. Now, a little change of plan. Emily and I will move to the brownstone as soon as it's ready. Emily will take care of the details." He looked at Emily. "The quicker the better, dear, we all need our privacy."

Emily nodded in agreement, she knew him well enough by now that he meant what he said.

"As regards the house in the Hamptons, I will take care of that. I will be having some renovations done, so you won't be seeing it for a while." Mary Norwood had an uneasy feeling that they would never be in that house again. "Well, that's about it! Oh, I bought all the furniture with the houses, and I would like you both to feel free to go and take your favorite things from both houses and bring them here. Consider it a personal gift."

"You mean that, Mark! I can have some of my things back?" Mary was totally confused. She would never understand this man.

"You can have everything in both houses if you can find the room, but I doubt that!" he said with a smile.

Jack Norwood had tears in his eyes. "Again, I'm speechless. How can we ever repay you, Mark?"

"Forget it, that's what families are for," Marcus replied.

Emily was hugging everyone in sight. 'What wonderful news! Now, Mother, we'll start first thing in the morning sorting everything out."

"Yes!" Marcus said. "I'd prefer if you started with the Hampton house, I'm anxious to get started on it myself!"

"Of course, dear," Emily replied.

Again, Mary Norwood got the feeling that she was going to the house for the last time. She knew she'd better not confide in her husband. He loved Mark, and it would just cause an argument, but the uneasiness persisted.

The next morning Marcus and Jack Norwood went out to buy a car. Marcus had never driven a car, but he liked the convenience of having a car available.

"I know you had to let your chauffeur go, Jack, can you drive yourself?"

Norwood laughed in glee. He had not felt so happy in months, for the first time since the crash he felt that after all, things might work out all right.

"Of course, Mark. I used to drive all the time till I could afford a driver of my own. Look, I really am grateful for all you're doing for us. If you're having second thoughts about buying a car for us I will understand perfectly, you've done enough already."

Marcus hailed a taxi. "Nothing like that, it's just that I've never driven a car myself." He leaned over to talk to the taxi driver. "Do you know where the Rolls Royce dealership is?"

195

The taxi driver shook his head. "No sir, but I can find out pretty fast!" Norwood interrupted. "No need, I'll show you where it is. Mark! You're not buying us a Rolls Royce?" They both got into the taxi.

"I'm not buying you anything, Jack. It will be in my name, you cannot own anything of value. Remember?"

Norwood had a slight sense of being put in his place. He gave the driver directions and replied uncomfortably, "Well, it will look odd, me driving around in a Rolls when I'm stone broke!"

Marcus patted his knee. "The Rolls is for me. We'll get you something more modest, all right?"

Jack Norwood nodded in agreement. For some reason, all the good feelings he had woken up with that morning seemed to have disappeared and left a sour feeling about the whole business.

The taxi dropped them off on Fifth Avenue north of 86th street across from Central Park. The dealer was at the corner. They opened the door and immediately the lone salesman straightened his tie and hurried over to greet them. Inside his stomach was churning. He had not sold a car in nine months and things were getting desperate. Everyone else had been let go and the dealership was about ready to close down. He had heard rumors that it could be as early as next week. These were the first people who had even come in the door in a month. Most people just looked at the Silver Cloud through the window. He put on his most charming smile. "Good morning, gentlemen, I'm Ben Bester. She's a beauty, isn't she?" he said, patting the Rolls and holding out his hand.

Norwood shook hands and introduced himself, and Marcus, who was walking around looking at the car, he didn't bother shaking hands.

"Is this the only Rolls Royce you have?"

Bester nearly tripped walking briskly over beside Marcus. All his years of sales experience were deserting him at this moment. He was feeling like a newcomer to the business who did not have a clue how to deal with a customer. He fought to get his emotions under control. If he could sell this car, he'd be all right for six months. At first he'd thought the older man was the one who would be doing the talking, but he quickly realized by their demeanor it would be Mark.

"Yes sir, it is the only new one. Normally we keep one in the showroom, and the customer has to order what he wants from England. This one here was ordered and, unfortunately, the gentleman had to cancel, so it is for sale, and at a bargain price too. There are more out the back, but they have all been repossessed." Marcus looked around the showroom. There were no other cars. There was a Ford Model T parked outside the dealership with a for sale sign on it. Marcus walked over to the window and pointed to the Ford.

"Are you selling that too?"

Bester's heart sank. Goddam Limey! He should have known he was too young to afford the Rolls. He had taken the Ford from his friend at the Ford dealer who was having as hard a time as him. If he sold it, he would get a small commission, nothing like selling the Rolls, but still, better than nothing.

"Yes, just as a favor for a friend, are you interested?"

Marcus shrugged. He looked at the salesman with an amused smile. He could practically smell the man's desperation. "Have you ever sold two cars in two minutes?"

Bester was taken aback by the question. Flustered, he stammered. "No, I don't think so."

Marcus looked at his watch. "If you know the bottom price for the Rolls and the Ford, tell my colleague, Mr. Norwood. If he agrees to the prices, you have a deal. If not, Mr. Norwood and I will be on our way. Now, may I use your phone?"

Marcus winked at Norwood and walked into the office. Bester looked at Norwood. "Is he serious?"

Norwood was as taken aback as Bester. "I guess he is." He looked at Marcus standing inside the office looking at his watch. Bester rushed over to his desk and frantically pulled the papers out for the Rolls. *To hell with the Ford*, he'd do without any commission on it just to sell the Rolls. He hurriedly wrote down the numbers and rushed back to Norwood.

Meanwhile, Marcus sat behind the desk and dialed a number that he read from a card he had taken from his wallet.

"Good morning, Henry Gardner speaking!" Henry Gardner was the president of Bank of America. Marcus had met him at a fund raiser before he had gone to Europe and Gardner had given him his private number. Marcus remembered what Gardner had said to him. "Remember Mr. Brown, anything at all, just call me!"

"Mark Brown here, how are you, Mr. Gardner. I have a problem that maybe you could help me with."

"Go ahead, Mr. Brown. Anything at all!" Marcus told him about his purchase of the houses and the furniture and Tweed's insistence that he sign the agreement to leave his funds in Bank of America.

"I felt like a fool, Mr. Gardner, being put on the spot like that. You see, my wife had her heart set on the houses, otherwise I would have walked out on the deal. Anyway, I thought I'd let you know that I'm very disappointed with Bank of America and I will be moving my assets as soon as the year is up."

Gardner sat bolt upright in his chair. "Is there anyway you would reconsider, Mr. Brown. We don't want to lose you as a client.'

"To put it bluntly, Mr. Gardner, I don't think I could do any more business with Gordon Tweed after what he put me through."

"And if Mr. Tweed was no longer with us?"

"Then I would leave my funds where they are."

"Rest assured, Mr. Brown, you won't have to deal with Mr. Tweed again. Please accept my apologies for your inconvenience and embarrassment."

"One more thing, Mr. Gardner. I always have been very impressed with John Reynolds, the young man who works in that branch. After all, it was due to him that I opened my account there."

"I'll certainly keep that in mind, Mr. Brown,"

"Thank you, Mr. Gardner, goodbye."

"Here you are, sir. This is the best I can do."

Norwood looked at the numbers blankly. What was Mark up to? He knew Norwood had no idea of the prices, so why would he leave the decision to him? Then it struck him. The decision had already been made. The whole charade was to get the lowest price. Bester had been left without any time to negotiate, that was why Mark had walked out! He looked up at Bester. "I guess you'd better go and get him."

Bester was overjoyed. The fact that he had fallen for Marcus' ploy would not strike him till much later.

Marcus came strolling out of the office.

"You have a deal, sir!" he said excitedly.

Marcus still had the slightly bored look about him. "Indeed! Well, let's get the paperwork done and I'll be on my way."

Bester held the door open for Marcus to go into the showroom.

As Norwood guided the Model T along Fifth Avenue, Marcus told him to call his old chauffeur and tell him he had a job for him. Also to hire all the staff back at the house in the Hamptons. They would now all be working for Mark Brown. Norwood had regained his happy mood of the morning and agreed to everything Marcus said. After all, he couldn't take the car back now. No matter how strange Mark was at times, he was being very good to the Norwoods, even Mary would have to admit that!

The next day Norwood was busy contacting the chauffeur and the staff to offer their positions back. Marcus had given him a budget to work with and left him in charge of the help in all three houses. It would keep him busy for a while, at least until something more was found for him to do. Norwood was ecstatic at being in charge again. Never mind that it was only a few housekeepers and gardeners, it was good to be needed again. Every one of them accepted their jobs back, and were glad to do so, because not a single one had found other employment.

Marcus had told Norwood as soon as he had hired the staff to have them assemble at each house to meet their new boss. It took a week to organize everything, but by the time Marcus was driven in the Rolls from the brownstone to the Hampton house to meet his staff, he had left Emily with instructions to do what she liked with the brownstone. He told her she'd be better staying there to oversee the decorating, and she would be closer to her parents.

Just before Marcus moved to the Hampton house he got a call from David Swersky. "Mr. Brown, I'm calling to let you know I'll be happy to accept your offer of employment, but there are a couple of issues I'd like to discuss with you before starting."

"Excellent!" Marcus replied jovially. "Unfortunately, I'm extremely busy at the moment," he said thoughtfully. "You are still working, aren't you?"

"Yes, I'm still working, but things are getting pretty slack around here."

"All right, this is what we'll do. You stay where you are until I call you. If you lose your job, call me immediately. If not, I'll call you when I'm ready and we'll set up a meeting. How does that sound?"

David was slightly disappointed but had no option but to agree. "Fine with me, I'll look forward to hearing from you, goodbye."

"Goodbye, Mr. Swersky. I'll be in touch." Marcus hung up the phone. Now he had his lawyer.

The Norwoods took Marcus up on his offer and took some of their most prized possessions home with them. Just at this time Emily had announced she was expecting their second child. Amid all the excitement of the family congratulating each other, Marcus thought it couldn't have been timed better. The fact that he was going to be a father again interested him only in so far as it would keep Emily away from his house even longer than he had planned. Now, as he sat in the Rolls watching the countryside go by, he was thinking of how he would run his business from the Hampton house and make sure the less the family knew about his affairs, the better.

As the Rolls came to a stop in front of the house, the entire staff was lined up waiting to be introduced to their new boss. Jack Norwood introduced everyone and they all waited expectantly for Marcus to say something. He looked up at the magnificent house and turned around to admire the beautifully landscaped lawns with the Atlantic Ocean in the background.

"Well, Jack, I guess you'll be wanting to get back home?" he said pleasantly.

Norwood grasped immediately he was being dismissed. "Yes, I'd better get back, I've got lots to do. Goodbye for now." He got into the Model T and drove off down the curving driveway.

Marcus turned to the staff. The head butler's name was Jennings. He was like a caricature of the English butler. He ran the household with an iron hand and made sure there never were any complaints from his bosses. He noticed everything and woe betide any member of the staff who did not do their job properly. Marcus knew the type well, he had been brought up with just such a man. Marcus realized that he must let the staff know immediately that Jennings still had full authority over them. That way he would gain Jennings' undying loyalty.

He walked over and shook Jennings' hand. "Glad to meet you, Jennings. You are very highly thought of. I'm glad you are on board." Turning to the rest of the staff, Marcus said casually, "I'm sure you all know your duties, but if you do have any questions or concerns, you will go to Mr. Jennings with them. Now, Jennings, will you give me a tour of my house, I'm anxious to see it properly."

Jennings bowed and dismissed the staff. Marcus thought he was going to burst out of his shirt, the way he preened himself. He stifled a laugh.

"This way, sir." Jennings led him through the front door.

Marcus took his time making plans for the complete renovation of the fifty-year-old house. He had an architect redesign the entrance to make it more grand and converted a large room on the ground floor to an office. He had skilled carpenters and tradesmen panel it with the finest woods available, and with the huge amount of fine furniture up for auction in those months after the crash he furnished it with the best of stuff under the guidance of an interior decorator. No expense was spared for the work and Marcus was always around making changes and suggestions.

During these months renovating the house, it was always at the back of his mind that he had decisions to make about his next venture. He knew that it would have to be something totally different from the stock market. People had no money left to invest. He took to going for long walks in the city after he had visited Emily, who was in her element doing up the brownstone and preparing for the new baby. Marcus was slowly extending the gaps between visits, making the excuse that he was too busy with the house. When Emily's mother brought it up, Emily just about told her to mind her own business. Emily could see no wrong in Marcus or in anything he did, so if he didn't come home so often, then he must have a good reason. After all, it was not as if she wanted for anything.

Again, Mary Norwood realized that she had better bite her tongue. Emily had her husband on a pedestal, and Mary might as well accept it. The fact was, Marcus held their future in his hands, and Mary was not prepared to jeopardize that, no matter how she felt about him.

On one of his walks one day Marcus noticed a long line up on the sidewalk. He had to walk on the road to get by because of the crowds. Marcus noticed that all of the people in the crowd were from all levels of society. There were children with parents, young couples, old people, all different backgrounds were represented. Marcus was curious. He asked a young man what the line up was for. The young man looked at him as if he was from another planet.

"We're waiting to get into the movies! Don't you be trying to skip in here! Get to the back!"

Marcus muttered a thank you and followed the line up right to the door of the movie hall. A uniformed attendant was controlling the crowds waiting for it to open. He looked up at the giant signs advertising the latest picture. Walking over to the attendant, he asked, "Is this a special opening or something?"

"Are you kidding? It's like this every day. Four shows a day! It's the same all over, pal!" He looked at Marcus with the same look the young man in the line up had. "Say, where have you been, mister? Everyone goes to the movies!"

Marcus smiled and walked across the street and turned around to watch the crowds. "Yes, everyone but me," he said thoughtfully. He stood for a long time watching the crowd slowly make its way into the movie hall. Now he knew he had found what he had been looking for. Still deep in thought, he hailed a taxi and went back to the brownstone where he had left the chauffeur with the Rolls. He went into the house where Emily was busy dealing with an interior decorator. Marcus told her to carry on and went into the study and lifted the phone. He pulled a card from his wallet and dialed the number.

A young female voice replied, "Good afternoon, Wills and Watson Solicitors. How can I help you?"

"May I speak with David Swersky, please? Tell him it's Mark Brown," Marcus asked.

"One moment, please," the girl replied.

A moment later Swersky answered. "Hello, Mark. I thought you'd forgotten about me. How are you?"

"I'm fine, David. I want to meet with you as soon as possible. You are going to be a very busy man."

Swersky could hardly keep the excitement out of his voice. Every week had the feeling it was his last with the firm. "Excellent, just tell me where and when."

They arranged to meet at the same place they had met before. The meeting would take place the next morning at eleven o'clock. It was the middle of September 1930, over a year since Marcus had gotten out of the market.

The two men met punctually at eleven, and after exchanging pleasantries Marcus got down to business. "The last time I spoke with you, you said you had a few issues to discuss. If you remember, I told you to write your own ticket! If you do that, then there will be no issues, will there?"

"Only if you agree to my conditions."

Marcus sipped his coffee. "So you have conditions?"

Swersky opened his briefcase and pulled a folder out. He opened it on the table and handed Marcus about five typewritten pages. "These are the terms of employment I would like. If you approve them, I'll start immediately. I won't have to give any notice, the office is dead right now."

Marcus slid the papers back across the table. "You'll have to let my personnel manager look this over. I leave all this legal stuff to him."

Swersky slowly put the papers back in his case. Puzzled, he asked, "Where will I find this person?"

Without a smile, Marcus said, "You are he! Along with your other duties. So, are you going to hire this man Swersky?" He laughed at the look on David's face.

David shook his head in disbelief. "I've never had this happen before! Sure I'll hire him, but don't you want to know the terms?"

"Only the salary."

Swersky looked at him levelly. "Fifteen-thousand a year plus bonuses."

Marcus finished his coffee and stood up. "Double it! Here's my address in the Hamptons. Be there at eight o'clock tomorrow morning and be prepared to stay for two days. It will take us that long to put a business plan together."

"I'll be there, Mark. And thank you." David stood up and shook hands.

Marcus left and David Swersky, for one of the few times in his life, was totally surprised by the turn of events.

David had talked to his parents before about Marcus' offer of employment and they urged caution before making any decisions. But time had elapsed since then and David knew he was lucky to get a job offer of any kind. His parent's tailors shop had started off not bad, but was going downhill fast. He didn't say anything, but he knew it was a matter of time before it went under. Nobody was buying new suits anymore. So it was as much for their sake that he made his mind up. He knew how proud Benjamin was and how hard it would be for him, after all the years of struggling to get his own shop. It was a matter of time before they needed his help and he wanted to be in a position to give it.

David showed up at the house right on time. Marcus had Jennings arrange breakfast for them.

"Nice place you've got here, Mark!" David opened the conversation.

"Yes, I'm doing a lot of renovations, but I'm very happy with it."

When they finished breakfast, Marcus took David on a walk round the property and they strolled along the beach chatting about the changes Marcus was making. As they made their way back to the house, Marcus turned to business.

"David, I want you to listen carefully. I will lay out my plans to create what should be an extremely profitable business. You will implement these plans. You will have full authority to run the business any way you see fit. You hire the staff you need to do so. I will stay here and you can report to me here. You can have an office in the city, we'll talk about that later. I am only interested in results, methods are unimportant. Is that clear?"

"So far you've told me nothing."

Marcus had forgotten how sharp Swersky was. He wanted to know what business Marcus was talking about. Marcus patted him on the back as they went up the stairs to the front door. "Let's go into the office and I'll tell you all about it."

They went into the newly decorated office and David could not help but be impressed. It was the last word in opulence. The walls were paneled with Brazilian mahogany with expensive oil paintings hanging in discreet locations to get the full effect of the lighting from the huge bay windows looking over the ocean. Marcus had the landscapers remove a large maple tree that was obstructing the view of the ocean. There were bookcases filled with the classics in leather bound editions built into the corners of the room. An Italian marble fireplace was situated at one end of the room. The ceiling had just been painted by an French artist and depicted scenes of the gardens at Versailles.

David looked around and nodded in approval. "Magnificent, Mark. Truly magnificent!"

Marcus sat down behind the huge hand-carved rosewood desk that had once belonged to an English earl.

"Thank you, David, have a seat." He gestured to an armchair to the right of the desk.

David sat down and waited patiently for Marcus to speak.

"I went for a walk the other day, and came across a long line up of people from all walks of life. Despite the hardships of this recession, they were lining up to see a motion picture. What does that tell you, David?"

David shrugged. "I guess they are going because it's cheap, and they have nothing else to do since there's no work for them."

"Maybe. But that's not the way I see it. They are looking for an escape from the problems of daily life. When they go to the movies they can forget all their problems, even if it is only for a few hours. So it follows that the longer this recession lasts, the more the people will go to the movies."

"So you want to get into making movies?"

Marcus stood up and looked over the ocean. "Not exactly. I want to buy the places they show them."

Immediately David Swersky saw the sense in what Brown was saying. "And you want me to buy these properties?"

Marcus turned around and faced him. "At present the movie makers set the price the movie halls have to pay to show their movies. Then the owners of the halls set the admission prices to make their profit. Let's say the halls were all owned by one company. It follows the situation would be reversed. The owner of the halls would then be able to set the percentages, not the movie makers. If they did not agree to the price, then the owner would simply not show their movies!" Marcus paused and leaned forward with his hands spread on the desk. "I want to own every movie hall in the country within a year. I will then rent them out to the highest bidder. Are you up to this job, David?"

Immediately David grasped the genius of Marcus' plan. If someone could pull this off, the profits would be enormous.

Carefully, David answered him. "You're talking about a lot of real estate, Mark. Most of these places are in prime locations. Your gold bullion could very well be gone by the time you're finished buying up such properties."

"The gold bullion will stay where it is."

David swallowed hard. "Are you telling me that you have other funds to use for this?"

Marcus opened his desk drawer and carelessly threw a folder labeled *Bank of England* across the desk. "Go on, open it David!" he said with a laugh.

David looked at Marcus and thumbed through the folder. When he saw the balance, he caught his breath. He looked at Marcus dumbstruck.

"Well, are you up to this job or not?"

David had recovered his composure. He flipped the folder back across the desk. "You bet I am! Mark. When do we start?"

"Right away. Form a company with yourself as president. When you do that we'll set up an account in the Bank of America. Get yourself a nice office in the city, they're going cheap right now. You have full authority to judge the values of the properties. I know you won't let me down. Every month you come up here with the figures. I mean the price we paid and the rent coming in. That is all I need to know." David got up to leave.

"One more thing," Marcus said. "I want you to deal only with John Reynolds from Bank of America. He will be chief financial officer, give him a seat on the board and a generous salary. Also hire my father-in-law, Jack Norwood. He used to run an investment house. I don't care what position you give him, but keep him busy. When you get things set up, come back here with John Reynolds and we'll go over the details. That's all for now."

"I haven't handed my resignation in yet. I'll use the firm to set up the company. Have you a name in mind?"

Marcus looked at the waves rolling into the beach. Absently he replied, "Yes. Call the company Atlantic Holdings."

It took a month for David to set the company up. He hired his brother Isaac as general manager, a move which delighted his parents. Then he rented a floor in the old Norwood building, which like most of the office buildings in Manhattan, was losing tenants every day. When he went back to see Marcus everything was in place for them to start acquiring the properties. He took his brother and John Reynolds to the meeting.

After introducing his brother, David sat back and waited till Reynolds thanked Marcus for giving him the job. Then he opened a thick folder and spread it on the desk. He passed a small folder over to Marcus with the company name and address on the cover.

"There are a few documents for you to sign, and then we can discuss where we want to start this venture." He pointed at the pile of papers, suppressing his excitement. "That's just part of the properties in New York alone!"

Marcus was looking at the cover of the small folder. "I see you are in the old Norwood building?"

"Yes, Isaac got us a good deal on the rent."

Marcus sat back in his luxurious leather armchair. "Would you excuse us for a moment, gentlemen?" He looked at Reynolds and Isaac. The two men glanced at one another as they nodded and left the office. When the door closed behind them, Marcus looked at David with a bored expression.

"David Swersky, I am surprised at you! Since when does a big company like ours rent a floor? Buy the Goddam building if that's where you want to have your headquarters."

Embarrassed, David replied, "I wasn't sure of my authority in that regard."

"When I gave you full authority, I meant it! The full amount in the Bank of England is available for use. I can't spell it out any clearer than that."

David sat quietly for a few minutes and digested what Brown had said. Now he realized just how big this venture was going to be. He looked at Marcus with burning eyes. "My fault! It will never happen again!" He didn't have to say any more.

Marcus now knew he had Swersky out to prove something. Exactly what he wanted. He knew that with Swersky's brains working for him he could not fail. He smiled disarmingly. "I know it won't, David. Now go and get the others, and we'll get on with it."

The meeting lasted just over an hour and the decision was made to start with New York City, then the big cities of the East Coast, and then the rest of the country. Jack Norwood would have the job of finding the properties and the owners. Isaac would be responsible for assessing the values. David would be in charge of purchasing negotiations and rental fees. John Reynolds would look after the accounting. Marcus walked out with them as they were leaving, and just before they left he called John Reynolds aside ostensibly to wish him well. They walked out of earshot and Marcus made sure he had his back to the Swerskys.

"John, David will report to me once a month with the figures. Just as a double check, I want you to make copies of every transaction and give me them once a week. David doesn't need to know. Can I trust you to do this?"

Reynolds shook his hand. "It's as good as done, Mark. And thanks again."

When they drove down the driveway, Marcus walked down to the ocean. As he watched the breakers rolling in, he allowed himself a moment to congratulate himself. Now everything was in place he just had to wait till it all came to fruition.

For the next three years Atlantic Holdings went from strength to strength. By the end of the second year all of the original investment of ninety-million dollars had been paid back. Now the profits were rolling in. By the end of the third year Marcus estimated his fortune at three-hundred million dollars.

He gloried in the power that money brought him. Everyone he dealt with was dependent upon him for their livelihood. In the atmosphere of the times, no one dared incur his animosity for fear it would cost him or her their job. When the staff at the house saw him coming they treated him with the deference he thought he deserved. Despite his friendly demeanor toward David Swersky, he was the one man whom Marcus knew was his equal, if not his superior intellectually, therefore it was prudent to have someone keep an eye on him. John Reynolds religiously brought Marcus all the dealings the company was making, and every month he would meticulously check Swersky's numbers. There were never any discrepancies, but Marcus was always on his guard and spent more and more time going over the finances.

Emily now had four children to look after. Marcus realized that a family was all she wanted from life and she showed not the slightest interest in his business. He spent most of his time at the Hamptons and the family visits were few and far between. The Norwoods were never asked to accompany Emily on her visits. When Emily brought the children to the house for long weekends, Marcus played the doting father to perfection. He always impressed on Emily how busy he was and as soon as he could he would spend more time with the family. He always brought gifts on his visits to the city, and Emily would not hear a word against him. Catherine Norwood gave up criticizing his long absences, and contented herself with enjoying her grandchildren. Jack Norwood was kept busy at work, and was happy except for the fact that he and Marcus seldom saw each other.

Marcus joined the New York Chamber of Commerce and attended all the functions, obtaining introductions to all the power brokers in the State. He gave a generous donation to the Roosevelt campaign and the new President invited him to the White house along with other businessmen to help implement the wide ranging work programs of the New Deal. A new plan was forming in his mind to get in on some of the billions of government money that was being spent to try and lift the country out of the depression.

The enormous profit that Atlantic Holdings was generating would pale in comparison to the profit to be made in some of these huge enterprises.

The trick was to be a supplier to the government. *The question was what to supply? What would the government need most?* Marcus spent many weeks pondering these questions. As the year 1933 ended, his empire stretched across America. The movie moguls in Hollywood had realized too late what had happened. They had to go along with Atlantic if they wanted their pictures to be seen, and they had no choice but to comply with the prices David Swersky set.

Chapter 10

As the train sped through the snow covered fields of western New York, Mary Ellen looked out of the window blankly. Her son was sleeping on the seat beside her. Again, she felt that fate had dealt her another cruel blow. Her faith was being tested to the limits, and now she knew things were about to get worse. She had just found out she was expecting a baby. Bitterly, she thought that given her present situation, her second child would be born under worse circumstances than the first. Her husband was in prison; she had a total of sixty dollars to her name, and nobody to turn to. Again, she looked at her little gold box and tried to lift her spirits, but it was no use. In her distress she tried to doze off but could not stop thinking of the abomination of Adam's trial. Ever since the judge had sentenced him, she had ran over every word that was said in her mind. Again and again, she pictured the bleary eyed judge hammering his gavel down and the sad faced lawyer mumbling platitudes to comfort her.

What was he talking about? Mary Ellen racked her brains to remember. Something he said had offered a glimmer of hope. What was it? Wearily she closed her eyes and tried to remember. As the steady clattering of the wheels on the tracks were at last sending her to sleep, she remembered what the lawyer had said. It was something about getting a lawyer who knew about Federal law. Mary Ellen sat bolt upright. She knew just the man who could help her. *David Swersky!* She had lost touch with the Swerskys, but it should be easy enough to find David's law office. Yes! He would help her. Suddenly she felt better and for now at least she had some hope that everything would be all right. She made herself more comfortable and at last dozed off into a fitful sleep.

David Swersky had prospered since joining Atlantic holdings. He had found that Mark Brown was very generous with the bonuses that came with the enormous profits of the enterprise. His relationship with Brown was strictly business and that was the way David liked it. He suspected that Mark had a way of checking up on him despite Mark's repeated assurances that he trusted him implicitly. As far as David was concerned it was just good business sense, personalities had nothing to do with it. Nevertheless, he always made sure his accounts were in perfect order when he presented them at their monthly meetings. He knew that he did not get the rewards for nothing, that he and his brother Isaac had made the company what it was. Still, he was satisfied with his position, which enabled him to help his parents. Benjamin and Rachel had to give up their shop at the end of 1930. Despite all their efforts, the customers had simply failed to appear. The same thing was happening all over the country. As people lost their jobs, they had no money to spend on luxuries like new suits.

When David told them about the job offer from Mark Brown, they were overjoyed. They were even more overjoyed when he hired his brother Isaac. At one of the Friday night family dinners, when the two sons were home, Benjamin eventually had to tell them that his dream of owning the shop had collapsed. He could no longer pay the mortgage and had no option but to close the shop. Fortunately, it was just at this time when David started his new job. He was able to rent a townhouse with four bedrooms so there was plenty of room for his parents to live with him and Isaac. Up to this time, Rachel had corresponded with Mary Ellen O'Neill in Detroit. After they moved into David's house, she discovered that she had lost Mary Ellen's address and phone number. Eventually they found Jimmy Switcher's address in a Detroit phone book at the library, but the letters they sent were returned. The family often talked about Mary Ellen and wondered how she was surviving during the hard times they were all living through.

By 1934 David was a millionaire. He lived in an apartment overlooking Central Park and he had bought the townhouse outright for his parents. Neither he nor Isaac had married despite Rachel's pleas to get her some grandchildren before she became too old to enjoy them.

When Mary Ellen walked out of Grand Central Station into the cold wind on that December afternoon clutching Patrick's hand, her first priority was to find a place to live. The lower east side where she used to live was about as far away from Sing Sing prison as you could get. She got on the subway and stayed on the northbound train till it reached its furthest point at 145th street. She then took a bus to Westchester county and easily found a room for rent in a well kept house, one of the many that had "room for rent" signs in their front lawns, hoping to keep the mortgage payments up. For ten dollars a week

Mary Ellen and Patrick had a roof over their heads and that included breakfast. The man had lost his job in the city, but like many unemployed, still went out every morning with his briefcase pretending to go to the office. Paradoxically, when people lost their jobs, in a lot of cases, they blamed themselves. After all, in America all you had to do was work to prosper, and if you didn't have a job it must be your own fault. That was the thinking that caused a lot of men to commit suicide at the time. The sense of failure at not being able to provide for their families drove thousands of men to despair. The couple made it clear to Mary Ellen that she stay out of their way as much as possible, as renting the room was bound to be a temporary measure. The house was handy for the bus route that went to Sing Sing, but Mary Ellen never mentioned the fact that her husband was in prison. The visiting hour was on a Sunday afternoon from two o'clock till three. As it was Thursday, Mary Ellen had to wait three days to see her husband. On the Friday morning she walked to the post office and started going through the phone book looking for lawyers offices in New York City. Her search proved fruitless, and she asked the assistant for help.

After looking under Swersky in the phone book with no luck, the assistant advised her to try the Manhattan phone book the next time she was in the city. Mary Ellen realized it would not be as easy as she thought to find David Swersky. Everyone did not have a phone, and some of those who had did not have them listed in the phone books. Maybe the Swerskys had moved away from New York, after all it was four years since she had lost contact. She decided to use Saturday to go down to the Lower East Side and go to the shop where Benjamin had started his business.

The Lower East Side looked the same as when she had last been there, except for the hundreds of boarded up shops and businesses. Everywhere she looked the people were milling about waiting for the food delivery trucks to come to the food stores hoping to get some damaged goods to eat. The Swersky store was boarded up, and nobody knew where they had gone.

In despair, Mary Ellen tried again looking through a Manhattan phone book. There were only ten Swerskys in it, and she wrote the numbers down and tried to call them. Five of them were disconnected and the rest did not know of a David Swersky. Wearily she got on the subway and made her way back to Westchester. On Sunday she left the house and walked for fifteen minutes before boarding the bus for Sing Sing. She did not want anyone to know her husband was in jail for fear of being put out. People were funny about these things, especially with the reputation the prison had in those days.

It was the first time Mary Ellen had been inside prison walls. The humiliation of being frisked by a leering guard unnerved her. Patrick was not allowed in as the prisoners were only allowed one visitor at a time. The prisoners were seated in a long line behind a double paned glass screen which ensured that nothing could be passed over to them. A guard constantly patrolled along the back listening to everything that was said. Adam was seated halfway up the line. There was a slit between the two panes of glass that enabled them to hear each other.

Adam was delighted to see her and was both happy and shocked to learn that she was expecting a baby. "Why didn't you tell me before?" he asked, his mind racing.

"I just found out last week. Anyway, there's nothing you can do from in here." She looked disconsolately around the grim visiting area with the armed guards glowering at them. She told him about her disappointing search for David Swersky and about the house where she was staying. Despite her efforts to appear brave, Adam sensed the desperation in her voice.

"What am I going to do, Adam? I've only got forty dollars left, and with you in here it's a matter of time before we're out on the street."

"God knows, Mary Ellen. I've got to get out of here!" he whispered desperately.

"Get out of here!" Mary Ellen replied angrily. "If you're going to talk nonsense like that I'm as well leaving right now. You know it's impossible to get out. So for God's sake talk sense!"

Adam had never seen her so angry. "I'm sorry, I just feel so helpless," Adam replied.

They sat in silence for a few minutes while Mary Ellen wiped her tears.

"Look, what's that lawyer's name again? Some of the guys in here get visits from their lawyers, maybe one of them knows him."

"David Swersky"

"I'll spread it around. I hope to God he can help us."

Mary Ellen sighed. "I hope to God we find him!"

The bell rang and the guard rudely banged his truncheon on the counter. "Time's up!" he roared. Immediately the prisoners stood up and said their hurried goodbyes before being marched through a door at the end of the room.

For the next two months Mary Ellen went to Sing Sing every Sunday. The room she was living in was becoming unbearable. The man of the house still went out every morning as if going to work, but at night Mary Ellen heard the cursing and arguing between husband and wife. Occasionally she heard the sound of blows and muffled cries and she knew the man was beating his wife. She pulled the pillow over her head and tried to block the noises out. Thank God Patrick was asleep when the beatings started. Her money had run out after six weeks and as a last resort she pawned her little gold box her brother had given her. She got thirty dollars for it. The breakfasts had gradually diminished in size so she started to give part of hers to Patrick.

She started to feel dizzy a lot and did not realize that she was losing weight instead of gaining during her pregnancy. Her cheeks were sunk deep in her face and she had dark circles under her eyes with the sleepless nights worrying about how she could not survive much longer. On the Sunday after Mass she counted her money and discovered she did not even have the bus fare to Sing Sing. It took her an hour and a half to walk it, and she was close to exhaustion when she got there. Desperate as she was, she decided not to tell Adam she had only one week left before she was put out in the street. Despite Adam's pleas, none of the other prisoners had talked to anyone who knew of David Swersky. After the visit was over, Mary Ellen started walking with the rest of the people who had been visiting. The bus stop was situated outside the main gates of the prison. Everyone stopped at the bus stop except Mary Ellen who held Patrick's hand and kept walking. A woman's voice stopped her. "Young lady, the bus stops here! There's not another stop for miles!"

Embarrassed, Mary Ellen called back to say she would walk home, as it wasn't far. The woman walked over to her. In a quiet voice she said, "There's not a house within miles of this place. If you've no bus fare, I'll pay it for you. In your condition you shouldn't be walking anywhere." Mary Ellen was so exhausted she accepted the stranger's offer. When the bus came, they shared a seat and the woman asked her where she got on the bus. Mary Ellen told her that she had walked it that day, but if she had bus fare, she got on at the last bus stop in Westchester. The woman, who did not ask her name or introduce herself, told her to get on the bus next week and if she had no money she would pay her fare as she got on the bus before Mary Ellen's stop. Mary Ellen thanked her and told her she would repay her as soon as she got some money. When the bus stopped at Mary Ellen's stop, the woman shook her hand and as the bus moved away, Mary Ellen opened her hand and saw a crisp new twenty dollar bill. She looked up to wave a thank you but the bus was already too far down the road. "Bless you! Whoever you are!" Mary Ellen said aloud. This meant she and Patrick still had a roof over their heads.

The twenty dollars helped her at the time, but she started to go to the soup kitchen at five o'clock every day as the breakfast now consisted of toasted bread and butter. The eggs and the occasional rasher of bacon had stopped altogether. Their clothes were becoming ragged, but they did not look out of place as most of the people were as poor as she was. In the long wait for the soup kitchen to open she heard horrific tales of what some people were doing to stay alive. One woman told her she should teach Patrick to pick pockets to see if he could pick up some extra money. Another told her to go to the rubbish dump where sometimes you could pick up some food that was still edible and maybe even something of value that you could sell for food.

Mary Ellen realized that most of these people slept in the streets and shuddered at the thought that if things did not change, she and Patrick would soon be joining them. She managed to get her landlady to reduce her rent to eight dollars a week because of the skimpy breakfasts they were getting. The soup kitchen did not always have enough to feed the increasing crowds and if you did not get there early enough you could end up going away hungrier than you were before. By the time Sunday came around, Mary Ellen was heading for a nervous breakdown. The constant hunger and worrying was wearing her down and the beatings at the house were nearly a nightly occurrence. She hated having to live there, but she had nowhere else to go. The woman who had paid her fare the week before was waiting on the bus for her and insisted on paying it again. Mary Ellen thanked her profusely, but sensed that the woman did not want to become any more familiar than they were.

Adam was sitting in his usual place when she walked slowly to her seat opposite him. Even though he was seeing her every week he could not help but notice she was failing badly. She was starting to look years older. He kept his thoughts to himself and greeted her brightly.

"It's good to see you, Mary Ellen. I have some news."

Wearily she looked up at him. She had decided she had to tell him she would soon be out on the street with Patrick.

"I hope it's better than my news!" she said morosely.

"What's wrong? Tell me! What's the matter?" Adam asked anxiously.

"Tell me your news first."

Adam pulled a slip of paper from his pocket and waved the guard over. The guard glanced at the paper and slipped it through the slit in the glass partition. Mary Ellen lifted the paper and read it aloud. "David Swersky, formerly of Wills and Watson is now an executive at Atlantic Holdings situated on Water Street near Wall Street."

Mary Ellen looked at Adam with shining eyes. "You found him!"

"Yes, one of the guys has a lawyer from Wills and Watson who knows Swersky. But how do you know if it's the right Swersky?"

Mary Ellen could not contain her excitement. "Because I remember those names! Adam, I can feel it, our troubles are over! David will help us."

"I hope you're right," Adam replied. *If you're wrong, I dread to think what will happen!*

The next morning Mary Ellen used the last of her money for the trip to Manhattan. The Atlantic building was easy to find as it was the biggest building on Water Street. It was after ten o'clock when she walked through the revolving doors clutching Patrick's hand. She looked around at the church-like marble columns and saw a semi circular desk with an inquiries sign on it.

The lady behind the desk looked askance at the ragged apparition heading toward her over the marble floor. The security guard was not in his usual place outside the main door. She would have to have a word with him. She hurriedly walked out from behind the desk and cut Mary Ellen off.

"Can I help you, madam?" she asked in a voice heavy with sarcasm.

"Yes, I'm looking for Mr. David Swersky," Mary Ellen replied. She noticed the other people coming and going looking at her curiously as they passed.

"Do you have an appointment?"

Mary Ellen realized immediately that she had to think of something fast. There was no chance of this one letting her go any further. Mustering all her courage, she replied coolly, "I don't need an appointment to see my cousin, do I?"

The woman looked at her disbelievingly. *A cousin with an Irish accent?*

"I wasn't aware Mr. Swersky had an Irish cousin."

Mary Ellen waved her hand impatiently and said. "Just tell him Mary Ellen is here, will you? I've no time to argue with you!" She turned her back and led Patrick to one of the armchairs that were scattered about the entrance hall. Her heart was beating so hard she was convinced the woman could hear it.

The receptionist thought fast. Her first instinct was to get that damn guard and have this woman thrown out. Obviously she was one of the thousands of street people who were crawling all over the city. *On the other hand, if she's telling the truth, it could cost me my job.* She made her decision and went back to her desk and called Swersky's office.

"Swersky!"

"Good morning, Mr. Swersky, sorry to bother you, but I have a woman here who claims to be your sister."

"Sister! I don't have a sister. What did she say her name was?"

"Mary Ellen." There was silence for a few seconds then Swersky's voice said urgently, "Keep her there! I'll be down right away."

The receptionist put the phone down and walked back over to Mary Ellen. Her manner had changed to a cool politeness. Mary Ellen nodded in acknowledgment. Suddenly she started to panic. It was years since Swersky had seen her. *What if he didn't remember her? Even if he did, why should he help her?* Her mind was going in all directions at once. *Oh God, why did I come here? I'll probably be thrown out!* A voice she instantly recognized shouted from the back of the hall.

"Mary Ellen O'Neill! By God, it is you!" David Swersky ran over to her and took her hands in his. He looked at her haggard face and her ragged clothes, and the little boy sitting on the chair. Tears welled up in his eyes, and unable to speak, he hugged her and said gruffly, "Let's go to my office, we can talk there." He led them toward the elevator. As they passed the receptionist, he said, "No visitors today, please." Neither of them said anything all the way up in the elevator. As they entered David's office he told his secretary, Alice Trent, to cancel all his appointments for the next two days and bring in a pot of tea and milk and cookies for the child. He seated Mary Ellen on a plush leather couch and pulled a chair over next to her.

She was crying into a rag which used to be a handkerchief. Between sobs she tried to tell him how glad she was to have found him. He stood her up and took her torn coat from her and calmed her down. In a soothing voice he said, "There's plenty of time, Mary Ellen. You're all right now! Here comes the tea. Now take your time and tell me how I can help you." She took a sip of tea and felt better immediately.

"So much has happened, I don't know where to start."

"We're in no hurry, why don't you start from the beginning."

As Mary Ellen started telling him everything that had happened to her since she had left New York, Swersky looked at her thin shoulders and haggard face. *By God, she must have been through hell. She looks like a woman of sixty. And pregnant too! I hope to God she's not been raped again.* He forced himself to listen to her till at last she finished.

"David, can you help get Adam out of jail, I've nowhere else to turn."

"I'll see what I can do. But first things first! I'll be with you in a minute." He lifted the phone and dialed a number. As he waited for an answer he held his hand over the speaker and whispered, "My mother. Hello, Mother, how are you today? That's good. Now listen carefully. I'm bringing someone over to the house, we'll be there in half an hour. Call Dr. Shapiro, tell him to come straight to the house as soon as he's free. I'll tell you everything when we get there!" He hung the phone up and shook his head. "She was asking a million questions at once! Come on, let's get you home."

"What's the doctor for, David? If it's for me I've got no money." Mary Ellen knew she wasn't well, but the last thing she could afford was to go to a doctor.

"Mary Ellen, listen to me! I'm so glad you found me, and so will the family when they find out! Don't be afraid anymore, we'll look after you and your little boy till your husband gets out of jail. Now, the first thing is to get the doctor to have a look at you both, and then we'll get you well again. You can stay with my parents, they have plenty of room now."

Meekly, Mary Ellen nodded her thanks. Swersky took them down to his private parking garage at the rear of the building where he kept his Packard Roadster convertible safe from the vandalism that was becoming more and more common as the Depression deepened. *He must be a millionaire! Look at this car!* Mary Ellen had never sat in such luxury. In the twenty minutes it took to drive to his parents, David told her that he no longer practiced law for a living but he still had his license if he needed to. He told her that the reason she couldn't find his phone number was none of the family had their numbers listed.

Rachel and Benjamin Swersky were overjoyed to see her. David sat in silence, listening to them pepper Mary Ellen with questions between outbursts of sympathy and the occasional tear. When the doctor showed up, they reluctantly allowed him to take her into a bedroom to examine her.

Rachel could not believe the state they were in. "David, it's just as well she found you. The woman is practically starving to death!"

"Believe it or not, Mother, but there are many more like her. And right here in New York."

"Thank God you got that job, David. That could be us if you hadn't helped us," Benjamin said quietly.

The doctor came back into the living room and lifted his coat.

Rachel rushed over to him. "Doctor Shapiro, will she be all right?" she asked anxiously.

"She's badly run down, and very weak. The child is in much better shape. But with a good rest and plenty of food, both of them will recover quickly. By the time she has the baby she should be in good health. But it's imperative she has the rest. Another week of living like that and she would surely have lost the baby and maybe even herself."

"But she will recover?"

"Rachel, you just look after them and I'll come by in a few days. By the way, what connection do you have to the young lady?"

"She's our adopted daughter!" Benjamin said.

The doctor looked at him doubtfully. "I see. Remember, give them both plenty to eat and I'll see you later. Have the woman take these pills three times a day. They will help her recover her strength faster." He handed Rachel a prescription.

When the doctor left, Benjamin went out to the drug store to get the pills. Mary Ellen came out of the bedroom looking weaker than ever. "What did the doctor say? He wouldn't tell me anything."

"Sit down!" Rachel said. "You're both going to be all right, but only if you do exactly what I tell you! You have to get plenty of rest, and more importantly, you have to eat everything I give you!"

"I never heard the doctor say that," David said.

Rachel swung around to face him. "That's because you never listen! Anyway, haven't you got work to do?"

David smiled at Mary Ellen. "I guess I'm being told to leave. I'll drop in on my way home." He went over and gave her a hug, and whispered, "I'll see what I can do about your husband as soon as I can." Mary Ellen nodded thankfully and David patted his mother on the back. "See you later, Mother."

When the door closed behind him, Rachel made Mary Ellen comfortable on the couch.

"I'm going to make some chicken soup for you, so while I'm working, you tell me everything that's happened since we last met. And don't leave anything out!"

David went back to his office and called Mark Brown. He had given David the job of making sure that his political connections were well looked after. David had a special checkbook with all the checks already signed by Brown. All he did was fill in the amount and the date. Brown would meet them at high priced dinners and meetings in Washington where he was laying the groundwork for his plans to get his hands on some Federal contracts. He would use his considerable charm on important members of the various committees, and after making sure they were in positions that may benefit him, would tell David how much to give to their various re-election campaigns.

"Good day, Mark, I have a favor to ask of you."

Marcus was surprised. Swersky was not one to ask favors. He did his job well, but always kept his distance, never speaking to Marcus unless it was necessary for business reasons. *It must be important, for him to call here, especially during the week. This could be good for me, Swersky would be a good man to have in your debt.*

"How can I help you, David?" he asked smoothly.

"I'll get straight to the point. I have a friend who's husband is in Sing Sing for a minor offence. The problem is that they made it a Federal matter. Therefore, it has to be appealed in a federal court. The bottom line is, Mark, do you know a Federal judge who could help. If you do, all you'd have to do is introduce me and I could take it from there." David knew that Mark had been donating generous amounts to at least two Federal judges. He knew Brown well enough to know that if he could, he would jump at the chance to put David in his debt. He liked everyone he knew to either work for him or owe him something. It consolidated what he regarded as his power over them.

That was what Marcus liked most about Swersky. *Straight to the point! No beating about the bush! Yes or no!*

"I think I may be able to help you. Let me make a call and I'll get back to you today." Marcus replaced the receiver and reached for his list of phone numbers. He never asked any details of the case, he figured if Swersky wanted to tell him he would have already done so.

Marcus was as good as his word. He called David back within half an hour.

"Hello, David. I think the man you need to talk to is Judge James Saunders. He will be in Albany next week to hear appeals. I mentioned your problem and if you could prepare an appeal by next week he might be able to squeeze you in. Here is his number. By the way, the good judge is preparing to run for the Senate next term, so why don't you kill two birds with one stone and take a check to Albany with you. It certainly won't hurt your chances."

David thought for a minute. *A week may not be enough time to prepare. He'd have to get the transcript of the trial from Detroit. But it could be done. Now the question was how much?*

"How much would you recommend?"

"Look, David. You've done good work for me. Take twenty-thousand in a company check. That should do it. But don't give it to him till he guarantees you will win your appeal. I can't do any better than that."

"And I couldn't ask for any more! I won't forget this, Mark."

"And I won't let you forget it, David!"

Marcus was laughing when he said it, but David knew he was dead serious. He had not expected Brown to pay what was nothing more than a bribe. He'd want his money's worth sooner or later. Still, he'd done what David had asked.

"Thanks again, now I'd better get busy."

The first thing David had to do was go to Sing Sing and have Adam Corbett sign a document making David Swersky his attorney. He drove up early the next morning. The night before he had visited with Mary Ellen and assured her he was doing his best to get her husband out of jail.

Adam Corbett was surprised at how soon Swersky came to see him. As he was an attorney, he had no trouble seeing Adam privately outside the normal visiting hours. He was happy to designate David as his attorney, but was honest about having no money.

"Look, Mr. Swersky. I really appreciate what you're doing, but I have to tell you up front that I'm broke. I simply can't pay you now, but I will as soon as I can afford it."

"I appreciate your honesty, Mr. Corbett. But the fact is I'm doing this for Mary Ellen, and there will be no cost to you."

"How are we ever going to thank you?"

David stood up and closed his briefcase. "Let's wait and see if we can get you out of here first. I'll be in touch once I get a date for the appeal to be heard. Goodbye, Mr. Corbett."

Adam went back to his cell with the first hopeful thoughts since he had entered the prison. *I hope it's sooner rather than later. At least Mary Ellen's being looked after. Yes, everything will be all right, it's just a matter of time before I get out of here.*

Unfortunately by the time David got the transcript from Detroit, it was too late for the court session to hear it. It would be another month before the next session. He went to Albany anyway to meet with Judge Saunders. The two men met for lunch in an upscale eatery.

After some small talk, David took the trial transcript from his briefcase and put it on the table. "This is the case we discussed, Judge. I've read it over and it looks like it could be overturned on appeal. The evidence was shaky to say the least, and the judge just wanted to make an example of our man."

Saunders looked at the folder. "Is that so, Mr. Swersky? Well, I'm really busy at the moment. I don't see me having the time to read this before the next session. I'm running for the Senate, you know. It doesn't leave much time for extra work in the judiciary." He sipped at his wine, looking at David over the glass.

So that's how you want to play it? This will be easier than I thought! "Yes, I imagine it takes a lot of time to run for office. And a lot of money too!" David pulled the checkbook with the pre-signed checks from his inside pocket. "I guess you can always use some extra cash. I hear these campaigns are very expensive?"

The judge eyed the checkbook greedily. "You've no idea how expensive it can get, Mr. Swersky."

"Indeed I have not! Perhaps you could give me some idea."

Saunders thought for a minute. "To give you an example. Traveling expenses alone can come to thousands of dollars over the course of a campaign. And that's not counting hotels!"

"Would ten-thousand dollars help?"

Saunders finished his wine. "It wouldn't hurt." He sounded slightly disappointed. David knew then that Brown had already agreed on a price.

"And another ten-thousand would really help?"

In answer Saunders took the transcript and put it in his briefcase as David wrote out the check. "I'll see you in court, Mr. Swersky. Bring your client here for the next session."

David decided to push his luck a little, as he gave Saunders the check. "Yes, here's hoping it works out well for him."

Saunders looked at the check and as he slipped it into his pocket, he said brightly, "Signed by Mr. Brown, I see." He ordered another drink. " I think I can guarantee it will work out very well, Mr. Swersky."

By the time Adam's appeal was heard, Mary Ellen had made a full recovery. She was now eight months pregnant. Both she and Patrick had benefitted from Rachel's care and attention. David had insisted that Rachel take them out and outfit them in new clothes. No expense was spared to make them feel safe and well. On the day of the appeal, David drove Mary Ellen to Albany to attend the hearing. Rachel and Benjamin looked after Patrick. On the way she peppered him with questions on how the process worked and what were Adam's chances of being set free.

David explained that it was a panel of judges and David had to give them good legal grounds to overturn the sentence. As for Adam's chances, despite his optimism David was cautious and told her just to wait and see.

Mary Ellen sat in the rear of the courtroom waiting for the hearing to begin. There was a case being heard before Adam's and it seemed to drag on forever. At last she saw Adam being brought up from the cells in an ill fitting suit. He looked at her and smiled and she waved back nervously.

David stepped up to a podium and started talking. A lot of it was legal stuff that she didn't understand, but the main grounds seemed to be that Adam had not been represented properly. When David finished, the six judges conferred with one another for a short time and then the judge in the middle, whom Mary Ellen assumed to be the one in charge, shuffled some papers and addressed Adam.

"Young man, this case should never have got this far. If your counsel had known Federal law he could have defended you better than he did. However, it is a serious matter striking a Federal agent. This court sentences you to time already served. You are free to go, Mr. Corbett." He banged his gavel on the desk. Mary Ellen cried out with joy and ran down to hug Adam. David packed his papers in his briefcase and glanced up at Judge Saunders. Saunders nodded slightly and David closed his case and turned round to tap Adam on the shoulder. "Come on, you two, we don't want to hang around here any longer than we have to."

They walked out of the courthouse and made their way to David's Packard. Mary Ellen was so happy she never stopped chattering about how good the Swerskys had been to her and Patrick, and now David getting Adam out of jail!

Adam waited till they got on to the main highway to New York before he spoke. "If you'll let me get a word in, woman. I've not had a chance to thank you, Mr. Swersky. As soon as I can find a job, I'll pay you back for your kindness to us."

David replied over his shoulder as he steered the Packard through the traffic. "I may have a job for you, but it must be on one condition."

Mary Ellen interrupted, "A job! Oh, Adam, isn't that wonderful. David you're too good to us!"

David laughed at her exuberance. *What a difference in her since that day she came into my office. She looks more beautiful than ever and the healthy glow is back in her cheeks.*

"Hold on, Mary Ellen, Adam may not want the job! And it is a conditional offer."

"All right, let's hear it!" Adam said. "I'll take any job I'm offered. Jobs are hard to find these days."

"The job is managing a picture house. It pays sixty-five a week. But there is that condition!"

"Come on, David, what's the condition?" Mary Ellen cried.

"Adam must promise that he will not try to unionize the workers. Can you promise that, Adam?"

Without hesitation, Adam replied, "You have my word on that! Look where I ended up because of the union! Their stupid lawyer was useless to me!"

"Excellent! I'm glad you said that. Now the next thing we do is get you a place of your own. You don't want to be living with my mother when the new baby comes along."

"David, you know we've no money! We'll have to wait till Adam gets some wages," Mary Ellen said humbly.

"And sentence this man to living with Rachel Swersky with an expectant wife!" He turned and looked at Adam with a grin on his face. "You'd be glad to get back to Sing Sing!"

"Don't you dare talk about your mother like that, David Swersky!" Mary Ellen scolded him. "She is the salt of the earth!"

"I know she is, but still you two need a place of your own and we will arrange it. Don't worry about the cost, you'll do me a favor by paying me back when you've got it, agreed?"

Adam and Mary Ellen reached for each other's hand and nodded in agreement. "Thank you again, David."

For the first time Adam called him by his given name.

Mary Ellen's baby was born on the sixth of June 1934. A healthy boy whom they called David. David Swersky had arranged for them to rent a flat one block away from Rachel and Benjamin. He had paid for their furniture and started Adam as a manager in a local movie house. As soon as Adam got his first paycheck, they both went to the pawn and redeemed her little gold box. They soon settled into a routine and Adam started to pay off the furniture at five dollars a week.

The money meant nothing to David, but he realized that Adam was a proud man and it did him good to feel that he was supporting his family. Rachel and Benjamin came by often, and strange to say, Adam and Benjamin took an instant liking to one another. Two men from different backgrounds discussing the relative benefits of communism and capitalism. They talked politics endlessly and argued into the night about the state of the country and the world. At last, Mary Ellen started to believe that the worst was over. She had her husband and children, and the friendship and support of the Swersky family. After a couple of months had passed, she decided to write and tell her family in Ireland how she was. She knew she had neglected them and it was time now to set their minds at ease.

Chapter 11

Marcus was finalizing his plans for his next and biggest venture. He had spent two years laying the groundwork and now he was ready to put his plan into operation. He called a meeting in the Hamptons with his executives. There were two United States Senators and the Governor of Michigan. David and Isaac Swersky, John Reynolds, and Jack Norwood were also asked to attend. It was only the second time Norwood had been in his old house since Marcus had taken it over. The meeting was held in Marcus' magnificent office. After the introductions, the servants brought in trays of sandwiches and coffee. When they left Marcus walked over and locked the double doors.

"Help yourself, gentlemen," he said as he poured himself a coffee. He sat behind his desk and waited till everyone was seated.

"Now, gentlemen, the reason I called you all to this meeting is because I have good news. I am pleased to announce that Atlantic Holdings has been awarded the contract to supply the Government of the United States with the concrete and steel required for some of the projects being built under the New Deal legislation!" He paused to see the different reactions his statement generated in the room. Immediately the three politicians clapped their hands excitedly.

"By God Mark, you did it! Congratulations!" The Governor leaned over to shake his hand. The rest of the men smiled uncertainly. Marcus stood up and held up his hand for quiet.

"I see I'll have to explain further what this means for all of us in this room. Senator Smith of Ohio, Senator Graves of Illionois, and Governor Deans have been lobbying for Atlantic for almost a year now. I have had some modest influence in making sure that their states got a piece of the pie. The projects entail the building of roads, power stations, dams and various other jobs. At the same time I have been buying shares in the major concrete and steel manufacturers in the Midwest, and one plant here in New York State. (He did not mention the two-million dollars he had spread around the various committees.) It means that there will be millions of dollars available for their states. Which means that Atlantic will make millions of dollars selling them the materials. And that's all there is to it. Any questions?"

John Reynolds spoke first. As he spoke, Marcus walked around and handed each of the men a folder.

"If Atlantic is selling concrete, it sure is news to me!"

"It's the first I've heard of it,"Norwood agreed. As Marcus knew he would, David Swersky immediately grasped what Marcus was planning.

"Isaac, I guess you'd better call our friends in Hollywood and tell them we're ready to sell our movie houses, except the ones in New York City. Jack, start negotiations to buy the remaining shares in the list of companies that I assume is in this folder. John, open accounts for Atlantic in Detroit, Chicago and Columbus. Put top people in charge of them, we'll discuss the amounts at our next meeting."

Marcus turned to the politicians and held his hands wide. "Gentlemen, didn't I tell you he was smart. Right on, David! All right, gentlemen, get busy. I want this done in three months!" As all the men shook hands as they filed out of the office, Marcus signaled David to stay behind after the others had left. He saw them off to their cars and he and David returned to the office.

"Well, Mark, you're in the big leagues now!" David said.

Marcus was looking through a pile of maps he had pulled from a large drawer under one of the bookcases.

"And so are you, David. The reason I held you back is because I want you to look after a separate project for me. One I will be totally involved in from start to finish. Ah, here we are!" He spread the map out on the desk. It was an up to date map of Manhattan. David joined him and Marcus pointed to a point just north of Battery Park. It was circled in red pencil.

"You want to buy some property?" David asked.

"Yes. And I want to build a skyscraper on it! Higher than the Empire State Building and the Chrysler building!" David was stunned. *Mark's ego was getting the better of him!*

"That certainly is a tall order in more ways than one."

"Well put, David. It will be called The Brown Building! Just imagine, when the ships from Europe come into the harbor, the first thing they'll see after the Statue of Liberty will be my building!"

David had never seen him so animated. "What exactly do you want me to do?"

Marcus stopped fantasizing and sat down.

"First, I want you to buy the land. Take care of all the necessary permits and legal stuff. Money will be no object in this project, David. I want it to be the best building in the world! Is that clear?"

Money will be no object? He's pouring everything into the government work! "Mark, I have to remind you that you have just about tied up your entire fortune in this Government scheme. A skyscraper like you are describing will cost millions of dollars! Not to mention the cost of the property."

"Yes, I'm aware of that! The money we make from the movie houses will buy the remaining shares in the manufacturing plants. Talk to Reynolds. He has the numbers. If my calculations are correct, there will be enough money there to buy the land for the building. That is all you need to worry about. By the time everything is ready for building, I will make sure the money is there."

He will make sure the money is there! He must have money someplace other than the company! Yes, David thought. *I should have known he wouldn't keep me informed of all his finances. But still, where will the money come from? He must have something going on that I'm completely unaware of! Perhaps overseas? Maybe that's the answer.*

"All right, I'll talk to Reynolds and I'll get back to you on how much we have left to purchase the land."

Marcus was looking out at the ocean. He replied casually, "Let me know immediately, David!"

David said his goodbyes and drove back to the city with his mind racing. *Was Mark Brown going too far? He'd need millions of dollars to build such a building. It was a huge risk he was taking! Or was he? It all depended on how much money he had and try as he might, David had no idea where or how much there was.*

Nevertheless, David decided to make sure he would be extremely careful of anything to do with the Brown Building!

The next day he went to see Reynolds at the bank. He told him that Brown wanted to know how much cash was available to buy some property. He did not mention what it was for. While Reynolds looked through the various accounts, he asked David what he thought about the big news.

"Mark has really gone big this time, David. If what he says comes true, he'll end up a billionaire!" David realized then that Reynolds knew nothing about the plans for the skyscraper.

"Well, with government contracts you can't go wrong, I think it's the right thing to do."

"I'm glad you said that, David. I noticed he'd been buying shares for a while, but when I asked him about them he told me to keep it quiet. Even with his record of successes, I was beginning to doubt the wisdom of putting everything into one thing. You've made me feel better." He stopped hammering at the adding machine and tore off the paper. He looked at the figure and shrugged.

"That's near the right figure, if he wants an exact number, you'll have to give me a couple of days."

David looked at the number. "Eight-hundred-thousand! I hope it's enough." He put the paper in his pocket.

"What property is he looking at, David?"

"You'll have to ask him yourself, John. I'll see you later."

David went back to his office and called Marcus with the figure. "I haven't inquired into the price yet, so first we'll have to see if the owner wants to sell, and then see if it's enough."

Marcus' voice turned harsh. "Listen well, David. Everything has a price! We will buy this property, do I make myself clear?"

"Of course, but if there is not enough money available…"

Marcus' voice became almost a shout, "If more funds are needed, sell the Goddam building you're in!" He slammed down the receiver.

David looked at the phone and laid it back on the cradle. It was the first time he had ever heard Mark Brown raise his voice. He steepled his fingers and pondered the situation. *The skyscraper had become an obsession with Brown. He had noticed the day before the exaggerated enthusiasm when he was talking about it. He never showed that kind of emotion, even when he talked about multi-million dollar deals. Obsessions often led to bad decisions. David resolved to do no more than was necessary in the purchase of the property. Let Brown make the decisions.*

David left the office and drove to City Hall. He filled in a form to search for the deeds for the property. A young woman accompanied him to the basement where the records were kept. She pulled out a box and thumbed through the papers. "You want to know the owner of all this property?"

"Yes, all of it."

The young woman pulled out a bundle of papers and carried them over to an empty desk. She started making notes as she looked through the legal documents. At last, she handed David the sheet of paper. "They are all owned by the same institution," she said as she lifted the papers.

David looked at the paper. The owner of the property was the Roman Catholic Church, represented locally by the Archdiocese of New York.

Chapter 12

Archbishop James Mooney sat behind his desk in his office just off Fifth Avenue. He had the job he wanted, the financial advisor for the Archdiocese of New York. The job gave him the freedom to travel around the five boroughs, and the power to control millions of dollars. Even in the middle of the depression, the faithful still put their money in the collection plates every Sunday. The job kept him busy, but not busy enough to curb his womanizing. He found that it was a lot easier for an archbishop to seduce women than a parish priest. As his duties entailed meeting a lot of powerful men, his affairs were mostly with women from the upper classes. He still had Bridie O'Connell as his housekeeper, who was more afraid of him than ever.

On Monday, September the tenth of 1934 the Archbishop was feeling particularly satisfied with himself. He had spent the night in the company of the wife of a businessman who was out of town. She was one of his regular visitors for "spiritual guidance" as he told Bridie was the reason for his many visitors who just happened to be well-heeled women. His secretary, a young woman of twenty, brought in his mail along with his coffee and laid it on his desk.

"Good morning, your Grace. How are you today?"

"Never better, Eileen, and you? Just a minute, don't be rushing away. Why don't you lock the door and sit with me for a while?" With her back to him, Eileen Donachie closed her eyes and gritted her teeth as she turned the key in the lock. *Not again! Please God get me away from this man. Her parents were so proud of her working with the Archbishop, it would break their hearts if they found out the truth about him.*

Later that morning, Mooney opened an envelope with 'Atlantic" embossed on it. It was a request for a meeting to discuss the purchase of some real estate. The letter was signed by a David Swersky. The name looked vaguely familiar to Mooney, but he could not remember where he had heard it before. He pressed the buzzer on his desk. Eileen Donachie came into the office, pen and notepad at the ready. Her eyes were still red from crying after her ordeal earlier that morning. Mooney shoved the envelope across to her.

"Reply to this and set up a meeting. Tell Father Mackowski to look after it and make sure you keep me informed." Father John Mackowski was Mooney's business manager in charge of real estate.

When David got the reply to his request, he noticed immediately that it was from the office of the Archbishop of New York, His Grace James Mooney. Immediately he rang for his secretary. *It couldn't be him! But I'd better check just in case. The bastard would remember me, and that would kill any deal before it got started.*

"Could you get me a recent picture of Archbishop Mooney? There's probably one in a newspaper somewhere." The secretary nodded and hurried out of the office. Alice never asked questions and that was what David liked about her. He started preparing a written offer to buy the property at ten percent more than it was worth. The quicker this business was finished the better. He had taken out a mortgage on the company building for two-million dollars to give him some leeway. The money was deposited in Bank of America. After lunch a brown envelope was delivered to David's secretary. She brought it in to his office.

"Here you are, Mr. Swersky. I called a friend at the *Times*." David opened the envelope and pulled out the picture. The handsome face of James Mooney smiled back at him. David threw the picture on the desk in disgust.

His hunch had been right. It was the damned rapist after all! *Well, well, this sure complicates matters. I'll have to get someone else to deal with him! But who will it be?*

At first David thought of letting Isaac take charge, but he was too busy dealing with the sale of the movie theatres. He reluctantly decided to let Jack Norwood handle it, after all he was Catholic, and that wouldn't hurt dealing with the Archbishop. Just before he left the office Mark Brown called him.

"David, it seems we have a little paperwork problem. I've just been informed that for Atlantic to get the government contracts, I have to be an American citizen. Would you look after it for me, I'm too busy with the architects designing the Brown Building."

"All right, I'll come up tomorrow with the forms. Have your passport and immigration papers ready."

"Fine, see you tomorrow."

On the drive to the Hamptons David decided to tell Brown that he was giving the land purchase to Norwood. He would not be pleased, but David had no choice. He had dropped in at the Immigration office to pick up the citizenship forms before heading out of the city. Marcus welcomed David into his office.

"Well, what do you think? My architect brought it up just yesterday. Isn't it beautiful?" he said, spreading his arms wide and looking at a large display set up on a table. It was a model of Lower Manhattan with the new building incorporated.

"Very impressive! The new building will certainly dominate the city!" David replied. He decided to tell Brown the news right away. "Look, Mark, I have some bad news about the property deal."

Marcus swung round to face him. "Bad news?" he said intensely.

"Well, the thing is, years ago I had a conflict with the priest who's in charge of this. It would be better if Jack Norwood looked after it."

"Oh, is that all? As long as you tell him what to do."

David noticed that Brown was having difficulty tearing his eyes away from his model. Relieved that Brown wasn't upset, David said brightly, "Well I'd better get back, I've got loads to do. So do you have your papers ready?" He pulled the forms from his briefcase.

"You just have to fill these out and sign them and I'll take them back today along with your documents. In two weeks you go to a swearing allegiance ceremony and that's all there is to it."

While Marcus filled in the forms, David walked around the display of the city. The proposed Brown Building towered over New York harbor. It looked so out of place, David wondered if it would ever be built. *I suppose they felt the same way when the Empire State Building was being planned.*

At last Marcus finished the forms and handed David all the paperwork. He stuffed them into his briefcase.

"I'll be in touch as soon as I know anything about the property deal."

"Yes David, The sooner the better! Give them what they want, just get it done! Okay?"

"Yes sir!" David said as he left the office. He noticed Marcus had already turned back to admire his display.

David drove directly back to his office to check that Marcus had filled out the forms correctly. He asked Alice to get him a sandwich while he looked over the documents. Absently he lifted the British passport and flipped it open. A younger Mark Brown looked steadily back at him. Suddenly David sat bolt upright in his chair. *Marcus Vicinius Browning w*as the name written on the passport. Instantly David knew that this was the man who had robbed Mary Ellen O'Neill. *Mark Brown! Very clever indeed! More like a play on words than a name!*

After the initial shock had passed, David put the passport in his pocket and hurried out of the office. He drove the Packard to Mary Ellen's flat and rang the doorbell.

Adam Corbett answered the door. "Why hello, David. Come in, it's awhile since you've been round."

"Yes, Adam, is Mary Ellen in?" Just then Mary Ellen walked in with the baby in her arms.

"David! How nice to see you," she said.

"You too, Mary Ellen. Now would you mind sitting down for a minute? Adam, hold the baby."

Adam took the baby and both of them looked at David expectantly.

"What is it, David?" Mary Ellen said worriedly.

David took the passport out and opened it. He spread it out on the table. "Mary Ellen, is this the man who robbed you?"

Dumbstruck, Mary Ellen looked at the picture. "Yes, this is Marcus Browning. Where did you get this?"

David felt strangely relieved. "Believe me, it's a long story, Mary Ellen. Make us a pot of tea and I'll tell you all about it."

Mary Ellen jumped up from the chair. "Don't wait for the tea! I can hear you! Hurry up, David! You're keeping us in suspense!" She rushed over to the stove.

David took his time and told them the whole story since he had first met Mark Brown in Tweed's office right up till he opened the passport. When he finished the story, the three of them sat round the table sipping the tea.

Adam was first to break the silence. "So, from what you've told us, and from what Mary Ellen told us about him, he made his millions off Mary Ellen's money?"

"It looks that way. I know he made a fortune in the stock market before it crashed, so it's likely that the stolen money was used to start him up."

Adam stood up and started pacing the floor. "Let's all go and confront him! He's got away with it long enough!"

"Calm down, Adam. He's a very powerful man now and, anyway, he'd only deny he ever knew Mary Ellen. We have to think this out very carefully."

Mary Ellen had sat in silence during their conversation. "Adam, why don't we let David look after this? He's a lawyer after all. David, do you think there's any chance of getting my Uncle John's money back from this man?"

"You should get more than that! He was the cause of all that happened to you! The bastard should be flung in jail!" Adam was raging with anger.

"Sit down, Adam. There's more!" David said quietly. He explained to them about the real estate deal and that Mooney was in control of the church's business in New York.

Adam threw his hands up in the air. "You've lost me, David. Are you telling me that you just found this out in the last couple of days?"

"That's what I'm telling you."

"Well, that makes two of them should be flung in jail!"

"It's not as simple as that."

"So they're going to get away with their crimes just because one's a millionaire and the other has the Catholic Church behind him?"

"I didn't say they would get away with it!"

Mary Ellen broke in. "You two stop bickering! Remember that I was the victim! It's all so confusing. Imagine after all these years you find the two of them at once. And involved in the same business deal too!" she said calmly to David. "I'm putting my trust in you, David. I'll leave it up to you how you deal with this. I only ask one thing. If you could at least get Marcus Browning to give me back my Uncle John's money so I could give it back to him, I would be happy with that."

"You're entitled to more than that!" Adam roared.

Mary Ellen patted his hand. "Sit down, Adam. Let's hear what David has to say." Adam meekly sat on the chair.

"Adam's right. You are entitled to more than your uncle's money!" He stood up and lifted his hat and coat.

"Why don't you both take a walk and tell my parents the whole story? I don't think I'm up to repeating the whole thing to my mother." He paused before he left and looked at them both for what seemed like minutes. "Believe me, you'll get more than your uncle's money, Mary Ellen. And by the time I'm finished with Browning and Mooney, they'll be sorry they ever met you!"

David left the flat and drove down to Battery Park. He parked the Packard and walked along the shore deep in thought. *It was easy for him to say Browning and Mooney would pay for what they had done, but it was a different matter putting his words into practice. He knew both of them were ruthless men, and with the resources they each had it would be difficult, if not*

233

impossible, to bring them down. He had seen the real Mooney for himself, the cold-hearted and callous way he dismissed Mary Ellen as a mental deficient. He had heard how Browning had crucified Walker and knew that he was behind Tweed losing his job. What they had each done to Mary Ellen was far worse. He had to make them pay, but how?

By himself he had no real chance of proving what they had done. If he tried to bring charges against them they would probably have them quashed before they even got to trial. There must be another way other than the courts, but what?

He stopped and looked out at the Statue of Liberty, and remembered that it must have been around where he was standing that his parents found Mary Ellen all those years ago.

To destroy Mooney or Browning, he had to be as cunning and ruthless as them. He knew he did not even have the means. But both of them had the means! Why not let them destroy each other? He had the perfect opportunity to set them against each other. It would not be easy, and would require perfect planning, but it could be done! It would be like walking a tightrope, one false move would be disastrous. Well, he'd just have to be extra careful, wouldn't he? Yes! You pair of bastards, your own arrogance will be your undoing, and David Swersky will make sure of it!

He lifted a stone and threw it into the Hudson. He had his plan of attack. Now he just had to set the wheels in motion. He drove back to his office and called Jack Norwood to tell him to come to the office in the morning.

The next morning David was in the office at six thirty preparing the offer for the real estate. By the time Norwood came in he had Alice typing it up for him.

"Well, David. To what to I owe the pleasure?"

"Good morning, Jack!" David said warmly. He had always liked Norwood and felt a little guilty for using him this way. The feeling soon passed when he thought of Mooney and Browning.

"I want you to look after a real estate deal for Mark. The owner of the property is the Catholic Church. As we'll be dealing with Archbishop Mooney, I thought maybe you could expedite things seeing as you're a Catholic yourself."

Norwood made himself comfortable. "Archbishop Mooney! I remember him when he was the parish priest at Saint Joseph's."

"So you know him! That's even better."

"Well, I can't say that I know him personally, but I've met him a few times."

"What kind of a man is he?"

Norwood thought for a moment. "As far as I know, he was very good at filling the church on Sundays. A good speaker, and smart too! I believe he was sent to Boston College for some course or other."

David was watching him carefully. "And that's all you can tell me?"

Norwood hesitated before answering. "There were rumors going around that he had an eye for the ladies, but to my knowledge they were just rumors!"

"Maybe there was more to it than rumors, Jack. Make a few enquiries and see if there's any truth in it."

"Okay. But he's an Archbishop now. He'd have to be crazy to do anything like that!"

"Or extremely careful!"

"Yes, I suppose so! Now tell me about this deal."

David handed the papers over. "We'll start off offering ten percent below the market value just to test the waters. Let me know how you get on. You'll be dealing with a Father Mackowski. You don't know him, do you?"

"No, I've never heard of him."

After Norwood had left David gave him five minutes start and told Alice he'd be out all day. He got the Packard and headed uptown. He had deliberately put a low offer in to gain time. He knew the offer would be rejected out of hand. He parked the car outside the Moore Detective Agency office and went up the stairs and rang the doorbell. He had used the agency when he worked for Wills and Watson and knew they were reliable, and more important, very discreet. A young woman answered the door and David introduced himself and asked to see Mr. Moore. Tom Moore was glad to see him and the two men reminisced a little before David told him why he was there.

"Tom, I have a job for you that will require the utmost discretion. If you decide to take the job, I'll pay you twenty-thousand dollars."

Moore let out a low whistle. "Twenty grand! I sure could use the money. But I can smell a rat here, David. Let's hear it!"

"Do you know who Archbishop Mooney is?"

"Of course I know who he is! What kind of a dumb question is that, David?"

David looked at him levelly. "I had to ask. Do you also know that he's a dirty Goddamned rapist that preys on young women?"

Moore was an experienced detective and nothing shocked him anymore. He had seen the worst of crimes in his thirty years on the job. "And the job is you want me to get you proof! Because if you had proof you wouldn't be here."

"Do you want the job or not?"

"How long will you give me?"

"No more than two months. If you can't give me proof by then, I'll pay you five-thousand for your time."

Moore held out his hand. "You've got a deal, David. Now, I sense there's something personal here. Can you give me anything to start with?"

David pulled an envelope from his pocket.

"In there you'll find affidavits from a cop and the priest's housekeeper. Both of them know what happened. Maybe you can get something out of them. The cop might talk for a price, but the woman is terrified of him, I don't think she'll be any help. As you know, I'm restricted by being a lawyer."

"Well, it's a start. This guy's a big shot, David. It's shooting high to try and bring down an Archbishop. I know how the church works. They protect their own." As Moore spoke he looked over the papers. "I see you even got one from the man himself."

"Yes, you know the poor girl had a baby and the bastard still denied it!"

Moore was going to ask what interest David had in the case, but decided against it. "David, in my experience, a little money goes a long way when you need a tongue loosened here and there." He looked up expectantly. David stood up and smiled grimly. He took an envelope from his pocket and laid it on the desk

"Twenty-thousand, John. Start with the cop. Use it well!"

By God, he wants this guy badly! "I'll be in touch, David," Moore said as Swersky closed the office door behind him.

David had one more thing to do to put his plan in motion. He went back to the office and called Mooney's office.

Eileen Donachie answered. "Archbishop Mooney's office. Can I help you?"

"May I speak with the Archbishop. You can tell him it concerns the Atlantic real estate offer. He'll know what I'm talking about."

"I'll put you through now, sir."

"Archbishop Mooney here, how can I be of service?"

David remembered the strong self-assured voice. He folded his handkerchief and put it halfway over the mouthpiece to disguise his voice. A trick he had learned from one of his clients.

"Listen carefully, I will not repeat myself. The man who owns Atlantic holdings will pay just about any price you want for that parcel of land. You can charge what you like and he will pay it."

"Who is this?" Mooney demanded.

"A good Catholic!" The phone went dead. Mooney put the phone down and looked at it reflectively. After a few moments he buzzed Eileen. She came in, notepad at the ready.

"Tell Father Makowski I'll be handling the Atlantic real estate thing myself. Direct all communications regarding it directly to me. Is that clear, Eileen?"

"Yes, your Grace," she answered as she hurried out of the room.

As soon as Marcus got his citizenship in January 1935, the government checks started coming in. The materials started flowing from the various plants to the work-sites that were scattered over the Midwest. He was right. The profit margin was astronomical. When David and John Reynolds went over the figures, they did it twice to make sure they were right. After two months they projected profits in excess of 50% per year. They decided to go to the Hampton house with the numbers to show them to Mark Brown. David had called John Moore a few times, but was asked to give him more time. He had told Mary Ellen and Adam to have patience and trust him to carry out his plan. They agreed even though he would not divulge exactly what he was going to do.

Reynolds was bubbling with excitement all the way in the car. He asked David did he expect a bonus off the profits. David said it was a possibility. To their surprise and disappointment, Mark seemed strangely disinterested when they showed him their projections. He merely nodded as they read the numbers.

"Aren't you excited, Mark?" Reynolds asked. "We thought you'd be delighted with these projections."

"Yes, yes, John, very good. Now could you give us a minute, please?" he replied absently.

Reynolds stood up abruptly and stalked toward the door.

"Take as much time as you want! I'll be in the car, David." He slammed the office door behind him.

David waited for Brown to say something, but he seemed not to have noticed Reynolds' outburst.

"Why haven't you bought that property yet?" Marcus' voice was edged with hostility.

"According to Jack Norwood they keep rejecting the offers."

Marcus leaned across the desk toward David, his knuckles white with gripping the desk. "Enough bullshit. Get Norwood off this deal today! I want you on it, and I want you on it now! Is that clear, or do I find someone else?"

David recoiled from the intensity in Marcus' voice. "I won't do any better! All we can do is up the offer!"

Marcus looked at him steadily. "Tell me the real reason you don't want to deal with this priest."

"It's a personal matter."

The two men sat in silence weighing each other up. *Do I fire him? No, he's too valuable; but I've got to get this deal completed; my building depends on it!* Marcus stared at David with burning eyes. "All right then, David. I'll look after it myself! Have Norwood meet me in your office tomorrow morning. I'll go and find out exactly what this priest wants."

Perfect, now the two predators can meet face to face, and if I play my cards right, they surely will destroy each other!

David returned Marcus stare and replied quietly, "I think you're doing the right thing. There will be no middlemen, just the two of you, *mano a mano!* I'll see you in the morning."* David got up to leave. Abruptly he turned back. "Don't you think the numbers are a bit high?"

"You'd better get used to it! The government pays high!"

David nodded and closed the door behind him. Marcus sat thinking for a long time after David left. He got up and went over to the display and walked around it slowly. *I don't care if it's the Pope of Rome, there's no damned priest going to stop this building being built!*

On the way back to the City, Reynolds complained to David about Marcus' behavior.

"After all the work we've done on this, and all he could think of was that building of his! Oh, I know that's why he wanted me out, don't deny it, David!"

"Calm down, John. Now think about it. Don't you think the profit projections look a little too good?"

"Yes I did, but it's bound to be lucrative when it's government orders, isn't it?"

"Why don't you go through all those material shipments again and double check them. It won't do any harm."

"Yes, I agree. I'll get right on it and I'll call you if there's any problems."

If I'm right, David thought, *there's a bigger problem than just profit margins!*

Norwood had all his papers ready when Marcus walked briskly into David's office. Without the usual courtesies, Marcus lifted all the documents and tossed them into the wastebasket.

"No more time wasting, gentlemen. I have two questions. First, what is the market value of the property, and second, what was our last offer?"

Norwood had the facts ready. He was relieved to be rid of this assignment. The Archbishop was a hard nut to crack. *By all means Mark, you're welcome to try yourself.* "The property is worth one point five-million. Our last offer was one point seven five."

"Right, let's go Jack. You can drive me to the priest. God, I hate coming into the City. There's just too many damned people! David, call him and let him know I'm on my way."

As soon as they had left, David called Mooney. Talking with the handkerchief halfway over the mouthpiece, he said gruffly.

"You know who this is. The boss himself is coming to see you. Do not take the offer he gives you, he'll go higher!" He hung up the phone and started going over the Government payments.

When Marcus and Norwood arrived at Mooney's residence, Marcus told him to stay in the car and wait till he came out. The housekeeper let him in and led him to the office.

Eileen Donachie nodded toward a door and said, "Go right in, His Grace is expecting you, Mr. Brown."

Marcus walked into the office and closed the door behind him. He looked at the big man behind the desk and recognized him instantly. As they shook hands, Marcus said, "Don't I know you from somewhere, Father?"

Mooney looked at him coldly. "I don't think so, and being an Archbishop, I prefer to be addressed as 'Your Grace.'"

Marcus smiled knowingly. "All right, Your Grace!" he said sarcastically. "Are you still going around groping your parishioners? I remember you! The Christmas party at the Waldorf a few years ago! You were groping a woman at the dinner table!"

Mooney stood up in a rage. *Who was this guy? I can't remember him.*

"How dare you talk to me like that! Get out before I throw you out! And you can forget about buying that land. As long as I'm here you'll never get it!"

Marcus leaned forward smiling broadly. With a mock bow he said sarcastically. "That wasn't a threat now, was it? I'm sure Your Grace will change your mind once I find out who your current plaything is! Because I'm sure the Church won't look very kindly on this sort of thing reaching the papers." His voice changed from mockery to deadly quiet. "You'd better be squeaky clean, my friend. Because if you're not, I'll make sure you hit every headline in the city!" His voice changed again as he opened the door to leave. "On the other hand, if you decide to sell, the offer is now reduced by half! You know where I can be reached." He closed the door softly.

Mooney sat down heavily in his armchair. *How could this man know what was going on? He couldn't remember meeting him before. Damn him to Hell! Even if he did see him with Clare all these years ago, that was water under the bridge. He'd just have to be extra careful from now on. Yes, Hell would freeze over before he'd sell the property to that little Limey.* He smiled grimly and reached over to the whisky decanter.

Half an hour after Norwood and Marcus had left, the phone rang in David's office. It was Tom Moore.

"Thank God, Tom, I thought you had disappeared! I was about to give up on you. What have you got?"

"Not much I'm afraid. There's no doubt this guy is a regular Casanova! He's having affairs with at least three married women. It's common knowledge that one of them is the Attorney General's wife. The guy's known about it for years, and is still friendly with Mooney. It seems they have an understanding. I staked the house out myself. I also suspect the secretary isn't there just to answer the phone. She's not a day more than twenty. These church guys usually have younger priests as office help."

"So what's the problem?"

"The cop is no use! He sticks to the story that he took girls to the priest, but only to get them shelter. The housekeeper is the key. If we could get her to talk, the guy's finished, but I spoke to her myself, and she's terrified of him. That leaves the secretary, but I've no proof there either. She goes to the same place for lunch every day. I tried to start a conversation with her but she brushed me off! She's probably as afraid as the old housekeeper. I'm sorry, David, but this guy's got his bases covered pretty well."

"Not that well, Tom. Hold on to the money till I get back to you. Something you said gave me an idea."

"All right, I'll keep on it till you get back to me."

David rang the buzzer for Alice. She opened the office door halfway and stepped inside.

"Yes, David, Do I need my notepad?"

"No, Alice. Get me Cardinal O'Leary on the phone please. I don't want any stories about how hard it is to get him! Just do it, Alice!" She nodded and let the door swing closed behind her. David lifted the phone and looked at his watch. *Everything depended on the timing! Brown would be back soon, and probably in a rage! Hurry and lift the phone, Mary Ellen!*

"Good morning, Mary Ellen here."

"Hello, Mary Ellen. Can you be ready to come with me in an hour?"

"I've got the children here and Adam's at work."

"Take them round to my mother's, I'll pick you up there."

"What's going on, David?"

"I'll explain when I see you. Goodbye for now." He hung up and immediately dialed Tom Moore. "Hello, Tom. David Swersky here. Listen up, this is what I want you to do. I'm bringing a young lady to your office about one o'clock. I want you to take her to where the Archbishop's secretary has her lunch. When you get there, just point her out. Okay?"

"Of course, David. What's going on?"

"I'll explain when I get there. What's the secretary's name?"

"Eileen Donachie."

"See you later, Tom." David had no sooner hung up than Alice came into the office.

"The Cardinal is on the phone."

David took a deep breath and picked up the receiver. "Good morning. Cardinal O'Leary?"

"Yes, this is he. What can I do for you, Mr. Swersky?"

"It's more like what I can do for you!"

"I'm listening."

"I have irrefutable evidence and three witnesses that one of your clergymen is a rapist and a philanderer."

"Go on." The voice was calm and steady.

"Rather than take this to the police, I thought if you want to save the church the bad press, I could give you the opportunity to punish him yourself!"

"We do prefer to deal with these matters internally, if at all possible." *Yes, I bet you do!*

"It will be possible if you want it to be."

"And what, may I ask, can make it possible?" The voice was heavy with sarcasm.

241

"Not what you think, Your Eminence. This is not about money! It's about justice! I presume you want this man removed as soon as possible?"

"If he's guilty of what you say, of course I want him removed!"

Let's see just how badly you want him removed, shall we? "One of the witnesses is terrified of him. She's Irish and believes she cannot testify against a priest. No matter how scared she is of him, I believe she'd be more terrified to lie to a Prince of the Church! Will you talk to her?" *This was the moment of truth! The whole plan depended on this moment and the Cardinal's answer.* The Cardinal remained silent for what seemed like an eternity.

"Yes, of course I'll talk to her. Can you bring her to the Cathedral?" he replied wearily.

This was not the first time the Cardinal had to deal with something like this! David sighed with relief, it was all falling into place. The Cardinal was a true Christian after all. "I'll get back to you on that, Your Eminence."

"May I ask who this priest is?"

"You'll find out soon enough, goodbye."

Ten minutes later the office door swung open and Marcus came striding in. He seemed strangely calm as he took a seat across from David.

"Well, Mark, did you buy the land?

"Not yet! We'll have to persuade this priest that it would be in his interest to sell." *He's taking this very well for a man who wants it so badly.*

"What will you do now?"

Marcus looked at him and started laughing. "You won't believe this, David. I've met this priest before! He didn't remember me, but I sure as hell remember him!" He was laughing harder now. "The last time I saw the Archbishop he had his hand up a woman's dress! Norwood was there at the time, but he never saw it." Marcus had to stop to steady himself. His voice turned to a deadly whisper, "A leopard doesn't change his spots. Get a private detective on to him right away. I want something on this bastard, and I want it soon!"

David sat looking at him with an amused look on his face. *I've got what you want, pal! Now all you have to do is pay for it!*

"What the hell are you grinning about?"

"Relax Mark, I'm way ahead of you. That private matter I mentioned is that I've known all along this guy's a womanizer. I just got the call five minutes ago from an old acquaintance of mine. He has two women who'll testify against Mooney!" Marcus broke into a broad smile.

"You never cease to amaze me, David. Now we can get the property for a song. I'll threaten him with the press!" He rubbed his hands in glee.

David shook his head.

"No publicity. The women want anonymity."

"If no publicity, then how can we get him to agree? That's the only thing that'll scare him!"

"No, there's something he's more afraid of than anything else." Marcus thought for a minute. He broke into a grin.

"The church! Yes, the church will crucify him if they find out! Good thinking, David." *Boy, I'll have to stop doubting Swersky! He's always one step ahead of me.*

"There is one issue that will need looking after."

Marcus looked at him anxiously. "What issue? We have got him! Haven't we?"

"The women want something for testifying."

"How much do they want?"

David shrugged. "Considering that the deal depends on them, I'd say it's up to you. How bad do you want it?" Marcus slapped his glove on his knee.

"You're right! I'll give them the difference between the two-million I was prepared to offer and what we pay for it."

"About a million dollars?"

"Yes, that's about right, the sooner you pay them, the sooner we get the land!"

"Good! I guess I'll take over the deal from here and let you get back home."

"Seeing I'm here, I'll spend the day with the family, it's been a month since I've seen them. Doesn't time fly?"

What a low life, the damned building is more important to him than his wife and children! "I'll keep you informed," David said.

Marcus stood up and looked at David shaking his head. "You know something, Swersky, you are priceless! You never cease to amaze me!" He walked out of the office still laughing to himself.

Priceless, am I! We'll see if you still think that when this is over! He looked at his watch and rushed out of the office.

He picked Mary Ellen up at his mother's house and as they drove uptown he explained what he wanted her to do.

"Listen carefully, Mary Ellen, and don't interrupt. We are about to bring Mooney down. He has a young woman working as his secretary. Her name is

Eileen Donachie and we believe he's abusing her. We are going to meet a friend of mine. He will take you to a restaurant and he will point her out to you. *Don't interrupt!* What I want you to do is convince her to testify with you against Mooney to Cardinal O'Leary. Now, both of you will remain anonymous. You will not even have to see Mooney! No one will know your names, and most important! After it's done he will never hurt any more young women. And remember, apart from yourselves, it's his future victims you're doing this for! Now, will you do it?"

Mary Ellen sat in silence for a moment and replied in a steady voice, "Of course I'll do it! He has to be stopped!"

"I never had any doubt, Mary Ellen. This is the place here." He parked the Packard in front of Moore's office.

The place where Eileen Donachie went for lunch was more of a café than restaurant. There was a lunch counter with a few patrons having coffee and four small tables for four scattered randomly across the remaining space. Tom Moore escorted Mary Ellen into the café at one fifteen, and as usual, the girl was sitting in her usual spot, alone at a small table next to the window.

"There she is, next to the window. Now it's up to you. Good luck!"

He pretended to have forgotten something and left the café. Mary Ellen looked around and, even though there were empty tables, she walked over and said brightly, "Do you mind if I join you? I like a window seat myself."

Eileen looked at her in surprise. She had finished eating and was sipping at a cold drink.

"No, I don't mind, have a seat. I'll be leaving soon anyway. What county are you from?" Mary Ellen ordered a drink and chatted about Ireland till she got her order. *How do I go about this? Asking a woman if she's being abused by an Archbishop? She'll think I'm insane. I'll start by asking her where she works and take it from there.* "Do you work around here? By the way, I'm Mary Ellen."

"I'm Eileen. Yes, I work around the corner."

"What do you do?"

"I'm a secretary. I work in the Archbishop's office." *It's now or never!* Mary Ellen sipped her drink and put the glass down, spilling some of her drink. "You work for Archbishop Mooney?" She looked askance at the girl.

"Yes, is anything wrong? Do you know him?"

Mary Ellen gathered her gloves and purse and said in a voice filled with disgust. "Do I know him? That man raped me, and he got away with it! If I were you I'd get out of there while you can!" *There! It's done.* She stood up to leave. *Please say something, don't let your chance slip away!*

"Don't go! Please! Sit down, please." The girl's eyes were filled with tears.

Thank God! Mary Ellen sat down and took Eileen's hand in hers.

"He's abusing you, isn't he?"

Eileen bowed her head and wiped her eyes. She looked up at Mary Ellen in anguish. "I don't know where to turn. He never leaves me alone. My parents would never believe me if I told them. I'm so ashamed." She started crying again.

He'll never touch you again! "Listen to me! You've nothing to be ashamed of! Now, let's get out of here and I'll take you to meet a man who will help us."

"You say he raped you! How did you ever get over such a horrible thing?" Eileen said between sobs.

Mary Ellen thought for a moment. "The hope of better days to come, I guess."

Moore was waiting for them in the car. He held the back door open and ushered them inside. He drove directly back to his office where David was waiting.

"Eileen Donachie, this is David Swersky, a friend of mine who is also a lawyer. He is here to put a stop to Archbishop Mooney's assaults."

David shook hands and guided Eileen to a chair. "You don't have to be frightened anymore, Eileen. You don't ever have to go near that man again. With you and Mary Ellen willing to testify…"

Eileen interrupted him, "Testify against an Archbishop? Impossible! My parents would kill me!"

David held up his hand. "Let me finish please! The whole thing is being willing to testify! You won't have to go to court or anything like that. The Church is going to deal with this matter."

"Then what is it you want me to do?"

David pulled a chair over next to her and sat down. "The housekeeper, Bridie O'Connell has known about Mooney's affairs for years. The poor woman is terrified of him. God knows how many girls he's assaulted. She is the key to the whole thing. All I want you to tell me is when she will be in the house alone. That is all you have to tell us."

"Most every afternoon. The Archbishop goes out nearly every day between two and four. Sometimes it's for business and other times it's what he calls ministering to the sick!"

"Yes, and I can guess what that means. All right, Eileen. Leave Tom here your phone number and he'll drive you home."

"I'd better go back to work. He'll think something is wrong if I don't show up."

"Listen carefully, Eileen. That man will never bother you again! You will have your job back as soon as he's gone. So if you like you can call in sick and leave it at that till Tom gets in touch with you." David stood up.

"How long will that be?" the girl asked.

"This is Tuesday. Tom will pick you up at your house at one o'clock on Thursday. I want you to be there to see Mooney get punished."

"I'll be with you, don't worry," Mary Ellen said gently.

"But who can punish him? He's an Archbishop."

"Cardinal O'Leary will punish him, so don't you worry. Mooney won't even know you're there!" David put his hand on her shoulder. The girl looked visibly relieved.

"All right. I'll call in sick, and then I just want to go home."

"Good! You can call from here. Tom, will you take these girls home please? I've got to get back to the office. I'll call you all Thursday morning with the arrangements. Goodbye, girls."

"Okay, I'll wait for your call," Moore answered.

David drove back to his office and called Cardinal O'Leary. "You know who this is. Now listen carefully, this is what you must do to get this cancer out of your Archdiocese. Send a priest to Archbishop Mooney's residence on Thursday at exactly one thirty and tell him to bring the housekeeper, Bridie O'Connell back to you.

"She's the one who knows everything. Now you'd better impress her with your authority if she's going to talk, because she's terrified of this man. Do you understand?"

"I understand perfectly. Why don't I just call and tell Archbishop Mooney to bring the woman here?"

David remained silent.

The Cardinal's voice became hoarse with shock, he had heard just about everything in his forty years in the priesthood, but this was different. "It is Archbishop Mooney you're talking about. Isn't it?"

"Yes it is! I will bring the other two witnesses. Now where do you suggest we do this?" David asked impatiently.

Cardinal O'Leary regained his composure. "Where better than the house of God! The Cathedral is empty most afternoons. Come to Saint Patrick's at two o'clock on Thursday."

"Fine, I'll see you there."

On Wednesday morning, John Reynolds came to see David at his office. He looked as if he had not slept a wink the night before.

"Well, John, what's so important that you had to come over here. You could have called, you know?" *If you've found what I think you've found, no wonder you look like that!*

"David, you'd better look at this. I hope I'm mistaken, but I've went over it three times. Tell me what you notice about these." He handed David a sheaf of printed papers.

Without answering, David started reading the papers. Reynolds sat nervously watching him. The silence in the office seemed to intensify with each passing minute. At last, David laid the papers on the desk. "What are we building in Lincoln Park? There seems to be more going there than anywhere else!"

Reynolds slumped in the chair. "I was praying you knew something I didn't. There is nothing being built in Lincoln Park, New Jersey, yet Atlantic has billed the Government three quarters of a million dollars for steel sent to that state! The order we have is for Lincoln Park, Michigan! What the hell is going on?" *What was going on was Mark Brown was double billing the government, sending steel to Lincoln Park in both Michigan and New Jersey. Nice work if you can get it, Mark!* David thought cynically.

"Why don't we go and see for ourselves? There's an address on the manifests."

Reynolds lifted the papers. "Yes, here it is! It's just outside Newark."

"Okay. Let's go. It's only half an hour in the car."

When they got to the address on the manifest, it was an old rusty railcar falling apart from disuse. Behind it, on a huge area of vacant ground were enormous stacks of steel girders. As the two men got out of the car, a tractor trailer full of girders drove past them into the yard. The truck stopped and the driver got out with a clipboard in his hand. He walked over to David and held out the clipboard. "Sign here, pal."

David took the clipboard and looked at the heading on the form. It read Atlantic Steel. It was one of the companies they had set up.

"Hey, What's going on?" A large red faced man came rushing out of the railway car. "Who the hell are you?" He grabbed the clipboard out of David's hand.

David held his hands up in apology. "The driver thought I worked here, that's all. We just took a wrong turn, sorry about that." The two men got into the Packard and drove off.

"What the hell's going on, David? There's a mountain of steel in that yard."

Yes there is! Just about enough to build a skyscraper! "If I'm right, that steel is going to be used to build Brown's building!"

Reynolds looked at him for a moment. "By God, David, he's going to build a skyscraper with government money!"

"It sure looks that way, doesn't it!"

"We'll have to go and tell him we know what's going on. If anyone finds out, we'll all go to jail!"

"That's true. Unless we're the ones who tell the Feds what's going on."

"You mean take this to the government! For God's sake, David, I don't know if I could do that! I owe everything to Mark Brown."

"Are you willing to go to jail for him? He committed the crime, not you!"

Reynolds sat in silence staring out at the city across the Hudson. "I just wish I'd never found it."

"What if you'd never found it? It was bound to come out anyway! Nobody could hide that amount of material."

"Still, I wish it had been someone else."

Perfect, John. Now I'm going to solve your dilemma. "Like me for instance?"

Reynolds looked at him sharply, "What do you mean?"

"Why don't you leave those papers with me and I'll look after the whole mess. You don't even have to know about it! Will that solve your problem?"

"You'd do that for me?"

"If you feel so strongly about Brown, sure I'll do it."

Reynolds leaned back in the seat. "Then it's all yours, David. And I know nothing about it!" He grabbed David's arm. "I'll never forget this, David. Thank you."

"Let go my arm or we'll crash! Forget it, John. I'm glad to help."

Bridie O'Connell was going through her regular routine of cleaning house when the doorbell rang. It was Thursday afternoon at two o'clock. She answered the door to see a young priest standing on the porch.

"I'm sorry, Father, but the Archbishop is out at the moment, he won't be back for a couple of hours."

The priest looked apologetic. "Bridie O'Connell?"

"Yes, Father, that's me. What can I do for you?"

"I'm here on an errand from Cardinal O'Leary. He asked me to tell you he needs to see you on a matter of great importance."

"Cardinal O'Leary! He wants to see me?" Bridie was both surprised and pleased that the great Cardinal O'Leary would remember her. *He loved my Irish stew! I remember when he was here for dinner he told me himself how much he enjoyed it! I bet he wants me to make him a dinner.*

"I'll just get my coat, Father." She rushed into the hall and grabbed her coat and hat.

David drove Mary Ellen to Tom Moore's office to pick up Eileen Donachie before they went to the Cathedral to see the Cardinal. "Do you want to come along, Tom?" he asked.

"Why not, I'd like to see how he handles the housekeeper."

"All right! Now what we will do is first, I'll tell him who I am and then introduce the ladies." He looked at the two women. "Now, don't be nervous, just tell him the truth. Nothing more, nothing less, all right now, let's go!"

The Cathedral was empty when the four of them went inside. The silence seemed eerie after the noise of the city. Suddenly they heard footsteps and saw Cardinal O'Leary emerge from a side door next to the main altar. Moore nodded to David and knelt down in the back row. The other three walked down the center aisle and met the Cardinal halfway.

David held out his hand. "I'm David Swersky. It's me who's been calling you. This is Mrs. Mary Ellen Corbett and this is miss Eileen Donachie."

"I am Cardinal Thomas O'Leary. I wish it were better circumstances. Now, ladies, you are both Catholics I take it?" His voice was sad and listless.

"Yes, Your Eminence," they answered in unison.

"Good. I don't have to remind you of the penalty for lying in the house of God, do I?" The two women nodded their heads. "Fine, now sit down here and you go first, Mary Ellen. I don't need any details, just tell me what happened to you as briefly as you can. Father Mahoney is on his way to pick up Miss O'Connell."

The car dropped Bridie off at the side door of Saint Patrick's.

"His Eminence will meet you in the Cathedral, just wait in front of Our Lady's statue for him." The young curate pointed to the door. Bridie was familiar with the cathedral and knew exactly where to go. The statue was at the side of the main altar. When she entered the vast church, she noticed it was empty except for two women kneeling in prayer and two men at the back of the church sitting apart from one another.

Hurriedly she crossed herself and knelt in front of the statue. Before she had time to start her customary rosary, a door opened to her left and Cardinal O'Leary walked slowly toward her. His red cassock seemed to make him look even taller than his six feet and the gold crucifix shone brightly in the sunbeams coming through the stained glass windows.

Awestruck, Bridie left her seat and knelt in front of him to kiss his ring.

"Up you get, Bridie," the Cardinal said kindly.

She stood up and looked at him in embarrassment. "I believe you wanted to see me, Your Eminence?"

"Yes Bridie, on a matter of great importance! You know the penalty for lying in church, don't you?" he said severely.

"Yes, Your Eminence. That's a mortal sin."

"No, Bridie! That is a sacrilege! Punishable by excommunication! Which means your immortal soul will burn in the fires of Hell for all eternity! Do you understand?" His voice was hard and insistent.

Bridie started to feel scared of the Cardinal. She sank to her knees in front of him. "Yes! Your Eminence. I would never lie in church!" she stammered.

"Then you will answer me truthfully, won't you, Bridie?" he asked softly.

"Of course, but what do you want to know?" She was trembling in fear.

The Cardinal towered over her and said in a hushed voice, "I have witnesses who tell me that you are aware that Archbishop Mooney has been abusing women for years." His voice was steadily rising. "Is this true, Bridie O'Connell? In the name of God Almighty, tell me the truth!" While speaking, he had grasped the gold crucifix and held it in front of her terrified face.

Bridie fell apart in front of him. "I've confessed it many times, but he told me it was the devil made him do it, and if I prayed hard enough for him, God would set him free. When a priest tells me to do something, I do it!"

"How many and how long has it been going on?"

Bridie started weeping. She shook her head. "I don't know how many, maybe fifty. I've been with him for ten years and it's been going on all the time."

Cardinal O'Leary took her hands and raised her to her feet. His voice was quiet and kind now. "Bridie, I want you to go and make a good confession, and after that say a prayer for Archbishop Mooney and one for me. Will you do that, Bridie?"

Bridie felt a great weight being lifted from her shoulders. "Yes, Your Eminence, I will! And will you pray for me, Your Eminence?"

"Of course I will. The car is waiting for you. Go and get your things and you can stay in my residence till we find another place for you. God bless you." He ushered her out of the side door.

The Cardinal walked back to the center aisle, genuflected in front of the main altar and turned and walked to the back of the Cathedral. Eileen Donachie, Mary Ellen, David and Tom Moore were waiting for him.

David broke the silence. "Now what happens?"

The Cardinal sighed. "Archbishop Mooney will be sent on what we call a retreat for an extended period. Again, I cannot express in words the sorrow I feel for both of you."

"What exactly does that mean?"

Before the Cardinal could answer, Tom Moore whispered in David's ear, "Go easy, David. Believe me, Mooney will wish he's in a jail rather than where he's going."

"All right, now Mary Ellen here is going to be looked after. But what about Miss Donachie, I think the church owes her more than an apology!"

"Believe me, Mr. Swersky, I will personally make sure Miss Donachie receives just compensation for what happened to her, but I think we should leave that till another time. Meanwhile, she will get her wages as usual."

"Fair enough, Your Eminence. I will keep in touch. Now when is Mooney going on his retreat?"

"I will have him announce it at Mass on Sunday. He will go shortly after that."

David held out his hand. "Goodbye, Your Eminence, and I must say, you handled the housekeeper perfectly." The Cardinal shook hands with David and Moore and held out his hand for the two women, who bowed and kissed his ring.

"It gave me no pleasure to do it, Mr. Swersky. God bless you all." He turned and walked toward the altar. Cardinal O'Leary had a lot of praying to do.

One down and one to go, David thought as he left the cathedral. Now he was ready to put the final part of the plan into operation.

Outside the Cathedral, Moore and David shook hands, and Mary Ellen said goodbye to Eileen. David was taking Mary Ellen home and Eileen was going with Moore.

"How can I ever thank you, Mr. Swersky?" she said.

"Call me David. And if you're serious, you can start by accompanying me to dinner tonight!"

"I'd be delighted, David."

"Fine, I'll pick you up at seven o'clock!"

On the drive back downtown, Mary Ellen jokingly said. "Well now, the lifelong bachelor is going out with a young lady! Wait till I tell your mother!"

David laughed out loud. "If you do that she'll have me married with kids in no time at all, and I'm only going out for dinner!"

Mary Ellen smiled knowingly. "Of course, David. It's just for dinner."

David, his face reddening, changed the subject. "Back to business, Mary Ellen. I need you and Adam to come to my office tomorrow morning at ten o'clock. Can you be there?"

"Yes, we'll be there. What is it about?"

"Patience, my dear! You'll find out soon enough!"

Chapter 13

Clare Morgan moved Mooney's arm and looked at the clock. She flung the covers back and jumped out of the bed.

"For God's sake, get dressed! Greg will be here any minute!"

Mooney laughed at her efforts at getting her clothes on. "So what! Do you really think he cares?"

"I care! I don't want him to catch us like this! Now get up and get dressed!"

Mooney shook his head and swung his legs out of the bed. He had been having an affair with Clare for ten years now, and even though the Attorney General had turned a blind eye, he had known for years what was going on.

"All right, I'd better be going anyway."

When Mooney parked his car in front of his house, he did not notice the Packard slowly leaving on the opposite side of the street. He rang the doorbell and waited impatiently for Bridie to open the door. After ringing again, Mooney opened the door with his key and stormed angrily into the hall.

"Bridie! Come here!" he roared. The house was silent. *Where was she? And where was Eileen?* He looked at his watch. *Quarter to four. The both of them should be here!* He started to look in different rooms, calling for Bridie as he went. Suddenly the ringing of the phone startled him. He picked up the receiver angrily. *This will be her calling with some kind of excuse!*

"Archbishop Mooney here."

"This is the last time I call you!" Mooney recognized the voice instantly. "Listen carefully and don't interrupt. It seems Your Grace has been very careless. You've got to learn to keep your pants buttoned. I don't know what you did to upset Brown, but he's been to the Cardinal about you! He is a very powerful man and does not like being crossed! You can expect a call from the Cardinal momentarily. I don't care about that, but I'll give you something on Brown. He had no right to get you that way!"

Mooney felt as if a brick was falling in his stomach. He tried to answer but the words stuck in his parched throat. *That bastard Brown! How did he find out? It was years ago he saw me. Good God, that's why the women are not here! He's taken them to Cardinal O'Leary! And the Cardinal was coming here!*

"Are you still there?" the voice asked insistently.

"Yes, I'm here." His voice was no more than a croak.

"All right, go to your mailbox. The contents will make interesting reading for your friend the Attorney General." Abruptly the phone went dead.

In a daze Mooney went outside and took the large brown envelope out of the mailbox. As he opened the door to reenter the house, the long black limousine with the small flag on the fender glided to a stop in front of the house. Mooney slumped and left the door ajar as he staggered to the lounge to find a seat. Grey-faced, he heard the door close, and as he looked up Cardinal O'Leary strode into the room. Mooney sat in silence waiting for the axe to fall.

"James, you have disappointed me personally, but we are all sinners. As the scriptures say, judge not and ye shall not be judged! We have decided it's time for you to go on a retreat. You will announce it to the faithful at Sunday Mass. Now I suggest you should examine your conscience and go and make a good confession." The Cardinal turned to leave.

"When will I be leaving?"

"As soon as possible. No later than next week."

Mooney held his head in his hands as he heard the door close behind the Cardinal. He sat for a long time letting the news sink in. *Where will they send me? Probably some monastery in the middle of nowhere! No more dinners at the Waldorf. No cars, no radio, no women! I'd be better dead than go to a place like that!* He stirred and went over to the small cabinet where he kept his whisky. He poured himself a large glass and took a good swallow. He sat down and opened the envelope. The contents were just a series of lists with some of the numbers circled in red. It was meaningless to him. He poured another glass of whisky, and suddenly the enormity of what had happened hit him like a sledgehammer.

The six foot four Archbishop, accustomed to the trappings of power, and of everyone around being in awe of him, broke down completely and cried bitter tears into the cushion on the chair.

Later that night, Clare Morgan was relaxing listening to the radio when the phone rang. Her husband was reading a report on one of his cases. Clare sighed and went into the hall and lifted the phone.

"Hello, the Morgan residence, Clare speaking."

"Hello, Clare, it's me. I've got to see you tonight! Can you come over?" The familiar voice was slightly slurred.

"For God's sake, James. You were here this afternoon! It's almost ten o'clock, and Greg is still up."

"I mean the both of you! Please ask Greg if he'll come?" The request sounded more like a cry for help than anything else.

"Just a minute and I'll ask him." She laid the receiver down and walked back to her husband's office. *What could be wrong? Mooney sounded more like a whimpering little boy than the big self-assured man she was used to.*

"Greg, it's James Mooney on the line. Something's wrong and he wants us to go over and see him."

"At this time of night? Are you sure it's the both of us?" His voice had a hint of sarcasm.

"Yes, it must be important or he'd never ask," Clare replied coolly.

Morgan threw his pen down and stood up. "All right! Tell him we'll be over in ten minutes."

Mooney was sitting at the kitchen table when the Morgans arrived. His eyes were swollen with weeping. He was not drunk, more like numb as the realization that his easy life was coming to an end was sinking in. He waved his hand at the chairs and they sat down across from him.

"Well, what's this all about? We don't have all night, you know!" Morgan said impatiently.

"I have something for you." Mooney slid the envelope across the table. Morgan looked at him quizzically and took the papers out. As he started to read them, Clare asked Mooney what was going on.

"It's all over, Clare. They're moving me away to God knows where."

"What are you talking about? For God's sake, tell us what's going on!"

Mooney told them the whole story about throwing Mark Brown out, the Cardinal coming to see him and the mystery man who had given him the envelope.

"That's about it, I guess." Greg Morgan laid the papers on the table. "You expect us to believe you're being sent away because you were seen with your hand on Clare's knee ten years ago? There has to be more to it!" Mooney looked at the ceiling. *It made no difference now.*

"Yes, there was more to it."

"Another woman?" Clare stared at him. He nodded. "More than one woman. I'm sorry, Clare."

Morgan laughed cynically. "Sorry, my ass! You're just sorry you got caught! Anyway, Clare doesn't mind, do you my dear?"

Clare lit a cigarette. "Not at all, now what's in the envelope that's so important?"

Mooney looked puzzled at her nonchalance. "I looked at it, but it means nothing to me. Do you know, Greg?"

Greg Morgan had spent years trying to expose corruption in the financial and political circles in New York. He had been modestly successful in bringing a few small fry to justice, but this was the mother lode. Mark Brown himself! The *Wunderkind* who had become a legend in a few short years. It was public knowledge that he had made two fortunes, one from stocks and the other from movie houses. Now he was selling building materials to the government. "You say you don't know who left this for you?"

"No, he just identified himself as a good Catholic. Well, do you know what it means?"

"I most certainly do! Thank you very much, Your Grace! This is enough to put your friend Brown in jail for a very long time! Come on, Clare, it's getting late."

Clare put her cigarette out and stood up. She held out her hand. "Well, James, it's been nice knowing you. Don't feel bad about a few other women! I've had a few other men too."

"Now, Clare, tell his Grace the truth! It was more than a few!"

The two of them walked away laughing together, leaving Archbishop Mooney sitting alone at his kitchen table.

The next morning at ten o'clock Adam and Mary Ellen showed up right on time. David was waiting for them.

"Good morning, come over here please." He guided them over to a long table on which were laid out ten checks side by side.

"As you can see there are ten checks here made out to different companies, all of which are fictitious. I have prepared bills from these companies for our records. Each of the checks is for one-hundred thousand dollars. That adds up to one-million dollars which Mr. Browning has agreed to pay you for the pain and suffering he caused by stealing your money."

"A million dollars! But it was two-thousand pounds!" Mary Ellen was in shock.

"The man made his entire fortune off it!" David said brusquely. "Believe me, he can well afford it, so take it and use it wisely, I suggest you deposit these checks in separate banks. It makes good sense not to have all your eggs in one basket."

The realization that she was not dreaming was beginning to sink in to Mary Ellen. "The first thing I have to do is pay my uncle back his money."

"I was going to bring that up next. Give me your uncle's address and I'll take care of it for you."

Mary Ellen remembered the last time she saw her uncle, and shuddered at the thought. "That will be fine by me, David. How much do you think I should give him? It should be lots more than two-thousand pounds."

"Why don't you leave that to me, Mary Ellen. I'm sure Mr. Browning will have no objections to the company paying it."

"Why not indeed! Thank you again, David. You are a true friend in need." Her eyes filled with tears.

"All right! Enough of that! Call me up with your uncle's address when you get time. Adam, get her out of here before she has us all crying. Remember, your money goes into different banks." He gathered the checks and put them in an envelope. "Here you are, now I've other things to do, so I'll see you later."

"It wouldn't have anything to do with Eileen Donachie, would it?"

Again David's face reddened. *How could she possibly know that he was seeing Eileen again today?*

"Maybe and maybe not!" he said as he ushered them out of the office. He waited till he was sure they were gone, then lifted the phone and called Marcus.

"Hello, Mark, I'm just calling to let you know your friend the Archbishop is finished!"

"Excellent! Now, how soon can we buy this property? I have a tight schedule and this is holding us up."

"Well, as soon as they put someone else in charge. I don't think the church is in the habit of rushing things."

"Keep on top of it and if nothing happens next week, let me know."

"One other thing. I paid off the women. It cost a million dollars."

"It was worth it to get rid of that priest! Call me as soon as you know anything." David hung the phone up. Now it was just a matter of waiting.

On the following Tuesday, Mary Ellen called and gave David her uncle's address. On Wednesday morning David went to Queens to see him.

The door of the small frame house was one of thousands in the borough which had been built during the boom times of the twenties.

David knocked on the door, which had seen better days, and Mrs. O'Neill answered it.

"Good morning, could I speak to Mr. John O'Neill please?"

"Whatever you're selling, we're not buying!" The door slammed in his face. David hesitated and knocked again.

This time O'Neill himself came to the door. "Can't you take no for an answer?"

David interrupted him. "I'm not selling anything! I'm here representing your niece, Mary Ellen."

"What the hell does she want? That stupid bitch lost everything I had. She cost me my chance at starting my own business! I've not worked for four years and all because of her!"

David waited in silence till O'Neill stopped ranting. "She wants to put things right as she sees them. I'm here on her behalf to give you your money! Now can we do this inside?"

Immediately O'Neill's manner changed. "You've got my money! Come right in!" He ushered David into the kitchen, which was small, but surprisingly clean, considering the state of the outside of the house. The two men sat at the small table, and Mrs. O'Neill, who had heard the exchange at the door, leaned against the sink to hear what was going on.

David opened his briefcase and pulled out a single sheet of paper and a checkbook. "I believe the amount lost was two-thousand pounds, equal to around eight-thousand dollars in 1926."

"Yes, but it cost me a once in a lifetime chance. It should be worth more than that now!" O'Neill said belligerently.

David sat back in the chair and looked at the huge man in front of him. He remembered the first time he had seen Mary Ellen and the black and blue mark on her face. "And how much would that be?"

O'Neill looked at him in surprise and turned and looked at his wife. She merely shrugged. O'Neill turned back to David and said, "I reckon it's worth at least double that, considering what it cost me."

"Sixteen-thousand dollars! If I give you a check right now for that amount will you sign this receipt putting an end to this matter?"

O'Neill hesitated. *This was too easy! She must have come into money.* "On second thought, maybe I could have made a lot more off that money. I'll have to think about it some more."

"I see. Well, if I were you I wouldn't think too long. Maybe your niece will decide to put other things right while we're at it!"

"What are you talking about? It was my money that was lost!"

David's manner changed. "There's the matter of a brutal assault against a defenseless young woman! Look, O'Neill, I don't particularly like bullies! I don't give a damn about you and your money!" He shoved the paper across the table and stood up. "Take it or leave it! You stipulated the amount. If you don't accept, believe me, my friend, I personally will make sure you'll do time for what you did! Now what's it to be?"

John O'Neill was not easily frightened. But there was something about this small man with the dark complexion that made him uneasy. "You'll give me a check today?"

"I have it right here." David opened the checkbook.

O'Neill hesitated and turned again to his wife. She turned away impatiently and said over her shoulder, "Take it and be done with it!"

O'Neill pulled the paper over. "Have you a pen?"

David smiled grimly and handed him his pen.

It took three weeks for the axe to fall. Marcus had been badgering David constantly about the land purchase, and when Alice put the call through, David expected the usual questions about how long it would take to get the deal completed. This call was different.

"David, you'd better get up here quick! I've just got a summons to appear before a Grand Jury!"

"What are they investigating?"

"As far as I can make out, it's for misuse of Federal funds."

"That is a very serious charge, Mark. I think you'd better come here, the Grand Jury will be convening in the city anyway. Bring the summons and let me have a look at it."

"I suppose you're right. I'll come down right away. Meanwhile, see if you can get someone from the Attorney General's office and see if there's any way we can have this revoked."

Revoked! You must be dreaming, this is the end of the road for you, my friend. "I'll see what I can do," David replied calmly.

Greg Morgan had taken three weeks to make sure he had everything correct. He had sent detectives to the plant in Ohio and seized the original manifests with all the shipping documents proving that Atlantic was double billing the government.

He had the accountants check everything before issuing the summons. If he could bring Brown down, his name would go into the history books. There was a groundswell of resentment among the public against the big money men, so if he won this case, his re-election would be guaranteed. As Mark Brown was the managing director, he was the one who received the summons.

Morgan was not surprised when his secretary told him there was a Mr. David Swersky from Atlantic on the line. He had been waiting for the call.

"Mr. Swersky, Greg Morgan here, how can I help you?"

"Mr. Morgan, it has just come to my attention that you are having Mark Brown appear in front of a Grand Jury. As President of Atlantic Holdings, and as Mr. Brown's attorney, I would appreciate it if we could meet for a little talk."

"Mr. Swersky, I have him dead to rights! If you're angling for a deal you can forget it."

"I'm not interested in any deals. If Mr. Brown has broken the law as the C.E.O. of Atlantic, then as an officer of the company, I will have to resign as his lawyer. On the other hand, if you could confine your charges to Brown and leave the company solvent, then I would be duty bound to report any discrepancies to the proper authorities." Immediately Morgan knew that the incriminating papers had come from Swersky.

"And how do you suggest I could do that?"

"Again, if Mr. Brown has broken the law, the government could confiscate Atlantic and all his assets. Taking over Atlantic would benefit both the taxpayers and the thousands of Atlantic employees who would all lose their jobs if the company went under."

Including yours, I bet. Still, this made a lot of sense. If I were the cause of thousands of people losing their jobs, then Swersky would make sure everyone knew about it and I could forget about re-election, even if I got Brown. And Swersky could guarantee that!"

"I think we should have that meeting, Mr. Swersky. Your office or mine?"

"Neither. I'll meet you in the lounge at the Waldorf at seven o'clock tonight."

"Fine, I'll see you there."

Marcus came into David's office with a scowl on his face. He threw the summons on David's desk and sat down. "There it is! You're the lawyer, have a look at it and tell me what you think."

David opened the summons and made a big show of reading it from cover to cover. At last he put it down and looked at Marcus seriously. "It is imperative you tell me the truth, Mark. Have you knowingly charged the government for extra material?"

Marcus stood up and started pacing around the office. "What if I have charged them a little extra? Everybody does it!" He stopped pacing and leaned his both hands on the desk facing David. "What I really want to know is how the hell did the Attorney General find out?"

"You never answered my question."

"All right, I told the shippers in Ohio to split the Lincoln Park Michigan order into two and ship half to Lincoln Park, New Jersey. I'm damned if I know how they found out! All the invoices were marked Lincoln Park."

"What about the cargo manifests? The delivery truck waybills would be marked Michigan and New Jersey."

Marcus stared at him. "Why would the Attorney General of New York check waybills from Michigan and New Jersey?" he asked quietly.

David shrugged his shoulders. "How the hell should I know?"

He's lying! For the first time in his life Marcus felt a shiver of fear run up his back. *What the hell was going on? Why was Swersky lying?* Keeping his composure, he said calmly, "What do we do now?"

"The question is, what do *you* do now? I suggest you get yourself a good lawyer."

Marcus struggled to keep from exploding. "You are my lawyer? What the hell are you talking about?"

"You've just told me you have broken the law! As an officer of Atlantic Holdings I'll be called as a witness. Therefore I can no longer be your attorney!"

Marcus realized he'd walked into a trap. Swersky was going to testify against him. *But why?* Keeping his voice calm, Marcus sat down again. He lifted the summons and put it in his pocket. "I don't know what your game is, David. But it's your word against mine, isn't it?"

David smiled and slid a sheet of paper off his phone console. With a sinking feeling, Marcus saw the red light. David pressed the button. "Did you get all that, Alice?"

"Yes, Mr. Swersky, I have it all," the voice crackled back.

Marcus was dumbstruck. He realized he'd been outwitted, but the war was just beginning. Recovering his composure, he looked at David with hate in his eyes. "Tell me why, Swersky. I think you owe me that!"

Casually, David pressed the button. "You can send them in now, Alice." He sat back with an amused look on his face.

Puzzled, Marcus turned toward the door to see Mary Ellen O'Neill walk into the office with a man at her side. It was as if he'd been hit a blow to the head. He staggered back and leaned against the desk, his ashen face staring in disbelief. David stood up and walked around the desk. He stopped with his face inches from Marcus.

"This is why! You Goddamned scumbag. Now what have you to say?" He was shouting in Marcus' face, his fists clenched in anger.

Adam Corbett pulled him aside and held his arm.

"Why did you do it, Marcus?" Mary Ellen asked softly.

Marcus' mouth moved, but no sound came out. He waved his arm in the air as he staggered toward the door, never taking his eyes off her. He stumbled out of the office and left the three of them looking at each other in silence.

The Waldorf Astoria lounge was half empty when David met Greg Morgan. They chose a corner table to give them some privacy. Both of them ordered a coffee.

"I've been thinking about what you said, Swersky. It does make sense to keep the company solvent, but that would be up to a congressional committee, it's a huge company."

"I'm sure such a committee would follow your recommendations, Mr. Morgan. After all, it's you who is prosecuting the case!"

"They would only do so if Brown were found guilty."

David sipped his coffee and looked up at Morgan. "You're not sure about that?"

Morgan looked uncomfortable. "I was a hundred percent sure we'd get a guilty verdict with the evidence we have, but now I'm not so sure. He was very cautious in the way it was done. We could not find a thing with his signature on it. Brown could tie us up in court for years."

"Not if you had a witness."

Morgan sat bolt upright. "Tell me he told somebody!"

"Not so fast. First, the company must remain solvent under government control with myself as C.E.O. I want written assurance that when Brown's assets are seized, his family get his townhouse to live in. At present his in-laws are living in it. After all, they did nothing wrong. The big money is in his brownstone and the house in the Hamptons."

"Done! But only if you give me a witness who heard Brown say he did it."

David took an envelope from his inside pocket. "In this envelope there is not one, but four depositions from people who heard him say just that, myself being one of them!"

Morgan smiled. Now he could not fail. He held out his hand for the envelope, but David put it back in his pocket.

"I said I wanted written assurance."

Morgan stood up and lifted his hat. "I'll be in your office first thing tomorrow with it. I don't know what your agenda is, Swersky. I do know what you've done is more than a disgruntled employee's revenge! But to tell you the truth, I really don't give a damn! See you tomorrow."

Chapter 14

Marcus sat in the back seat of the Rolls with his eyes closed. He was on his way to the Hampton house, forgetting about visiting his family. He was still in shock after meeting Mary Ellen. *How did Swersky know her? What possible connection could he have with her?* He opened his eyes and looked blankly out of the window. He felt a deep feeling of anger building up inside him. *To Hell with Swersky! To Hell with Mary Ellen O'Neill! To Hell with all of them! That treacherous bastard could cost him his building! Well, he'd soon find out Marcus Browning was no pushover.* He rapped his knuckles on the partition and the chauffeur opened it.

"Yes sir?"

"Turn around and go back into the city." Marcus took a card from his wallet and read the address aloud. The driver knew better than to ask questions. He turned around as soon as he could and headed back into New York. Marcus looked at the card thoughtfully. It was the card Swersky had given him the first time he had met him in Tweed's office.

It took an hour to get to the office of Wills and Watson. It was four forty five and the door was open. Marcus strode in and walked over to the receptionist.

"Please tell whoever's in charge that Mark Brown is here on a matter of great urgency!" The receptionist jumped out of her seat and almost ran to the oak door with the brass nameplate. She knew who Brown was and wasn't about to question him.

"Of course, Mr. Brown, right away!" She knocked once and opened the door and said in a hushed voice, "Mr. Watson, Mark Brown is here to see you!"

George Watson looked at her over his spectacles. "THE Mark Brown?" The girl nodded dumbly. Watson stood up and put his jacket on.

"Well, don't just stand there! Send him in!"

The girl turned around and called to Marcus, "This way please, sir." She ushered Marcus into the office.

The two men introduced each other and sat down.

Watson opened the conversation. "How can I help you, Mr. Brown?"

Marcus took the summons from his pocket and laid it on the desk.

"It looks like I'm in trouble with the Federal Government. I would like to retain you as my counsel." He leaned over toward Watson. "Money is no object, just do what you have to do to have this matter dropped."

Watson held up his hand and reached for the summons. "May I?" Marcus nodded. Watson took his time and read the blue papers carefully. At last he put them down and looked over at Marcus.

"I'm sure you are aware of the seriousness of these indictments. I can't promise anything, but there will be no way to have this matter dropped, as you put it. But without witnesses, the government will have a hard time convicting you. I think I can safely say we can win this case, Mr. Brown."

"Hypothetically speaking, what if I told you they had witnesses willing to testify they heard me admit to the charges?"

Watson looked at him calmly. "Hypothetically speaking, I'd say your ass is in a sling!"

Marcus smashed his fist on the desk. "You've got to get me off! I'd lose everything I've got."

"Yes, you would, Mr. Brown, and you would surely go to prison for a long time if convicted of these crimes."

Marcus slumped in the chair. "So there's nothing you can do for me?"

"I didn't say that. Look, if you want me to represent you, you'd better tell me everything! Leave nothing out, including why David Swersky is not representing you. Then and only then will I decide if I can help you with this case."

Marcus sighed and nodded. "All right, I'll tell you all of it." He told Watson the whole story except for the part about meeting Mary Ellen O'Neill. While he spoke, Watson made notes on a pad of paper. "Well, what do you think, can you help me?" Marcus asked anxiously.

Watson was the consummate professional. It mattered not to him that Marcus was as guilty as sin. As a client he was entitled to the best defense he could give him. "Difficult, but not impossible. There are two major problems in this case. The first problem is Swersky testifying against you."

Marcus interrupted, "And what's the other?"

Watson looked over his spectacles. "The other is much more serious, Mr. Brown. Public opinion will be against you!"

Marcus never answered him, he felt a sense of dread overcome him. *Watson was right, I never even thought of that! Public opinion! Yes, the papers would have a field day! The bastards were just waiting for a chance to bring a successful man down!*

Watson's voice interrupted his thoughts. "Before we make any plans for your defense, for this case my rate will be a hundred dollars an hour."

Marcus laughed in relief. "I told you money was no object, didn't I? How much do you want up front?" He pulled out his checkbook.

"Five-thousand should get us started."

"Here's ten." Marcus scribbled a check and slid it across the desk. "Leave nothing to chance, I must be acquitted of these charges."

Watson stood up. "Listen carefully, Mr. Brown. Don't presume to lecture me or give me orders! I will give you the best defense I can possibly give you. I will leave no stone unturned in my efforts to do it. But I am promising nothing, do we understand each other?"

Marcus was not used to being talked to like that, but he had to swallow it. Chastened, he replied quietly, "Understood, Mr. Watson, I'm just a bit worried about it."

Watson escorted him to the door. "And so you should be, Mr. Brown. I'll be in touch."

The newspapers used their "end of the world" print to report the indictment of Mark Brown. Gordon Tweed saw it in the *New York Times* and positively gloated as he walked to his teller's job in Bank of America.

In London, Jeffrey Walker sat in his council flat having breakfast when he read about it. *Wonderful news! Because of that bastard I'm living in a pigsty and working as a clerk. I hope he gets life!*

In Oxford, Sir Derek Browning walked over to the fire and carefully slid the paper into the flames. He had managed to stay out of jail, but his good name had been ruined when the news broke about his wartime activities. He did not gloat, but felt a kind of sadness. *Greed! Marcus. Nothing but greed brought you down!* He stood for a long time watching the paper burn. He did not want his bedridden wife to see it.

Chapter 15

Four months later there was a party in the Swersky house. It was the Fourth of July. They were celebrating the engagement of David Swersky to Eileen Donachie and little Patrick Corbett's eighth birthday. It was also a farewell party for Mary Ellen and Adam Corbett, who were going on a holiday to Ireland and Scotland. The trial of Marcus Browning had just finished with the accused being sentenced to ten years in a Federal prison. Atlantic Holdings continued in business under the control of the government. Greg Morgan had become something of a folk hero for managing to get a conviction against the best lawyers money could buy.

Late in the evening, as the guests were starting to leave, a slightly tipsy Benjamin Swersky called for silence. He wanted to make a toast to Mary Ellen and Adam, and David and Eileen. He started with the day he and Rachel had found Mary Ellen down at the battery.

"Remember how she looked, Rachel?"

Before he could say any more, Mary Ellen walked over and grasped his arm. "Benjamin, there's only one toast tonight! It's to the man who made this night possible. Without who's help none of us would be standing here! Raise your glasses to David Swersky!" Everyone raised their glasses. "To David Swersky!"

The great depression had not been kind to the O'Neill family. The plan Robert had come up with to take a mortgage had backfired badly. All of the O'Neills had lost their jobs in England and the bank had foreclosed on the mortgage. Now they were merely tenants on land which had once belonged to them. Like thousands more of their countrymen they worked the land and were allowed to stay in the house and feed themselves from the crops in lieu of wages. In the nine years since Mary Ellen had gone to America, her brothers Liam and John had married and had six children between them. There were eight adults and six children living in the farmhouse. Patrick had built two extra rooms in the attic for the married members of the family.

When they got word that their daughter was coming home for a visit, all their troubles were forgotten, and now the big day had arrived. The whole family was gathered outside the house waiting for the car which Mary Ellen said they'd be arriving in. In that remote area they were lucky to see one car in a week, so the whole family was beside themselves with excitement.

"She must be a millionaire! Coming home in a private car!" Liam said in anticipation.

"Don't talk rubbish, Liam! Just because they can afford to hire a car doesn't mean they're millionaires!" Suddenly they all became quiet as the sound of the motor broke the stillness of the morning.

"Here she comes!" Patrick started running down the path to the roadside. The whole family crowded around and the hugs and tears did not stop for a good five minutes. When everybody caught their breath and the introductions were finished they all settled in the living room and Adam opened a bottle and brought a case of beer in from the car.

After things had calmed down, Patrick told Mary Ellen about the boys losing their jobs and the bank foreclosing on the mortgage.

"Patrick! Mary Ellen's here for a holiday, not to listen to our problems! Now, Mary Ellen, tell us, how are things in America?" Martha scolded him.

Mary Ellen broke into a broad smile. "First thing I want to do is thank Robert for this little box." She held the box out for everyone to see. "It gave me strength when I most needed it." She walked over and hugged her brother. "Now! Mother, Father, listen everybody. Remember when I used to dream of going to America and coming back a millionaire? Well here I am, and I am a millionaire! So your worries are over!"

The hum of conversation stopped and everybody became quiet. They were all staring at her.

"Have I grown horns or something? What are you all staring at? Haven't you seen a millionaire before? Tell them, Adam!"

"She means it!" Robert shouted. Suddenly everyone started talking at once.

"Is everyone in America a millionaire?"

"Are the streets really paved with gold?"

Patrick started thumping the table till everyone became quiet. "Now everybody keep quiet and let Mary Ellen talk. Now, child, take your time and tell us all how you became a millionaire?"

Mary Ellen looked at her husband and then turned to her father. "It's a long story, Pa. I'll tell you some other time. Now, who's for a song?"

Leavenworth Federal Penitentiary August, 1935
The nightmare was always the same. It started with the secretary, Greta, throwing a dollar bill in his face. Then it was Jeffrey Walker hitting him with handfuls of banknotes. Gordon Tweed was showering him with bundles of checks. Next, it was his mother and father joining in till he was smothering in the mountain of money. Finally, as he climbed out of the money, Mary Ellen O'Neill appeared, asking him the same question over and over, *Why did you do it, Marcus?*

"That's the Limey screaming again, the son of a bitch will cause a riot in here. It's happening every night now!"

The old guard nodded. "I've seen his type before. They usually get worse. He'll have to go into solitary."

Pluscarden Abbey, Scotland. 4:00 a.m. November, 1935
The monks filed in for morning prayers as they had done for centuries. The only sound was the drumming of the rain on the slate roof. The Abbot knelt in front of the large crucifix and crossed himself. He turned to lead the monks in prayer and saw that the penitent was missing again. He sighed and nodded to one of the monks. Brother Benedictus pulled his cassock tighter to keep the cold out and left the chapel. He walked slowly along the freezing stones and stopped at the cell door. He slowly opened the door and entered to awaken the penitent. He dropped to his knees and crossed himself hurriedly as he stared in horror up at the silhouette of the swinging corpse of Archbishop James Mooney.

Printed in the United States
65661LVS00003B/148-195